Mt. Lebanon Public Library
16 Castle Shannon Blvd.
Pittsburgh, PA 15228-2252
412-531-1912
www.mtlebanonlibrary.org
Children's Library   02/2023

CATHEDRAL OF TIME

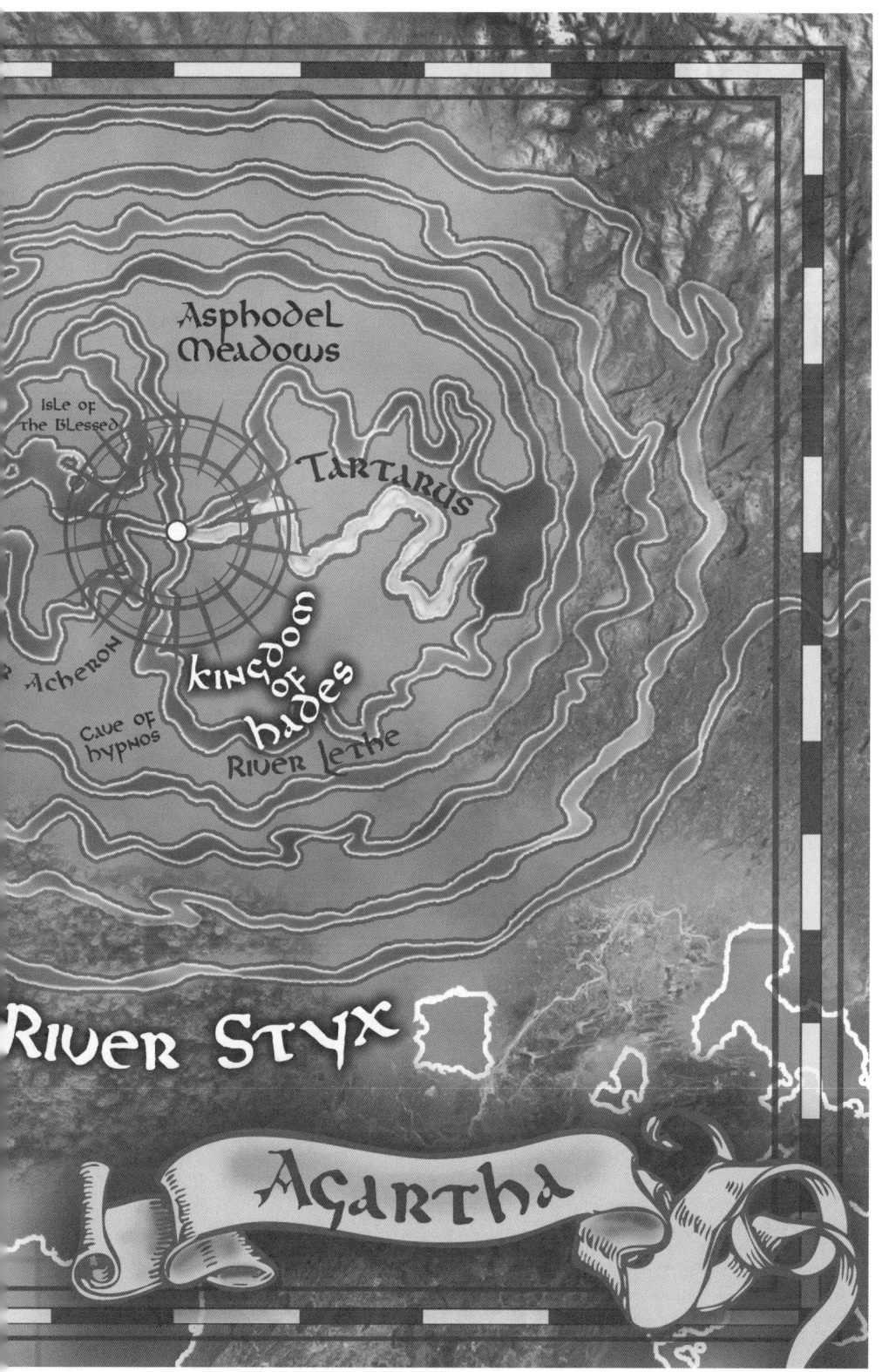

THIS BOOK IS AUGMENTED-REALITY ENABLED

TAKE THE STEPS BELOW TO GET THE MOST OUT OF YOUR READING EXPERIENCE:

CATHEDRAL OF TIME

Stephen Austin Thorpe

CONTINUUM MULTIMEDIA / SLC

Copyright © 2017 by Stephen Austin Thorpe.

All rights reserved. No part of this publication may be reproduced, distributed or transmitted in any form or by any means, including photocopying, recording, or other electronic or mechanical methods, without the prior written permission of the publisher, except in the case of brief quotations embodied in critical reviews and certain other noncommercial uses permitted by copyright law. For permission requests, write to the publisher, addressed "Attention: Permissions Coordinator," at the address below.

Stephen Austin Thorpe/Continuum Multimedia, Inc.
PO Box 160473
Clearfield, Utah 84016

www.continuummultimedia.com

Publisher's Note: This is a work of fiction. Names, characters, places, and incidents are a product of the author's imagination. Locales and public names are sometimes used for atmospheric purposes. Any resemblance to actual people, living or dead, or to businesses, companies, events, institutions, or locales is completely coincidental.

Book design © 2013, BookDesignTemplates.com

Ordering Information: Special discounts are available on quantity purchases by corporations, associations, and others. For details, contact the publisher at the address above.

SLC / Stephen Austin Thorpe – Third Edition

ISBN 978-1-7327835-1-5

Printed in the United States of America

For my wife Maria, and daughters Jenny and Mary - without whom this book would never have seen the light of day!

CHAPTER 1

THE LEGEND

(MICK)

Makayla "Mick" Brown was about as all-American of a girl as there was at Edmonson County Middle School. It was said she had the Midas touch—whatever she touched seemed to turn to gold, from her straight A assignments right down to her reddish-brown hair that always had just the right amount of curl. Only Tanner and Andrew, who knew her best, saw firsthand that she wasn't just being favored by the gods. Mick worked her tail off.

Her so-called charmed life wasn't all it was cracked up to be, though. There was the whole middle school hierarchy, and the popular girls were becoming increasingly angered by how a bookworm nerd like Mick could be so well-liked by the boys. And worse than that was Mick herself. Mick was a perfectionist, and she was becoming more and more frustrated with hiccups on her relentless pursuit of a perfect life.

"It's got to be around here somewhere," Tanner said as he, Andrew, and Mick crept deeper into the darkness of Mammoth Cave.

Mick turned her flashlight onto the map she was using for navigation.

"The librarian's going to kill you," Andrew said, pointing at the adjacent page, which was half-missing.

"It was that way when I checked it out," Mick replied. "According to the caption, it was a pencil sketch of the murderer."

"I've always wondered what he looked like," Andrew said.

Mick glanced back and forth between the book and her surroundings. "If this map is right, the marker should be right over there." She swung her flashlight across the cave and abruptly stopped as it illuminated a small brass plaque on the ground.

"That must be it," Tanner said.

The trio approached the marker.

Burial site of the Shawnee girl murdered as a result of the Brownsville Bank Robbery of 1810.

"Why do you think he killed his accomplice too?" Mick asked.

"That's easy," Andrew replied. "He got greedy, and she knew too much. That kind of money can do strange things to people."

"When did they find her remains?"

"Just five or six years ago," Mick said. "Don't you remember? It was all over the news."

"Must've been before we moved here," Andrew said.

"Got *national* attention, though," Tanner added. "By the way, did you hear there was another sighting?"

"Of the murderer?" Andrew asked and then answered his own question. "Yeah, but the whole thing's such a big hoax—the guy would have died like a hundred and fifty years ago."

Mick shook her head in disgust. "It's embarrassing that the only thing Brownsville is known for is the whole Legend of the Caveman thing."

"I think it's cool," Tanner said.

Mick came from a long line of Brownsvillians, including a grandfather who had been mayor for as long as she could remember until his death a year and a half earlier. Her family encouraged everyone to forget about the legend and recognize Brownsville for what it really was: a great community with one of the most spectacular natural wonders on earth—Mammoth Cave.

"Why would people think the Caveman's still alive, anyway?" Mick asked.

"Some say he found a fountain of youth down here," Tanner said. "Or that it's just his ghost everyone's seeing."

"Someone's just trying to get more tourists to Brownsville," Andrew said.

"But there are so many stories, and they come from reputable people," Tanner said. "There has to be something to it. You know, where there's smoke, there's fire."

"It can't be the Caveman, though," Mick replied. "Probably just a homeless guy living down here."

"I think somebody's trying to scare people away from the cave while they search for the money," Tanner said. "It never was recovered, you know."

"We should get out of here." Andrew winced as he panned his flashlight back and forth around the cave.

"Come on." Tanner laughed. "You were the one saying it was a big hoax."

"The whole Caveman thing is, but like you said, there have been a lot of strange things happening . . . yeah, let's go."

"Not yet," Mick said, pulling her camera from her backpack. "We've got to at least get a picture for my presentation."

"Yeah, that way we can prove we found the place," Tanner said.

"What happened to the guy's family after he went psycho?" Andrew asked as they snapped some pictures.

"I heard they were driven out of town," Mick replied.

"I heard they were . . . what's that?" Tanner yelled in a panicked tone, pointing off into the distance.

Andrew and Mick jumped and whirled around in the direction he'd pointed. Tanner began to laugh.

"Very funny," Mick said disgustedly.

"You're a real riot," Andrew added.

Mick looked at her watch and sighed. "I've got to get home."

"Me too—big game today," Tanner said.

The three of them wound their way through the cave to the exit. Tanner shared Caveman lore as they went. They hopped on their bikes and headed for home.

"So was Donald Carlton the first one to discover the cave? Is that why they called him the Caveman?" Mick asked as they stopped before turning onto the main road into town.

Wheeeoooooweeeeooooo Weeeeooooo Weeeeooooo.

"Looks like Sheriff Gardiner hasn't had his donuts today," Tanner said, chuckling as the sheriff's car sailed past.

Wheeeoooooweeeeooooo Weeeeooooo Weeeeooooo.

"Something pretty serious must be going on," Andrew said as police cars two and three streaked by.

"You're right," Tanner replied with a grin. "I think they were chasing the Caveman on an invisible horse."

CHAPTER 2

BEGINNINGS

(DONALD CARLTON)

Late 1700s

Nine-year-old Donald sat on a tree stump listening wide-eyed as his father described his latest adventure. It had been a tough day on the farm, and Donald wiped the sweat from his brow as he leaned forward, re-energized by every word.

"John turned just in time to see a massive black bear lumbering toward him. He took off into the trees. After a short chase, I lost sight of him. I fired a couple of shots, and the bear took off. The crisis over, I went searching for John."

Donald's father continued, "Come to find out, he had found the entrance to a cave and hid inside. When I arrived, we decided to explore it."

Donald's eyes lit up like a Christmas tree. His imagination began to run wild when his father mentioned the cave. He asked question after question as he was told of underground streams, cavernous rooms, and endless passageways.

"Will you take me there tomorrow?" Donald eagerly asked.

"On one condition, son. We'll have to work extra hard the next day."

"I promise I will, Pa!" he said.

Donald had trouble sleeping that night. He lay in bed thinking of what his father had described. When he finally fell asleep, he dreamt of the secrets the mystical cave would reveal.

His father woke him earlier than usual. They quickly did their required chores around the farm, so they'd have plenty of time to explore this marvel of nature. It was a day that would change Donald's life forever.

When they entered the cave, the cool air was an exhilarating contrast from a normal hot and humid day on the farm. The flickering light from their lanterns danced along the cavern walls, adding to the enchantment as Donald excitedly scanned every formation, chamber, and passageway. He knew he would never forget the feeling of entering the cave for the first time.

Donald and his father had never spent much time together—outside of work on the farm, that is. His father was a hardworking man who rarely had time for his son other than giving him instructions and explaining how the chores could have been done better. The fact that Donald was exploring and discovering with his father added to the incredible atmosphere. They passed a stunning rotunda of white limestone and then a dome that Donald could barely see the top of. As they positioned their lanterns in just the right way, he was able to estimate its height to be nearly forty times his own. He stood looking up and shaking his head in awe.

I can't believe I live so close to the greatest place in the world. He passionately absorbed everything he saw.

Continuing on, they reached a massive block of limestone nearly forty-five feet long along the right-hand wall of the cave.

"Looks like the coffin of a giant," his father said as they examined it more closely. Behind the "coffin," where it had broken free from the wall, was a low arch and narrow crevice. They squeezed through it, winding their way to a pit so deep they were unable to see a bottom. After nearly five hours, they began to work their way back through the labyrinth to the entrance.

Donald was practically skipping as they walked home.

"Thanks, Pa," Donald said as they neared their log cabin. "That was the best day of my life!"

"Aren't the creations of God spectacular?" his father said. "Always treat them with great respect, son."

"I will." Donald replied.

Donald lay in bed that night for hours, reflecting on his experience. He imagined Blackbeard and his swashbuckling pirates hiding and defending treasure in remote regions of the cave. The formations he'd seen evoked images of that and other tales he had heard. The day had been exhilarating, but exhausting. He fell fast asleep giving names to each of the magical features.

CHAPTER 3

BREAKING NEWS

(TANNER)

"Tanner! You're going to be late for your game," Mrs. Hunter said as he bolted through the front door.

"Naw, I got it."

He dropped his backpack and sprinted up the stairs, down the hall, and into his bedroom. What seemed like only seconds later, Tanner was racing back down, fully dressed in his red, white, and blue Brownsville Braves uniform.

"Let's get going. A trip to the state tournament is on the line," Mrs. Hunter said.

"Do you think Dad will show up if we make it to the tournament?"

Tanner's father had thrown the family a curve ball when he abandoned them a little over four years earlier. Everyone saw it coming, but that didn't make it any easier to deal with. Tanner blamed himself. His dad was an avid sports fan, and Tanner knew he was trying to live his sports dreams through him. No matter how hard Tanner tried, no matter how well he did, he braced himself for a tongue lashing after every game—no matter the sport.

There were many times he wanted to throw in the towel, but he desperately craved his dad's acceptance, so he just kept working harder. It consumed him. Tanner quickly became the best athlete in town despite his dad's not so pep talk advice after each game.

Tanner still wasn't sure what caused his dad to split, but he held on to the belief that his hard work would eventually bring him back.

They pulled into the parking lot just as Tanner's team was running from the dugout onto the field.

"Ahhh," Tanner said as he stepped out of the car. "I didn't wear my lucky socks."

"You don't need 'em," his mother replied.

"Hunter!" the coach yelled. "Where have you been? You were supposed to pitch. You haven't even warmed up!"

"I'm good," Tanner replied, swinging his arm in wide, arcing circles.

The coach shook his head. "I really should bench you."

Tanner ran to the pitcher's mound, picked up the ball, made sure everyone was in place, and fired his first pitch.

"Stiiiiiirrrrrike one," the umpire hollered.

Tanner was by far the best player the Braves had. There were many times the coach had wanted to bench him for his tardiness, and his 'fly by the seat of your pants' attitude, but everyone knew he couldn't afford to.

The game was a pitcher's duel. Tanner, as usual, had played a masterful game. In his three at bats he had a double, a home run, and a walk, and as pitcher, he had allowed only four hits scattered across the game.

When the top of the ninth inning arrived, the score was 1–0 in favor of Brownsville. Tanner struck out the first two batters. He knew exactly who was up next—Smith's Grove's best hitter.

Tanner was excited for the challenge. One last out and the Braves were on their way to the tournament. He reared back and let the pitch fly.

A single into right field.

With two outs and the go ahead run standing in the batter's box, Tanner's coach called time out.

"Can you finish this off?" he asked as he approached the mound. "Are you tired? I can swap you out."

"Naw, I'm good."

"Okay," the coach replied, leaving the mound.

Tanner eyed the catcher's mitt.

"Throw him the dark one." One of his teammates yelled as Tanner began his windup.

Crrrrraaaaaaack. Tanner watched dejectedly as the player from Smith's Grove rounded the bases, giving them a 2–1 lead and in the end the victory.

"Good thing Dad wasn't here," he said to his mom as he approached the stands. "I choked."

"Stop worrying about your dad. You played an amazing game. You could not have played much better."

"Yeah, but . . ."

"There's no 'but.'"

"Dad wouldn't have talked to me for a week if he'd seen it. Well, after chewing me out, that is." Tanner climbed into the car and sat hunched over in his seat.

"Chin up," his mother said.

Tanner continued, with his head down, to think about how things would have been different if he could have only lived up to his father's expectations.

If I would have just worked harder. Been stronger, more committed. He rehashed in his mind the clichés his father used on him over and over.

I've got to make it big. Then maybe he'll come back.

"I wonder where he went."

"You know I don't know that, Tanner."

He was grasping at straws, hoping this time there would be a clue, something he could latch on to. Even just the smallest thing that would allow him to believe his dad would come back and give him another chance.

Maybe next year if I can send him a picture of me winning the state championship or pitching a no-hitter. I guess the no-hitter thing wouldn't work, though. I already did one of those, and he still left.

"Honey, we both just need to forget about your father and move on," Mrs. Hunter said as they pulled into the driveway.

They entered the house, and Mrs. Hunter turned on the TV to watch her favorite cooking show while she made lunch.

"BLT okay?" she asked.

"That's fine." Tanner pulled his shirt up over his head as he stumbled upstairs to change.

When he came back down, his mother had relocated from the kitchen to the family room, where she sat glued to the television.

"What's going on?" he asked as he saw Sheriff Gardiner standing in front of his police car with a *Breaking News* banner superimposed on the screen.

I guess it wasn't donuts after all.

"Do you remember the star of that reality show on the *Treasure of Mammoth Cave*?

"Yeah."

"He's been reported missing."

"I was just in the cave with Andrew and Mick this morning."

"I know. I'm glad you guys are safe. Speaking of Andrew, it's a shame what people are saying about the Wheelwrights. How is he doing?"

"Why? What are they saying?" Tanner asked indignantly.

"Well, you know, they've been talking about all the sightings and strange things going on in and around the cave."

"What does that have to do with Andrew's family?"

"All those things started to escalate after the Wheelwrights moved into town."

"You've got to be kidding me," Tanner said. "People are actually saying they're part of the Caveman legends? No way. They're some of the nicest people in town."

"I'm not saying *I* believe any of it, but nobody really knows a lot about them, and Andrew's dad *has* been involved with some buried treasure stuff in the past with his archaeological digs, you know."

"That's ridiculous," Tanner said. He was livid. "I wish everyone would take the time to get to know the Wheelwrights instead of just gossiping about them."

CHAPTER 4

A Surprise in the Loft

(Mick)

"Where's Dad?" Mick asked as she opened the front door and entered the kitchen for lunch.

"He's at work," her mom replied.

"Again?" Mick had become frustrated with all her father's business travel and with how many nights he had to work. "Now he's even working weekends?"

There was no response, but Mick sensed there was something about her question that didn't sit right with her mother, so she changed the subject.

"We found the Shawnee burial site today."

"I don't think it's a good idea for you kids to be hanging around that cave, what with all the rumors goin' around."

"Oh, it's fine," Mick said.

❖ ❖ ❖

After lunch, Mick grabbed a notebook and pencil and went out to the barn to work on her presentation. She climbed the wooden ladder up to the loft and sat on a bale of hay in the corner. She began to document her expedition to the gravesite and the tales she learned from Tanner about the Caveman. There had been sporadic sightings ever since the murderer disappeared in 1810, but since the Shawnee's remains were found, they were happening with much more regularity. Residents and visitors alike claimed to have witnessed a strange man in or around the cave. Many Brownsville citizens vowed to never go near the place.

Tanner's right. Mick thought after writing the last of his stories. *"Where there's smoke, there's fire. And there is a lot of 'smoke.'"*

The solace Mick normally loved about the loft quickly dissipated the more she reflected on the local lore. She stiffened at every scratch or creak. Her eyes darted from side to side in an attempt to find each source, until she had sufficiently frightened herself. She closed the notebook, stood up, and tiptoed toward the ladder.

Thunk.

What was that?

She had never heard one of the boards under foot make a noise like that. She stepped on it again.

Thunk.

Mick was scared and wanted to get out of there, but curiosity got the best of her. She scanned the barn in every direction and, satisfied she was alone, knelt down and brushed the hay away from the board.

Unlike the rest of the barn that was hundreds of years old, this board looked almost new. Carefully, she lifted the plank and in stunned silence knelt looking down at a weathered leather satchel, latched shut with belt-like straps. A shudder ran down her spine as she lifted the bag from its hiding place.

This has to be as old as the barn itself, she thought as she looked at the rusted buckles. Slowly, she undid the straps, lifted the worn flap, and looked inside.

The bag was filled with small rectangular pieces of paper that were similar to one another in shape and size.

She pulled one out.

Agricultural Bank of Tennessee . . . Pay on demand to the bearer TEN DOLLARS.

Oh my gosh! It's money. She gasped as she grabbed a small stack of bills from the early 1800s out of the bag and stared in awe at their varying designs.

Mick was captivated by the money but couldn't make sense of what it was doing in her barn. Bank of Tennessee. The banknote read 1810. And then it hit her.

It's the money from the robbery!

This was the find of the century, and to think it had been hiding in her barn all these years. She looked at the floor again—the new board, the shiny nails. It didn't add up. The stories about the legend flooded her mind simultaneously as she tried to piece it all together. There was a scratching noise behind her, and she spun around, but saw nothing. The anxious feeling she'd had returned. This wasn't an ancient find; someone had recently put it there. Fear enveloped her.

No one can know I've been here.

She put the money back in the satchel, buckled the straps, placed the bag exactly as she found it, and reached for the board. Below, her favorite horse let out a screeching whinny. Mick would have known that sound anywhere. Something—or *someone*—had spooked her.

"Hello?" Mick said, nervously looking in every direction. "Who's there?" She placed the board quietly over the opening and brushed the hay over the boards, making it look as close as she could to how it had before she'd made her discovery.

Bzzzz, Bzzzz.

Bzzzz, Bzzzz.

Mick's phone vibrated. It was Tanner. *Impeccable timing Tanner,* she thought angrily. *Although, if someone really is here, it would be good to have you on the phone.*

"Hey, T," she whispered.

"Mick, turn on the news."

"I'm not by a TV. What's going on?"

"You know that treasure hunter, Harvey Wilkins, I was telling you about that's been trying to find the money from the robbery?"

"Yeah," Mick replied slowly.

"He's missing. We must have left the cave right before the whole thing broke. The place is crawling with police."

"I've got to go," Mick said. "I'll call you later." She hung up. A million thoughts raced through her mind as she scrambled down the ladder.

Has Wilkins been hiding in our barn? Or did someone kill or kidnap him over the money and then stash it here?

The hairs on the back of her neck stood up. Head down, she sprinted out of the barn without looking back.

I've got to call Dad and tell him about all this, she thought as she got to the back porch. *He'll know what to do.*

She reached for the doorknob just as the back door opened. Her dad stood in the doorway.

"I thought you were at work," she said, panting as she jumped backward.

"I had to leave early. But it's okay. I finished up everything I needed to do. Oh, and good news: no more late nights."

Mick swallowed and opened her mouth to tell her dad about what she had found.

"Hold on," he said putting his hand up in a stop motion. "Before I forget. Don't go up in the hayloft. Some of the boards are loose up there, and I don't want any of you kids falling through."

"Dad," Mick said still out of breath. "I . . ." She paused as it registered in her mind what her father had just said about the loft. What did he know? Could the hidden money have something to do with her father? Her stomach twisted in a knot. "I'll stay out of the loft." She tried to gaze as deeply into her father's soul as she could, looking for answers.

"I've had a crazy morning," she finally said.

"Same here," he replied. He strode purposefully past her and headed for the barn.

"Think I'll take a nap," Mick said, looking over her shoulder at him. She quickly made her way to her bedroom and locked the door behind her.

CHAPTER 5

DAD

(MICK)

Mick was reeling. Telling her father she had a crazy morning was the biggest understatement of her young life. She sat on her bed trying to put some meaning to it all.

Why would Dad have said to stay out of the loft? I don't think he even knows I go up there.

It's just a coincidence. Yeah, coincidence.

But why today? It's too much of a coincidence. Dad's involved somehow with the Caveman legends. What if it's him everyone has been seeing? What if he's the cause of all the rumors?

Maybe he hasn't been working late nights at all—well, not at the office.

No. What am I thinking? It can't be Dad. I'm crazy.

But the money. It's in our barn, and he obviously doesn't want anyone to find it.

And what about that Harvey Wilkins guy's disappearance? Was Dad involved? Andrew said, "That kind of money will do strange things to people." What if Dad finds out I know about it?

And what about Mom? Does she know? She gave me that strange look when I was asking about Dad working late so much, but then she also told me to stay away from the cave. She wouldn't have said that if it was Dad who was in there, or would she? Maybe she just wanted to make sure I didn't get tangled up in their web.

And what happens to me, Nathan, and Addie if one or both of them end up in prison?

No way. Stop. It's crazy. Mom and Dad couldn't. They just couldn't.

Mick put her head in her pillow. Her all-American perfect world that she'd worked so hard to create was collapsing around her.

What if Dad knows I've been up there? What if he could see it in my eyes? I never was good at keeping secrets from him. And he was headed to the barn. What if he notices the money's been tampered with?

I'm just being paranoid. All that talk about the legends got me worked up, that's all. But what if...

Bang. Bang.

Mick froze as she heard a couple of gunshots coming from the direction of the barn.

CHAPTER 6

THE GUNMAN

(MICK)

Dad! She ran to the bedroom window. Afraid of what she might see, she nonetheless put her face against the curtains and parted them just enough that the barn came into view.

Nothing unusual.

But that didn't change what she heard. She backed away from the window, but stopped when the barn door slowly began to open and the barrel of a gun emerged. Someone or something had definitely been shot at. Mick's jaw dropped as her father appeared from behind the door. He looked left, right, and then snuck around the side of the barn.

He's okay. Relief flooded her thoughts but then slowly turned to fear.

Did Dad just shoot someone?

In an instant home no longer felt safe. She had to get away.

The library.

She would be safe there. Plus, her Caveman research had suddenly become very personal. It was no longer just a school report.

I've got to figure out how, and why, Dad is connected to this whole thing.

"Where are you going?" her mother asked as Mick made a beeline for the front door.

"The library," she responded.

"I don't want you walking around Brownsville alone. You heard about that treasure hunter who's gone missing, didn't you?"

"Yeah, I heard."

"Call Tanner or Andrew; one of them will go with you."

"I don't have time to wait for them," she said, feeling frantic. She had to get out.

"Makayla Ellen Brown!"

"I'm going, and you can't stop me!" Mick said as she pushed her way for the door.

"What has gotten into you?" her mother asked, shock filling her voice.

Eek, Mick thought. *I've got to act normal, like nothing ever happened.*

"Sorry. Don't know what came over me. I'm sure I'll be fine going alone." Mick tried to assess the look in her mother's eyes.

"No."

To Mick's frustration, she was forced to call Andrew and wait nervously until he got there to escort her to the library.

"Remember who you are!" Mrs. Brown said giving Mick the Look as they left.

Mick had heard that statement every time she went anywhere with anyone, but it seemed exceptionally odd this time.

"What's the deal with the whole 'remember who you are' thing?" Andrew asked as they walked toward the center of town.

"My parents can't deal with the thought of any of us kids damaging the family name, I guess," Mick replied. *Although it looks like they've completely destroyed it themselves,* she thought.

Andrew talked about flaws in parenting techniques all the way until they entered the library. Mick barely heard a word.

"I'll meet you over at that table," Andrew said as he went to the biography section.

"Excuse me, Mrs. Watson," Mick said as she approached the counter.

"Yes, Makayla. How can I help?"

"I just needed to renew this." Mick handed her a copy of *A Dark Day for Brownsville*. "Oh, and the torn picture was that way when I checked it out."

"Yes, I know," Mrs. Watson replied. "Been that way ever since I've worked here."

"Do you have anything else on the legend of the Caveman?"

"I didn't know you were so fascinated with that."

"Well . . ." Mick replied. The last thing she wanted was for anyone to think she was overly interested in the legend. "I just have to do a class presentation for history and thought I'd learn a little more about some local stuff."

Mrs. Watson leaned her head in toward Mick and whispered. "Did you hear there was a sighting just a couple of weeks ago? And then Harvey Wilkins disappears."

"Yeah, it's all just a bunch of hogwash," Mick replied, knowing it was in her best interests to downplay the whole thing. "I'm sure the two are completely unrelated."

"I'm not so sure." Mrs. Watson turned to go in the back. "Give me a couple of minutes. We keep a box full of articles back there. Let me see if anyone has checked it out."

The librarian disappeared, and Mick fidgeted as she waited.

"You're in luck," Mrs. Watson said as she handed a box of news clippings to Mick.

"Thanks." Mick took the box.

"Good luck with your presentation. Let me know if there's anything else I can get for you."

"Did you find what you were looking for?" Andrew asked as his arm shot out and grabbed an article from the box. "Oh yeah, you're doing your presentation on the Caveman. Not a bad idea, I guess, with all the excitement around town."

Mick just mumbled.

"You ready to go?" he asked.

"Sure." She looked at the door of the library. Where could she go? Not home. The two of them checked out their items and exited the library.

I should tell Andrew. He won't tell anyone. But what if he does? If Dad really did just shoot someone—no one can know what I saw.

"Is it okay if we go to your house?" Mick asked, desperation filling her voice. "There's always so much noise at my house. Hard to study."

"Study? Mick, I know you're obsessed with being the perfect student, but I don't study on Saturdays."

"I just want to get a good start on my presentation. Go ahead and do whatever you were planning. I just want someplace quiet to read."

They made their way to Andrew's house, where Mick found a secluded place by the pool while Andrew went to his room and tinkered with a mish-mash of disassembled electronic components.

Andrew's family was an anomaly in town. His father was an extremely wealthy philanthropist, which had given Mick, Tanner, and Andrew the extraordinary opportunity to tag along on some of the archaeological digs he had sponsored. The townsfolk were baffled at why the Wheelwrights chose Brownsville to build their mansion. Mick had always appreciated how completely unfazed Andrew was by his father's wealth. It was one of the things she liked most about him. That and how he was always willing to help her out—even if he refused to study on Saturdays.

She opened the box that he had carried for her and began to pour over its contents, hoping to find anything that would give her clues on how to prove or disprove her father's involvement with the whole thing.

How could he have been so cold-blooded? Mick wondered as she read about Donald Carlton and the murders in the Brownsville Bank that had started the whole legend. Mick became so engrossed in the articles that she was shocked when she looked up and saw the sun was going down. She had no idea that much time had passed.

"Mick, your mom's on the phone." Andrew yelled from the back door.

Mick looked at her own phone wondering why her mother hadn't called her directly. It was dead.

"One second," she said as she marked her place in *A Dark Day for Brownsville* and walked to the porch.

"Hi, honey!" her mom said when she took the phone from Andrew. "Sorry I didn't call you for dinner. There's been a lot going on over here today."

Yeah, I know, Mick thought. "Is everything okay?" she asked tentatively—prepared to listen intently for anything unusual even in the tone of the response.

"Everything's fine. I'll be over to pick you up in a couple of minutes."

"I already ate." Mick lied, knowing she would be too tense to sit at the table.

"All right, but I still want you home. We have church early tomorrow."

Church? Mick thought. *You're taking us to church?*

Mick's family went to church every Sunday, but seeing her parents in a new light, she couldn't picture them sitting innocently in the pews.

"Can Andrew come over?" Mick asked, hopeful there would be a buffer between her and her parents.

Dad has to know I was in the loft by now. No one else would have disturbed the money and not taken it.

"No, we want it to be just our family tonight."

That was not what Mick wanted to hear.

"Come on, can't he at least come over for a while?"

"Your father got called to go out of town for a few weeks on an impromptu business trip. I'm sure he's going to want to spend time with just the family."

Dad's skipping town. That just confirms everything. If I can just get through tonight, then I've got some time to figure out exactly why and how he's connected to all of this.

She stuffed her book in the back of her pants, pulled her shirt over it, tucked the box under her arm and nervously waited for her mom to arrive.

The normally short ride from Andrew's seemed like a cross-country road trip as Mick sat quietly in the passenger seat, trying in vain to read her mother's mind. Her normally talkative mother was completely silent other than a cursory "hello" when Mick first got in the car. The tension was thicker than the waters of the Stygian Marsh. It was the worst ride of Mick's life, but at the same time she didn't want it to end. After all, she wasn't sure her mother was even part of the whole scandal, but her dad on the other hand, who apparently was waiting at home for their return, was a different story.

CHAPTER 7

THE ATTIC

(MICK)

"Hey, Mick," her dad said as she opened the front door.

"Hey." Mick muttered as she looked away and made a beeline for her room. She threw the box and book onto the bed, shut her door, and sank back against her pillows. A firm knock on her door startled her.

"Mick?" Her dad's voice came from the other side.

She stood quickly and shoved the box and book onto the floor on the opposite side of the bed. She turned just as he cracked the door open.

"I don't want you kids out in the barn at all for the next few days. I'm working on some repairs, and it just isn't safe. I wouldn't want any of you getting hurt." His eyes bore into hers, sending a shudder down her spine.

"Um, sure, okay, Dad. I won't go out to the barn," she said. If there was any doubt before in her mind about his involvement, it was obliterated now.

He smiled and shut her door. She paced back and forth across her room, stopping once to look out the window at the barn. Did he know she had seen the money? No, he would have said something. But that look. He was hiding something. This was the second time he'd told her to avoid the barn.

I've got to check the attic. Dad goes up there all the time, and he's always saying it's not safe for me. Maybe he's got maps of the cave or documents about Donald Carlton stashed there.

Mick waited until everyone was asleep, then slipped into the hallway. She pulled the string that lowered the ladder and quietly climbed up. The contents of the attic were stereotypical. Mick saw her science fair project on the layers of the Earth and a box full of old college textbooks of her dad's. There was an antique mirror and a small chest of drawers. Mick snooped and scoured the attic contents for hours, sifting through boxes and opening drawers but was sadly disappointed to find absolutely nothing that connected her father to the recent sightings. She looked at her phone. It was 5:00 a.m.

Church starts in four hours. I better try to get some sleep.

Turning, she noticed the Bible her grandmother used to take to church with her every Sunday sitting on top of a dusty dresser. She picked it up, and a thousand memories flooded her mind. It had only been six months since her grandma had passed away, but right now, it felt so much longer. The book was well-worn and marked, and there were lots of notes written in the margins. Finished with her search, she carried the Bible down the attic ladder and quietly pushed it back into the ceiling.

I wish you were here, Grammy. I could talk to you. You'd know what to do.

An intense feeling of isolation swept over her.

There's no one I can talk to. No one.

Mick had never minded keeping to herself, but *this* was forced isolation, and she didn't like how it felt.

"Mick?" Her father's voice pierced the darkness, and she dropped the Bible. "What are you doing up so early?" He flipped on the light. "I've been wanting to talk to you."

Not wanting to make eye contact she looked down at the Bible on the floor. The leather cover had torn away from the book itself and a folded piece of paper that had apparently been hidden between the layers fell out.

Her father bent down and picked it up.

CHAPTER 8

GRAMMY'S SECRET

(MICK)

"Now's not a good time," Mick said as her father handed her the paper. She bent down, grabbed the Bible, and stuffed the paper randomly inside. "I'm going to try to get a little more sleep before church."

"Good time or not, we're talking."

She tried to stifle her fear by looking only at his feet.

"Your mother tells me she's been warning you not to go down to Mammoth Cave, but you've been ignoring her." He gently grabbed her chin and made her look at him. "Do not go down to the cave while I'm gone. You hear?"

"Okay," she said, breaking away from his grip and moving toward her bedroom in an attempt to cut the conversation off. That was two places he'd now forbidden her to go—and both of them were connected with the Caveman mystery.

Mick entered her bedroom and locked the door. She desperately wanted to turn on the light and see what the paper was that had fallen out of her grandmother's Bible, but she had just told her father she was going back to sleep, and she definitely didn't want to give him an excuse to barge in and continue their discussion.

Exhausted, and unable to turn on the light, Mick fell fast asleep. She was shocked when her mother woke her up.

"Mick, you're going to be late. Church starts in fifteen minutes. Get up!"

She groaned and looked at the alarm she had forgotten to set for the first time in years. She hurriedly ran around the room finding socks and shoes and the matching bow for her dress, in too much of a hurry now to remember the odd piece of paper in her grandmother's Bible.

"Mick, we're going. We'll meet you there."

Mick scrambled to finish braiding her hair and took one last look in the mirror. Her eyes looked as tired as she felt. On the corner of her nightstand she spotted her grandma's Bible. She grabbed it as she ran out of the room.

When she walked in the back of the chapel, she could see her mother, Nathan, and Addie sitting near the front next to Andrew's family. She made her way to the pew.

"Where's Dad?" Mick asked as she wiggled her way past her mother.

"He already left on his business trip."

"Hey, Mick," Andrew said.

"Oh, hey," she said, as she sat next to him.

As they were singing the opening hymn, Mick was shocked when she looked over and saw Andrew skimming through her Grammy's Bible.

"Where did you get this old thing?" he asked.

The book fell open exposing the hidden paper.

Mick tried to grab it away, but didn't want to cause a scene as Andrew held it away from her.

"What is this?" he whispered taunting her. "Some kind of love note?"

"Very funny."

Stretching his arm as far away from Mick as he could, he unfolded the paper.

"Why were you being so secretive about this?" he asked, showing Mick a pencil sketch of a man. "It's just your dad." He paused. "Wait." He pointed to the corner of the paper where there was a book title and page number. "This is that missing page from the book you had in the cave. It's not your dad." He paused again. "It's Donald Carlton. Why did your grandma have a picture of Donald Carlton in her Bible?"

"Give me that," Mick said, reaching over him.

"Shhhhh." Her mother scowled in their direction.

Andrew turned the sketch over. On the back was a hand-sketched genealogy chart.

"Mick, you're a *descendant* of the Caveman?" Andrew asked, flabbergasted.

"No, I'm not." Mick whispered angrily as she grabbed the paper away from Andrew.

She examined the diagram.

Hannah Gould and Donald Carlton had six children. Mick looked at the diagram's two boxes. One with Hannah's name, birthdate, and place of birth and one with Donald Carlton's. A line fanned out to six boxes representing their children.

"Bridget McClusky," she read, *"was the oldest."* Mick let out a small gasp. Bridget was her fifth great-grandmother. *No, no, it can't be.*

She looked at Donald's name and panicked. *I'm actually a descendant of that murderer?*

Even though everyone's family tree includes some type of charlatans and shysters, Mick didn't expect to find that her family was descended from the town's most notorious scoundrel. And this, coupled with what she had witnessed about her father, put Mick over the edge.

She put her head in her hands as a strange feeling of despair swept over her.

What does this all mean? She wondered. *Maybe the legend has been running for generations through my family.* She flipped the paper over and looked at the sketch of Donald Carlton in disbelief. *He does look just like Dad. It makes perfect sense now why everyone believed the Caveman himself had returned. But wait, was Grammy in on the whole thing too?*

Mick felt even more alone than before. Even though her grandmother was dead, Mick had taken comfort that she could, in her mind, say things as if she were talking to her, but now she didn't even feel like she could do that.

Why would she have torn the image out of the book and concealed it in her Bible? Maybe she was just as horrified as me about both her ancestor and her son.

The meeting was nearly over when Mick raised her head and turned to Andrew. "Don't say anything. You've got to promise." She was afraid of the embarrassment and bullying she'd have to endure once word got out about how the golden girl of Brownsville was a descendent of Donald Carlton. But more importantly she knew if word did get out, the full story might unfold and she may end up with a parent or even parents in jail.

"You can't tell anyone. Not even Tanner," Mick implored. "Swear it!"

Andrew agreed, but it was going to be a difficult promise to keep. Mick, Andrew, and Tanner had been nearly inseparable since elementary school, and they knew everything about each other.

"We're going to be run out of town," Mick said as they walked down the hall of the church.

"No, you won't," Andrew said with a look of disgust. "Those murders happened over 200 years ago. Are you sure the chart is even right? Seems like your parents would have said something."

There's a lot of things they're not telling me.

"Maybe they don't know," she said as a cover. "Obviously someone didn't want anyone to find out."

"I definitely wouldn't want anyone to know, if it was me," Andrew said.

"You're not helping, Andrew."

Mick took the torn page and put it in her pocket as they left the church building.

CHAPTER 9

THE SYMBOL

(TANNER)

"Mick!" Tanner shouted when he saw Mick and her family crossing the street on their way home from church. "Why'd you hang up on me yesterday?"

Mick tensed up, pursed her lips in a "shut it" shape, and gave him an angry look as her eyes moved to the side nearest her mother.

He got the message.

Mick broke away from her family and ran over to him.

"What's the deal?" he asked, confused at the way Mick was acting.

"Nothing. I just hate it when my mom knows everything that's going on with my life."

"Gotcha." Tanner smiled. "But why didn't you call me back?"

"Sorry. Things got crazy. Dad had to go out of town on an emergency business trip so everyone was in panic mode around our house."

Tanner nodded in understanding. "So what do you think about the whole Harvey Wilkins thing?"

"Pretty crazy."

Tanner was stunned at the dismissive way Mick replied.

Something's going on. In the cave, all she wanted to do was talk about the Caveman. Why is she acting so uninterested?

"Come on, Tanner," Mrs. Hunter yelled. "I want to swing by the cemetery on the way home."

"Okay." Tanner groaned. "See you later," he said to Mick as he ran back to his mom.

I don't think I can do this.

His five-year old sister had passed away just a couple of years earlier from a battle with leukemia. He had never fully recovered. With her death, two of the three most significant people in his life were gone. "Can we maybe go another time?" he asked. "I'm not feeling great."

"Come on we need to go. Tomorrow's her birthday."

He wanted to talk to his mother and ask her a lot of questions. *Why did it have to happen? Will I ever see little Maggie again?*

Memories of how much fun he had with Maggie streamed through his mind. He had never known a kid as vivacious as she was. She was so full of life, and then he had to watch it all drain away until she was gone. How was that fair?

"Here we are," his mother said.

Tanner followed her with his head down as they walked toward Maggie's grave. Lying on the ground in front of the marker was a single white daisy. His heart stood still.

Dad's been here! There was no question in his mind that his father had left the daisy. It was his trademark with Maggie. When the daisies were in bloom, his dad would come home almost every day with a daisy for her.

"Mom, did you see that? It's got to be Dad."

"Yes," she said with a sad smile.

Tanner had gone from near despondency to soaring hope. He stared at the small flower with its white petals and yellow center lying on the ground. He had no idea that something so small and insignificant could change his whole world in an instant.

Maybe he's coming back.

Tanner was filled with anticipation. He began to walk around the cemetery thinking about what he had just seen.

I'm so much better than I was before he left. And maybe he's changed. Maybe he'd be okay with me now.

Tanner strolled through the cemetery glancing at the different gravestones as he poured through scenarios in his mind. If Dad came to a game, he would win for sure. There was no doubt about it. And they would be a family again. He imagined Sunday dinners and movie nights—his mind was on a completely different planet until one of gravestones in the oldest section of the cemetery caught his attention.

Hannah and . . . it was hard to make out the rest. It looked like it had been vandalized on multiple occasions, and part of the gravestone had been broken off at the top. Finally, he was able to make out the other name . . . *Donald Carlton.*

I thought he disappeared. Why would he be buried here, then?

He looked more closely at the headstone.

December 7, 1785–

Ah, okay. Now it makes sense. No death date. I better take a picture of this. Mick may want to use it in her presentation.

Tanner stepped back and framed the headstone in his phone's camera. As he looked at his camera's display, a symbol he hadn't seen with the naked eye became visible. It was centered below Donald Carlton's name. It looked like the helmet of a warrior. The sides had the horns of a ram, and on the top were curved spikes on each side and a much smaller spike in the middle. The eye holes reminded Tanner of the eyes of a screech owl. He put the phone down and walked over to the tombstone, trying to understand why he couldn't see it without the camera. He rubbed his hand along the stone and realized that the symbol was recessed ever so slightly and the camera lens had accentuated the indentation more than the natural lighting.

He sent the image to Mick. *Could it have something to do with the cave? I wonder why he was so obsessed with that place.*

CHAPTER 10

Healing

(Donald Carlton)

Late 1700s–Early 1800s

"Please, can we go to the cave again today?" Donald pled.

His father reminded him they had committed to work extra hard to make up for the previous day. After milking the cows, they returned home for breakfast. Donald, who was normally quiet, hardly stopped talking long enough to breathe. He described his adventure to the cave from the day before in fanciful terms.

After a hearty meal, Nathan sent his son to feed the hogs while he went to work their crops.

Donald quickly finished and moved to other chores. He still held out hope his father might take him to the cave if they finished early.

Pa must really be working hard to make up for yesterday, he thought when his father hadn't checked on him after a few hours.

Maybe he finally trusts me, Donald thought, beaming with new confidence after another hour went by. *Maybe he doesn't feel like he has to check my work anymore.*

But after yet another hour passed, Donald decided to go look for his father. When he got to the corn patch, he saw his father lying awkwardly on the ground.

He ran into the field. "Pa! Pa!" He shook his father's broad shoulders, but there was no response. Donald's mind raced.

What should I do?

He sprinted to their home.

"Ma! Come quick! It's Pa!" Donald's mother tore off her apron and threw it on a chair near the door as she sprinted for the field. Donald and his sister, Elizabeth, followed behind.

"Nathan!" He could sense the terror in his mother's voice. She arrived at her husband's body in the field and cradled his head in her arms.

"Oh, Nathan. Don't leave me! Don't leave me!" She hugged his limp body and looked heavenward. "No! Please."

❖ ❖ ❖

The death was a severe blow to the Carltons. Donald and Elizabeth were forced to grow up in a hurry. They had to put in longer, harder hours just to survive. The family relied heavily on one another for support through their struggles. His mother was tough as nails through it all, but Donald knew her heart was broken. His parents had been so in love.

Donald's trips to the cave became more significant to him as time passed. It was a key to his healing process. His favorite place became the limestone block his father had referred to as the Giant's Coffin. He would go there whenever possible to think and reflect and remember his adventure with his dad. He could almost feel his father at his side whenever he was there.

CHAPTER 11

MRS. BARRETT

(MICK)

"Time to get up," Mick's mother said as she knocked on her door.

Mick couldn't believe it was morning. She had fallen asleep reading. *A Dark Day for Brownsville* was lying open on her bed along with the articles about the legend. She had completely struck out. There was nothing to indicate anyone other than Donald Carlton had committed the murders and no clues that would help her understand exactly how or why her father was involved. Everything pointed to the two of them. Even the dates of all the recent Caveman activity matched up with her father's "late nights at the office."

I've got to find another source. Something that gives Donald Carlton's side of the story.

For the first time in her life, Mick didn't want to go to school. She felt sluggish and thick as she got ready. Looking in the mirror, her reflection was somehow different than before, now that she knew her ancestry. It was hard to look at herself, even to braid her hair. Her normal tasks took longer than usual, and she had to sprint out the door at the last second in an effort to catch the bus.

"Makayla, that's not like you to miss the bus," her mother said as she walked back in the front door, an uncharacteristic mess of papers under one arm and a couple of books about to fall out of her other hand.

"Rough night."

"Where's your backpack?"

"Didn't have time."

"All right, go get in the car. I'll take you."

Mick couldn't stay focused in school, oscillating between exhaustion and distraction. After school, Andrew cornered her and tried to subtly check in.

"How's your presentation coming along?"

"Don't want to talk about it."

"Mick, it's not that big of a deal."

"What if you found out you were a descendant of Bigfoot?" she whispered angrily. "How would you feel?"

"But the Caveman wasn't some hairy monster."

"Yeah, but Bigfoot wasn't a brutal killer who devastated our community." Mick walked to the bus and isolated herself in the back.

❖ ❖ ❖

Over the next few days, she became more and more obsessed with the legend. She neglected her studies entirely as she spent her down time devouring anything she could find about it. Her life was in a tailspin. The esteem she relied on from her rich heritage had been obliterated, and the confidence she had from social interactions with family and friends was imploding as she isolated herself more and more. Even her unspotted history of report cards was in jeopardy. The more she focused on the murders, the worse things got.

Most of the new sources Mick found about the Caveman were articles from tabloids. She questioned their reliability, but she was desperate.

One afternoon, as she continued to pore over articles, she read:

One of Mr. Carlton's descendants, a Mrs. Barrett of Brownsville, insists that all the evidence in the case is circumstantial and that since no murder weapon was ever found, the killings shouldn't be attributed to him.

Finally, something to work with, Mick thought as her spirits leapt. *I had no idea Mrs. Barrett was a descendant of Mr. Carlton, too. Maybe she'll have some information that will help clear his name. I've got to call her. She'll help me out.*

Mick was one of Mrs. Barrett's favorite students in third grade, and when Mr. Butler retired, Mrs. Barrett began teaching fifth grade, and Mick was in her class again.

Mick looked up Mrs. Barrett's number, pulled out her phone, and dialed.

"Mrs. Barrett?"

"Yes?"

"This is Makayla Brown," she said quickly, wanting to get to the heart of the conversation.

"What can I do for you, Makayla?"

"I'm doing a presentation on Donald Carlton. I understand you're one of his descendants."

"Yes, I am."

"I was wondering if you might have any information that could help me with my research."

There was a long pause on the other end.

"Why do you wish to do a report on Mr. Carlton, Makayla?" Mrs. Barrett said defensively.

"Well," Mick stalled. She knew she couldn't say anything about the legends. "I want to prove he was innocent."

Mrs. Barrett replied, the tone in her voice much brighter, "Why don't you come over and we can discuss what I have."

"I'll be right there."

Ten minutes later, an out of breath Mick knocked on Mrs. Barrett's door.

She opened the door and shook her head in disbelief. "Makayla! How did you get here so quickly?"

"Just anxious, I guess," Mick replied. "Thanks for having me over."

"Come on in. I apologize for being defensive on the phone. It's just that I've been persecuted over the years for my relationship to Donald Carlton."

And that's just what's about to happen to me. "I, um, didn't know you were a relative until I saw your name mentioned in an article about him."

"Most of the citizens of Brownsville don't know I'm a descendent, but those who do have shunned me entirely. It's refreshing that someone actually wants to hear his side of the story."

Mick sat down on the tufted high back chair Mrs. Barrett motioned to and looked around the dimly lit room. It looked like a museum display of artifacts from the early 1900s. Crocheted doilies adorned the French provincial furniture, gaudy wallpaper covered the walls, and it was impossible to ignore the distinctive old musty smell.

"So what is it you would like to know?" Mrs. Barrett asked.

Mick was unsure how to broach the topic of Donald Carton, her relationship to him, and her father's involvement. And so she began with the typical history report questions, fidgeting as she asked for information she already knew. Finally, she got up the courage to ask what she really wanted.

"Why do you think he was innocent?" she asked.

"Can I trust you with something extremely valuable to me?" Mrs. Barrett said after some time. She stared deep into Mick's eyes.

"Sure."

Mrs. Barrett picked up a small book from the end table next to her.

"This is Donald's journal." She handed the book to Mick. "I had the pages digitized about a year ago, and I'd be willing to let you copy the files if you promise you won't let anyone else see them or make copies."

"Oh, I promise."

"Makayla, I've never believed the rumors. Just because no one found another suspect doesn't mean Donald was the perpetrator. I actually respect and look up to the man, and I think you will too, once you've read this."

A small seed of hope broke open in Mick's heart. "I'm looking forward to it. Thank you. Thank you so much." Mick said. "You have no idea how much this means to me."

"I pasted a poem inside the front cover," Mrs. Barrett said. "It expresses my perspective on Mr. Carlton, notwithstanding what others might say."

Mick opened the front cover and read the Edgar A. Guest poem pasted inside:

> *My Creed*
> *To live as gently as I can;*
> *To be, no matter where, a man;*
> *To take what comes of good or ill,*
> *And cling to faith and honor still;*
> *To have no secret place wherein*
> *I stoop unseen to commit a sin;*
> *To be the same when I'm alone*
> *As when my every deed is known;*
> *To be without pretense or sham*
> *Exactly who you think I am.*

Encouraging, Mick thought.

"What does this go to?" Mick asked as she grabbed an old key on a weathered piece of twine that was taped inside the back of the book.

"Oh, that." Mrs. Barrett replied taking the book and key back. "It was attached to the diary when it was given to me many years ago. I've never found what it goes to. Anyway, let's send you those files."

Mick gave Mrs. Barrett her email address, and Mrs. Barrett sent the files.

"Can I take the key in case I come across whatever it goes to?" Mick asked.

Mrs. Barrett shook her head slowly. "I'm sorry, Mick, you must understand. I can't take a chance on it getting lost."

CHAPTER 12

THE LAST PARAGRAPH

(MICK)

I'm going to regret not having that key. I know it, Mick thought. *But I can't steal it. Mrs. Barrett would never trust me again. I've never stolen anything in my life. But who cares. My family might be at stake.*

Mick eyed the book in Mrs. Barrett's hands and then looked her in the eyes.

"Mrs. Barrett, do you think I could have a glass of water? It was a long run over here."

"Sure, Makayla." Mrs. Barrett sat the book down on the coffee table.

Mick watched as she made her way to the kitchen. As soon as she was out of sight, Mick reached for the book. She opened it and stared at the key.

I can't do it. But it's my family. The key's probably not important, anyway. She started to close the book. *But what if it is?*

She grabbed the key and gave a gentle tug.

"Do you want ice?" Mrs. Barrett called out.

"Yes, please."

My phone. I'll take a picture. I can replicate the key. Mick reached in her pocket. *Ahhh, I was in such a hurry to get here that I left it at home. I've got to just take it. It's for a good cause, and I'll bring it back.*

Mick gave another tug, and the yellowed tape broke free from the book. Mick looked at the key in her hand.

Nope, I can't do it.

She tried to secure the tape again to the back page, closed the book, and set it back on the table.

"Here you go." Mrs. Barrett returned to the room with the water.

Mick guzzled the drink and handed the glass back. They said their goodbyes, and Mick left. She could hardly wait to get home to begin reading. She sprinted the half mile and flung open the screen door.

His side of the story.

Finally, Mick thought excitedly. *No one has ever included that. It's my best chance to find anything that may connect this to Dad or prove both of them innocent.*

The family computer was in the kitchen. Mick rushed there to check her email. Her mom was paying bills online.

Mom, do you have to do that right now? She couldn't stand the wait. *How am I going to do this? Someone's going to ask me what I'm doing, and they'll see the images of Donald's old journal. I'm going to have to wait until everyone's asleep.*

"Mom, what time is it?"

"It's one minute after the last time you asked me. What are you so anxious for?"

"Um. I'm just tired. Anxious to go to bed."

"You don't have to wait. Just go to your room and get some sleep, if you're so tired."

"Okay." She gave her mom a quick peck on the cheek and made her way to her room. While she waited for everyone to fall asleep so she could use the computer, she lay on her bed, staring at the ceiling as she speculated anxiously about what Donald's journal would reveal. Relaxing on her bed began to make her tired. She tried to fight it, but long before anyone else went to bed, Mick was fast asleep.

Around five a.m., she jolted awake.

Oh my gosh. I must have fallen asleep. I've got to hurry. Mom will be waking up before long.

Quietly, Mick went to the kitchen and accessed her email. She scoured the journal as quickly as she could, listening for any kind of sound from her mother's bedroom. From everything she read, Donald appeared to be a God-fearing man who loved his wife and children. As she made progress through the journal, she became more encouraged.

Someone like this is not a murderer.

Carefully, she scanned for clues that would shed light on the scandal, only to find nothing . . . nothing, that is, until the last paragraph.

"I often visit an area of Mammoth Cave my father named Giant's Coffin. There is a unique feeling in that place. It has become a spiritual retreat for me. I go there to ponder and reflect. It was near this spot that I uncovered the path I needed to pursue. I would encourage anyone who is looking for direction, for answers, for truth, to find a spiritual spot like the one I found where they can uncover truth for themselves."

The closing lines of Donald Carlton's journal hit Mick like a bolt of lightning. There was something in it for her. She wasn't exactly sure what, but she felt like it was important.

Was this his turning point? Was this when he went from God-fearing to cold-blooded? Was that the path he felt he "needed" to pursue? And his advice—am I supposed to find a spot where I can find answers and truth?

Mick could hear her mother's alarm.

She quickly exited out of the account and tiptoed back to her room. Just as she quietly closed her bedroom door, she heard her mother open hers and enter the hallway.

Mick reflected on the closing lines of Mr. Carlton's journal over and over until she actually felt like she could hear Donald's voice repeating them in her mind.

A few days later, she was hiking the cave with Tanner and Andrew.

"This place is kind of creepy, don't you think?" Mick asked.

"The legends finally getting to you?" Tanner asked.

Andrew looked at Mick. She gave him a "you better not say anything" stare. "You know, I've been working on that presentation about the Caveman."

"Don't tell me you're starting to believe all that stuff," Andrew said.

Mick didn't respond. She was thinking about Donald's journal and his comments.

"Let's go to Giant's Coffin," Mick said.

The three of them made their way to Donald's spiritual retreat.

When Mick arrived, a shudder ran down her spine. "Whoa."

"What is it?" Tanner asked.

"Nothing. Nothing," Mick said. A million thoughts raced through her mind. She imagined the Caveman standing there, wondering which path to pursue. She could picture the noble

Donald Carlton of his journal standing next to the brutal killer Donald Carlton of the newspapers.

What did he decide?

Her whole body shook.

"Are you okay?" Andrew asked.

"I'm fine," she said.

I've got to come back alone. There really is something about this spot. I can feel it. Tomorrow. Mom will be working, and Nathan and Addie will be in school. It's perfect.

Mick was completely detached from the world for the rest of the evening. The boys and her family tried in vain to bring her back to earth, but all she could think about was returning alone to the cave the next day.

❖ ❖ ❖

"Today's the day," Mick said quietly as she looked in the mirror the next morning. "I'm going to get some answers."

"Who are you talking to?" her mom asked as she walked past her bathroom.

"No one. Just practicing for a presentation I have to give."

"Oh. That's right. I forgot that was today. Good luck. I'm headed out. Don't miss the bus."

"Okay."

Stupid presentation, Mick thought. *There's no way I could stand in front of the class and give a presentation on the legend, anyway. Too risky. Andrew might say something.*

Mick never had a blemish as big as missing a presentation. But she justified it as she thought about how the current situation was going to destroy her family's life, so what was a little presentation? She ran to the window and watched her mom drive away.

"Here we go." Her adrenaline was pumping from excitement and terror at the same time. By the time she arrived at the cave, she was straddling a massive chasm in her mind.

This is so stupid. I can't go in there alone. But I'm just a few minutes from answers. Maybe I can prove Donald innocent. There's something magical about Giant's Coffin. Is it good magical or bad magical? Curiosity killed the cat. Mick paused, *But I'm not a cat, so here goes.*

An overwhelming sensation ran through Mick's entire body when she finally arrived and sat down at Giant's Coffin. A voice in her head repeated the closing lines of Donald's journal.

"I know. I know," Mick replied to the voice. "Now, *how* am I supposed to uncover the truth?"

No sooner had she asked the question than she pointed her flashlight at something she hadn't noticed before. Not far from where she was sitting was a stone that looked too perfect to have been randomly placed. The shoe prints of Tanner and Andrew were visible from the previous day. Mick approached the spot and began to brush away the dirt. Once the sides were clear, she was able to get her hand under the stone and pry it up. A small metal box about the size of a three-ring binder had been carefully placed underneath the stone. Mick's heart stood still as she bent down and removed the box.

My answers, she thought, *are in this box!* She moved the box around in her hands, trying to find where it opened.

Ahhh, the key. I knew it! She thought angrily as she looked at a small lock on the front of the box. *What do I do now? Just go over to Mrs. Barrett's? No. I may not want her to know about whatever's in here. Do I go back and steal the key? Actually, I wouldn't even have to. I could just sneak in, use the key, and sneak back out. What if I get caught, though? I could just smash it open, but Mrs. Barrett might not be happy if I destroy her box. Wait, it's just as much my box as it is hers. I'm a descendant, too. I have just as much right to this as she does.*

Mick began looking for a rock big enough that she could smash the box open.

This should work.

She set the metal box on the ground and dropped the rock on the edge with the lock. She reached down and moved the rock out of the way. The lock lay smashed on the ground.

CHAPTER 13

THE UNEXPECTED CONTENTS

(MICK)

Mick picked up the damaged metal box and slowly opened the cover.

Her heart skipped a beat as she looked down at a black book with gold lettering that simply said, "Journal." The closing words of Mr. Carlton's journal ran through her mind again.

I would encourage anyone who is looking for direction, for answers, for truth, to find a spiritual spot like the one I found where they can uncover truth for themselves.

It was a clue to help someone find this book, she thought. *I've uncovered the truth!*

Anxiously but respectfully, Mick removed the journal and tossed the box to the ground. As she held it in her hands, her mind raced. *He really did hide out here.* Mick opened the journal and shone her flashlight on the first page.

A strange noise startled her before she could read anything.

"Who's there?" she asked, her voice faltering. "Who is it?"

More noise.

Did someone follow me? Did whoever got rid of Harvey Wilkins come back to the scene of the crime? I should have listened to my dad. I was so stupid coming down here alone.

Mick hid behind the rock formation of Giant's Coffin as the noises grew louder.

It's just my imagination, yeah...

A ray of light came toward the space where she was hiding.

Someone really is here. It can't be Dad. He's out of town. Or...

She strained to see the figure in the darkness. It was difficult, given the bright light from the flashlight panning the space. All she could see was the silhouette of a man who looked to have a similar build to her father.

Oh, no.

The man stepped closer to where Mick was hiding. He had a distinctive limp. *Not Dad.*

Mick tried to position herself better so she could see his face when he passed in front of her. There was just enough light reflecting in the cave that Mick could make out his features as he walked in front of the coffin.

Mick was stunned. It was Tanner's dad.

What's he doing in the cave?

She tried to process what she'd just seen. Tanner's dad had been gone for four years.

Maybe Dad's not the Caveman after all. But why is Tanner's dad walking with a limp? Did Dad... she paused as she thought about the possibility that Tanner's dad was hiding with the money in her barn and that her dad may have shot him.

Mick waited until she knew the coast was clear, then sprinted, journal in hand, out of the cave, through the woods, and back to her home.

Once she arrived at the porch, she scanned her surroundings. Feeling confident that no one had followed, she entered the empty house. She would have felt safer if everyone had been home and she could have just locked the door and read, but she was happy she wouldn't have to face any awkward questions.

Disappointed that she couldn't absorb the whole journal by osmosis and instantly know its secrets, she turned to the first page and began to read.

July 30, 1810
Today I made one of the greatest discoveries in history. As I was exploring the cave, I stepped into one of the underground streams. To my surprise, I fell through and found myself in a river in the middle of a large meadow.

"What?" Mick said out loud.

There's a meadow inside Mammoth Cave? What does he mean "fell through?"

August 7, 1810
I waded in the river until the rapids became too difficult to navigate. The banks were swarming with people fighting one another in an attempt to cross the raging mess on foot. A ferryman was extracting coins from the mouths of would-be passengers who boarded his small boat and began a treacherous journey down the river. Those who had no coin were unable to even access the pier.

August 9, 1810
This morning I went to the library. Many things I saw in this new land reminded me of legends I had been told about the underworld of Greek mythology.

If this place that is located "under this world" is truly the underworld of Greek mythology, I want to be better prepared the next time I visit.

August 17, 1810
I confirmed that what I discovered is actually the underworld of the Greeks. With what I learned from the library, I was able to navigate the Styx, appease Cerberus the three-headed dog, and enter and exit the Great Hall of Judgment with relative ease. I pity anyone who enters without being prepared as I was.

Mick was stunned. She continued to read as he documented in great detail everything he encountered.

This has to be a fraud, she thought. *An elaborate scheme. But why?*

A distraction? If someone was on his trail, this journal could completely throw them. Make them think he was crazy. But why would he have made the journal so hard to find?

Mick argued back and forth in her head as she continued to read.

What if it's true? Maybe that's why they were never able to find him. The only way to find out is to try to pass through the stream myself.

I could take Tanner and Andrew. No, not Tanner. I'd have to tell him about my connection to Donald Carlton. And not Andrew either; there's no way he could keep this a secret. I'm going to have to do this alone. I just have to prepare like Donald said.

CHAPTER 14

SCHOOL'S OUT

(MICK)

"Hey, where were you yesterday?" Tanner asked.

"I was sick."

"You were supposed to give your presentation you know. It was a quarter of our grade."

"I know," Mick said, her voice full of apathy.

"Who are you?" Tanner asked, looking like he had encountered a complete stranger.

Mick wondered the same thing. She wasn't the same person she'd been just a few days earlier. She looked Tanner in the eyes.

He would be so excited if I told him I saw his dad, but if his dad ends up being the cause of all the trouble around the cave, he'll be devastated. Ahh, what to do?

"What did you decide to write your mythology papers on?" Tanner asked, breaking the awkward silence.

"I'm thinking about the Greek underworld." Mick wondered for a moment if she would have firsthand knowledge for this report as well. At least she would be prepared with the knowledge that Donald Carlton said she would need if his journal turned out to be true.

"You're not going to flake on that, too, are you?"

"No way!" she replied.

"That's more like the Mick I know."

By the time this report was due, Mick planned to know everything she could about the underworld.

❖ ❖ ❖

"How do you think you did on your paper?" Tanner asked as he and Mick sat down for their final class of the year.

"Pretty good," Mick said.

"Makayla these are the best papers on the underworld I've ever received from a student," Mrs. Beck said as she handed a stack of papers to Mick.

"You realize we only had to write a one page summary of our topic, right?" Tanner asked as he grabbed Mick's papers and started reading.

"It never hurts to go the extra mile," she said. *Especially when knowledge may be the key to a safe journey through the underworld.* She shook her head. Preparing for the report had brought some sense of normalcy back to her life. A hidden world in Mammoth Cave? She wasn't sure what she'd been thinking.

Why did I let the whole Caveman thing ruin me? she asked herself, full of regret as she waited for her report card.

Mrs. Beck placed Mick's report card on her desk and gave her a sympathetic, better luck next time kind of smile. "Have a nice summer."

Mick looked down at her grades. She was devastated. For the first time in her life there were not only blemishes to her perfect history, there were deep gashes.

"I always knew I was smarter than you," Tanner said as he smugly looked over at Mick's desk.

"Shut it," she replied.

Rrrrrrriiiiiiiiinggggg. The final bell was a welcome relief. She'd have the summer to set things straight, to get her perfect life back on track. Everyone eagerly abandoned their desks and fled for the doors.

"Come on Mick, we're going to miss the bus," Andrew said.

"Oh, yeah, okay," she said, trying to snap herself out of the funk she was in. The bus ride home wasn't much better. Tanner and Andrew argued back and forth about what to take on their scouting activity that night. Everyone else discussed summer plans and passed yearbooks around. Mick could think only of the mess her world had become. *At least I succeeded in making sure no one found out about Dad or that I'm related to Donald Carlton.*

But even that thought lost comfort as the bus pulled to her stop.

"Hey, Brown!" a voice called as she stood to gather her belongings. "Is it true you're related to the Caveman?"

There was a collective gasp and then, "Nice genes!" someone else yelled sarcastically.

"Does that make you a half-blood or pure-blood killer?" came another cry.

Mick looked in disbelief at Andrew who was in the seat in front of her.

"How could you?" she hissed in his ear. "You're the only one who knew. You betrayed me."

"But . . ." Andrew started to defend himself.

"Did you tell *him* too?" Mick nodded at Tanner as she pushed her way through the mocking crowd.

"Mick, I swear, I never . . ." Andrew tried to shout.

"I'll never trust either of you again."

Nearly the entire bus was taunting Mick. Tanner and Andrew made a feeble attempt to push the other kids aside, but it was too little, too late. The damage had been done.

She reached the door, stepped off the bus and sprinted for home while listening to the continued jeers coming from the bus windows. She exhaled as she shut the front door behind her and began to sob as she ran to her room and locked the door.

"What's up with Mick?" her younger brother called from the hallway.

She wiped the tears from her eyes. Yanking open the top drawer of her dresser, she reached to the back and felt around until she pulled out her box of clues.

This is what's up with me, she thought. *I'm obsessed with this whole thing.*

She threw the secret journal in the trash.

Life was so much easier before. Now, I have to prove he was innocent. That's the only thing that will fix this. Nothing will be normal until I can do that.

Bending down, she pulled the book back out of the trash. Her love-hate relationship with the book tore her soul in two. When she'd found the journal, Mick had hoped it would answer her questions about the man and somehow prove his innocence. Instead, it just created more questions. Lots of them.

If the things this mysterious man wrote are true, Mick thought, *this book could turn the world as we know it inside out.*

She pored over the pages again, searching for something–anything–she may have missed, until her mother called her for dinner.

"Just a sec," Mick said.

Is it worth the risk to follow the clues? she asked herself as she looked at the stack of supplies she'd been gathering for such a journey, neatly organized in her closet. *If I can find the murder weapon and prove both he and my whole family line are innocent, it is.*

I have to talk to someone about this whole thing. I can't just go it alone. Not Andrew. I still can't believe he told someone about the Caveman. Tanner, though—somehow his family is already mixed up in this. Maybe keeping quiet about his dad hasn't been the best decision. I'll call him as soon as he gets back from his scouting activity.

Mick placed the box back in its secret location, stepped into the hallway, locked the door behind her, and made her way to the kitchen. As soon as she entered the kitchen, she could tell something was wrong. Her mother's entire demeanor was different.

"What's wrong, Mom?" Mick asked, a sickening lump forming in her gut.

"Kids, I have some bad news." Her mother motioned for Mick and her brother and sister to sit down. "You know your father has been away on business, right?"

"Yes," the three of them answered. Mick braced herself, preparing for the worst.

"He was arrested today."

"What?" Nathan and Addie said in shock, unable at their ages to fully understand the significance of what was going on.

Mick tried her best to act totally surprised herself, but was sure her acting probably left something to be desired.

"So until this whole thing blows over, we're all going to Virginia to stay with your grandma."

"May I be excused?" Mick pushed herself away from the table. "I've lost my appetite."

"It'll be all right Mick," her mother said. "We'll get through this."

Mick didn't stay to hear more. How would they get through it if they ran away? What exactly had her dad been arrested for?

Is mom going to be a fugitive? She wondered, convinced even more now that her mother was entangled in the whole mess.

Well, that decides it. I can't wait for Tanner. I've got to go tonight.

She stormed around her room, pulling out the items she'd already prepared for such a trip and adding new last-minute things to her bag.

Have I got everything? She frantically pawed through her backpack. *An obol, sweetcakes, the journals, plenty of food, a tunic . . .* She reviewed her numbered list one last time. Carefully, she put the journal in an outside pocket of her backpack. As she sat on her bed listening to every move outside her door, she read through her papers on the underworld one last time, trying to make sure she was prepared.

Why doesn't everyone go to sleep? What's taking so long? Mick feared that unless she could leave soon, she might chicken out.

"Good night, Addie, good night, Nathan." Her mom was working her way down the hallway. Her footsteps stopped just outside Mick's door.

"Mick, sweetheart?" Her mother knocked softly.

"I don't want to talk!" Mick said. It wasn't the truth. She wished she could just ask her mom everything, but all the secrets, all the lies had hardened her beliefs. The only way she would know the truth of any of this was to follow the journal herself.

Her mother didn't answer right away. Mick worried that she would try to talk to her, to reason with her. Instead she finally sighed and began to walk away. "Good night, Mick."

"Good night," Mick said too softly to be heard. "And goodbye."

It wasn't long before she could faintly hear her mother snoring. Her heart began to race.

It's now or never.

Quietly, she stood up from her bed and tiptoed to the door. She slowly turned the doorknob and stepped into the hall. After glancing around, she quickly made her way to the back door.

"Breathe," she coached herself.

Mick carefully opened the screen door. It was a dark, overcast night. Mick could hear the sound of thunder in the distance.

"You can do this," she whispered as she stood on the edge of the woods behind her home. She stepped into the trees as if she were breaking a magical plane.

This is crazy. I shouldn't be doing this alone, she thought as she reflected on her belief that the kidnapper was still at large. *What if someone follows me?*

She entered the cave, knowing there was no turning back. If her dad really wasn't responsible for Mr. Wilkins's disappearance, she was running the risk of coming face-to-face with a murderer in the depths of the cave—by herself. But she had to prove her father's innocence and the only thing she had to work with at this point was Donald Carlton's secret journal. Every noise made shivers go down her spine as she made her way to the underground stream described in the journal. When she got there, she shone her flashlight around in every direction, and, finding herself alone, she looked at the sketch in the book one last time. "This is definitely the place," she said as she looked over the edge. She stared at the water in front of her. Could it really lead to another world?

CATHEDRAL OF TIME

I can't do it, she thought, frustrated by her fears. She looked away.

An exaggerated image of the school bus bullying broke onto the stage of her mind. More and more students were flooding into the fray. "Half-blood murderer!" they shouted.

Mick snapped herself back to her present reality. More noises.

"Who's there?" she demanded of the darkness.

It's so risky, but I've got to jump!

"Hey!" a deep voice yelled in the darkness, startling her before she could make the leap.

CHAPTER 15

Makayla is Missing

(Tanner)

Tanner was jolted out of bed by his ringing cell phone. He certainly didn't expect a call at six a.m. on a Saturday. He stared at the caller ID through half-open eyes. It was Mrs. Brown. He groggily answered.

"Hey, Mrs. Brown, what's goin' on?"

"Makayla's gone. When we got up this morning, there was no sign of her anywhere. You haven't seen her, have you?"

"No," Tanner replied.

"I thought maybe she had gone somewhere with you and Andrew."

"No, we were at scouts until late last night. Maybe she went somewhere with Andrew this morning?" He didn't want to sound alarmed. He could tell Mrs. Brown was worried enough as it was. But he also knew that Mick had been more than a little upset with Andrew the day before on the bus. He was certain she wouldn't be with him, which made the pit in his own stomach swell.

Word spread quickly that Makayla was missing. Brownsville, Kentucky, was usually a pretty quiet place, but Mick's disappearance, combined with Harvey Wilkins's disappearance and the urban legend of the Caveman, changed all that. Rumors ran rampant that the Caveman was involved. Reporters descended in droves. The media set up camp outside the Brown's small farm, making it nearly impossible for them to have any privacy or carry out their daily responsibilities.

"There are no signs of a break-in," her mother told the national news. "But her room was disheveled, which isn't like her."

It was painful for Tanner to watch the broadcast. They showed Makayla's yearbook picture and described her as being about 5'4" with olive-colored eyes and wavy, shoulder-length hair. Before the story was over, he threw a pillow across the room and bolted for the backyard, where he picked up a basketball and began shooting. He played with an angered determination as he tried to deal with the idea that his best friend and longtime sidekick was missing. Yet another person in his life torn away.

CHAPTER 16

FINDING COVER

(MICK)

The voice startled Mick, and she instinctively jumped forward into the small underground stream. Everything went dark. When she felt herself breathe again, she cleared the water from her eyes and tried to assess her surroundings. She was in a babbling brook, but it was too dark to see much else. There was a large moon-like object in the sky that was obscured by smoky clouds.

It really exists! Mick thought excitedly. *Donald Carlton was telling the truth!*

Her excitement quickly changed to fear as she heard noises she didn't recognize.

This is so stupid. I know nothing about this place. Why am I doing this? I should just go back home and forget about the whole thing.

But I can't.

She thought about the voice in the cave.

I've got to get moving. Someone's obviously following me.

She took her flashlight out of a Ziploc bag and panned across the landscape. There was nothing hostile in sight—only a vast meadow surrounded by woods on every side. *Whew.*

I'll find a hiding place over there and wait until morning.

CATHEDRAL OF TIME

The farther Mick ventured from the entrance point, the more it sunk in that she was in a completely new world. Even though she had thoroughly read Donald's journal, she still felt unprepared. Someone would have thought she was an owl the way her head swiveled back and forth with every noise as she made her way through the tall grass to the edge of the woods. She found a rock outcropping in the trees, where she deposited herself, untied her sleeping bag, and tried to get comfortable. It was after several hours of alert listening that Mick finally fell asleep from exhaustion.

CHAPTER 17

A Surfacer

(Mick)

"Hey! Over here. It's the Surfacer."

Mick was awakened to growling voices and blinding beams of light. As she looked around for a place to escape, she realized there were lights surrounding her in all directions. She sensed she was in danger, so she sprinted for a small gap in the lights. Instantly, she was grabbed by a pair of large men.

"Bind her, and let's get her to the king," a raspy voice said in the darkness.

"We'll be rich men by morning," a man directly in front of her said in a sinister way while wringing his hands.

Mick kicked and screamed, fighting with all her might, to no avail. There were far too many of them. She continued to struggle as the men loaded her into a hovering craft.

"How do we make sure no one takes her from us? The stakes are so high."

"We'll go straight to the palace. Even though we can't have an audience with the king until morning, it should offer us some protection."

"Unless the guards themselves turn on us. There's nothing preventing that. You know how desperately the king wants a

Surfacer. It's been like a gold rush ever since he announced his plans."

"What do you want with me?" Mick protested.

"Gag her," the leader commanded one of the men as the craft began to speed away through the darkness.

Mick struggled again as she tried to fight the gagging. As she thrashed her head back and forth, she noticed lights in the sky growing larger and brighter. She was able to make out hosts of aircraft approaching the craft she was in.

What is going on? Mick wondered. *There was nothing about any of this in Donald's journals. Am I in the wrong world?"*

"Surrender the Surfacer!" a thunderous voice came from one of the aircraft.

"Never!" the craft Mick was in lurched forward in an attempted getaway and then jolted as her captors fired their weapons on the incoming vessels. Looking at the surrounding aircraft, Mick could see her kidnappers had no chance. She braced herself for certain death. There was no response. Her craft jerked again as the men fired another round. This time an explosion occurred, lighting up what looked like a transparent sphere surrounding the small vessel. Mick wasn't sure if the sphere had been created as a protection by her captors or as a defense by the assailants.

A booming voice bellowed from one of the other aircraft. "Your weapons have been disabled. Your craft will be brought to Delfi, where you will be allowed to plead your case before the great High Priest."

Still bound and gagged, Mick wondered what was going to become of her.

These guys were so anxious to capture a "Surfacer." Are they going to dispose of me to keep me out of their enemies' hands? Thousands of possible outcomes played in Mick's mind, and she had to admit that nearly all of them were bad. As she contemplated her possible fate, the lights of a spectacular city came into view.

Doesn't look like anything I've ever read about in mythology, she thought. *I've got to be in the wrong place. Donald's journal was all about mythological places.*

"Welcome to Delfi," a piercing yet peaceful voice announced. "We'll be arriving at the Palace of the Great High Priest shortly."

Mick looked down on buildings that were unlike any she'd ever seen. Brassworks and green glass, gears and gadgets of all kinds integrated into the buildings. Transportation devices and various types of hovercrafts dotted the sky. She had not fallen into a world of Greek mythology—she'd been transported into a science fiction novel.

"Please make yourselves comfortable as we approach the palace," the voice declared as the ship began to descend.

Mick was surprised at the calm nature with which the enemies of her captors were treating the whole situation. It was as though they never truly felt threatened. There was no fear, anxiety, or apprehension in the tone of their voices. Only quiet confidence.

The convoy of aircraft landed gently just to the right of the entrance to a stunning palace.

"You will now untie the Surfacer and disembark from your craft." The commanding voice announced. "The Presiding High Priest will entertain you momentarily."

The men reluctantly freed Mick from the bonds she found herself in and were escorted into the palace. She stared in amazement as they walked down the main corridor of flying buttresses made of brass and iron, past moving artwork so realistic it looked as though you could step right into any frame and find yourself in a completely different world.

She was distracted from the artwork by the creaking noise of the massive throne room doors opening in front of her. The doors were an elaborate combination of glass and brass with beautiful carvings of astronomical elements in the metalwork and etchings in the glass.

Seated on a sumptuous throne in front of her was a man nearly twice her height.

"Great High Priest, these men captured a Surfacer and were heading to Anatok." One of the pilots announced. "We were able to stop them and have brought them before you to be tried for their crime."

"We have committed no crime," one of the captors brazenly barked. "You have no jurisdiction over the citizens of Anatok."

"But we do have jurisdiction over our own lands, and you were trespassing," one of the guards replied.

"Is this true?" the High Priest asked.

"It is true we were on your lands, but so was this woman. Expel us all together."

Even Mick, who knew so little about what was going on, was savvy to what the man was trying to do.

"Do not attempt to deceive the Great High Priest." The great leader's powerful voice reverberated through the chamber.

"I'm not being deceptive. We were all trespassing, expel us all."

"We know what you want with the woman and will assure that none of you come near her again," the guard replied.

"Take them to the dungeon," the Great High Priest said, pointing at the captors. "We'll finish with them later."

The kidnappers were escorted out of the throne room, leaving Mick alone with the Great High Priest and his guards.

"State your name," one of the guards said.

"Makayla Ellen Brown."

"And why Makayla, were *you* trespassing on Delfian lands?"

"I'm sorry, but I didn't know I was." She tried to stand as bravely as she could, not sure what the punishment for trespassing would be. None of this was like the world described in Donald Carlton's journal. All her preparation had done nothing for her.

The High Priest spoke up. "Makayla. These are very dangerous times for Surfacers. For all of us, actually. You shouldn't be wandering around alone. Why did you come here?"

"I'm searching for clues about an ancestor who came through these lands many years ago."

"And how do you know he came here?"

Mick held up Donald's journal. "He documented his travels in this book."

"May I see the book?" the High Priest asked.

Mick handed the book to the guard, who brought it to the High Priest. The majestic leader intently scanned its pages.

"We'll help you." The High Priest seemed satisfied with Mick's cause and handed the book back to her. "Where is it you wish to go?"

"One second," Mick said as she shuffled through her backpack. "Ah, I forgot my papers," she whispered to herself. "I can't believe it." She gritted her teeth and jolted her head in self-directed anger.

"What's that?"

"Nothing. It's just . . ." Mick wasn't sure it was wise to admit just how unprepared for all of this she was. Where did she want to go? Where had Donald Carlton gone? She thought about the journal—the last entry—and flipped the book open. "The Cathedral of Time," she said with more confidence than she felt. "I'm looking for the Cathedral of Time." It was written in the last entry. It was as good a starting point as any.

"Ah, Mount Olympus," the High Priest said. "I do have the authority to escort you to the judgment platform of the gods on Olympus. I will have one of my guards take you there. If you pass judgment, you will be permitted to remain on Olympus temporarily. It's rare, but if the gods find you and your cause worthy enough they may grant you access to the Cathedral of Time."

"How do I know I can trust you?" Mick asked.

"You don't," the High Priest said. "But you saw what happened when you were wandering around the interior alone. That's your other option."

I'm not sure I like either option, Mick thought. *I can't do this. What was I thinking? I'm not spontaneous. That's Tanner.*

Mick had spent hours mapping where she could go and what she would do, and now, all her extensive research was lying on her bed. She shook her head in disbelief that she had left something so important behind.

I'm lost.

"Could you just take me back home?" she finally asked.

CHAPTER 18

ASPERGAR

(MICK)

"We *could* take you home," The High Priest replied, "but I thought you wanted to find information about your ancestor."

"Yes, I do."

But the farther I get from the entrance, the less chance I have of getting back home. Besides, what do I think I'm going to find? So I found an entrance to the underworld and could go to Mount Olympus—it's awesome, but it's not going to help Dad.

"You must go to Olympus for that very reason."

Mick looked up. What reason? To help her dad? "Wait, are you reading my mind?"

The High Priest smiled but didn't respond. A calm feeling swept over Mick, but her logical mind wasn't in sync with it.

"Okay. Take me to Olympus," she said to the High Priest as she closed her eyes and braced herself.

The High Priest looked at the guard to Mick's left, and without any words being spoken, the man nodded once and turned to her. "My name's Aspergar. I'll have the privilege of escorting you to Olympus." He clasped forearms with Mick and bowed slightly. "Follow me."

She followed him through a door behind the throne of the High Priest onto a platform with a small aircraft. He stepped onto a piece of metal on the pavement. A flat square light ascended from the metal and continued to rise until it reached the top of his head. The light made an electrical buzzing sound as it descended back down to its point of origin.

"Pilot recognized," a voice announced, and the glass dome on top of the craft opened.

"Climb in," Aspergar said as foot hole steps formed in the side of the vehicle.

Stunned at the technology, Mick climbed into the aircraft.

"Brace yourself," he said as Mick sat down, and the dome closed above them.

In a flash, the two were airborne. Mick watched as the spectacular city faded into the distance. She tried to create a mental picture, a way to remember everything for when she finally got a chance to write it down. Had Donald Carlton had a similar feeling the first time he had stepped through the river?

"Do you enjoy music?" Aspergar asked.

"Yes," Mick replied, intrigued by the question.

"It's a long flight." A small platform emerged from the seat in front of Mick, and a three-dimensional image of a singer appeared above the surface that looked real enough that it could have been a sculpture, except for the fact that it was moving. "Just swipe your finger across the stage to find a song you like."

Mick stared in awe as she moved her finger along the platform, and the image changed to different artists, bands, orchestras, and more. She settled in to a station whose music she enjoyed and looked out the window. The craft was hurtling through space at an incredible rate of speed.

A peaceful voice filled the craft. "You are leaving the realms of the underworld and are about to enter the domain of Mount Olympus."

"We'll be arriving shortly," Aspergar said as he turned and looked at her.

"I thought you said this was a long flight?" Mick asked, confused. They couldn't have been in the air for more than fifteen minutes.

"Yes, I hope you didn't grow bored."

"No, it was very entertaining," she said shaking her head as she thought of some of the long flights she had experienced on the Surface. A throbbing reverberation shook the craft, and Mick covered her ears, thinking her eardrums might explode.

"What was that?" she hollered.

"We've been hit by enemy fire," Aspergar said. "We're going down. Hold on." Frantically, he tried to continue to navigate the craft, but Mick could see they were heading for a crash landing.

"Your seat's an escape pod," Aspergar said. "Hold on."

"Can't we both use it?"

"It's not big enough. There's barely room for one. You *must* survive."

Mick was surprised at the forcefulness with which he insisted.

"But–" She couldn't just leave him, could she?

"I'll be fine," he added.

"Okay." The small hatch between the two seats closed. There was a rush of pressure as she was ejected from the craft. Aspergar's craft began to spiral out of control and plummet toward the surface.

"Makayla, can you hear me? I only have a few seconds so listen closely."

"Yes, I hear you." A few seconds until what? She shook the thought from her head, trying to concentrate on what was important enough to tell her in those last few seconds.

"You will land in the outskirts of the Kingdom of Hades. You must go to the Great Hall of Judgment immediately. Don't stop for anything or anyone. Ask for Persephone. If she's around, she'll help you pass the Judgment and get to Olympus. If she isn't—"

Mick saw a small explosion where the craft impacted the surface. And then there was silence.

Her own craft shook violently as something impacted with it.

"I'm under attack."

She braced herself and covered her ears. Her pod shook again. *I'm not going to make it either.* Her plummet was faster than she thought, and her pod decelerated rapidly right before impact. She found herself surrounded by pine trees as large as the Empire State Building. She looked around wildly for signs of where Aspergar's vessel had gone down.

I've got to see if I can save him.

She took a step in the direction she thought she'd seen the smoke and then stopped.

But he was so insistent about me going immediately to the Great Hall. He seemed so worried about my survival, and there are obviously hostile forces hidden in the forest. If I go farther into the woods, I'll be risking my own life. They had to have seen where his craft went down as well. They'll be heading there too.

Mick was completely torn on what to do. He'd sounded desperate when he said she must survive.

I can't just leave him, though. I have to see if I can save him.

She sprinted through the trees, dodging and weaving between the trunks and jumping over and ducking under the branches.

Strange voices in the forest swirled around her, talking loudly and excitedly.

I've got to beat them there.

It was the race of her life. Trees to her left and right were exploding and collapsing to the forest floor. Her neck jerked up, down, sideways, and slantways as she ran, trying to avoid the trees that crashed violently around her.

I can see it. Almost there.

She slid under one final felled tree and into the side of the craft. Aspergar wasn't in the pilot's seat.

Where are you? She looked rapidly around the craft. Spotting him, she ran to his side, grabbed the neck of his jacket, and pulled him under cover of the spacecraft as it lay on its side.

"Aspergar can you hear us?" came a voice from the cockpit. "We sensed trouble with your craft."

"He can't respond," Mick said. "We're under attack. The enemy is on us."

"See the small glass dome directly in front of the pilot's seat?" the voice said.

Mick climbed into the cockpit. "Yes."

"Place both hands over it."

One of the large trees was falling toward them. *We're done for!* She placed her hands on the dome, tucked her head under her arms, and braced herself for impact. A protective shell quickly formed around the craft, and the tree broke apart as it crashed into it. Mick breathed a sigh of relief, then gasped as soldiers emerged from the woods in every direction.

"We're being fired on from all sides!" Mick said.

"The shell should hold long enough for us to arrive and dispel them."

"Wait, should?" Mick cried. The odds didn't appear to be in her favor. She kept her hands on the dome, afraid that if she let go, the force field would collapse, and they would be prey to the enemy that surrounded them.

CHAPTER 19

THE ARCTIC?

(ANDREW)

Andrew knew Tanner was devastated about Mick.

I have to create a distraction. Something to get Tanner's mind off the disappearance before he self-destructs—and Dad's the one who can make it happen.

He approached Tanner's house and rang the doorbell. Tanner answered in his pajamas. It was obvious he hadn't used a comb in days, and there were dark circles under his eyes. He looked sloppy.

This may be harder than I thought.

"How's it going?" Andrew asked.

"Okay, I guess," Tanner said, not bothering to even look up.

Andrew hesitated as he thought through his plan one more time, but then he decided to go for it. "Look, Mick's disappearance has been hard for all of us. But she wouldn't want us wasting away doing absolutely nothing. You and I are going on an excursion to the Arctic Circle!"

"What?" Tanner said, finally looking up.

"You heard me. We're going to the Arctic! My dad's working on a project there, and he got permission for us to visit his site! Don't you remember how much fun we had when we went to Rome with him?"

"How can you even think about something like that with Mick missing?" Tanner sounded agitated "Do you *really* think it would be right for us to be out having fun when we still don't know what she might be going through or even if she's still alive?"

"Did you hear me? The Arctic Circle—as in the North Pole! This is a once in a lifetime opportunity." How could Tanner not be jumping at the opportunity? What kid ever got to go on this type of adventure? Andrew looked at his friend closely. The weight of his grief at losing Mick was even greater than he'd first suspected.

"It's not that we don't care about her," Andrew continued, trying for a less grand adventure approach. "We're *all* hoping and praying she'll be found alive and well."

"It would be a disgrace to her memory to go off on an adventure like nothing ever happened!"

"No, it wouldn't! You've got to listen to me. We've tried to help in every way possible with the investigation, and we'll continue to, but we can't just shrivel up and die. We'll keep in touch with what's going on here, and if we're needed for some reason, we'll come back."

Tanner walked out the front door and onto the porch. Andrew just waited. Finally, Tanner turned around, looked Andrew in the eyes, and in a resigned voice said, "You're right. I have to move forward. It's just so hard. But the Arctic?"

Andrew could see more emotion in Tanner's eyes than he had ever seen.

"We would need to do a lot of preparation if we're going to go. What do you think?" Andrew asked.

"If you promise we'll keep up with what's going on here, I'm in."

Andrew couldn't restrain his excitement. He gave Tanner a shove that sent him sprawling off the porch. With a big grin on his face, Andrew looked down at his friend and said, "Let's get planning. There's a lot that needs to be done. I'll email my dad and tell him we're coming."

Andrew immediately saw glimpses of the old Tanner. For their past trips, Tanner would research the destinations and suggest things the three of them could do while their parents were playing cards or talking politics. Finally, Tanner had something to research, something to plan, something to distract his mind from Mick's disappearance.

CHAPTER 20

JUDGMENT

(MICK)

Mick sat in Aspergar's vehicle, watching her enemies fire relentlessly on the protective dome that had formed over the craft.

"Yes. The dome should hold," the voice over the radio said. "We'll send a force to extract you immediately."

Large metal projectiles smashed against the protective shield and electrical charges exploded from the location of impact.

"Do I have any weapons I can use to defend the craft?" Mick asked.

"No. That craft only has defensive systems."

Great.

Enemy forces continued to fire on the shell, and Mick could see the angered and determined faces of her enemies as she climbed out of the cockpit to check on Aspergar. She hadn't had time to even check to see if he was alive when she pulled him under the spacecraft.

He's breathing.

It had taken nearly fifteen minutes to fly from the Palace of the High Priest to where they currently were, and after waiting for ten minutes, Mick was beginning to see why the response was "should hold." The shell was weakening under the continued barrage.

"We're almost there," the voice inside the cockpit said.

"Please hurry." Desperation filled her voice.

Crack.

One of the projectiles partially penetrated the shell, and Mick watched helplessly as the surface cracked in all directions.

It's over.

Just as she had resigned herself to certain demise, a brilliant shaft of light from above formed around the shell.

"Climb back in the craft and place your hands on the glass dome again. That will allow us to levitate you into our ship."

"But will the enemy fire penetrate the light shaft once the shell is gone?" Mick asked.

"We'll resolve that now."

She watched as a strange visual wave emanated from the shaft of light and the soldiers were blasted into the trees.

"Quickly. Remove the shell now!"

Mick covered the glass dome with her hands. The shell disappeared and the craft, Mick, and Aspergar were gently but swiftly levitated into a mother ship.

"Is he going to be okay?" she asked as Aspergar was placed on a suspended bed and removed rapidly from the area.

"Yes, he'll be fine," the man who escorted Mick out of the light shaft said.

"Why are these people so desperate to kill me?" Mick asked.

"Kill or capture. They'd be happy with either one," the man replied. "The Kingdom of Anatok has been at war with our people for many years. All I'm at liberty to say is that they see you as a potential weapon to accomplish their sinister designs. However, do not worry. You'll be on Olympus soon. You'll be out of harm's way there."

Mick was only on board the spaceship for a couple of minutes when the man informed her they were nearing their destination. She felt a surge of heat rush through the craft.

"You should be able to see the judgment area now." The man pointed to a large circular amber platform in the mountains below. "We were told your book instructs you to access the Cathedral of Time. Prepare to justify your need to access the sacred building. The gods are very particular about who they allow to use that holy facility."

"Thanks," she said as she began to rehearse in her mind her reasoning for pursuing Donald Carlton. She panicked as the craft hovered directly over the platform.

"It looks as though the gods are in session. They're prepared to hear your argument."

I need more time to prepare. I'm not ready. It was as though a giant clamp was squeezing her brain. *I can't think straight.* She was about to give the most important presentation of her life—before a panel of the gods. And she hadn't even given her argument two minutes thought. Highly un-Mick-like.

As she looked out the window at the majestic platform, she felt silly thinking about a quest she was sure the gods would see as trivial. A narrow stairway formed, and she slowly began to descend from the craft. Afraid to look at the gods, she focused her eyes on the transparent amber floor.

Oh my gosh. I can see the entire Inner Earth. That must be the River Styx.

As she stared at the river making its circular passes, she realized her view was zooming in on the area her eyes were focused on until she could see the expressions on the faces of individuals clamoring as they tried to cross the river.

She glanced elsewhere, and the view instantly zoomed back out.

That must be the Kingdom of Hades. Wow.

Again, her view zoomed as she continued her gaze.

As she stepped off the final stair and set foot on the platform, she tore her eyes away from the enchanted floor and forced herself to look up to see the twelve gods of Olympus seated in a circle around her.

She steadied herself like a tightrope walker about to fall off the wire.

I'm actually about to the meet the gods. Breathe.

The gods were talking amongst themselves as the craft departed, leaving her stranded alone in the middle of the platform. Mick felt completely vulnerable as she found herself isolated with gods in every direction.

Oh my gosh, I'm actually standing in front of Zeus. The zapping electrical thunderbolt in his hand less than ten feet away tipped her off. With his other hand, he was petting a lion Mick could only describe as being too large. Perched on top of his throne was a golden eagle whose flapping wings looked as though they were made of actual gold.

Why did they have to leave? She looked up at the spacecraft, which was nothing more than a speck. Mick had done enough research to know the mythological gods ran the gamut of emotions and passions and was fearful of how they might respond to her. She wanted to flee, but at the same time was soaking in the most incredible experience of her life.

The conversation between the gods stopped, and the platform became deathly silent.

What am I in for? Mick cringed as she braced herself for the worst.

"Makayla Ellen Brown, please state the purpose of your visit to Olympus." Zeus's voice thundered. Awe swept over her as she attempted to muster the courage to speak.

"So yeah, I'm Mick . . . Makayla Brown. But you already know that. Yeah, so I was . . . and then he disappeared . . . and then my dad with a gun, and then Donald Carlton . . . the secret journal. . ." Words tumbled from her mouth faster than she could think.

"Slow down. Just relax, child," the goddess Hera said as she stroked a peacock sitting on her golden robe. "We're not going to hurt you. What do you ask of us?"

Mick took a deep breath and tried again. "I'm following the trail of an ancestor. I'm trying to figure out if he murdered four people in my community, and if he did, why." She exhaled.

Ares leapt to his feet, sword and shield positioned like he was ready to do battle. "And this is important enough that you would approach the gods about it?" The snakes on the head of the Medusa that adorned his shield hissed wildly.

Hera motioned sternly in his direction, and he turned away and sat down.

"I know it may not seem important to you," Mick fidgeted nervously. "But trying to learn enough about the history of this man that I can prove my father is not involved in certain things that have led to his arrest is very important to me."

"And why do you think your pursuit of this ancestor will help?" Hera asked.

"Honestly, I don't know if it will. But I had no one I could turn to for answers. No one I felt I could safely even talk to about the situation without endangering the people I love. So I went in pursuit of answers myself and somehow ended up here.

"Is that the only reason you left your home?" Hestia, goddess of home and hearth asked.

"No." She sighed. Why had she really left? What exactly was she hoping for? "It's partly selfish as well. When I learned of my connection to these horrible murders and terrible things my father may have done, I felt like it was going to ruin my life."

"Makayla, just because someone in your family tree might be less than worthy, it doesn't have to affect your future." Zeus chastised her.

"I was also afraid of becoming an outcast."

Apollo spoke up as he gently played his lyre, "Mockery is a powerful tool used by those who would have you become less than you are capable of. But to act for yourself is the greatest gift you've been given. At times, you may feel that your environment, circumstances, and background stand in the way of your ability to reach your potential, but the truth is, the gods are merely providing you with opportunities to advance from who you are to who you can become."

The owl perched on Athena's shoulder hooted softly, and Makayla turned to look as the goddess advised her. "We will help you to continue your quest, and once you master the lessons you must learn from this situation, you will succeed. But remember, success as measured by the gods is often something far different than what you would consider success."

Mick nodded, not sure she understood, but filled with relief that they were willing to help her.

"Anatolia," Zeus beckoned in the direction of the gated entrance to the platform. "Will you please escort Makayla Ellen Brown to the Cathedral of Time?" A flaming red-haired goddess glided gracefully onto the platform. "Makayla, this is Anatolia, the goddess of the sunrise, one of the twelve goddesses of the hours of the day. Show her the drawing from the book you shared with the High Priest of Delfi, and she will assist you with the next phase of your mission."

CHAPTER 21

AGARTHA

(TANNER)

Tanner fired up his computer. He searched for sample itineraries, forecasts, and more. In the midst of his searches he came across a link titled "Admiral Byrd: Diary of my exploration flight over the North Pole."

Someone else's journal would probably give me some good ideas.

The site explained that Admiral Richard B. Byrd was an American naval officer who specialized in exploration. He received the highest honor for heroism given by the United States. *This guy was amazing*, Tanner thought.

He began to read the diary.

Shortly after nine a.m., the compasses on my plane began to act strangely. Within an hour, we were flying over a small mountain range and could see a green valley with a small river. We should have been over ice and snow. At about 10:30, our temperature indicator read 74 degrees Fahrenheit! A message came through the radio saying "Welcome, Admiral, we shall land you in a few minutes. Relax, you are in good hands." We saw a beautiful city like something straight out of a science fiction movie and were brought before the leader of this strange land who explained we were in "the Inner World of the Earth."

It took Tanner a while to get his jaw off the floor.

The guy was crazy. And yet everything other than the journal was so legitimate. Tanner checked to confirm the website wasn't a hoax. Everything he read confirmed in his mind that Admiral Byrd truly believed what he'd written. Intrigued, Tanner continued to research this idea of an Inner Earth. It had to be fake, and yet it sounded so real—and it gave him the feeling that it was something he'd always known.

The more he read, the more he opened his mind to the idea that maybe, just maybe, what he had learned in science class wasn't true. He remembered that in the center of Mick's science fair model on the layers of the earth, there was a yellow and orange object representing the hot core. According to the articles he was reading, it was actually a sun-like object that gave light and warmth to "Inner Earth" dwellers. Mick's model had a semi-transparent fluid between the inner core and the crust.

What if that space was actually an atmosphere?

Before he knew it, his mother was calling him for dinner. He'd gone through three peanut butter and jelly sandwiches and an entire bag of chips learning about this Inner Earth and the legends surrounding it.

Over dinner he continued to try to dismiss what he had read.

There's no way. It's impossible. And yet he had a nagging feeling that what he was reading was real.

By the time he went back to his room, he decided he'd stick with widely accepted information about the North Pole, not articles that seemed like tabloid material. As he was about to enter a new search term, he saw an image that caught his eye.

Passageways to Agartha (the Inner Earth).

He scanned the diagram. The first entry point was at the Pyramids of Giza.

Maybe we can get Andrew's dad to take us to Egypt as well, he thought wryly.

Next, he saw Mount Epomeo in Italy. He wasn't quite as quick to dismiss this entry point.

The Romans and Greeks were always talking about the underworld in their myths. Had the authors actually been to the underworld through this point of entry? Were the things they wrote about not myths at all, but based on events that had actually happened inside the Earth?

He shook his head. No, that was ridiculous. Things like this didn't exist. As he went to shut the computer down, one last point of entry grabbed his attention.

Mammoth Cave.

Wait, what?

Suddenly a wave of information started falling in place. Mick's obsession with the cave, her way too in-depth report—even for Mick—on Greek mythology, and the papers she left on her bed the day she disappeared that were either about the cave or Greek mythology.

A surge of excitement suddenly jolted through his body. What if Mick hadn't been kidnapped? What if she hadn't run away? Mick was always so careful, so perfect. None of those scenarios had made sense. But this, crazy as it was, made sense.

"I know where Mick is!" he said out loud.

CHAPTER 22

TRUST YOUR FEELINGS

(MICK)

Anatolia and Mick left the judgment platform and began their journey to the Cathedral of Time.

"You must be extremely careful when you travel back in time," Anatolia said.

"So it's true? Donald Carlton really did go back in time?" Mick's eyes widened. "When I saw the drawing in his book, the only thing I could imagine was that he had found a time machine, but it was hard for me to comprehend."

"Anything is possible for the gods," Anatolia said. "Like I started to say, when you travel through time, you must pay close attention to your feelings before you act."

"Why?"

"Makayla, you live in a time thousands of years after the time you will be visiting. Your present is a product, in part, of decisions you made when you went to the past. You see, your trip to the past already took place. If you do anything differently than you did in the past, your future and the futures of millions of others could be changed dramatically. You'll feel a certain harmony with the actions you take that will give you a calm confidence. If you feel a sense of discord, you must immediately stop what you're doing. Understood?"

"I guess, like if you kill a mosquito in the time of dinosaurs it will change the whole future?" Mick said recalling a science fiction book she and Tanner had read last summer.

Anatolia nodded.

"But where will those feelings come from?" Mick asked. It was easy to make sure not to hurt anyone or anything, but to follow her feelings? They had been all over the place recently. She wasn't sure if she could trust them.

"The gods will be watching over you. You won't see them while you're on the Surface, but they will see you and will be able to whisper their guidance and direction. They'll guide your actions for good if you'll let them."

"How will I know if I'm being given guidance or if it's just my own mind?"

"Your feelings. Listen to them. If you feel right, deep in your soul, then act."

Am I going to be able to do this? Mick wondered. *I've never let my feelings get in the way of reasoning and logic.*

"That's not true," Anatolia said.

"Excuse me?"

"You *have* let your feelings get in the way of logic."

"Wait, you can read my thoughts?" Mick tried to clear her mind. What had she thought since she'd gotten here? Did the gods know how unsure she was about all of this?

"Here on Olympus we can communicate either by voice or thought. It's so much easier to understand someone when they aren't constrained by finding the right words to use."

"Why do you say it's not true that I've always relied on reason?"

"Was it logical for you to jump into the River Styx back in Mammoth Cave?"

"Wait how do you know about that?"

"Let's just say that you and your friends have already been receiving guidance. You have important missions to fulfill."

"We do?"

"Yes."

I should have brought Tanner and Andrew. I knew it.

"No, it's best that they didn't come with you."

"Sorry. This whole reading minds thing is going to take some getting used to," Mick said.

"Just like what happened when you jumped in the Styx, there will be times when you will feel you need to do something that defies your own logic. But, if you feel that harmony I spoke of, you must do it. Your mind will be at ease, even though it may not make sense."

"Okay," Mick said, not sure if she could really do such a thing, especially now that she would be second guessing every idea or feeling she had. Still, she'd come this far, and she had to continue.

"We're almost there." Anatolia pointed to a building on a small hill in the valley below that looked like a cross between a cathedral and a spaceship. It had blue stained glass windows with a modern pattern and a framework straight from a medieval gothic church. It looked like a glowing, white UFO that might take off at any moment. There were three spires on top and six surrounding it on the outside. A semi-transparent dome covered the whole building. It resembled heat waves that rise above an asphalt road on a blistering hot day.

Mick stared in awe. When they arrived, Anatolia placed her hand on the translucent dome that surrounded the structure, and it dissolved. She pulled Mick closer to the building, and the dome re-formed behind them. They followed a dirt path up a gentle slope until they were at the foot of the cathedral.

"Step inside," Anatolia said, pointing to the door of an elevator-like device.

When the back doors of the elevator opened, Mick was escorted into a gothic style building filled with hi-technology.

"The controls for the Time Room are over there." Anatolia pointed to a small domed structure inside the cathedral. "Can I please see the drawings from your book?" she asked as they made their way to the control room.

Mick handed the journal to Anatolia. She looked around the room, and a surge of excitement overcame her. She recognized the controls from the drawing Donald had made in his journal. She was here, where he had been; she was following in his footsteps—footsteps that she hoped would lead her to answers.

"What does that say?" Anatolia asked, pointing to the date setting on the drawing.

"Looks like Rome—August 22, 64." Mick strained to read the small writing. The book was weathered, and the writing wasn't clear.

"Are you sure?"

"That's what it looks like to me."

"That's what we'll set it for, then." She entered the control room and began to adjust the settings. Mick recognized the map on the display as being a map of Italy, but the characters on the screen may as well have been Greek.

"Everything is set," Anatolia said as she pressed a pulsating green button on the large display screen. "Just follow the arrows."

She pointed to flashing arrows along the walkway, which Mick began to follow. "And remember—trust your feelings."

CHAPTER 23

THE ENTRANCE

(TANNER)

The police found a metal box with Mick's fingerprints in the cave. She must have found the entry point to Agartha. That's why there aren't any traces of her. She's actually somewhere inside the earth.

Tanner began pacing around his room at almost a sprint.

I have to tell the police.

No. They'll think I'm crazy.

I have to tell Mick's family.

No. They'll think I'm crazy.

I have to call Andrew. He'll think I'm crazy too, but he's the one who put me on to the Arctic idea in the first place. He'll at least humor me.

Tanner grabbed his phone and dialed.

"Come on. Pick up!" The phone hadn't even rung yet on Andrew's side, but Tanner was going crazy. He had to tell Andrew everything right away. After what seemed like an eternity, Andrew picked up.

"Andrew, you've got to get down to my house. Now!" Tanner shouted.

"Whoa. Hold on. What is it?" Andrew asked.

"Taaaaannnner? Are you home?" Mrs. Hunter had arrived home from work.

"In my room!" Tanner yelled down the stairs. He could hear the sound of his mother bringing groceries into the house.

"Listen," he whispered quickly to Andrew. "Don't say anything to anyone, but I know where Mick is. Grab your backpack and anything you could possibly need for at least a few days. I'll explain when you get here."

"Wait. Did you say you know where—"

"I'll tell you everything when you get here," Tanner interrupted. "Just hurry up, and remember, you can't tell anyone."

While Tanner waited, he continued to be haunted by the one hole in his theory.

I've explored that cave so many times. But I've never seen anything that looked like a passage to the Inner Earth. I have to be wrong. But what else could have happened to Mick?

He kept going back and forth in his mind as he paced around his bedroom.

That has to be where she is. Nothing else makes sense. Just 'cause I can't think where there's an entrance doesn't mean it's not there. The cave's huge.

The doorbell rang sooner than he anticipated.

Oh my gosh! I've got to get the door before mom does. She'll see Andrew with all his gear and start asking a million questions. It's going to ruin everything.

"I'm coming!" his mother yelled.

Fear coursed through Tanner's veins. He ran out of his bedroom, down the hall, and to the top of the steps, but he was too late. He could see his mother opening the front door.

"Hi, Andrew," she said. "Where are you boys headed this time?"

Tanner panicked.

Andrew, please don't say anything. Please. He held his breath waiting for Andrew's response.

"We're just doing a gear check, Mrs. H. You know how it is, summertime and camping and all. We'll probably head out hiking sometime in the next few weeks."

Tanner waited for his mother to start a round of questioning, but she just shrugged and motioned up the stairs. "Go on up. I think Tanner's in his room."

Tanner exhaled in relief.

The boys entered Tanner's bedroom. "Sit down," he said as he closed his door behind them. Andrew sat on the bed, and Tanner rolled the chair from his desk so he was sitting directly across from him.

He leaned forward and looked Andrew in the eyes. "You're not going to believe me on this, but you've got to hear me out. I know where Mick is—sort of." Tanner watched a puzzled look ripple across Andrew's face. He launched into a detailed account of everything he'd found, about the papers on Mick's bed and the box in the cave—everything.

Andrew listened dutifully, but when he didn't even react to the idea that their favorite destination was a passage to the Inner Earth, Tanner knew it wasn't adding up.

"Look, we all wish we could find Mick," Andrew said, "but it doesn't make sense. If there really were an Inner Earth, we'd have discovered it by now. I mean, we've sent men to the moon—over fifty years ago—and you're trying to tell me there may be an entire civilization right underneath our feet, and we don't know anything about it?

"Why not?" Tanner asked.

"Because it's crazy. How could no one, no scientist, know about this?"

It *was* strange, but Tanner wasn't going to let Andrew know he thought that too. He was trying to come up with an additional argument for his belief that Mick was there. Then he had it.

"That's why she did her science fair project on the layers of the Earth."

"She did that because she loves geology. You and I both know that."

For a brief moment, a hollow, sunken look crossed Tanner's face.

"And her project on mythology. Who puts that amount of research into a project?"

"I'm not buying it." Andrew replied. "And Mick puts that type of research into a project."

"You're just going to have to trust me. Let me grab my gear, and I'll prove it to you."

The boys opened Tanner's window and climbed into the tree in the backyard, as they had done many times in the past. Tanner had no idea what might come of this whole thing and didn't want anyone to know what they were up to. If anyone other than Andrew knew, he could only envision the whole thing blowing up in their faces.

As they rode their bikes toward the cave, Tanner braced himself for the moment Andrew would ask where the entrance to the Inner Earth was, and sure enough, as soon as they entered, he asked.

Tanner had to break the news. "I don't know. I can't figure that part out."

"Well, that seems like a pretty important missing detail."

"I know," Tanner said dejectedly.

"Maybe it's at the bottom of Bottomless Pit," Andrew said, referring to one of the deepest holes in the cave.

"Very funny! There is no bottom to Bottomless Pit. That's why they call it that."

"Exactly. They may have named it that, because everyone who has been to the bottom never came back."

Tanner could tell that Andrew was just patronizing him, but it was worth trying the pit. "Good idea. Let's start there," he said. "Do you have some rope?"

"Come on, this is me you're talking to. Of course I brought rope."

"Shine your flashlight down there," Tanner said when they reached the pit.

"Okay, but you know we're not going to see anything."

"Wishful thinking, I guess. Let's get this rope secured, and I'll head down," Tanner said. They busied themselves securing the rope, and Tanner began to descend into the darkness.

"Do you see anything?" Andrew yelled.

"No."

"Well, we're out of rope. We'll have to go home and get more."

"Okay. I'm coming up then," Tanner said, resigned to the fact that they'd had no other options. I mean he could let go and see what happened, but that didn't feel right–not like he felt when he'd decided to believe in Inner Earth.

"I can't see Mick scaling down that thing any farther than you did, especially by herself," Andrew said, pulling Tanner up the last few feet.

"Yeah, you're right. Any other ideas where there might be an entry point?" Tanner asked, not ready to give up just yet.

"Well, there's the River Styx," Andrew said, referring to the underground stream named after the mythological river. Or Symmes' Pit."

"Let's try Styx."

The boys made their way to the River Styx and began walking along the banks.

"Maybe we should be walking *in* the river," Andrew said. "You know, since Styx is supposed to be the boundary between earth and the underworld, I think the entrance would be *in* the river."

"Good thinking. I knew there was a reason I brought you along." Tanner was sure Andrew was just playing with him, but he still liked the idea.

❖ ❖ ❖

They trudged along in the river for about fifty yards when Tanner turned around to say something. Before he could speak, he stumbled on a rock and fell face first into the river—and was gone.

"Tanner!" Andrew said as he ran to the spot where his friend had disappeared. There was no sign of him. Andrew had watched him trip, saw him fall in, and yet when he looked in the stream, there was nothing. He could clearly see the bottom, but no Tanner.

Andrew grabbed a stick he saw along the bank and stuck it into the water. When it reached what should have been the riverbed, there was no resistance. The stick continued to disappear deeper into nothingness. But it *looked* like a riverbed.

Is it only an illusion?

Andrew stuck his stick in the water again. Same result. He'd always been the least adventurous of the three friends. He didn't have the same "go down swinging" attitude as Tanner. Or the same "everything is going to work out" attitude that Mick had. But still, two of his best friends were missing—one right before his eyes. Maybe being skeptical was no longer acceptable.

What if I follow him, and we can't get back? Maybe I should just tell the authorities. But if Tanner is in danger, there's no time to lose.

It was like a giant math problem was formulating in Andrew's head. There were lots of variables he was trying to solve for, but this equation had many elements he knew nothing about. Finally, he decided to do the only logical thing he could think of . . . or perhaps it wasn't logical at all.

CHAPTER 24

A Fatal Mistake?

(Mick)

It had been two days since Mick exited the Cathedral of Time, and she found herself trapped in a small cave with no apparent way out. She sat on the damp floor shivering with her arms wrapped around her knees. The sound of her growling stomach and the slow drip of water from above were the only things breaking up the eerie silence.

Mick had reviewed every aspect of her quest with a fine-tooth comb many times before she embarked, but somewhere there had been a flaw. A potentially fatal mistake. Unless she could compensate for it, the small cave was destined to become her tomb. She needed a miracle or intervention by the gods themselves to save her now. She closed her eyes and tried to listen to her feelings like she'd been told, but the only things she felt were cold and hungry. She scanned the space again through tear-filled eyes in an attempt to find something that could change her fate. To her left was the techno-gothic metal door through which she had entered the cave. She had tried many times to open it and re-enter the Cathedral, but for whatever reason it wouldn't budge.

I have to press forward. But how?

She pointed her flashlight up and to her right. It flickered. She shook it hoping that the batteries just weren't making a good connection but knowing they were about to die. In the flickering light, she could see a stone covering that looked like an exit. She viewed it as the only thing between her and solving the mystery that had been haunting her for weeks. If it were moved, she would be able to exit the cave, something she wanted desperately, but it was far too heavy to move alone. She had tried many times in vain.

Someone should have opened it from above today. What did I miss?

She looked again through her notebook.

The Mundus is opened on August 24, October 5, and November 8. She could picture herself in the library jotting down notes about how the Mundus was used as a place to safely store seed corn from the harvest until it was time to retrieve the seeds for fall planting.

Where did I go wrong?

She tore the page from her notebook in frustration, crumpled it up, and threw it across the cave.

Again, she looked at the stone.

Do I really even want it open?

She knew what waited on the other side was a race whose atrocities were well documented.

My fate might be worse than starvation if I do get out, but it's my only shot. Why didn't I just leave well enough alone? Just because Donald's journal led me here doesn't mean I'm going to find anything that will help prove him or my father innocent.

CATHEDRAL OF TIME

Mick pulled the journal out of her backpack. She illuminated it with her fading flashlight and looked at the sketch on the last page.

It all checks out. What could I have done wrong?

In frustration, she threw the journal against the wall.

"What lesson am I supposed to learn?" she cried out to the gods. "Patience? Long-suffering? Hurry up and teach me then!"

Something moved in the shadows. Mick leapt to her feet and screamed as a small rat ran across the ground in front of her. The flashlight fell from her hand and landed in such a way that it created a large silhouette of the rat scurrying away on the opposite wall. Then it went out. Mick scrambled in the darkness to higher ground along the side of the cave.

Rats. That's the last thing I need! She'd always hated them since she'd found that nest in the barn. Mick freaked out thinking about her history with rats.

Disgusting. Filthy creatures.

As she stood against the wall, she revisited her recent decisions.

What was I thinking? My stupid pride is going to end up being the death of me. If only Tanner and Andrew were here. They'd know how to get out. But they betrayed me. I couldn't bring them. I should have at least left a note for Mom, though. I'm so stupid.

Hunger pangs nearly doubled Mick over when she heard the rat scurrying across the ground again.

Am I going to get desperate enough to eat him?

CHAPTER 25

New Paradigms

(Andrew)

"Here goes nothing!" Andrew yelled as he belly-flopped into the underground stream. He tried to mimic as closely as possible what Tanner had done to assure his own passage into another realm.

I can't believe I'm doing this.

The next thing he knew he was lying on his back in a stream surrounded by a lush green meadow. He looked up at something that resembled the sun, only it was much closer and not as bright. It was more like a bright moon, because he could stare at it without burning his eyes. It was close enough that he could see solar flares and what looked like molten lava on the surface. The sky was more colorful than on the surface, and towering clouds in shades of black, tan, and off-white billowed majestically above. There was also something similar to stars, but in a much greater range of size and brilliance. Andrew sat up and could see that

Tanner was about ten feet away, standing in the middle of the stream with a big grin on his face.

"You have got to be kidding me!" Andrew exclaimed in disbelief as he sprang to his feet and ran up to Tanner and started shoving him in the chest. Tanner was shoving him back.

"You have got to be kidding!" he repeated. Andrew had only gone along to humor his friend. He never believed for a second there was any truth to it, and yet there he was standing in what could only be Inner Earth.

"We found it," Tanner said excitedly. He bent down and slapped the water with the palm of his hand. "I knew it! I knew it! I knew it! Now, let's go find Mick."

"Wait! We've got to mark this spot," Andrew said. "Make sure we can get back." He trudged to the bank and found a stick, then shoved it into the riverbed a few feet from the entrance.

"She's here somewhere," Tanner said. "We've just got to find her."

Andrew didn't reply. Beyond the meadow that flanked the stream on both sides were woods. The grass was about four feet tall, and the trees looked like those you would see in a tropical rainforest, only much taller. It was much more vivid than any place his dad had ever taken him.

"Let's head for the trees," Tanner said.

Crack.

The boys whirled around in time to see a family of woolly mammoths crash through the trees and emerge into the clearing. The ground shook beneath their feet as the massive creatures lumbered through the tall grass. Andrew stumbled backward, nearly falling into the stream. Yes, this was much more vivid.

"That thing must be fifteen feet tall," Tanner said looking at the male.

"And look at those tusks," Andrew whispered in response.

The male's tusks were at least as long as he was tall and curved around toward each other in the front. The mammoths seemed docile, but Andrew was glad they were about seventy-five yards away. He wouldn't have wanted an up close encounter. The creatures stopped and began to graze. There was no indication they had noticed that two intruders had entered their world.

As Andrew silently admired the huge beasts, he lost the grip on his backpack, and dropped it into the stream. Both boys stiffened as the mammoths turned and looked their way.

"You idiot!" Tanner said, doing his best to talk without moving his lips.

Andrew's heart was about ready to jump out of his chest. After a few seconds, the mammoths went peacefully back to their grazing.

"I think I might need some clean underwear," he said as he carefully picked up his backpack.

"Hold that thing tighter from now on, would you?" Tanner said.

"Yeah, okay."

"Do you think this means there are dinosaurs down here?" Tanner asked fearfully.

"No. Dinosaurs were extinct by the time mammoths showed up."

"Yeah, and there's no such thing as the Inner Earth, either. We better be on guard just in case the scientists are wrong."

"Nah, carbon dating proves that dinosaurs and mammoths didn't coexist."

"Okay, believe what you want, but I'm going to be on the lookout. I wouldn't want a non-coexisting T. rex to come crashing through the trees or have a pair of velociraptors who didn't get the memo that they were supposed to be extinct chase us down, because we weren't prepared."

Though he would never admit it, Andrew knew he had to throw some of his scientific belief system out the window. Roaming around the Inner Earth had more than rocked the foundations of what he trusted in.

Boom.

"What was that?" he asked.

"No idea, but there's no time to stick around and find out." Tanner pointed at the mammoths that were thundering toward them. "Head for the woods!"

Andrew watched Tanner quickly out-distance him as he fled for the dense jungle. As Tanner entered the forest, Andrew turned just in time to see the male mammoth closing fast.

Seconds later, the mammoth in full stride gave a quick flick of his head, scooped up Andrew with his tusks and carried him to the edge of the woods, where he gently dropped him. The mammoth turned and lumbered to a larger opening in the trees where the other mammoths had disappeared. Tanner grabbed Andrew's arms and dragged him into the trees.

Andrew sat in stunned silence.

Safely hidden behind the dense foliage, Andrew looked intently for an indication of what could have created such panic in the mammoths. There was something moving in the tall grass near the opening where the mammoths disappeared, and it was moving toward the opening.

"What is that?" Tanner pointed toward the commotion.

"Not so loud," Andrew said. "We've got no idea what's lurking around here. We can't give away our position."

Suddenly, whatever spooked the mammoths turned and was heading back to the other side of the meadow.

"What do you think that was?" Tanner asked.

"Not sure I want to know."

"Maybe a raptor?"

"I told you, they didn't coexist," Andrew said. "Maybe a sabretooth." He knew he could continue to deny the coexistence of dinosaurs and mammoths, but internally he wished he didn't know as much as he did about dinosaurs.

"Neither one sounds like a very good option," Tanner said, biting his lower lip.

"Agreed."

The boys sat down, and Andrew pulled some snacks out of his backpack and began to nervously munch.

"Shhh," Tanner said looking around. "Do you have to eat so loudly?"

"Sorry." Andrew replied. "You know I have to eat when I'm nervous."

They were on high alert for several hours before the effects of the adrenaline rush began to wear off, and Tanner fell fast asleep. Though equally exhausted, Andrew couldn't sleep. He was utterly disoriented. His entire soul had been ripped out. Science was what he lived for. It was who he was. His ability to spew scientific facts whenever they connected to his current situation defined him. And yet there he sat inside the earth.

When he finally did fall asleep, he watched prominent scientists on trial for their theories parade through his dreams.

CATHEDRAL OF TIME

❖ ❖ ❖

"Did you hear that?" Andrew was jerked awake by the sound of aircraft overhead.

"Huh, what?" Tanner replied half-awake.

"Don't move."

The boys listened intently and scanned the sky through the trees for the source of the noise but were unable to determine its origin.

"Check out those vines," Tanner said pointing up to the trees.

"I don't think they're vines." Andrew winced as he realized they were the longest snakes he'd ever seen. Again, a deafening noise like the sound of jets pierced the sky.

"We've got to get moving," Tanner said. "Grab your stuff."

The boys sprinted across the undulating surface of the forest floor, over moss-covered rock outcroppings, and through spectacular ferns. The deeper into the forest they got, the louder the sound of the river became as it crashed against the rocks, and a slew of unfamiliar sounds filled the air. As beautiful as the terrain was, Andrew couldn't enjoy it. Not only because of the apparent threat from above, but also since he had no idea what could be lurking behind the trees or if a horde of giant poisonous insects would emerge from beneath the ground cover.

As the thunderous sounds of aircraft began to occur less frequently, the boys began to slow their pace.

"I wonder if Mammoth Cave got its name because of the mammoths living beneath it," Andrew said.

"Hmmm," Tanner murmured. "Maybe so. After all, we're not the first to discover the passage. The cave was listed on the map of Agartha."

"Agartha? What's that?" Andrew asked.

"It's the name for the lands of the Inner Earth," Tanner said. "Enough about that, though. We've got to start looking for Mick."

"If Mick did come here, there's no way she's still alive," Andrew surmised. "We've been running for our lives ever since we got here, and she's been gone for weeks."

"Listen. Mick is one of the smartest girls I know. I've never seen her in a situation she couldn't handle. We've got to have faith and get moving."

"But we have no idea where to go."

"Well," Tanner said, "I think that just changed. Did you see that sign over there?"

"No. What sign?"

Tanner pointed to a sign along the river's edge. It was covered with strange unrecognizable characters. As Andrew was trying to determine what it said, he noticed among the unusual symbols the word *Styx*.

"Whoa! That's a coincidence," Andrew said.

"I'm pretty sure it's not a coincidence. I think it may actually be *the* River Styx. Think about it—every Greek myth about the underworld talks about the River Styx, and that sign clearly says *Styx*. I think the authors may have been here and wrote about things they experienced in the Inner Earth."

"Come on T! There's no way that's the *actual* River Styx."

"Why not?"

"It's completely ludicrous."

"Yesterday you thought the Inner Earth was ludicrous." Tanner reminded him. "Think about it. Styx was the border between earth and the underworld. And how did we get here? We jumped in a river on earth and ended up in a river in the underworld."

Andrew looked away sheepishly.

"So it looks like I not only discovered the Inner Earth but also the lands of Greek mythology!" Tanner said puffing out his chest.

"Uh, I think you mean we," Andrew said. He might not have believed at first, but he was here now, and that had to count for something. "So what do we do with this information? How do we find Mick?"

Tanner looked up and down the riverbank and then scratched his head. "I wonder . . ."

"Yes?" Andrew asked expectantly.

"Remember how passionate Mick became about mythology before she disappeared? She always liked it, but her term papers were super realistic. Almost like she had been there!"

"So? How does that help us?"

"I think if we can get our hands on those papers, they'll lead us right to her."

"The police have all of her stuff," Andrew said. "They're not just gonna hand them over. Especially if we say anything about the underworld! We'll be spending time in an asylum if we mention any of this to anyone."

"We've got to steal them," Tanner said. "I can't see any other way. Are you in?"

"You're not actually considering breaking into the police station and stealing evidence? You're even crazier than I thought!"

A smile crept across Tanner's face. He put on his sales hat and went to work trying to convince Andrew to at least come a long.

CHAPTER 26

Mundus is Open

(Mick)

"I'm going to have to do it," Mick said, staring at the rat. "It probably tastes just like chicken, anyway. Talking to myself again. Not a good sign."

I'm really not learning anything from this, she said in her mind to the gods. *In case you were wondering.*

She pulled her pocket knife out of her backpack.

"Now to catch you."

She had no light. Her flashlight had died, and the backup batteries she brought were also dead. *Who put dead batteries back in the kitchen drawer, anyway?* She angrily pictured the faces of her family members, trying to think who might have done it, but her thoughts quickly turned to how much she missed them and whether she would ever see them again. She had made the biggest mistake of her life not involving anyone else in her quest.

She listened intently to determine the rat's current position, but instead heard the fingernail on chalkboard sound of rocks scraping against one another. A small ray of light entered the chamber from above.

"The Mundus is open!" someone shouted as the stone that blocked the exit slid open.

Mick's heart leapt. She had been waiting for those words for days. She had imagined them being said over and over in her mind. She pinched herself to make sure she wasn't dreaming.

As her eyes adjusted to the light, a magnificent being appeared. A woman who emitted an unusual glow stood near the techno-gothic door. The woman waved her arms in sweeping motions, and a rock formation assembled itself, covering the entrance to the Cathedral of Time. Another sweep of her arm, and she began to fade from the bottom of her flowing robe to her torso.

"Wait!" Mick said trying to be sure she was heard only by the woman and not the men she could hear through the opening above. The being gestured with her arm and the fading stopped. Only the upper torso and head of the woman were visible.

"Who are you?" Mick asked.

"I am Demeter, goddess of the fruitful earth and guardian of its underworld portals."

"You're the mother of Persephone."

"Yes. And how do you know of my daughter?"

"I read about her. So if you guard the entrances to the underworld, did you know I was here?"

"I did."

"Then why didn't you help me?" Mick asked, exasperated. Had the gods really just been watching her the whole time? Maybe they had even placed bets on when she would crack and eat the rat. Perhaps she should have tried for him sooner.

"If I helped you immediately you wouldn't learn anything."

"What's that supposed to mean?"

"If we were always bailing out Surfacers, they'd never grow from the challenges they face."

"We?"

"The gods."

"Will you please help me *now*? I'm starving to death." *Please don't make me eat the rat.*

Demeter gave a swift jerk of her head and a plate full of fruit appeared suspended in the air in front of Mick. "Help yourself."

"This isn't the kind that will condemn me to live in the underworld forever, is it?"

In a powerful rebuke Demeter said, "Do not speak of that horrible curse!" Mick stumbled backward.

"Sorry." Mick steadied herself, reached for an apple and took a bite. "Oh," she muttered. "Can I ask you one more thing?"

"Of course."

"Since you're the guardian of underworld portals, do you keep track of everyone who comes and goes through these points of entry?"

"I do."

"Great. I was expecting someone to arrive here at the same time I did. Has anyone else come through recently?"

"No. In fact, you're the first Surfacer to come through here in nearly a decade."

"A decade? That can't be—"

"I'm sorry child. I must be off. My work here is done." Demeter made another waving gesture with her hand.

Mick babbled a few vowels trying to get her to stop, but she was gone.

What now? Donald should have shown up at exactly the same time I did. But, no one in a decade? His journal must have been a hoax. But it couldn't have been. It was too accurate.

Maybe he adjusted the settings on the time machine like he sketched in his book and never ended up going. That must be why he didn't write about anything after the Cathedral of Time. This whole trip has been a complete waste. I'm never going to get answers.

Mick approached the rock wall that Demeter had created to cover the entrance to the Cathedral. In angered frustration, she grabbed and heaved at the massive stones in an attempt to access the door.

"Let me out. I'm going back home." She cried out to the gods.

CHAPTER 27

THE PAPERS

(TANNER)

It took longer than usual for Tanner to convince Andrew to follow him. But it was breaking and entering into a police station they were talking about. Finally, Andrew succumbed to his pressure. After all, they were using Mick's notes for a good cause. Once they rescued her, no one would care what they'd done.

They returned to the clearing and scanned the meadow for any indication that whatever had frightened the mammoths was lurking in the tall grass. Once confident nothing was there, they ran back upstream. When they arrived at their marker, Andrew grabbed it and began poking around until he found the point of entry and the two of them belly-flopped back into Mammoth Cave.

"We need to leave a marker on this side as well," Andrew said.

They moved a uniquely shaped rock adjacent to the spot.

"Let's get those papers," Tanner said.

"I've been thinking, and we shouldn't have to steal them."

"What do you mean?"

"Well," Andrew said, "don't you think we could sneak in and just take pictures of them with our phones?"

"That's perfect. No one will even know we've been there." Tanner smiled, nodding his head in acceptance of the idea.

"We've got to be careful, though. The whole town may be looking for *us* now," Andrew said.

When they emerged from one of the remote entrances to the cave, it was pitch dark.

"This couldn't have worked out better," Andrew said after a quick glance at his phone. "One a.m. Plenty of time to get in, get the pictures, and get out. Let's hit my house first. I want to grab my night vision goggles. Then we'll head for the station."

"Sounds good," Tanner said.

"We should grab a solar charger for our phones, too," Andrew said. "Not that we're likely to have service in the Inner Earth, but we may want access to some apps."

"Don't worry. I already have one in my backpack." Tanner patted the large pack on his back. "Guess I've learned something about preparedness from Mick over the years."

The boys snuck into Andrew's house and ravaged the pantry, stocking their backpacks with snacks and other miscellaneous supplies, then quickly ran back outside. It was only a mile to the police station, but Tanner was interested in getting back to the cave as fast as possible.

"Let's get your dad's Vespa," he said.

"You're kidding, right?" Andrew whipped around and gave him his most unbelieving look to date.

"No. Why would I be kidding? It will get us there and back to the cave a lot faster than we could walk. Time is of the essence. Mick needs us." He was certain of it.

"We don't have driver's licenses! If I keep following your suggestions T, I'm going to end up spending the rest of my life in prison. Driving without a license, breaking and entering, obstruction of justice..."

"Come on. Where's your sense of adventure?" Tanner replied. "Besides it's for a good cause."

Andrew sighed and held up his hands in a gesture of giving up. He led Tanner to the garage, and they pushed the Vespa away from the house before starting it up.

There usually wasn't anyone out this time of night, not in a town as small as Brownsville, but still Tanner felt it important to remain as inconspicuous as possible. He turned off the scooter headlight and drove with Andrew's night vision goggles, taking back roads when he could. Andrew held on, but Tanner could hear him mutter about bad ideas the entire ride.

Brownsville's police station didn't get much action. The boys were confident they could get in easily. When they arrived at the back door of the station, they gave it a pull to see if it happened to be unlocked, but they wouldn't be that lucky. It had started to rain lightly, interrupting the absolute silence of the small town.

Andrew had disassembled just about every mechanism he could get his hands on. His bedroom was living proof. He took out his student ID and a pocket knife and began to work his magic. In less than ten minutes, they were in. A bit wet, but in.

"Her papers have to be in that file cabinet," Tanner said. "Andrew, do your stuff."

Some locks were not as easy to pick as others. After trying for about 30 minutes, Andrew finally gave up on the locked cabinet. "We're either going to have to take an axe to it or find the keys."

As they began to search for the keys, Tanner noticed a newspaper clipping pinned on the bulletin board about Mick's disappearance. He walked over and began to read. When he finished, he saw another, much older article, the paper yellowed and curling. The headline read: *Murder Suspect Missing*.

August 27, 1810—Donald Carlton, the prime suspect in the murder of three Brownsville National Bank employees, has been missing for a week. Local law enforcement combed the area looking for Mr. Carlton but haven't turned up anything.

Mr. Carlton, a well-known explorer, was influential in naming both Mammoth Cave and the underground river that flows into it.

Why would someone like Mr. Carlton have turned to a life of crime? Tanner wondered. *He was one of the most successful men in Brownsville.*

Tanner glanced down at his cell phone. 3 a.m.—they needed to get going. He looked back at the article. It talked more about the mythology of the cave and what to do if you saw Donald Carlton. He chuckled.

Don't think I'll be running into Donald Carlton anytime soon.

But he did hope to run into Mick.

"Got 'em," Andrew said.

Tanner turned around to see his friend unlocking the file cabinet.

"Let's find the papers, and get out of here."

CHAPTER 28

THE RESTLESS EXPLORER

(DONALD CARLTON)

Late 1700s–Early 1800s

A little over a year after Nathan's death, things began to change for the Carltons. Elizabeth met a young man, and the two were married. Ten months later, she had her first child. They lived with Donald and his mother. Thomas, Elizabeth's new husband, was a strong and hardworking man. Donald's mother still missed her own husband, but the birth of her first grandchild brought a new excitement to her life.

Thomas's arrival took a lot of pressure off the workload. Donald was fourteen, and the two of them, with occasional help from Elizabeth, were able to manage. Donald finally began to have some free time to spend in the cave. Over the next few years, whenever he would go into town to sell their goods, he would share stories about his discoveries. His visits to Brownsville became an attraction for the town folk. Word would spread that Donald was in town, and everyone would gather to listen to his latest adventures—which wasn't bad for business, either. The names he gave the features of the cave began to stick, and the locals began to refer to the place as Carlton's Cave.

On one of his visits, he met a beautiful young lady from Virginia named Hannah. The two courted briefly and were married. Thomas and Elizabeth had built a small home, and Donald and his bride moved in with his mother.

By this time, Thomas and Elizabeth were the parents of two children, with a third on the way. It didn't take long before Donald and Hannah passed them. Within a few months of their marriage, they were pregnant with twins and had a child each year after for the next three years. Donald's mother was extremely busy with her grandchildren. The farm was prosperous, and Donald continued his exploration. The townspeople continued to gather to listen to his stories, but there was a growing sentiment that because of his lust for adventure, he would grow bored with life in Brownsville. His mind was too active. He appeared restless.

Donald began to refer to the cave as Mammoth Cave, and the more he explained the extensiveness of the place, the more the name stuck.

By the time he turned twenty-five, Donald had become one of the most prestigious men in town. His children were active and enjoyed playing on the farm with their cousins. Hannah surprised him one day in the spring when she informed him she was pregnant with number six. Everything was looking up for the Carltons—until the tornado.

CHAPTER 29

DON'T MOVE

(TANNER)

The boys opened each drawer of the file cabinet and Andrew scanned the folders, looking for Mick's stuff. The lights were off, and he was struggling to find the folder using his goggles.

"Got it!" he finally whispered. As he started to pull a folder from the drawer, someone inserted a key in the front door. A chill ran down Tanner's spine.

Why would someone be here at three in the morning?

He looked over at the door, and noticed the clock on the wall showed 6:00.

How could that be? It was barely 3:00 when I last checked my phone.

The doorknob began to turn, and the door swung open. The lights flipped on, and there the two of them stood, folder in hand, petrified like a victim of Medusa.

"What the . . ." Sheriff Gardiner looked as shocked as they did. The Sheriff had always been nice to the boys. They hadn't been troublemakers, after all. But they always considered him intimidating and thought it best not to get on his bad side. He was at least 6'2", and had a stern look and a marine haircut. He would have made a good linebacker.

"Have a nice day!" Tanner blurted out not quite knowing what to say. The two criminals, scrambled for the back door. Sheriff Gardiner shouted, "Stop! Don't move!" They slammed the back door and sprinted for the woods. The light rain had turned to a downpour. It was still dark, but it wasn't long before Sheriff Gardiner's flashlight was illuminating their escape.

"Stop!" he yelled as they continued their flight.

The light disappeared.

"This is the worst," Andrew said. "I can't believe I let you talk me into this."

The sirens of Sheriff Gardiner's car blared in the distance. Tanner was sure he'd called for reinforcements, not because the two of them were hardened criminals, but because the neighboring communities had become so involved with the disappearances that whenever anything out of the ordinary happened, the whole county became involved—and Tanner and Andrew had just done something very out of the ordinary.

"We've got to get to the river!" Andrew yelled. "With this rain, it will be way too easy to track our footprints. If we can get to the river, they may find where we entered, but they'll never find where we exited."

"Eventually, they'll find it," Tanner said.

"No, the River Styx forks off the Green and then disappears into the cave. We'll follow that all the way to the Inner Earth. Once we're in the Green, we'll never have to exit."

CHAPTER 30

THE RIVER STYX

(TANNER)

"The sun's coming up. We're in trouble," Tanner said, trudging through the shallows of the river. He checked the time on his phone. 3:30. "What time does your phone say?"

"3:30." Andrew replied.

"That's so odd. Why are our clocks so far off? It was just six at the police station."

"It's strange," Andrew said. "Although, after the last twenty-four hours, I wouldn't call anything strange."

"Hurry up!" Tanner said. "Once the sun's up, we're going to be easy to spot." Behind them, a barking dog was getting closer. They should have fled on the Vespa like he'd originally planned. They would already be at the cave. Now, they were playing fugitives, and if they got caught, they might never get to Mick. He tried moving faster, but the cold current pushed forcefully against them.

"How long can you hold your breath?" Andrew asked in a panic.

"I don't know."

"Quick! Over by the bank. Stay under as long as you can," Andrew said right before submerging himself.

Tanner took a huge gulp of air and dove under the icy ripples. When they came up, they could tell that the dog had gone past them.

"Oh, great. Here come the copters," Tanner said as the whirling thump of metal blades sounded overhead. Brownsville had grown accustomed to them since Harvey and Mick disappeared. "We've got to get out of the river. They're going to spot us."

"We can't. If our footprints are found this close to the Styx, they'll search it above and below ground, and someone's bound to fall through the entrance. We've got to stay."

"Over there!" Tanner pointed to a couple of fallen trees that were crisscrossed slightly above water level near the bank. They deposited themselves below the trees and listened as the helicopter approached. The copter went straight for the cave entrance and began zigzagging back and forth along the Styx and over to the Green River until it was directly overhead. Once it passed, it circled back repeating the same pattern.

"They must know we took the river," Tanner said. "How many times is that stupid thing going to circle?" he asked as the copter made another pass.

This time it continued to crisscross downstream. As soon as it was out of sight, the boys made for the Styx. With the sound of the copters gone, they could hear barking dogs and the sirens of multiple police cars.

"I can't believe we did this," Andrew grumbled. "We're dead meat."

Tanner scowled. "We've got to pull this off. We don't have a choice. Mick's life is at stake. If we get caught, no one will ever find her."

They waded as quickly as they could through the river. The sound of the dogs grew louder, but the cave's entrance was in sight. They darted into the cave and moved even quicker, looking for the marker they'd left behind earlier. The sound of barking dogs now echoed off the walls of the cave.

"They're in the cave," Andrew whispered.

Tanner breathed a sigh of relief as they reached their point of entry. He belly-flopped down, but to his surprise, he didn't fall through.

"I know this is the rock we used," Andrew said in a panicked tone. "I would know it anywhere. And I'm sure it hasn't moved. What do we do?" The two boys paced rapidly in circles around the location trying to find the passage, but nothing. The sound of the dogs was growing louder.

Andrew continued. "You're kidding. We've come this far, and now we can't get back in?" He jabbed a stick into the river over and over. Each time it hit the bottom. Was the passage only open at certain times? Had they been extremely lucky the last time?

"If we wouldn't have gone back, we'd be on our way to Mick right now," Tanner said in a muted yell.

"Hey, it wasn't my idea to get the papers." Andrew tried to remain levelheaded. There had to be something they'd missed. "We'll get back in. I know we will."

"And if we don't?" Tanner asked. "We'll have to live with ourselves knowing we could have found Mick and blew it." The dogs were beginning to growl as they closed in on their prey.

"Maybe the portal moves?" Andrew said. He began to run farther down the river.

The light from the police flashlights panned the cave walls in front of them. Tanner was certain this was the end, but he still chased after his friend. Suddenly, he wasn't there anymore. With a grateful sigh Tanner threw himself toward where Andrew had vanished.

"Whew. That was close," Andrew said as they emerged in the meadowed river of Inner Earth.

"Do you think the police are going to find the passage?"

"I don't think so. I doubt they're walking in the river."

"I hope not." Tanner stared at the entrance watching for a dog or policeman to fall through. "I didn't think we'd make it."

"Do we have everything?" Andrew asked nodding in agreement.

"Too late now if we don't."

Tanner grabbed Mick's folder out of his jacket, thankful for the protective plastic of the evidence bag. "These papers are going to be a lifesaver."

"They better be, after what they just cost us!"

"What are you talking about?"

"We can't go back to Brownsville unless we bring Mick with us. We've obstructed justice. Tampered with evidence. Everyone's going to accuse us for Mick's disappearance. So we better get used to this place 'cause we're never going back." Andrew dragged himself out of the river and plopped on the muddy bank.

"Shut up," Tanner replied forcefully. "We're going to find her. Now, where does the first paper say we need to go?"

"It's about the River Styx, but I don't know if they're in order."

"Of course, they are. That's the first landmark we saw down here. Now, let's get going."

"Don't you think we should stop and read what it has to say first?"

"No time. Who knows what kind of dangers Mick's facing. Down the Styx!"

And with that they were off again.

"What's that?" Tanner asked as he heard Andrew mumble something behind him about not liking this.

"Nothing," Andrew replied.

"What do you know about the river?" Tanner asked.

"If you'd let me stop and read her paper, I'd know a lot more than I do."

"No time. If you want to read while we're walking that's fine, but we can't stop. What do you remember from class?"

"Well, wasn't Achilles dipped in the River—making him invincible?" Andrew asked.

"Hey, I am feeling pretty invincible myself, now that you mention it."

"That's nothing new," Andrew said. "But before you start feeling too indestructible, I think certain parts of Styx are supposed to be poisonous."

"Poisonous? Maybe you *better* read the paper. That's a pretty important detail."

Andrew pulled the paper out and tried to read what he could while they were walking, keeping the paper well above the water. Unfortunately, it wasn't long before the water level was above their waists and was becoming more and more difficult to navigate.

CHAPTER 31

THE GLEAMING CITY

(TANNER)

"We can't stay in here much longer," Tanner said.

The boys climbed up on the banks and began to walk through the forest, which was becoming much denser.

"I can't fit between the trees anymore," Andrew said.

"You're going to have to hold your backpack in your hand and sidestep."

"We may have to go back down to the river."

They sidestepped here and there, arguing about the best path to take for a few more minutes. Just as Andrew had made a clear case for returning to the river, they found themselves emerging into a massive clearing. Sprawled out before them was a spectacular city.

The entire place looked as though every building, every structure, every object, had been designed by a single architect. Not because everything looked the same, but because everything was so well coordinated. The city gave the impression of a single, incredibly elaborate edifice. The building windows were a deep shade of green, a glistening gold, or a charcoal black; and the metalwork that framed the structures was either bronze or black and was engineered with an industrial retro look. There were gears and gadgets of every kind incorporated into the design.

Masses of people moved on walkways. A train system was suspended in mid-air. Flying transportation mechanisms of every shape and size dotted the sky. There was no smog. Everything was immaculate. It was Oz meets steampunk meets *Star Wars*, Tanner decided.

"Well Toto, I don't think we're in Kansas anymore," he said.

"That's for sure. This place is amazing. It's . . . it's hard to put into words." Andrew continued to gawk. "Let's go check it out."

"See if there's anything in Mick's papers about it before we waste any time here."

Andrew pulled out Mick's folder and scanned the documents.

"I don't see anything."

"So what's the next paper?" Tanner asked.

"The Gate of Erebus, and it doesn't sound like anything you'd see here. Maybe it's on the other side of the city."

"Let's just bypass this place, then." Tanner's focus on rescuing Mick had him more dialed in than usual.

"I agree." Andrew looked longingly at the city. For the first time, the boys looked down at the pavement, which was made of perfectly spherical dark grey stones.

"Whoa. Do you think this is safe to walk on?" Andrew asked.

"I hope so, 'cause I don't see another option." Tanner pointed out that access to the woods had been blocked by a wall that had appeared out of nowhere. "Do you think we can climb over it?" he asked.

"No way. Looks like we've got no choice but to approach the city."

Tanner pointed to a section of wall across the open plaza. "That might be an exit over there by the river. Let's make a run for it."

"Okay. I'm right behind you."

"What the heck?" Tanner shouted as the stones under their feet began to roll. Regardless of how fast—or in what direction—they were running, they were being rolled toward the main entrance.

"I can't control where I'm going!" Andrew yelled.

"Me neither." Tanner shouted back.

The harder they tried to run away from the entrance, the faster the stones rolled them toward it. They were being transported at a constant speed in the direction of the city gate. For the first time ever, Tanner's athleticism made no difference. He was running as fast as he could toward the river, but the way the pavement moved, both of them were still side by side as they moved closer and closer to the city.

"What's that pattern in the stones?" Andrew asked.

About halfway between the woods and the main gate was a design made from different colored spherical stones. It was three circles that overlapped in such a way that in the very center there was a curved triangular shape.

"I don't know, but whatever it is, that's where we're headed."

"It's no use trying to fight it," Andrew said.

The stones stopped as they arrived in the center of the symbol and a light shaft matching the shape of the triangle quickly formed around them.

"I don't like this," Andrew said.

"Can you see where the light's coming from?" Tanner looked up.

"It's too bright," Andrew said, shielding his eyes. "I can't tell."

A mild but penetrating voice from above pierced their souls.

"State your purpose."

"We . . . We have a friend we've . . . um lost. We have come here l-l-looking for her." Tanner stammered.

"Have you no other purpose?"

"N-No. In f-fact, . . . uh . . . we would l-love to see your b-beautiful city, but time is . . . um . . . critical. If you can help us . . . um . . . it would b-be greatly appreciated. But if not, please let us . . . a . . . continue on. She may be in d-danger."

Tanner braced himself for the response. He expected some type of Victorian storm trooper to appear and haul them off to the Emerald Palace.

"Our help will be provided. As you have witnessed, severe measures have been taken that we might protect our city from forces that threaten our very existence. We recognize full well the risks that exist in this land for your friend. Do you have an image we can scan to verify whether your associate is in our fair city?"

The confirmation of dangers lurking beyond the city walls had Tanner begging in his heart that, once Mick's image was scanned, the voice would tell them she was safe within the city.

"Yes, I have a picture." He pulled out his phone and navigated to a picture of Mick posing on a rock just outside Mammoth Cave. A more focused and brighter beam appeared within the light shaft, and Tanner's phone was pulled from his hand and levitated slightly above his head. A flat green beam of light scanned the picture from top to bottom. Tanner expected to wait while Mick's image was checked against a database, but the voice responded almost immediately.

"We have no record of the current whereabouts of Makayla Ellen Brown."

"I never said her full name. Did you?" Tanner whispered to Andrew.

"I forgot she even had a middle name."

"The fact that we cannot pinpoint her current coordinates would indicate one of two scenarios. She is either on Mount Olympus, an area the gods prohibit us from monitoring, or on the outer surface, and her precise location prevents us from being able to track her at this time."

"But she's definitely not in the city?"

"That's correct."

"Can you please let us go, then?"

"You are free to leave the city if you wish," the voice said. "But I must warn you of the dangers you face."

"We know," Tanner said.

"Where would you like to go?"

"The River Styx."

"So it shall be." No sooner had the voice spoken than the round stones began to roll the boys toward the river.

"We've got to head back home," Andrew said.

"What are you talking about?" Tanner replied angrily.

"You heard the voice. She's either on Mount Olympus or on the surface. You don't really believe she's on Mount Olympus, do you?"

"Of course. It makes perfect sense," Tanner replied with enthusiasm. "This is Mick we're talking about. Where else would she go except straight to the gods?"

"Back home," Andrew replied matter-of-factly.

"When are you going to wake up?" Tanner asked. "Check her papers. They lead us straight to Olympus, don't they?"

Andrew looked, and sure enough, Mick's last mythology paper in the folder was about Mount Olympus.

"Just think. Mick might be chillin' with Zeus right about now," Tanner said. "That is so like her."

"I'm still trying to wrap my head around the fact that there's an Inner Earth. But gods? Mount Olympus?" Andrew shook his head as if to clear it of all the unexpected new information they'd received. "Hey, how do you think they knew Mick's full name?"

Tanner shrugged. "That was kind of creepy."

"Do you think they're monitoring people on the surface?"

"Sounds like it. He said Mick might be on the surface and that they just couldn't monitor her exact location. Talk about stalkers."

"Careful, T. They're probably monitoring our conversation."

"Yeah, you're probably right. They seem pretty peaceful though," Tanner said. "Still I'm worried about Mick. I really don't think she would have stayed here this whole time if everything was fine."

"Me too," Andrew said. "You don't think they can't track her because she's dead, do you?"

Angrily Tanner stared down his friend. "Don't even think that!"

"What do you suppose they're trying to protect themselves from?"

"No idea," Tanner said, "but for them to be that paranoid, it must be something pretty bad. With the kind of technology they must have, why would they need to fear anyone—or anything?"

Tanner looked back to the city but was knocked off balance as a massive explosion shook the ground. They turned to see a fireball in the sky and rapid firing from a host of spacecraft.

A booming voice from above announced, "The city is under attack. Man your stations. Protect your families."

Another explosion in the sky.

"We know you're harboring Surfacers." A sinister voice reverberated through the sky. "Surrender them immediately!"

"We've got to get out of here!" Tanner yelled.

"Are they referring to us?"

"I'm not going to stick around to find out."

"The passage is closing." Andrew pointed to the space in the wall they'd been headed for.

"Run for it."

It didn't do any good to run. The boys had forgotten their speed was controlled by the stones below them.

"We're not going to make it!" Andrew yelled.

"Dive!"

They were close enough to the passage that they both lunged through the narrow opening a split second before it completely closed.

"We have scanned the city and verified there are no Surfacers here." The same voice that had spoken to Tanner and Andrew earlier rang out across the sky.

"That's a lie. We tracked them here."

More thunderous explosions.

Tanner and Andrew descended down a paved staircase to the river's edge. On each side of the stairs were rock outcroppings; and the trees, whose exposed roots were clinging to the rocks, formed a canopy above their heads.

"I'm not sure we should have left," Andrew said.

"Why not? They were under attack."

"Yeah, but I would have felt safer with them protecting me. We've got no idea what we're going to run into out here. Plus it sounds like whoever was attacking them was after us."

"Then we've got to get as far from here as we can. If they think we're in the city, then the further away we are, the better off we'll be. How did they know we were here anyway?" Tanner asked.

"And why would they care?" Andrew replied.

The boys scampered down the stairs to the river's edge. Once they arrived, the stairway closed behind them leaving no trace of the path they had travelled. They quickly glanced around in every direction, and not seeing anyone they slipped into the Styx.

CHAPTER 32

PAYING THE TOLL

(TANNER)

The Styx had widened significantly from the small creek the boys waded through when they first entered Inner Earth. Their surroundings had grown significantly darker. The sun hadn't gone down—there was no place for it to go—but there was a dark fog surrounding the area.

"The darkness should provide some cover," Tanner said, shivering. "Get out your night vision goggles."

The sound of the explosions had become more and more distant.

"I'm surprised we haven't run into any troops on the ground," Tanner said.

"Me too—knock on wood."

"Why do you think they're after Surfacers?" Tanner asked.

"No idea, but we better not tell anyone where we're from."

The canopy of jungle became denser, and the pace of the Styx began to accelerate as well. The rocks cropping up in the river had created some serious rapids, and it became more and more difficult for the boys to walk or to hear one another. Gradually, the steep rock walls along the sides of the river began to level off, and the fog dissipated. Ahead was a mostly flat clearing on each side of the river. In the darkness, Tanner could see the distant silhouette of a pier. As they got closer, they realized there were several dozen people swarming around the pier.

"What's going on?" Andrew asked.

"Looks like mud wrestling to the death."

It was a horrible sight. There was biting and yelling, punching and grappling as a mass of people tried to cross the river on foot. With all the commotion, it was hard to tell if some were actually drowning, but Tanner was convinced they were. Hoards were attempting to cross, but he hadn't seen anyone successfully exit on the other side.

"Excuse me," came a voice from behind.

Andrew jumped. He turned around and saw a weathered elderly woman.

"Could you spare an obol?"

"What's an obol?"

"A coin. Any kind of coin."

Andrew began digging through his pockets.

"I need it to pay Phlegyas," she said as she pointed to the dark silhouette of a figure standing on the pier. "He won't ferry anyone across without it. Been roaming the banks for sixty-nine years now. Still another thirty-one to go unless someone'll give me an obol."

"Tanner, you got any change?" Andrew shouted above the din. "Oh, hey, never mind. Looks like I've got a couple of quarters." Andrew pulled them out of his pocket and held them high in the air.

"Don't give 'em to her!" Tanner yelled, lunging for Andrew.

"Why not?"

"We need them ourselves," he said as he reached out and grabbed one of the quarters.

"But she's been waiting sixty-nine years."

"Andrew, now's not the time to be a philanthropist. We're trying to rescue Mick. We need those."

"They've got obols!" Someone yelled from a few yards away. There was a mad rush toward the boys as they tried to hold the coins away from the zombie-like mob.

"T! Help me!" Andrew screamed. Tanner wrestled him loose from the grasp of a couple of men.

"Run for the pier!" Tanner yelled.

They slashed their way through the masses kicking and clawing to get free as hands grabbed them and the smell of bodies and sweat surrounded them on all sides.

"Get 'em," another yelled.

"Put the coin under your tongue," Andrew said as they ran.

"What? You're making that up, right?" Tanner said, a disgusted look on his face.

"No. Mick's paper said the obol had to be under your tongue."

"Seriously. Can you imagine how many germs there are on a quarter?" Tanner said as they continued to fight their way to the pier. "Who knows where it's been. That's probably why people die doing this. It's disgusting."

Andrew gave a quick gesture at the throngs around them. "Not any worse than this. Just do it! Focus on the fact that you're doing it for Mick."

"She better be grateful when we find her." Tanner reluctantly stuck the coin in his mouth.

They leapt onto the pier and made a dash toward Phlegyas.

"Where'd everyone go?" Tanner asked when he realized no more dirty hands were reaching for him.

They turned around to see the masses attempting to step onto the pier and being electrocuted by a strange force field. It wasn't stopping the throng from trying, though. The desperate looks on their faces were horrifying as they attempted over and over to force themselves through the electrical charges.

"Aren't you glad you put that coin under your tongue?"

"Not really. Couldn't we have just held it in our hand?"

"You're the one who keeps saying we have to follow Mick's papers."

"Well, maybe we don't have to take everything literally. Anyway, let's find this Gate of Erebus place. We've got a boat to catch."

Phlegyas had moved so he was standing directly behind them. When they turned and saw him staring them down, Tanner thought he might prefer to just go back and face the zombie horde again. The ferryman was close to eight feet tall and had one eye loosely stitched closed with some course, black twine. The other was open wider than normal. His skin was grey and leathery, and he had a long face with hollow checks and high cheek bones. His short, scraggily, gray goatee on his protruding chin matched his unkempt shoulder length hair. He was wearing a tattered cloak made from a short-haired animal skin that had been patched many times and was splattered with mud. The hood was off his head and resting on his back. A series of prominent scars protruded from his neck in the shape of a sabre-tooth tiger skull.

As they stared fearfully, his hand shot out and grabbed Tanner's face. Tanner let out a yelp. Phlegyas squeezed his cheeks and pried his mouth open to get the obol. Tanner thought he was going to hurl. Not only was there a dirty coin in his mouth, but the filthiest being he'd ever seen was reaching in to remove it. After Phlegyas secured the obol from Tanner, he moved to Andrew and did the same thing. Tanner watched as Andrew dry heaved. Having secured both coins, Phlegyas turned away and walked down the pier. The boys looked at each other in disgust and spat onto the ground over and over trying to remove the horrible taste in their mouths. Phlegyas motioned for them to follow and climbed down the ladder into the rocking boat. As Tanner and Andrew descended, Phlegyas held out his bony hand to help the friends one at a time. There was a flurry of zapping electrical noises, and the boys looked back to see the jealous onlookers desperately trying to access the pier again through the electrical charges.

The boat reminded Tanner of a Venetian gondola in its basic shape. It was far more weathered, though. The wood was cracked, broken, and covered in mud. It had a dark and fearsome looking sea goddess carved on the front like the ones on Viking ships and a mermaid's tail on the back.

Phlegyas hadn't said a word. He had only gestured. He pulled the hood over his head making it extremely difficult to distinguish any expressions in the darkness. Their ferryman turned away, looked heavenward, and yelled with an Inner Earth-shattering voice.

"Curse you Apollo!" He turned around, leaned over, got right in the boys' faces, and shouted while spraying them with glowing, green spit. "Never. Never. Never confront the gods."

The boys backed away, cowering in fear. He grabbed their shirts near the neck and shoved them backward, then turned around and stormed to the front of the boat. They shook themselves off and timidly returned to their seat.

Andrew whispered to Tanner. "Well, Apollo should be happy."

"What?"

"Mick's papers said Phlegyas was cursed by Apollo and forced to warn anyone he ferried to not confront the gods."

"If that's how you turn out by confronting them," Tanner said, "he makes for a pretty compelling case not to do it. Why was he cursed in the first place?"

"I guess his daughter was one of Apollo's lovers. When she cheated on him, he had her killed."

"Hardly seems fair that Phlegyas was cursed for that."

"Well, Phlegyas was furious about his daughter's murder and burned down the Temple of Apollo."

"Important safety tip," Tanner replied. "Don't mess with the gods."

Phlegyas untied the rope that was holding the boat to the dock, and they were on their way. It was like a whitewater rafting trip except there was no white to the water. Throngs of people in the river clamored in the darkness to climb into the boat. Phlegyas bashed their arms and hands relentlessly with his oar, and their cries added to the commotion.

Amidst the chaos of screams, Tanner recognized Andrew's cry for help. He whipped around to see that a grotesque man had reached into the boat and grabbed Andrew's arm. The figure yanked hard, and Andrew scrambled to keep from falling overboard. Phlegyas began beating the man with an oar in an attempt to force him to let go. Tanner grasped Andrew's leg and pulled with all his might to keep him from being dragged into the river. Unable to withstand the pounding, the man finally let go, and the boys watched him sink into the depths.

The farther they got from the dock, the number of people attempting to get in the boat and fight their way to the other side dropped. The rapids had become far too intense for anyone's survival. Periodically, the boys could see the silhouette of Phlegyas's head turn to look their direction, and he would break into a maniacal laugh.

After what seemed like hours, the boat finally began to stabilize. They sailed through occasional rapids, followed by periods of calm. The river was still very muddy, and its speed was extremely high, even in the calm areas. Eventually, the rapids were gone entirely, and the boys took turns sleeping in the darkness.

❖ ❖ ❖

While Tanner was sleeping, Andrew pored over Mick's papers. He still wasn't convinced Mick was in the underworld, but he'd seen enough things that matched his knowledge of mythology that he wanted to brush up on what she'd written.

Could it really be true? Are the myths actually a reality?

Even though he was on the River Styx being escorted by Phlegyas, who was cursing Apollo, Andrew struggled to accept it all. He kept pinching himself to see if he would just wake up and find it all had been a dream. But each time he pinched, it definitely hurt.

After several hours of calm, they were jolted again by the heaving of the boat and found themselves traveling through rapids larger than those they'd originally encountered.

"Look over there. It's more people trying to cross the river. We must have made one complete pass around the underworld"

"You think?" Tanner asked.

"Yeah, they're the ones that successfully crossed the first section and are attempting to cross the second section here," Andrew said, remembering what he'd read in the papers. "We've got to stay away from the water for sure from this point on."

"Why?" Tanner asked.

"Didn't you read Mick's papers?" He was a little annoyed at what a big deal Tanner had made about him needing to read the papers.

"Well, I might not have read everything. Anyway, why do we need to stay out of the water?"

Andrew furrowed his brows at Tanner and then sighed. There was no use in getting mad at his friend. They needed to keep calm and help each other in every way possible if they ever wanted to get back home. "She said once Styx makes a complete pass the water becomes *entirely* poisonous, will dissolve most anything, and will fry your brain for a year if you drink it."

"Another important safety tip," Tanner said. "Stay away from the water."

"The good news is we only have six more passes to go," Andrew said.

"What?"

"Styx makes seven passes around the underworld before we hit the River Acheron and the Gate of Erebus."

"Okay," Tanner said. "Sit back, relax, and enjoy the ride. Oh, and keep your arms and legs inside the ride at all times."

It was a few hours later when Tanner yelled, "This has got to be it!"

High above the river was a spectacular gate. The boat was in incredible torrents for the fourth time—the heaviest rapids yet.

They had been traveling in the darkness for some time, but in this area of the river, there was a palpable mist in the air. It was like fog, but extremely patchy and black. Emerging in and out of the mist was a smattering of bats flying in erratic patterns.

"But we haven't gone around seven times," Andrew said. "Mick's paper definitely said seven. And I don't see the River Acheron. This can't be Erebus."

"She also said if you stay on the Styx too long you'll end up in the Stygian Marsh. I don't know about you, but I don't feel like being reincarnated and sent back to earth. Check again, this has to be it."

"Okay. Okay. I'm looking." Andrew quickly scanned the papers.

"I can't find anything," he cried out as he frantically searched to locate more information on the Gate of Erebus.

Tanner didn't appear to be listening or care what the papers said. He stood up and ran to the side of the boat as they neared the gate. "Jump! Now!" he screamed before taking a flying leap.

CHAPTER 33

CERBERUS

(ANDREW)

The boys leapt off the boat onto a small rock precipice far below where the gate stood as it towered above the cliffs. A second later, and they would have missed the ledge and plunged into the poisonous Styx. As it was, Tanner had one foot on the rock and the other hanging above the rapids. He made a grab for a plant dangling out of the side of the cliff.

"My shoe!" Tanner yelled as the water splashed up. There was a sizzling noise and the sole of Tanner's shoe was gone.

"The plant's coming loose."

"Don't fall in!" Andrew shouted. "Mick said the water—"

"I don't care what Mick said! Just get over here and help!" Tanner screamed. "Unless you want your brain fried by my *fist*!"

Andrew lunged for him as the plant dislodged, and he began to fall off the rock.

"Got ya," He said as he pulled Tanner safely onto the ledge.

"Whew, that was close."

"Never confront the gods!" Phlegyas yelled above the noise of the river. "Never!"

"I hope you're right about this being the Gate of Erebus," Andrew said. "Mick's paper definitely said seven times around and that Charon the ferryman would be waiting at the gate."

"We couldn't take the chance of continuing to the Stygian Marsh. The last thing I need is to be waddling around Brownsville as a penguin or something."

"Good point," Andrew said.

"Hey, have you got anything to fix this shoe?"

"I think I've got some duct tape." He rummaged through his backpack. "You can fix anything with that stuff." Andrew grabbed his tape and wrapped it around Tanner's shoe. "So what do we do now?"

The boys were in a precarious position. The small ledge they were on was the only thing between them and death in the Styx. Above them was a cliff that they would have been happy if it had actually been straight up.

"We've got to climb it."

"Are you crazy? I can't climb that thing."

"Sure you can," Tanner said. "At least you better be able to."

"No way."

"Come on, remember that rock wall at the state fair last year? You climbed that."

"Yeah, but I had a spotter and was tied to a rope."

"And you only fell twice," Tanner said, trying to grab the words and pull them back into his mouth, but it was too late.

"Exactly. It'll only take *one* fall here and life is over." Andrew did not like those odds. He'd only agreed to join this excursion to help Mick—not to find his skin burned from his bones by an acid river. If the fall didn't kill him first, that is.

"Well, we can't spend the rest of our lives on this ledge."

"I think we just wait for the next boat. I'd take reincarnation over trying to scale this."

"Come on. Just stay close. I'll tell you where to step. We'll go slow."

Andrew looked up the cliff wall that Tanner had already started to scale. If he lived through this, he and his so-called best friend were going to have words. "All right." He sighed. "But I still think reincarnation might be better."

"Don't look down," Tanner said as Andrew inched his way behind him. It was too late. Panic set in, crawling over every inch of Andrew.

"One step at a time," Tanner coaxed. With some additional encouragement, Andrew began to climb again.

"Ahhhhhh!" Andrew screamed as his feet slipped off the rock they were braced on. His legs dangled high above the river. *I'm going to die. I'm going to die.*

"Swing your legs back toward the cliff," Tanner yelled.

"I don't think I can without losing my grip."

"You've got to. You'll never be able to pull yourself up any farther with just your arms."

Slowly, Andrew swung back and forth. His thoughts swung also between remembering the fall from the rock wall last year and the thought of ending up a fried fish.

"A little farther," Tanner encouraged.

Andrew swung again and was able to anchor his feet. He pushed off and continued his ascent.

"Look out!" he yelled as a boulder from the cliff broke free and careened toward Tanner. He pulled himself flush against the cliff and the rock snagged on his shirt, ripping it, and nearly pulling Tanner along with it into the river. "We're never going to make this," Andrew exclaimed shaking his head in disbelief. But after a few more close calls, the boys finally reached the top and found themselves in front of a dark and ominous gate.

"I knew you could do it," Tanner said as he gently shoved Andrew in the shoulder. "You just need more confidence."

"Had my life flash before my eyes a few times, but here we are I guess."

"Aren't you glad you didn't choose reincarnation?"

"If my heart recovers, I will be," Andrew said as he exhaled. "Have you given any thought to how we're going to get back? 'Cause I won't be climbing *down* that cliff, if you were wondering."

They stood in silence, looking at each other and realizing there was no way back. Finally Tanner broke the silence. "Stop being so negative. We'll figure it out. Come on."

The massive gate consisted of two doors that made a shape like the neck and head of a cobra. Ram horns wrapped around the upper portion of the doors, and goat horns extended above the gate in the center. A golden cobra emerged above the doors. Along the sides were a series of sloping walls topped with mammoth tusks that gave the impression of a giant rib cage.

"It's incredible," Andrew said.

"For sure. It *has* to be the entrance to the underworld." Tanner sounded a bit unsure.

"Now, we need to figure out how to get through it."

As they gazed at the gate, a trap door they hadn't noticed on the ground in front of them flung open and a massive beast leapt out. It was a black three-headed dog that snarled angrily as it stared down at the boys. It foamed at the mouth and looked anxious for its next meal.

Tanner screamed.

Andrew groaned. "Why does it have to be dogs?"

Around the necks of the creature was something that at first glance looked like the manes of a lion. The creature lurched at the boys but luckily, the chain restricting it stopped the beast inches from their faces as they stumbled backward.

As Tanner and Andrew attempted a backward crab crawl, the manes flared out. To their horror, it wasn't fur at all. It was venomous snakes that had been lying docile against the dog's necks, but now looked poised to strike. The razor-sharp fangs of the dogs were snapping ferociously in the boys' faces, and the snakes began to strike as well.

"Reincarnation would have been better," Andrew cried in a frantic tone.

The creature began to swipe rapidly at the boys with its lion-like paws. Tanner took another crawl backward and felt the edge of the cliff. The earth beneath his hand broke off and careened into the river below.

"Don't back up!" Tanner shouted recognizing the danger behind them.

"The chain! It's coming loose!" Andrew screamed.

The dog's eyes had turned fiery red, and it looked more bent on their destruction than ever. Just when they thought they might have a few seconds to formulate an escape plan, since they were still barely beyond the beast's reach, the ground began to crack beneath them. The thunderous lurching was causing large sections of the earth around them to slough off into the Styx.

"We're dead!" Andrew screamed.

A snake struck at Andrew's face, and he thrust himself back as far as he could. He heard something in his backpack break. Music began to emanate from below him.

"What is that?" Tanner asked as a classic rock song about the grim reaper began to play.

"Must have turned on when I fell on my backpack."

"Not the best time for a song about the grim reaper," Tanner replied. The dog lunged again, and more earth broke off into the river. "I think we're about to meet him," he added.

"What's going on?" Andrew asked as the snakes began to lie back down on the necks.

"The music," Tanner said as the dog appeared to be getting groggy. "Whatever you do don't stop it." Tanner looked over at Andrew's backpack.

"Look out!" Andrew yelled.

Tanner turned just in time to see the huge dog collapsing toward them. He rolled away as the beast slammed to the earth right where he'd been. More earth cracked and plummeted into the Styx.

"We've got to get out of here before he wakes back up," Tanner said.

The boys ran for the gate.

"You need to change your tastes in music," Tanner said.

"It worked, didn't it?"

"Yeah, I guess so. I just hope that song wasn't some kind of omen."

"So do you believe me now?" Andrew asked.

"About what?"

"That Mick isn't here. Her papers clearly said seven times around the underworld. We only went three. Plus, she didn't say anything about a three-headed dog."

"She's down here," Tanner said gritting his teeth. "I know it. Now, figure out how to get that gate open would you."

Andrew began to rummage through his backpack.

To their surprise, the gate opened on its own, and a figure emerged out of the mist.

"Oh great. You actually *summoned* the grim reaper!" Tanner whispered.

"Very funny, you idiot. Actually, I think that's Charon the ferryman of the River Acheron."

"Then we *are* in the right place. This *is* the Gate of Erebus," Tanner said enthusiastically.

Charon was hunched over and elderly. He had a scraggily gray beard and was thin and brittle. He wore a rust-colored hooded cloak made of wool that was tattered and frayed along all the edges. His eyes looked hollow and distant. Tanner and Andrew would have felt sorry for him had they met him on the streets at home, since he looked like a worn-out homeless man. However, they had no idea what to expect from him here in the underworld, and they weren't sure whether to be apprehensive or sympathetic.

He beckoned, and they hesitantly followed through the gate and down a set of stairs to their right.

"Are those bats?" Andrew asked, moving to the side opposite the moss-covered gothic archways where the huge creatures were hanging.

Crack.

One of the wooden plank stairs snapped, and Tanner's leg plunged into the hole.

"You all right?" Andrew asked as he helped Tanner pull his leg out.

"I'm fine."

A massive thicket covered everything like a canopy. As they got to the bottom of the stairs, Andrew looked to his left and could see a river thats source was the Styx. A portion of that river was flowing through an underground tunnel. Swarms of bats were diving up and down; occupying the space between the thicket and the water.

A large bat flew directly toward Andrew and landed on his chest. He flailed his arms wildly.

"Get him off of me!" he yelled.

Tanner rushed over, waving his arms like an overgrown bird.

"I hate this place," Andrew said as frustrated tears made their way to the corners of his eyes.

Charon motioned for the boys to get in his boat. It was similar to the one on the Styx, but the carvings were of multiple sea goddesses that were more lifelike and threatening. Andrew did a double take, convinced he saw one of them move. The craft was newer and not nearly as dirty and weathered. The friends got on the boat and were soon being ferried down the Acheron. The darkness was heavier and damper than the mists they'd experienced before. Andrew grabbed a lighter from his backpack and tried to flick it again and again, but it went out immediately each time. On one of his attempts he fumbled it into the river.

Tanner reached for the lighter.

"No!" Andrew screamed as his arm shot out and slapped Tanner's hand away from the water.

There was a sizzling noise, a few sparks, some flames and hissing, and thick bubbles as what little remained of the lighter submerged in the mud.

"I had no idea your reflexes were so good," Tanner said in amazement. "Thanks."

"I wonder if it dissolves steel." Andrew reached for his water bottle.

"Of course, it does. You saw what it did to your lighter."

"Yeah, but that was plastic."

Andrew couldn't restrain himself.

"What are you doing?" Tanner sounded incredulous as Andrew lowered his water bottle carefully scooping in some of the poisonous water.

"Just gonna run some tests on it when we get back to Brownsville."

"Just don't drink it on accident. We don't want your brain fried any more than it already is."

After the brief interruption, the Acheron returned to its glasslike stillness. The farther they sailed, the more their terrified anticipation grew. At any moment, something might spring out and attack or pull them into the destructive water. Their heads jerked with every small sound. There was the faint sound of a few crickets and the fluttering wings of the bats, and that was it. Gradually, the bats began to disappear, and even the crickets stopped their chirping. Everything had become completely still. The boys were paralyzed with fear and unable to speak. They could see glowing objects in the darkness of the thicket and couldn't determine if they were the eyes of creatures or not. The silence finally broke with horrific shrieks and bone-chilling cries. When the howling subsided, there was an eruption of cackling laughter. It was as if someone was taking great joy and pleasure in torturing another. Tanner and Andrew looked at each other. Nothing was said, but each knew what the other was thinking.

Am I next?

It happened again. Blood-curdling screams, then evil laughter. The trip down Styx was harrowing, but this was worse. Andrew remembered reading something in Bible study about the weeping, wailing, and gnashing of teeth of the wicked. This sounded a lot like what he had imagined that would be. He couldn't imagine a worse fate, until it reached out and grabbed him from the inside.

CHAPTER 34

THE TORTURE OF ACHERON

(TANNER)

Tanner stiffened as he heard Andrew's blood curdling scream. He spun around to look at his friend, who was writhing in pain.

"Andrew!" he yelled. "Are you okay?"

No response. Tanner watched helplessly as his friend winced, hollered, screamed, and thrashed about. He tried to reach down and steady him to no avail. Finally the torture stopped. Tanner heard more cackling and laughter. But this time he felt a sense of rage knowing that whatever or whoever had done this was laughing and cackling at the pains his friend had just endured.

Andrew wailed as he shook his head like he was still trying to snap himself out of what he'd experienced.

"What happened?" Tanner asked.

Whimpering, Andrew said, "It was the worst experience of my life." He was so limp it looked like his entire skeletal structure had been removed from his body.

"I don't know how to describe it," he continued. "It was like I felt every type of suffering I've ever experienced all at once. Every stomachache, every heartache, every sorrow. Broken bones, headaches, and guilt for anything I've ever done wrong.

They were all there. Then I started to feel pain for things that hadn't even happened yet, but it was as though I knew they were going to happen. It was weird, T. I wanted to die, but I knew I had to make it through. I tried to concentrate on how badly I wanted to find Mick, and somehow I survived."

"That's crazy! Every pain? All at once? Any advice? 'Cause I'm sure my turn is coming."

It was too late. The torment descended on Tanner and he began screaming. The strong, athletic Tanner curled up in a fetal position and began writhing in pain and hollering. Tanner was re-living the horrible sorrow he felt when his sister, who was only five at the time, battled and lost her fight with leukemia. He felt the pains he endured when his father constantly belittled him over the years and told him he would never amount to anything. He re-visited the pain he felt when his father abandoned him and his mother. He experienced the sorrow he felt as he watched his mother sob for her daughter and husband who were both gone. He pictured himself on the basketball court trying to relieve the anger, sorrow, and confusion.

Mixed with the emotional trauma was the physical suffering he'd endured over the years, and he certainly had his share of that as well. Every cut, every broken bone, every illness all mixed together like a stabbing needle through his chest. When the ordeal ended, Tanner weakly propped himself back up into his seat the best he could.

"Oh man," he said feebly. "That was horrible. I took your advice though. It was much easier to endure my own pains when I was thinking of someone else. Do you think we'll have to go through it again?" Tanner asked.

"I hope not. I'm not sure I'd survive."

There were several more rounds of screams and cackles, but gradually, the thicket above became less dense and the mist of darkness began to dissipate.

"Is that the sky?" Andrew asked finally.

"We survived it," Tanner said.

The boys shielded their eyes as they tried to adjust from absolute darkness to incredible light.

"What's that?"

"Looks like another city."

As they emerged from the thicket, they could see a beautiful garden with gazebos, a large greenhouse, and other structures in front of them. Beyond the garden were two spectacular buildings.

"T, we've got to stop this madness. We're never going to find Mick down here, and frankly I'm not sure *we're* going to survive. Plus think about what our parents must be going through."

Tanner wobbled like a staggering boxer. He had been so bent on rescuing Mick that he hadn't considered the impact being missing was having on his mother who only had him to lean on. There was a long pause as he relived the pains he had just witnessed his mother endure during his torture on the Acheron.

I will not let her lose me too.

"We're going to find Mick *and* survive," Tanner said more resolved than ever. "Besides, we can't go back without her. You said it yourself. We'll end up in prison."

"Prison sounds pretty good right about now."

"We're going to find her"

"What makes you so sure?"

"Just trust me," Tanner said. "I feel compelled that we can't back down."

"But so far, I've been guilty of breaking and entering, was almost killed by a three-headed monster, and just thought I was going to die from excruciating pain."

"We can't go back," he said, pausing for emphasis after each word. "Are you planning on telling Charon you want a round trip ride on the Acheron? It's going to be easier to go forward than back at this point, and we're almost there. The only other thing Mick mentioned in her papers between where we are and Mount Olympus was the Great Hall of Judgment, and how hard could *that* be?"

"I don't know, but people always talk about Judgment with fear and trembling, and I've done enough of that already on this trip."

"Come on. We're almost to Olympus. Even if you don't think Mick's here, you wouldn't stop when we're that close to the home of the gods would you? The worst is behind us. Hey, speaking of breaking and entering, did you see that article in the police station?"

"No, what article?" Andrew asked.

"There was an article about Donald Carlton. I guess he was the one who named Mammoth Cave."

"What does that have to do with anything?"

"Come on, don't you get it? He did a lot of exploring in the cave and named it Mammoth Cave. Do I have to spell it out? He must have gone through the portal. He must have seen the mammoths."

"You think so?" Andrew asked. "Well, if you're right about Mick *and* Donald, we now know two people who entered this place . . . and neither one of them ever returned. I'm not sure I like those odds."

"But if Donald Carlton named the cave because of the mammoths, he obviously was in and out of this place before he disappeared for good," Tanner said. "We just have to make sure we figure out the secret to exiting the underworld the same number of times we enter it."

"Just a minor detail." Andrew was clearly irked.

CHAPTER 35

THE TORNADO

(DONALD CARLTON)

"Take cover!" Donald yelled. "Everyone in the storm cellar!"

The winds howled fiercely, and Donald could see the funnel cloud had touched down and was heading straight for his farm.

"Is everyone accounted for?" Thomas asked as he began a headcount.

"Little Bridget's missing," Donald said, climbing the ladder and thrusting the door of the cellar open.

"Bridget!" His voice was filled with terror. *Where could she be?* He ran to the barn. "Bridget!" The swirling cloud raced toward their fields.

"Dad! I didn't know where to go." Bridget was running from the barn to the house. Donald ran to his oldest daughter, grabbed her hand, and raced to the storm cellar. He picked her up and handed her down to Thomas and then stepped inside himself before closing the door.

A furious sound like a locomotive roared overhead as the tornado meandered through their fields, and then everything went quiet. Donald was closest to the door, so he slowly pushed it open, fearful of what he would find. His fears were realized as he saw that their crops were completely destroyed. The home and barn were damaged, but were repairable.

Thomas climbed out of the cellar.

"At least we're all safe," he said.

"How are we going to survive without a harvest?" Elizabeth asked.

"We'll find a way," Donald replied.

CHAPTER 36

PERSEPHONE'S GARDEN

(TANNER)

Charon pulled the boat alongside the river's edge, and the boys disembarked, careful to not touch the water.

"Where to now?" Tanner asked.

"Well, Mick's next document is about the Kingdom of Hades."

"Wait, isn't Hades a bad guy?"

"That's what I thought," Andrew said. "He *is* the king of the underworld, and from what we've seen, there are some pretty terrifying things here."

"So what's in the Kingdom of Hades?"

"Persephone's Garden, Hades's Palace, and the Great Hall of Judgment."

"Who's Persephone?" Tanner asked.

"Come on, T, even *you* should remember that. We talked about her in English just before summer break."

"Pretend for a moment I wasn't paying attention."

"That'll be easy." Andrew shook his head in obvious frustration.

"Persephone was Zeus's daughter," Andrew explained. "She was kidnapped and taken to the underworld by Hades. Don't you remember? Zeus intervened and forced him to return her to the surface."

"So why does she still have a garden down here?" Tanner asked.

"Hades tricked her into eating pomegranate seeds before she left."

"What's so special about pomegranate seeds?"

"It's any food. If you eat or drink anything in the underworld you're doomed to spend eternity here."

"Wait. Have we eaten anything since we've been down here?" Tanner asked.

"No. You almost ate some berries when we first arrived, remember?"

"Yeah, I don't even remember why I didn't—that was lucky."

"I don't think it would have mattered," Andrew said. "How could eating something affect your ability to leave? It's not logical."

"Go ahead and take a chance, then," Tanner said. "Eat something and see what happens. Not me. It's not worth the risk."

Andrew nodded, agreeing with Tanner on this one.

"So back to Persephone. Does she have to stay here forever?"

"No. Zeus, Hades, and her mother, Demeter, negotiated a deal so she only has to be here a few months every year. That's when we have winter on the surface."

"Because her mother is goddess of the harvest and is cursing the earth."

"You got it. See T, you can learn when you apply yourself."

"You don't think Mick ate something while she was down here, do you?" Tanner asked.

"First of all, I don't think she's here. But if she were, there's no way she would have eaten if she could help it. She wrote about all this *and,* unlike you, she paid attention in class."

"She's been gone for weeks, though. She would have had to eat."

"If she did come here, I guarantee she was much better prepared than us. You know how she is."

"So what was the other place you said was here?"

"The Great Hall of Judgment?"

"Oh, yeah. What's the scoop on that?"

"It's where you're judged. If you're evil you go to Tartarus; ordinary, you go to the Asphodel Meadows; and if you're good, to the Isles of the Blessed."

"So where do we go?"

"Probably Tartarus for you." Andrew laughed.

"No, you idiot, I mean where do we go right now?"

"Well if you still believe the papers are a map to Mick, then Mount Olympus."

"That wasn't one of the options you listed."

"Once you're judged, Hades can give you permission to go to Olympus. If you're worthy, you can dwell there with the gods."

"Then we're off to Olympus. I'm not sure either one of us will be judged worthy to go there, though, so we're going to have to fool the gods and break in," Tanner said with a furtive look on his face.

"Wait a second, wouldn't that violate the 'don't mess with the gods' safety tip? Remember Phlegyas?"

"Hello, how can I be of assistance?" A beautiful voice startled the boys, and they turned around quickly. What they saw was a woman who truly looked like the daughter of a god. She wore a jewel encrusted white robe, and her blonde hair was flowing in the gentle breeze. Her eyes were crystal blue, and she had a colorful headband of flowers and a freshly picked bouquet in her hands. She had the poise and grace of a ballerina.

"Earth to T, earth to T, come in, T." Andrew nudged his friend.

Tanner was frozen. It wasn't only the woman's beauty that had him paralyzed, but he didn't know if she heard him talking about fooling the gods and breaking into Mount Olympus.

"I'm Persephone. Welcome to my garden. How can I help you?"

"I thought you were in the underworld only in the winter," Andrew said.

"I come here for a few weeks in the summer as well to visit my son, Zagreus."

"But doesn't Demeter cause it to be winter on the surface whenever you're down here?" Tanner asked.

"Only when I'm *forced* to be here against my will," Persephone said. "Where are you from?"

"Well, we're from the Surface," Andrew said.

"We don't get many Surfacers," Persephone replied. "How did you get here?"

"It's a long story. But we entered Inner Earth through Mammoth Cave."

"Even more rare," Persephone said. "As you may have heard, I resided on the Surface World as well, before my kidnapping."

"Then you'd be willing to help some fellow Surfacers, wouldn't you?" Tanner asked.

"I'll do what I can. What do you require assistance with?"

Tanner decided to try to leverage what he knew about Persephone in order to win her over to their cause. "We're looking for a lost friend. She mentioned your beautiful garden in her writings, so we think she must have come through here. But we're afraid she may unknowingly eat something and be forced to spend eternity in the underworld."

"What does she look like?" Persephone asked.

"She has reddish-brown hair that she usually wears in a ponytail, and she's about this tall." Tanner held his hand up at about the 5'4" mark.

"I haven't seen anyone matching that description come through here recently."

"Our friend actually entered the underworld a few weeks ago," Andrew said.

"She must have eaten something by now, or she'd be dead." Persephone gave the same response that Andrew had given.

Tanner's heart sank. He'd known Andrew was right, but Persephone stating it so clearly made him realize that there was no way Mick had survived this long without eating. They were just going to be lucky if she survived.

"Well, we're hoping we can at least see her," Andrew said. "You must understand. You know how devastated your mother was when she thought she might never see *you* again, and we don't have the leverage to negotiate with Zeus like she did. Could you at least help us find Mick? Have you seen anyone matching her description in the last *five or six weeks*?"

"No, I don't remember seeing her. But I'm not always here, and I don't see everyone who comes through. I'm sorry."

"We're pretty sure she was heading to Olympus," Tanner said. "Can you help us get there?"

"Certainly. But it won't be easy."

"That's okay. It hasn't exactly been a cake walk to get this far," he replied.

"Those with pure hearts can get to Mount Olympus using the normal methods. However," she looked them up and down, and a small smile played across her lips, "I sense with the two of you, we may need to resort to alternate methods."

"What's that supposed to mean?" Tanner asked wondering exactly how offended he really had the right to be.

"Well, let's just say *your* hearts might still need some purifying."

The boys looked at each other wondering how Persephone could tell.

"I'll go and make sure Hades is distracted," she said. "The other judges aren't in the Great Hall right now, so your timing is perfect. I'll meet you at the entrance in a few minutes. It's the larger building over there." She motioned to the massive building perched on a rock cliff beyond the gardens in front of them.

"Thanks for your help," Tanner said.

The world seemed to disappear as Tanner watched the beautiful Persephone walk away.

"T!" Andrew said, snapping him out of his mesmerized state. "Let's head over to the Great Hall."

Tanner was first to talk about the bad news. "Persephone's right. Mick has to have eaten something, and if that's true, she's trapped here forever."

"Do you think there's any way around it?" Andrew asked. "Because if there isn't, we're gonna spend eternity here too 'cause I'm famished, and I'm not sure how much longer I can go without eating something of substance."

"Same here. We've got to find a loophole. I'm not planning to spend forever in this hellish place. I've only been here a few days, and I'm not sure I could handle much more."

"But if Persephone couldn't negotiate a way out of it with her own father, Zeus, we don't have a chance."

"You're underestimating our skills, Andrew." Both boys smiled at Tanner's brash statement.

The garden they crossed through had a staggering number of flowers that were meticulously cared for and arranged. There were orange and purple tulips mixed with white roses, and hibiscuses with pink flowers as big as soccer balls surrounded with purple and white hyacinths nearly four feet tall.

"This place smells like an international perfume convention," Tanner said as a gentle breeze blew in his face.

Animals peacefully strolled the grounds, and macaws, flamingos, and other birds chirped melodious tunes. There were stunning marble architectural elements and small buildings. Adjacent to their path was a small greenhouse filled with exotic plants and an array of butterflies like they had never seen before. As they neared a greenhouse, a large snow leopard emerged from behind the structure.

"Don't move," Tanner whispered.

The boys were paralyzed with fear. The leopard walked directly up to them and began rubbing itself against their legs as if it were a small house cat. They watched as a bobcat bound across the garden, playfully chasing a butterfly. None of the animals seemed as frightening as they'd originally thought. It was like a piece of magic in the portals of terror.

They approached a small orchard along the outskirts of the garden and sat down on a bench. There were fruits of all kinds including those Tanner and Andrew had only seen on rare occasions and many they had never before seen. The mood changed immediately as they looked at the massive Great Hall of Judgment directly in front of them. At the base of the rock cliff was a forest of dead trees.

The hall itself was a blackened cylindrical-shaped building that had twelve wall sections jutting out like spokes of a wheel. These sections were curved like a crescent moon and attached to the building on the convex side. At the narrowest point of the curved walls, near the vertical center of the building, was a transparent ring that reminded Tanner of the rings of Saturn. Flowing along the top edge of four of the wall sections were small streams that formed waterfalls, with the water landing on the lower portion of each crescent.

Resting on top of the cylindrical core of the building was a transparent dome.

"Look at the clouds inside that dome," Tanner said.

"It's like the building has its own environment," Andrew replied. "And look at that 'sun.'"

On top of the dome was a magnificent golden sphere with cone-shaped rays extending from it. It looked like a representation of the sun. Directly under this object was a clear tube that could be seen through the glass dome. The tube extended down from the orb into the building.

Ki-kaw, ki-kaw.

Tanner looked up and saw a large bird swooping toward the path to the Great Hall. The peaceful silence they had enjoyed in the garden was broken as more and more of the great birds joined the angry cawing chorus.

"What are those?" Andrew asked.

"They're griffins," Persephone said from behind rejoining them. "They're a hybrid of an eagle, king of all fowl, and a lion, king of all beasts. They're protectors of the divine."

"That building doesn't look very divine to me," Andrew replied.

"It may not look divine, but it's the only way to access Mt. Olympus, so it must be heavily guarded."

Persephone motioned for them to walk with her in the direction of the Great Hall. The giant birds began to scatter as soon as Persephone walked out onto the path as if revering her very presence.

"I was successful in distracting Hades," she said as they hiked up the rocky trail to the hall. "The other judges won't be in their seats for about an hour. You'll have to move fast."

The three of them walked up a semicircular staircase that ended looking over a moat filled with hot lava. Persephone waved her arms and a small footbridge emerged from the building, connecting it with the staircase. The three of them approached the massive doors in front of the Great Hall. They were bronze with intricate designs of planets, stars, and other astronomical objects.

"Um, quick question," Andrew said. It was obvious by the look on his face that something was weighing on his mind. He spoke with hesitation. "We're pretty much out of food and water. I know this might be a sensitive topic, but is there anything we can eat or drink without being forced to spend eternity here?"

"Ah, yes" Persephone responded. "Thank you for being sensitive, and obviously I understand the importance of the question. The rule of the Fates is absolute as far as food goes. However, you can drink the water of either the Lethe or Mnemosyne Rivers without that effect. The rivers originate as four small streams in the Great Hall behind the judgment seat of Hades. I would recommend you drink near the judgment seat because the effects of the water are more pronounced the farther downstream you are."

"What do you mean effects?" Tanner asked.

"Well, the water from the two rivers has opposite effects. The water from the Lethe has a soothing effect that causes forgetfulness as opposed to the Mnemosyne, which heightens awareness and improves one's memory. You will find both to be the best water you've ever tasted."

"Thanks," Andrew said.

"I shall now grant you access to the Great Hall of Judgment. I've confirmed that none of the gods are there. That's the only way you have a chance to get to Olympus without being judged."

"What do you mean, have a chance?" Andrew asked. "If you let us in, and we don't have to be judged, won't that guarantee we'll get to Olympus?"

"If you aren't willing to prove yourselves worthy through judgment, then you'll have to prove yourselves worthy another way," Persephone said.

"How?" Andrew asked.

"That, I cannot tell you. It's forbidden. You'll have to use your own wit and skill. Everyone is *capable* of attaining Olympus, but not everyone is *willing*."

"Oh, we're willing," Tanner said, having no idea what they were about to face.

"We shall see," Persephone said as she opened the massive doors and let the boys into the Hall. "Remember, set your sights high!"

CHAPTER 37

THE JAWS OF HELL

(TANNER)

Tanner gazed in awe at the interior of the Great Hall and found it far more great and terrible than he'd envisioned based on the exterior. He had never been in a building large enough to have its own canyon inside. A narrow rocky trail led from the front entrance upward and toward the back of the hall. It created a semicircle on each side that was open to a nearly bottomless pit that looked like the entrance to hell.

The ragged cliff-like drop-offs plunged into this dark abyss, and the path itself was jagged and formidable. In the depths was a labyrinth of passageways, tunnels, and pits visible only when periodic bursts of fire illuminated them. There was a lava river that wound its way like a snake through this hell.

"Not the best place to have a duct tape shoe," he said as he sensed how the rocky path would feel without the dissolved sole.

At the back of the building was a platform with three thrones and a single chair positioned to face them. On each side of the platform were staircases leading farther up and back toward the center of the building, where there was another, more stunning platform at the base of the glass dome. On this upper platform was a single throne with a small seat centered perfectly in the middle.

"Those must be the thrones of Minos, Aeacus, and Rhadamanthus," Andrew said pointing to the back of the building.

"Who?"

Andrew shook his head in disgust. "The throne up above must be Hades.'"

"Maybe we should have just taken our chances with being judged."

"I guess if we caught the gods on a good day, but based on the mythology I've read, I still think we have a better chance by keeping our destiny in our own hands."

"You're right," Tanner replied. "We couldn't risk having them send us somewhere different than where Mick is."

"We've got to get to that sun." Andrew pointed up at the golden orb visible through the glass dome. "Persephone said we need to set our sights high. I bet it's a transportation device that will take us to Olympus."

"Easier said than done."

The two were exhausted, hungry, and thirsty. Still, Tanner was sure they were close to reuniting with their lost friend since the paper after the Great Hall of Judgment, in Mick's folder, was her essay on Mount Olympus.

"No missteps or we're going to hell," Tanner said.

"Now's not the time for jokes."

"It's not a joke," Tanner said. "I can't believe there's no handrail."

Tanner had a quick flashback to a similar hike the three friends had done the previous summer in southern Utah. "At least Angel's Landing had that chain to grab on to."

"And we didn't have the jaws of hell gaping wide open below us," Andrew said.

"I actually thought I might fall to my death at Angel's Landing," Tanner said. "It was the first time I really felt vulnerable—not indestructible like I always felt before. But *that* would have only been death. This would be death *and hell*. Definitely not something I want to face."

"Agreed," Andrew said.

As Tanner was about to step out onto the path, a thousand echoes from the past rang violently in his head.

"What's the matter with you, boy? You can't do this. You're so weak. You'll never amount to anything." The alcohol impaired voice was so clear Tanner looked around to see if his father was actually there.

"T. Are you okay?" Andrew asked.

Tanner shook his head in an attempt to cast out the memories. "I'm good. I've got this."

Andrew frowned, and Tanner knew his friend understood the thoughts racing through his head without him having to explain. Only Andrew and Mick knew how vulnerable Tanner was when his dad's words haunted him. Only they had seen him cripple in despair.

"Don't listen, Tanner," Andrew said. "You can do anything you set your mind to. It's not you. It's just all your father knew. He was lashing out at the pain of his own failures. Plus, it's how he was treated when he was a boy."

As had happened so many times before, his father's demeaning remarks gradually began to fade, and he could hear his mother's gentle voice encouraging him on. He nodded in thanks to Andrew and stepped onto the path. The path would have been harrowing enough had they been able to completely focus on *it*. But periodic bursts of flames and mighty creatures whose shadows they could see lumbering in the pathways below created disturbing visual distractions. Horrific noises reverberated in the vast chamber.

"We're not even supposed to be here," Andrew said. "Messing with the gods never ends well."

"Come on. Where's your sense of adventure?" Tanner tried for an encouraging smile.

"It would be one thing if Persephone was helping us, but she only let us in because she has a soft spot in her heart for Surfacers."

"This isn't any worse than that cliff in front of Erebus."

"Maybe you can't see the beasts down there or the lava river, or maybe you don't realize that Hades himself might walk in on us at any time."

"Okay, maybe it is worse, but we've got to do it, so come on."

The adrenaline was unlike any Tanner had ever felt before. After completing about a third of the hike, their hearts stood still as they heard the loud creaking noise of the gigantic doors opening behind them. Both boys froze.

Is it Hades? Tanner panicked. *Did we run out of time already?*

They carefully looked back and were relieved to see Persephone. She was standing on a small, round metallic disc with a translucent, cylindrical panel of light that extended to her waist where a metallic railing hovered. The device was transporting her gently but swiftly in their direction. In an instant, she was hovering next to them. There were elaborate carvings on both the metal disc and railing.

"You can do this," she said emphatically. "It may seem impossible, but I have confidence in your abilities. Never lose sight of why you're doing it. Having a vision and noble purpose is one of the great keys to accomplishment. Each of *us*, that Surface mortals consider to be gods, was once just like you. The things we have learned and attained in our progression have come about through our ability to face difficulty head on and to defeat our weaknesses through continued efforts."

Words of encouragement from the most beautiful woman I've ever seen seems like a greater key to accomplishment to me, Tanner thought.

"You have no idea how much it pains me that I am forbidden to assist you any further, but crossing this chasm under your own power is the only way someone who hasn't been judged can prove himself worthy to access the lands beyond. I promise what you find on the other side will make whatever you endure here worth it."

The boys thanked her as she departed. Moments after she closed the doors, the entire interior of the building began to darken. The beautiful cumulus clouds they had seen drifting peacefully in the dome earlier became black and threatening. No light entered the building. Suddenly a flash of lightning illuminated the darkness. The boys nearly lost their footing as they were jolted by the explosive clap of thunder that echoed simultaneously through the chamber.

"Grab the headlamps!" Andrew yelled as the noises within the building grew louder.

Tanner held on to a ragged piece of rock to steady himself as he sifted through their backpacks. Another flash of lightning, a thunderous boom, and the pair found themselves in a downpour. The thunder gradually subsided and was replaced with the sound of the pouring rain.

"Is this punishment for confronting the gods, or does it happen to everyone?" Tanner asked.

"Maybe it's just bad timing."

Andrew, who was following Tanner's lead, suddenly slipped, and a boulder under his feet broke free—tumbling into the darkness below. To prevent himself from falling, he leaned away from the falling stone but overcompensated.

"Taaaaaaaanner!" he yelled as he was losing his balance and began to fall. Tanner lunged to grab Andrew's arm. He latched on to his forearm just as his friend began to plummet to certain death.

"Hang on!" Tanner screamed.

Another explosive clap of thunder.

"T! I'm slipping! Don't let me fall!"

Tanner grabbed more tightly, but the rain had everything impossibly slick. He began to slip himself. "Andrew! I'm sliding! Grab something! Can you get your feet on anything? I'm going down!" Tanner's headlamp illuminated a ledge about three feet from Andrew's dangling feet. "That ledge! Over there. See it?"

"Swing me over to it."

Tanner swung Andrew toward the ledge, but he was unable to reach it.

"I can't hold on any longer. We're both going down. You have to jump. You can reach it!"

Andrew jumped. He hit the ledge but relief was quickly replaced with terror as Tanner watched him slide across the wet stone toward the edge. Unexpectedly, Andrew hit a dry patch, which slowed his momentum enough for him to get a grip on a stone outcropping. He slid to a stop, precariously perched on a narrow ledge over the chasm.

Tanner grabbed some rope from his backpack and fastened it securely to a boulder. "Grab this," he said as he lowered the rope.

"Are you sure it's secure?"

"I'm sure."

Andrew pulled himself back onto the path. The boys looked at each other, both shaking their heads. Andrew clasped Tanner's arm in gratitude. They knew they were lucky to be alive. They also knew there was no time to waste.

"We've got to keep moving. We can't be here when the gods return," Tanner said. "Be more careful from now on." It came across a little harsh, but the reality was that Tanner couldn't bear the thought of losing Andrew. He was already unsure if he would ever see Mick again, and only a few hours ago on the River Acheron, he'd been reminded of the pain of losing his little sister and father. He couldn't lose Andrew too.

An increased soberness settled in as they continued up the path. There were a few more harrowing moments, but through sheer determination, they reached the other side. The weather cleared the instant they set foot on the back platform.

"We did it!" Andrew yelled throwing his arms up in the air.

"That was terrifying," Tanner said.

"That's an understatement," Andrew said. "I can't believe I actually made it." He shook his head in disbelief as he brushed himself off.

"I can't believe you did either!" Tanner said.

"The way the weather cleared as soon as we finished makes me believe it really *was* a test," Andrew said. "It was a way of seeing how committed we were."

"I agree. It definitely wasn't a coincidence. We must really care about Mick."

"Yeah, about that," Andrew said. "Remember how Persephone said one of the great keys of accomplishment was having a vision and a noble purpose?"

"Sort of. Actually, I think all I remember were those eyes and that dazzling robe she was wearing."

"Shut up," Andrew said in a mock disgusted tone. "Is her beauty the only thing you can think about?"

Tanner grinned, and Andrew punched him in the shoulder. "Anyway, as I was saying, I don't have the same vision you do. Mick isn't down here. I never really believed it, and I can't keep risking my life for something I don't believe in. It's not fair to either of us. I'm sorry, T, but I can't go any farther. I'm done."

CHAPTER 38

THE SHAWNEE

(DONALD CARLTON)

Things became desperate for the Carltons after the tornado. Donald gathered his personal effects and went to town hoping he could sell or exchange them for food and supplies. Moments after leaving the mercantile, having been able to sell only a few things, a beautiful Shawnee girl entered asking for Mr. Carlton. She was young and turned more than a few heads when she walked in.

"He just barely left," the store owner told the girl. "Was heading back to his farm."

She ran out of the store, jumped on her horse, and set off after him. The men stood in the doorway watching her ride into the distance, her jet-black hair flowing behind her.

"Who was that?" someone asked.

"Never seen her before." Another replied.

"What do you suppose she wanted from Donald?"

"Good question," the store owner replied.

There was a lot of buzz about this beautiful young woman in the ensuing weeks. On and off there were sightings of her with Donald but they were never in public places. Donald seemed even more animated than usual when he was with her. Rumors ran rampant. Someone spotted them talking under a tree, another riding horses, and still another walking in the woods. Everyone was convinced that the flamboyant adventurer was about to abandon his wife and family and disappear from Brownsville.

In the midst of all the speculation, the most heinous crime in the history of Brownsville occurred—the Brownsville Bank robbery. Three bank employees were killed and the robbers made off with hundreds of thousands of dollars. Everything pointed to Donald and the Indian girl as the murderers. The last time anyone saw either of them was the night before the robbery, and not only were they missing, but their horses were tied outside the entrance to Mammoth Cave where some of the money from the robbery was found. Donald Carlton, town hero, plummeted from grace in Brownsville and became the exact opposite of what he had been.

CHAPTER 39

THE JUDGMENT SEATS

(TANNER)

"How can you not believe in what we're doing?" Tanner asked, not sure if he was more shocked or angry. "Mick's papers have matched up almost perfectly with what we've experienced. She totally left them as a breadcrumb trail to find her." Sure it was scary, but how could Andrew not believe after all they had been through?

"Almost isn't good enough for me to keep risking my life. Besides she just got that information from her research. Someone else probably went through this stuff, and she found their work and used it for her papers. We've asked everyone we could if they've seen her, and no one remembers her."

"But she came here several weeks ago. There may have been thousands that have come through since then. She's here somewhere. My gut tells me we're on the right path, and we're going to find her."

"How can you say that? You have no proof. There's no evidence other than those stupid papers. I want something tangible."

"Fine. Go ahead. Cross the chasm and go back home. I guarantee you it would be a lot harder going *down* than it was coming up. If you even try to go back down by yourself, you know I'll be watching you take a swim in that lava river down there. Or you could just wait here on the platform until Hades shows up. That would be fun to watch." Tanner scoffed. "Look, the worst of this is behind us. I mean, try to think—can you come up with anything worse than that climb, the River Acheron, and the three-headed dog?"

"No, I guess not. But maybe that's just because my imagination isn't that good."

"Come on. We've been through some pretty bad stuff, and we made it. Together. Are you ready to just go back on your own? How long do you think we'll last without having each other's backs?" He knew they couldn't make it alone, which left him even more apprehensive about how Mick had survived on her own. But right now, he needed Andrew to stay; he couldn't make it farther by himself.

Andrew looked at him, full of apprehension.

"I know you don't want to cross that chasm again, so just humor me. Let's keep going. I guarantee we're going to find Mick soon."

"All right." Andrew nodded slightly, not looking one hundred percent convinced, but still willing. "But I'm coming along only 'cause I don't want to go back alone."

Tanner slapped him across the back in an encouraging gesture. He hoped he was right and that the worst was over. They turned and gazed at the three spectacular thrones in front of them. Up until now, they hadn't paid much attention to their amazing details. The center throne was the most imposing. Looming behind the seat was a weathered bronze Minotaur. He had a threatening expression, was holding a double-sided axe, and looked ready to spring into action. Fire sporadically erupted from his horned armor. Red electrical charges encircled the horns on his head, sizzling as they flickered on and off. The seat was a crimson satin, and the seatback was about twice the height of the boys and rose slightly above the Minotaur's knees. Suspended above the seat were the letters MINOS.

On the left was an equally impressive, though shorter throne with a statue of a jaguar and a sign reading AEACUS, and to the right another with a statue of a dragon and the name RHADAMANTHUS.

"Mick wrote about the thrones," Andrew said.

"See. She must have been here." Tanner nudged Andrew in the ribs with his elbow. "Just think how intimidating it'd be if you were actually being judged by the three gods."

"Agreed. They're scary enough as it is," Andrew said.

On each side of the building, three waterfalls formed small streams that merged into a river of fire in front of the thrones. The fiery river turned and flowed beneath the throne of Minos, where a small boat was anchored, ready to escort a passenger out the back of the building.

"That must be the boat to Tartarus—home of evil souls."

Small bridges crossed the flaming river on each side of the thrones and gave one access to the stairs leading to the suspended platform.

"Let's cross here," Tanner said.

"Wow, that's hot," Andrew said as he crossed over the flaming river.

They began to walk up the staircase toward Hades's throne. The railings were made of intricately designed silver, and the stairs were made of ice.

"Be careful, T. The stairs are slippery. Make sure to hang on to the railing."

"You sound like my mother," Tanner said, but gripped the railing nonetheless.

They placed each foot carefully, making sure not to slip and fall. They were about halfway up when cracking noises started behind them. They turned just in time to see that the stairs beneath them were breaking loose and careening one at a time into the depths of hell.

"Whoa!"

"Run for it!"

The boys sprinted for the top.

"Hang on!" Tanner yelled as the remaining stairs began to pivot and form a slippery slope to the pits below. "Grab the railing! We're going to have to pull ourselves to the top."

The boys had already burned through their adrenaline supply. There was nothing left in the tank for either of them. They were running on fumes. The drink Persephone had told them about was so close and yet not close enough to revive their parched spirits.

"Just this final stretch, and we're on our way to Olympus," Tanner said, his mouth as dry as the desert floor. But he wasn't sure even he believed it. Then the clouds in the dome began to back up. It was going to continue to be one thing after another. He refused to give up.

"We're in for another storm!" he yelled. "Climb as fast as you can! We've got to try to beat it!"

And then it began to snow.

"You've got to be kidding." Andrew groaned. Within seconds a blinding blizzard wrapped around them, dropping the temperature of the railing until the cold steel almost burned their hands.

"We've got to get to the top. Our hands are either going to freeze to the railing, or we're going to get frostbite and won't be able to hold on."

"Well, if our hands are frozen to the railing, at least we won't fall." Tanner tried to keep up his optimism, but it was failing fast.

"Enough with the wise cracks, T. In case you didn't notice, we're about to die."

Tanner pulled harder, the pain in his hands each step of the way incentive to finish as soon as he could. He reached the top first and turned around to help Andrew. "You can do it, you're almost there."

The snow turned to hail. The boys were being pelted by pea-sized hailstones that pummeled their skin, causing small welts to instantly appear.

"I'm not going to make it. My hands are freezing," Andrew said through chattering teeth.

"You've got to hurry. The hail is growing. With our luck, golf ball sized hail is on its way next. A couple more pulls, and I'll be able to reach you. Think about Mick."

Andrew kept pulling and got himself to where Tanner could grab him.

"You did it!" Tanner said as he pulled him safely to the upper platform.

As quickly as the storm had started, the atmosphere in the Great Hall cleared and it was sunny and warm again. Andrew collapsed on the platform.

"We're almost there," Tanner said. "We can't stop now. The gods could show up any minute."

"Hold on T. Let me catch my breath, would you? Seriously. I don't have anything left."

"Just follow me to the water. Remember how Persephone said it would invigorate you? We're so close."

Hades's throne was directly in front of them and was the most spectacular yet. It was silver with embedded emeralds and amethyst stones. The seat was a luxurious green velvet and silk. It was integrated into a silver statue representing Hades's capture of Persephone. The carving was intricate, and the green and blue flames that illuminated the surface accentuated the gems. Scripted letters above the throne read HADES. Between the central judgment chair and this throne was a small river. Instead of dirt, stones, and weeds, this riverbed was lined with silver and precious stones matching the statue. It was filled by fountains springing up in regular intervals. Like the other rivers, it contained a small boat and flowed to the side of the building where it exited.

"That must go to the Asphodel Meadows—where ordinary and indifferent souls go," Tanner said, proud he remembered some of his mythology.

Behind Hades's throne were the four riverheads Persephone told them about. Two of which would eventually form the Lethe and the Mnemosyne rivers. Tanner and Andrew crossed the stream using the small bridge to the right of the judgment chair in order to access the drinkable water.

"Hallelujah!" Andrew said he bent over the stream and began devouring the water. "Don't forget to fill your water bottles."

"Good thinking," Tanner replied. "Persephone was right. This *is* the best water I've ever tasted."

"I'm definitely thinking more clearly and feel totally reinvigorated. It's like I've been healed. And after what we just went through, that's a miracle."

"Where do you think these go?" Tanner pointed to the place where the rivers exited the building.

"To the Isles of the Blessed—where the gods send heroic souls."

"Speaking of the gods, we better get moving. We've got to be close to our one hour limit."

"Yeah, it'd be a shame to get busted now!"

They walked to the central judgment chair with its surrounding cylindrical glass tube that led to the golden sphere shaped like the sun. A section of the orb was missing. It matched the outer shape of the chair.

"The chair must become part of the sphere," Andrew said.

Tanner nodded. "That's our ride to Olympus." He walked around the chair slowly.

"Let's go check Hades's throne" Tanner said. "There's got to be a button or lever or some type of trigger that sends the judgment chair into the golden sphere." He climbed into Hades's throne.

There was the rumble of thunder, an instant darkening of the room, and another flash of lightning. The boys looked around, expecting that Hades or one of the other judges had entered the hall, but there was no sign anyone had entered. Tanner saw what looked like a button on the armrest of the throne.

Boom!

Another clap of thunder and multiple flashes of lightning.

"Andrew, get in the chair! I'm not sure how this button works, but I don't want both of us to miss out on going to Mount Olympus if it shoots up into the orb."

"Wait. What about you?"

"There may not be time for me to push the button and get over to the chair before it's sucked into the orb."

"Well, let *me* push the button, then, and *you* sit in the chair. I don't want to go alone."

"Andrew, your problem-solving ability is better than mine. We have to think about what would give us the best chance of rescuing Mick. I'm putting it in your hands. Now, don't let me down!"

"Tanner. It has to be you. I don't even believe Mick's there. You're just as good at solving problems as I am when you apply yourself, and right now, you're fully committed. Now, get in that chair."

Tanner was stunned by Andrew's forcefulness. "Okay."

"Get in the chair!" Andrew shouted again.

"Okay. Okay. I'm going."

"I'll push the button and run for the chair, but if I don't make it, good luck." Andrew jumped onto Hades's throne.

"Wow, did you see this helmet?" Andrew asked as he reached for an intricately designed helmet resting on a stand next to the chair. As his hand touched the helmet, he noticed his fingers begin to disappear.

"Andrew!" Tanner yelled. "That's . . ."

"Persephone! What have you done?" A thunderous voice came from below. The boys looked down and saw that Hades had entered the building.

"Push the button!" Tanner yelled.

Andrew pressed the button and raced for the chair. He could hear the sound of equipment starting up. He lunged for Tanner, and the moment he landed on the chair, they were both sucked up the tube into the golden sun-shaped orb. Straps automatically secured around them as the seat integrated itself into the orb.

"Did you see Hades?" Andrew asked.

"Yeah, we're dead." He jerked up in the seat hoping to get the orb to shoot up, taking them away from the hall—and from Hades.

"Persephone will intervene."

"No way," Tanner said. "And face the wrath of Hades? She won't do it."

"Yeah, she will. She's not afraid of him."

"What's wrong with this thing?" Tanner slapped the side wall of the orb. "Come on, we've got to get out of here."

CHAPTER 40

THE GOLDEN ORB
(TANNER)

"Why isn't this thing moving?" Tanner asked in frustration.

"You're not thinking we're going to be safer once we're in the air, are you? This is a god we're talking about. We just ticked off a god."

"I know. I'd just feel better if we weren't so close to where he is."

A series of loud noises began to ring through the orb in synchronized intervals.

"That has to be a countdown."

The boys began to count from ten in their minds, bracing for takeoff. Ten, nine, eight . . . The anticipation grew as they neared zero. Five, four, three. Then an explosive noise. Tanner was completely caught off guard as they were flung into space.

"Welcome aboard the transport of the gods. Tanner and Andrew, you have been deemed worthy by the judges of the underworld to approach the gods and plead your case before them. If found pure, you will be able to reside with them forever on Mount Olympus."

The sound was so crystal clear Tanner looked around to see if someone was with them in the orb.

The instrumentation in the craft was more sophisticated than any technologies Tanner was familiar with. It was like a holographic projection with more substance. There were representations of the Great Hall, the orb they were in, and what appeared to be Mount Olympus. According to these objects, they were rocketing through space, rapidly approaching the home of the gods.

Suddenly clouds descended on the orb representation.

"Oh great, another storm," Andrew said as the actual orb began to be batted around like a ping-pong ball.

"Hades is behind this, I guarantee," Tanner said. The color drained completely from their faces while they tried to keep from retching. Even with the safety restraint, they were tossed around like rag dolls. "We're completely at the mercy of Hades."

"Phlegyas warned us," Andrew said. He grabbed at the air and wrapped his fingers around the representation of the 3D clouds enveloping the orb. The ship stabilized.

"What did you do?"

"I don't know I just reached out to steady myself and everything stopped."

The ride smoothed out to the point that it felt like they weren't moving at all. But their brains still felt squishy. Tanner pulled his cell phone out of his pocket. "That helmet you touched back there. That was the symbol I saw on Donald Carlton's headstone."

He showed Andrew the picture. "Donald Carlton must have been to the Great Hall of Judgment."

"Hmm," Andrew replied. "Yeah that's definitely the same helmet."

"Why do you think it was on his gravestone?"

"Maybe it symbolized he'd gone to the underworld?"

"Tanner and Andrew, you have left the realms of the underworld and entered the domain of Mount Olympus," the voice in the orb announced.

"I guess we were crazy thinking we could sneak into Mount Olympus," Tanner said.

Andrew laughed for the first time in a while. "So what do we do once we get there?"

"I wish I knew," Tanner said hoping that Andrew's smile meant he was going to stick around for a while and Tanner could stop worrying about when he might leave. "I don't have any idea what to expect from *these* gods."

"Mick didn't really say much about them."

They watched the hologram as the ship continued to approach Mount Olympus.

"Kinda weird how Olympus looks like it's suspended in the air like that," Andrew said. He reached out and gently put his finger on the image of Olympus. It zoomed in allowing them to see it more clearly. Their projected landing point was on a flat area atop the highest mountain of the land. There was a circular, crystal-encrusted amber surface surrounded by marble pillars. The pillars supported a series of arches forming twelve niches.

"Those must be for the twelve gods that sit in judgment, and we're heading right for the center of it."

Both boys had their lives flash before them. Literally. On each side of the hologram that displayed Mount Olympus and its judgment platform, three-dimensional movies appeared and were replaying their lives at high speed—straight from birth. The boys sat in awe. It was hard for them to comprehend how quickly the action was happening, and yet they were able to stay with it all.

"There's no way I'm going to pass this judgment," Tanner said.

Some things he had seen in his movie made him nervous about standing in front of the gods. He was sure that if they had the technology to display every moment of his life at that kind of speed, he wasn't going to be able to fool them into thinking he was worthy to live on Olympus. Not that he had done something that would have landed him in jail or anything (except maybe stealing Mick's papers), but every little lie, every time he was less than courageous or didn't stand up for his beliefs like he should have—all those things were magnified to him now.

"I'm not going to pass either," Andrew said. Tanner was certain his friend knew exactly how he was feeling.

"Mick must have passed though," Tanner said.

"Why do you say that?"

"Well, she described things beyond this landing area. She must have landed, been judged, and was able to explore Olympus. She always was a better person than us."

"Listen Tanner, I don't want to burst your bubble, but Mick's writings are not based on personal experience."

"They are!" Tanner blurted out. "I wish you'd quit being such a skeptic."

"They can't be personal experience. Think about it. First of all, they aren't completely accurate. Like when she said Styx went around the underworld seven times. We only went around three."

"Maybe we actually went around seven times. We were asleep for parts of it." Tanner refuted.

"Secondly, she would have had to disappear once *before* she wrote the papers. We know she didn't disappear twice."

Tanner opened his mouth to refute Andrew's argument when it donned on him that Andrew was right. Mick hadn't disappeared twice. After a brutal pause, he finally said, "Don't talk to me."

His world had just come crashing down on him. So much of his assurance about Mick's location rested on her papers, and apparently, they meant absolutely nothing. He sat in the orb, reeling mentally far more than he'd just done physically because of this devastating realization.

I was too hasty. Everyone's right. I don't look before I leap, and now we're stranded in the middle of the underworld. Mick's probably been found and is home enjoying her summer vacation, and Andrew and I are going to die—or worse.

It was true Tanner wanted to rescue his lost friend, but he also desperately wanted to be a hero. Wanted to be successful. Wanted to prove his father wrong. For years he'd wanted that so badly that he often acted rashly. He would do anything that he thought might give him the positive reinforcement he craved from the depths of his soul.

After several moments of very thick silence, Tanner spoke up completely disoriented. "What now?" His foundations had crumbled, and he felt his world collapsing around him.

"We've got to try to land this someplace other than that judgment platform," Andrew said, not recognizing the depth of Tanner's question. "What transportation device doesn't have a method for steering? Maybe we can avoid being judged if we can land this thing somewhere else."

Andrew reached out and grabbed at the three-dimensional object that represented the projected path of the orb they were in. He dragged it over to a mountainous region far away from the central platform where they were originally destined to land. The boys felt a quick but smooth change in the direction of the orb.

"You're a genius, Andrew."

They felt the orb gently touch down. A pleasant voice announced their arrival.

"Tanner and Andrew, welcome to Mount Olympus. You have chosen not to be judged at this time. Due to this decision, your stay will be temporary. You will be monitored, and if your behavior is inappropriate, you will be expelled. You will not be permitted to meet or dwell with the gods. We must remind you that due to your choice, you will return to the Great Hall of Judgment at a designated time and will be required to pass judgment again before being allowed to dwell on Olympus."

"Hopefully we're not going to want to come back, then, because I'm not up to repeating that."

"Amen, brother!" Andrew said. "The good news is that it seems like whoever runs Olympus is okay with us being here."

"Good thing. I hadn't worked out how sneaking in and hiding from the gods was really going to work out." Tanner felt the tension leave his body as the orb opened and he looked out onto the harmonious land of Mount Olympus.

"Whoa, check this out." He pointed to the ground as he stepped onto the surface. The beautiful grass and the ground around him in a ten-foot radius had become completely invisible, and he could see the lands of the underworld in the distance far below. "Look, there's the River Styx. It looks so small from here." The River clearly made three passes around the underworld before disappearing into what he realized must have been the Stygian Marsh.

"That must be the Isle of the Blessed over there," Andrew said pointing to a beautiful island rising up out of a massive lake.

"This is going to take some getting used to," Tanner said as he began to walk across the meadow. "I'm not usually afraid of heights, but this is like standing on the moon and looking down on earth."

"You don't think we're going to fall through do you?" Andrew asked as he gingerly stepped onto the surface for the first time.

Tanner bobbed carefully on the balls of his feet. "No, Olympus is probably just designed this way so the gods can keep an eye on the people of the underworld."

"They must have much better eyesight than me."

"They're gods," Tanner said, tiptoeing gently across the landscape. "It looks like this path leads to that waterfall over there." He pointed to a small path about twenty feet away. "Let's follow it."

They crossed through a flower-sprinkled meadow filled with lush grasses, ferns, and moss. Birds so spectacular they would have made even macaws hide in shame swooped in and out of the surrounding trees, painting the sky with their colorful feathers.

"Wow!" Tanner exclaimed. "We are actually on Mount Olympus. Can you believe it?"

"It's crazy," Andrew replied. "I mean, I've heard of Mount Olympus ever since I was little. It's the most talked about place in Greek mythology. And we're here."

"I can see why everyone talks so much about it," Tanner said.

"It's everything Mick's paper said it would be."

Tanner sobered up immediately as the fresh Olympian air thickened between the boys. "Don't talk about Mick's papers."

They walked over the crest of a rolling hill. Tanner silently berated himself for believing the papers were a trail to Mick. He began to question whether she was even in the underworld. He was so long in thought that he almost ran headfirst into a woman whose beauty matched that of Persephone.

"Excuse me," Tanner said.

She stood up and turned around to face the boys. Her hair was black, and her stunning green eyes briefly mesmerized the two of them as they looked up at her. And they really had to look up—she had to have been at least seven feet tall. She wore a robe covered in peridot gems that complimented her eyes.

"Can I help you?"

Tanner stammered briefly, not sure what to say, but figuring that even without Mick's papers, they still needed to find her. "We're looking for a friend. She may have come here a few weeks ago. She's not very tall." Tanner had never really thought of Mick as being short, but in comparison to this woman she would be pint-sized.

"Can you tell me more about her?"

"She has reddish-brown, wavy hair," Tanner said moving his hand back and forth by his head. "And she's always smiling. She usually pulls her hair back."

"Yes, I saw someone who looked similar to your description,"

Tanner's heart started racing. Had they finally got something right? "Where can we find her? Is she okay?" He jabbed Andrew in the ribs. "I told you. Now do you finally believe me?"

"She entered the Cathedral of Time several weeks ago." The woman gestured at an unusual structure perched on a small hill in the valley below. "But she hasn't come back."

Tanner thought this was a peculiar response.

"What do you mean she hasn't come *back*?" Tanner inquired.

"We never saw her return."

"So are you saying that you think she's still in there?" Andrew jumped into the conversation.

"I guess, in a manner of speaking, you could say that."

"Thank you," Tanner said. 'Thank you so much."

"You're welcome," the woman replied and went back to picking flowers.

"See, I told you Mick was here. Let's go get her."

"I'll believe it when I see her," Andrew said skeptically.

"Aw, come on! You're kidding, right? I mean that woman just said she saw her a few weeks ago. When are you going to wake up to reality?"

"She saw someone who matches that description. It's only speculation until I see her," Andrew said, shrugging.

"Come on doubting Thomas, let me prove it to you."

The boys began the hike down the hillside to the unusual structure.

"Are you hungry?" Andrew asked as he passed a patch of bushes laden with luscious berries. "We're no longer in the underworld. Do you think the no eating rule still applies on Olympus?"

"I don't know, but look at those berries," Tanner said salivating. "They look amazing."

Andrew's stomach growled in reply. He put his hand on it and frowned. "But still, we can't take a chance until we're sure they're safe." His stomach rumbled again. "Although, I'm not sure it matters, anyway."

"What do you mean?"

"According to Mick's papers," he rolled his eyes when Tanner scowled, "less than ten people in history have ever made it out of the underworld, and the only way to guarantee you can get out is to have some golden bough thing."

"Ten bucks says Mick has one," Tanner said, full of confidence.

"I'd go fifty bucks since she's not here."

"What's that?" Tanner asked.

"Nothing."

The building they were approaching looked like a cross between a cathedral and a spaceship. It had blue stained glass windows with a modern pattern and a framework straight from a medieval gothic church. It looked like a glowing, white UFO that might take off at any moment. There were three spires on top and six surrounding it on the outside. A semitransparent dome covered the whole building, looking like the heat waves that rise above an asphalt road on a blistering hot day. And nowhere did there appear to be a door on the dome.

Tanner tried to stick his hand through the dome but was unable to penetrate the substance. He took a few steps back and ran toward it, lowering his right shoulder. There was a slight shift as he made impact, but he bounced off as if it had pushed back.

"T, I don't think brute force is going to work on this."

Tanner's selective hearing allowed him to completely ignore the comment. He moved still farther back and ran full speed into the dome. There was a larger shift in the waves but Tanner was flung back even farther in a slingshot effect.

"Mick's less than fifty feet away. We've got to ask someone how to get in."

"I'm not up to walking back up that hill. I'm exhausted," Andrew said.

"Me too." Tanner sat on the ground next to where Andrew had already plopped down. "Let's just rest for a minute. Maybe someone will come by." The grass was cool, and a soft breeze brought a pleasant scent that wrapped around them like a comfortable cocoon. Within minutes they were both fast asleep.

"Good evening!"

The boys startled awake looking at a man towering above them. They shook their heads as they tried to wake themselves up.

"Good evening," Tanner said through a yawn.

"You're obviously not from here. Are you just visiting?" The stranger asked.

"We are. We're looking for a lost friend. A lady over there told us she had seen her entering this building, but we can't seem to get through this shield."

"Unfortunately, the Cathedral of Time is reserved for the twelve gods of Olympus. They are the only ones who can enter and exit the building."

"But our friend—"

"The woman must have been mistaken," the man interrupted.

"But she's a goddess. She couldn't have been wrong," Tanner said, remembering how beautiful she'd been. And how tall. She had to be a goddess.

"We're not all gods or goddesses. She's probably just in training. She didn't want to disappoint you, so she made something up."

"So you're sure our friend's not in there?" Tanner asked, the discouragement thick in his voice.

"For sure. Only the gods. It's a very sacred building you know."

"See. I told you," Andrew said. "I can't believe we've wasted all this time. Let's just figure out how to get back to Brownsville, have a nice big steak, and get back to planning that Arctic trip."

Tanner was devastated. They were back to square one. He felt like a balloon someone had just let the air out of. Darkness began to descend on Mount Olympus and on Tanner.

Maybe Andrew's been right all along. Maybe Mick isn't here. Maybe I just talked myself into it. The investigation wasn't going anywhere so this was my one hope she was still alive. I just didn't want to lose her too.

"Um, maybe she's just roaming around Olympus somewhere," Andrew said patting him reassuringly on the back.

"Thanks for trying to cheer me up. But I think you're right. This whole thing has been a wild goose chase."

"Why don't you get out your night vision goggles, and let's at least have a look around," Andrew said. "We'll take turns watching for Mick and sleeping."

"I know what you're trying to do," Tanner said.

Andrew just gave him a grin and motioned for him to follow. They climbed a short distance up the hill, where there was a good view of the Cathedral and surrounding area. Tanner volunteered to take the first watch while Andrew slept. About an hour and a half into Tanner's watch, he was just about to fall asleep when he saw some commotion on the other side of the building. He focused the night goggles the best he could. It was a man with a white flowing beard. It was completely dark outside, but the man was navigating the path as easily as if it were midday.

How can he see where he's going?

"Andrew!" Tanner shook his friend.

"What?" Andrew groggily replied.

"There's someone over there across the clearing. It looks like he's heading for the dome."

"Let me see." Andrew took the night googles from Tanner and looked to the other side of the clearing. The man was looking around as though he wanted to make sure no one was following him.

"I bet it's one of the twelve gods," Tanner said. "Let's get down there. Maybe he's about to dispel the protective sphere and we can sneak in."

"I don't think that's a good idea. Remember 'never confront the gods'? Plus they said they were going to be monitoring our behavior."

"Then you stay here. I'm going." Tanner still had a glimmer of hope, but he didn't want to say anything. He didn't want Andrew's logic to shoot it down.

Maybe the guy was wrong. Maybe Mick is in there. The lady said she was. We've come this far. Might as well give it a shot.

Quick as a flash Tanner worked his way down the hill toward the mysterious dome on the opposite side of the building from where the man was heading.

"Wait for me," Andrew said like he had so many times throughout his life.

"Keep your eyes on the dome. Watch for anything to change."

Like his words were magic, the boys watched as the dome dissolved.

"Jump in!" Tanner said grabbing Andrew by the arm.

No sooner were they in than the dome re-formed behind them.

"We did it!" Tanner said.

"I'm not sure what good it will do. You heard that man—he said it's only for the gods. Mick's not here."

"But *we're* in, aren't we? So why wouldn't Mick have been able to get in? The woman said she saw her."

Andrew rolled his eyes. "Don't you think it's odd how easy it was for us to sneak in? If it's only for the gods, there should have been more protections."

"We're on Olympus. They don't have to protect stuff. It's not like there are a bunch of thugs running around trying to break into places—besides us." Even Andrew laughed at Tanner's statement.

They watched the god enter an elevator on the outside of the building that lifted him to an entrance about sixty feet in the air.

"Let's wait and see if he comes back out," Tanner said. "I'd prefer not to confront him directly.

CHAPTER 41

The Cathedral of Time

(Tanner)

They waited patiently for what seemed like hours, but as the dawn began to set in, they knew they couldn't wait any longer. Now that they were through the dome, they could see things even clearer. The path to the cathedral looked rarely used, and the grounds had been given meticulous and constant care. A series of doorways was evenly distributed around the exterior and opened into midair above them. As Tanner and Andrew approached the elevator in front of them, it opened, and they cautiously entered. The door closed behind them, and they could hear the creaking of gears and the whirr of electronics as the elevator began to ascend. Seconds later, they felt a small jolt as it came to a stop. The back door opened, and the boys walked inside.

The interior was a single large room and, like the exterior, looked like a gothic church from a sci-fi movie.

"Do you see him anywhere?" Andrew whispered.

"No, and it's not like there's a lot of places he could hide."

A slight haze filled the room, and the blue glow from the stained glass gave it an air of mystery. In addition to the long, narrow stained glass windows on all sides, there was a large round stained glass window on the ceiling. Stairways descended from each of the six entrance doors to a hexagonal walkway. In the center of the room, a raised platform contained four glass chambers filled with an amber colored, bubbling fluid.

Tanner could see Andrew's eyes light up as he spotted a small domed structure across from where they stood. One of the six walkways passed through the center of the structure. It was filled with computers, holographic devices, and other sophisticated electronics.

"Let's go check that out," Andrew said, leaving before waiting for a response.

Tanner uncharacteristically tried to keep up as Andrew excitedly made his way down the stairs to this command center.

"Look at this." Andrew pointed at two holographic 3D systems that reminded Tanner of the technology in the golden orb.

"What do you think *this* is?" Tanner asked as he approached a large glass surface in front of the window that looked out on the center of the building.

Andrew pushed Tanner aside and centered himself in front of the massive display. A pulsating three-dimensional sphere rested over the northeastern section of an image of India. Below the sphere was a date in the year 273 BC.

"T." Andrew paused. "This is a time machine."

"Come on."

"It must allow the gods to travel to different places and times. The god we saw must have gone to India."

"You're not really serious, are you?" Tanner asked.

"Of course, I'm serious," Andrew said. "Maybe the mythological gods throughout history were just people from the Inner Earth that travelled back in time and were so much more advanced that they were viewed as gods."

"Hmmm," Tanner replied. "Interesting thought."

"I mean, think about it. If we used this machine and showed up in 273 BC with our cell phones, they'd probably treat us like gods too."

"Let's do it, then," Tanner said with a big grin. "I'd like to see how it feels to be treated like a god."

Andrew had moved on. "Look at that button," he said pointing to what looked like a start or go button. "Do you think if we pushed it, we'd be on our way to India?"

"Probably."

Tanner reached out to push the button.

"Hold on." Andrew pushed his hand away.

Andrew touched his finger to what looked like a back arrow. The screen now displayed a map of China.

"Mick has travelled back in time!" Tanner shouted out.

"What are you talking about?"

"The woman we met said Mick came in this building and never returned. It makes sense now."

"No way."

Tanner ignored him. "I can't believe Mick didn't tell us about this! Why would she keep *this* a secret?"

"Maybe because she didn't really do it?" Andrew replied sarcastically.

Andrew might just as well have been a thousand miles away. Tanner had latched on to new hope and wasn't about to listen to any contrasting points of view.

"We've got to figure out where she went," Tanner said. "I don't think its China."

Tanner touched the back arrow. This time it showed the Yucatan Peninsula.

"She might have gone there. Remember how fascinated she was with Mayan culture after she went to Chichen Itza?" Tanner asked.

Tanner touched the glass again. Italy.

"That's it!" Tanner said excitedly. "Didn't you say there was a stray paper in Mick's folder that was about some ruins of Ancient Rome?"

"Yeah, but . . ."

"And here you thought it didn't belong," Tanner said. "Let's go find Mick!" He touched the green pulsating circle on the glass. Instantly the screen changed to a countdown timer with symbols they didn't recognize. Lights flashed in sequence along the floor.

"Follow those lights!" Tanner said.

"Wait!" Andrew called. "If it is a time machine, how will we get back? We need to think this through first." Andrew had been burned a few too many times already for following Tanner's impulses.

"Too late! Follow me."

Tanner grabbed Andrew's arm and pulled him out of the control room.

"Follow the arrows."

The lights directed them to a set of stairs on the side of the platform, which they quickly climbed. The boys had no idea how much time they had. Andrew slipped and his shin slammed into the metal surface of the stair. He cried out in pain.

Tanner screamed at him "Andrew, get up here! This timer is going to go off, and I'm going to be in Rome by myself!"

Andrew hobbled up the remaining steps and arrived in the center of the platform. The boys caught a blast from six floodlights that rotated from the ground to shine in their eyes. A burst of energy entered and exited their bodies, and they were encompassed by a glowing sphere of light. Then everything went dark.

"T, are you there?"

"I'm here, but where is *here*?"

"Are we in Rome?"

"No idea."

The lights came back on. They were standing in the exact same place as before.

"Did we do something wrong?" Tanner asked.

"Pushing that button," Andrew said clearly angered.

Just then, arrow shaped lights began to flash on and off along the floor.

"Follow the lights!" Tanner exclaimed.

They followed the lights, which led them to the stairs below one of the exit doors. There was a glass surface above the door that had the same image of Italy they had seen in the command center, with a pulsating green circle over Rome. Tanner and Andrew continued up the stairs.

"Maybe when we exit the building we'll be in Rome," Tanner said.

"A giant building like this landing like a UFO in an ancient civilization? That doesn't seem very logical." Andrew scoffed.

"That's true, but according to some of the TV shows I've seen, early civilizations did have encounters with aliens and UFOs."

"Well, if you saw it on TV, it must be true." Andrew shook his head in disgust.

"Did you look at the date on the screen?" Tanner asked.

"You pushed the button before I had a chance to look at much of anything. Do you think we should go back and check?" Andrew asked.

"I don't think so," Tanner replied. "We need to just follow the arrows. We can't take the chance of doing anything different. Who knows what would happen."

"You're right. We better stick with the obvious."

"By the way, how was Roman food in the past?" Tanner said, his mouth watering.

"Well, if it's anything like the food in modern Rome, we'll be in pretty good shape," Andrew responded, sounding cheerful for that at least.

"That's for sure. Actually, I don't care what it tastes like," Tanner said. "As long as it's edible! We *will* be able to eat it right?"

"We won't be in the underworld any longer, so we should be able to eat anything," Andrew said.

"Okay. Here goes." Tanner slowly pushed the door open.

CHAPTER 42

ANASTASIA OR PRISCILLA

(MICK)

Mick sat frustrated in the cave, wishing she could clear away the stones Demeter had placed to block the entrance into the Cathedral of Time. Having learned from the goddess that no one had passed through that portal from the underworld in a decade, she really just wanted to go home.

If Demeter isn't coming, I guess I'll have to move the other direction.

Mick turned her attention to the opening above. She pulled out her notes and tried to reconstruct the plans she'd devised to get into Rome before she found out Donald Carlton hadn't been there. She could hear men's voices.

I can actually understand what they're saying. Mick was shocked. She knew the men were speaking Latin. *Is that some sort of gift from the gods?*

When the men's voices subsided, Mick positioned herself just below the opening and cautiously poked her head up into the chamber.

Seeing the coast was clear, she pulled herself through the opening. She could see a ladder that led up to the open door in the cylindrical wall that surrounded her.

Just as I expected. Outside that door is Ancient Rome.

Mick was disheartened, but as she thought about her love for history, she wanted to just run up the ladder and into the city.

I have to follow my plan.

Mick quietly approached the ladder and carried it to the opening she'd just climbed through. *If I lower this into the Mundus, but leave enough exposed for it to be visible, the guards won't be able to resist climbing down to see who moved it.*

Mick changed into the tunic she'd made back home and waited patiently in the Mundus until it began to grow dark.

They should be here any minute to lock this thing up.

"Hey, what happened to the ladder?" One of the guards said.

"There it is, over there," the other replied.

"How did it get *there*?"

"No idea."

Mick heard the two men jump down the ten feet to the floor of the Umbilicus.

"Grab it, and let's get this place locked up."

They're not coming down. What now? They'll lock me in here, and I'll die for sure.

"Help me," Mick moaned from below. "Please help me."

"Did you hear that?"

"Yeah, who do you suppose would be down there?"

"I'm not sure I want to know. You know the Mundus is an entry point for evil spirits."

"Come on. It's just a legend. What if someone's really hurt or in trouble?"

"I'm not going."

"Come on, don't be a Carthaginian."

"All right, but you go first."

It worked!

She carefully hid along the cave wall below the opening opposite the ladder in the shadows as the men moved the stone to widen the opening and began to descend down the ladder into the Mundus. Once the men reached the cave floor, they stepped away from the ladder and began to look around. Mick leapt from her position to the ladder, climbed the last few rungs and pulled the ladder back up through the opening.

"Hey! Halt!" yelled one of the guards.

They'll be right behind me. Got to move fast.

She leaned the ladder against the cylindrical wall and climbed to the door.

Element of surprise. She dashed out the door and into the city. *Don't slow down. No one is expecting you.*

Mick had researched the area near the Umbilicus prior to leaving home and knew exactly where she was going. She fled up a nearby staircase. When she arrived at the Tiber River she sprinted down another staircase to the river's edge and hid in the shadows of a bridge.

Quietly she waited.

What now? I've got to find someplace to stay. But where?

Mick sat under the bridge trying to come up with answers on where to go and what to do.

The Christians. I know the stories from the Bible well enough that I could blend in with them. But where do I find them?

Mick racked her brain trying to remember anything she had learned in history classes or church about Christians in Rome.

There are the catacombs, but I don't think they were built until later.

Peter and Paul were held as prisoners here. I could try to find them, but probably better to stay away from prisons. Maybe I can get some ideas from my guide book.

She rummaged through her backpack and pulled out the guide book she used when she and the boys had gone to Rome with Andrew's father. There had to be something in there about the early Christians. She flipped to the index.

A house church. That's perfect. The homeowner has already agreed to allow other Christians to use their house as a church since it's not safe to have public meetings. Surely they'd be willing to help me. Now, which one? Remember, follow your feelings, Mick thought as she looked through a list of house churches. *Let's see, Anastasia—something about that seems familiar or right, but so does the house church of Priscilla. Which one?* Mick was asking the gods in her mind. *Those two stand out for some reason. Maybe either one's okay? Anastasia is close to the Circus Maximus. It seems like it would be safer to be farther away from all the action around the Circus. Okay. House church of Priscilla it is.*

Following the book's map Mick made her way toward the house church of Priscilla. As she passed the house church of Anastasia, she again questioned her decision briefly, but shook it off.

The location of Priscilla just seemed to make more sense. She paused. *I hope I'm doing the right thing. Anatolia said to follow my feelings. Why is it so hard?*

At length, she decided to continue on to Priscilla's.

"Hi," Mick said timidly to the woman who answered the door. "I'm a Christian and have come here from a faraway land. I'm looking for a place to stay. Can you help?"

CHAPTER 43

Almost There

(Mick)

Tomorrow. A big smile crossed Mick's face as she sat alone in the atrium of Priscilla's house church. *I'll finally be able to try again to get home.*

She'd been in Rome for over a month. The place was amazing, but Mick kept thinking about her family. Did they think she was dead? What were they going through?

I was so sure I'd be able to get back into the Umbilicus before now, but they're so worried about spirits of the underworld escaping into the city when the Mundus is open, that they guard it heavily to make sure it's not open more than three times a year.

"I've learned my lesson." Mick said picturing the gods of Olympus in her mind. "Yeah, my perfect world was shattered, but I've made my life so much more complicated by not just accepting the imperfections and moving on. Please, just let me succeed now in getting back home."

Crash! The front door burst open and two legionnaires stood glaring at Mick.

"You there, girl. You will come with us," the larger man said.

Mick quickly assessed the men, the distance between herself and the side door, and her success at her last track meet.

"Oh no, I won't," She said as she bolted out the door and into the alleyway.

I even said please. Mick thought, looking up at the gods as she ran for her life.

The men split up, and soon Mick found herself trapped in a dead end side alley.

"Oh yes, you will," one of the man replied with a sickening grin.

Soon Mick was in chains and being escorted to prison. "What is this about?" she asked. "I haven't done anything wrong."

"You're a Christian, aren't you?" one of the legionnaires asked.

"Yes, but . . ."

"That's enough," the man said with an arrogant air of finality.

I said I'd learned my lesson. Mick thought as the guard grabbed her and restrained her arms behind her back.

She was led through town and thrown into a filthy prison cell. She'd tried to do everything the gods had told her. She'd followed her gut, and it had led her nowhere. In all her time here she had not gotten any information on Donald Carlton. She had not figured out a way to show her father was innocent. The gods had abandoned her.

What do I do now? She listened intently for an answer from Olympus.

"Do exactly what you're told," the guard said. "Don't give us any trouble." Mick gave him a puzzled look.

It wasn't until the guard left and she spoke to her fellow captors that she realized something was not right. Everyone else was also Christian. That in itself wasn't strange. Christians were always being imprisoned for one thing or another. But in this case, no one had any idea why they were being held.

CHAPTER 44

THE BELLY BUTTON OF ROME

(TANNER)

"Where are we?" Tanner said apprehensively as he stepped into a dark cavern.

The boys shined their lights around the space. Looking behind them, there was no sign of the Cathedral of Time, other than the door they had walked through surrounded by jagged cavern walls.

"Rome?" he questioned, full of uncertainty.

"I have no idea," Andrew said. "But I know for sure Mick didn't come here."

"What makes you say that?" Tanner was tired of Andrew's negative comments. They were in a cold dark cave, starving and tired, and it was all his fault. He got that. Why did Andrew have to keep rubbing it in?

"We didn't adjust the time settings at all. If she came here, she would have arrived at the same time we did."

Tanner's heart sank. Andrew was right—again. Mick definitely should have been there.

"Mick", Tanner softly called, hopeful she was just hiding somewhere out of sight, but there was no answer. "Mick." He raised the volume but still nothing. "Keep looking," Tanner said, hoping that for once he could be right and say told you so to Andrew. "Maybe this place is bigger than it looks."

They walked around the space, but it wasn't bigger than it looked, and there definitely was no Mick. Tanner sat down on the cave floor.

"You were right," he said resignedly. "I was so sure we were on the right path. This whole thing has been a disaster."

"It's all right," Andrew said.

"No, it's not. I've messed everything up—and dragged you along despite your better judgement."

"Hey, at least we survived. And you did promise me an adventure. But what do we do now? There's no way we can survive a return trip through the underworld."

"I guess we try to get out of this cave and into Rome," Tanner said. "We can work to regain our strength. I'll be able to think better if I'm not so hungry."

Andrew's stomach rumbled in agreement. "Let's figure out how to get out of here." He shined his light around the space.

"Hey, shine your light over there again," Tanner said.

A crumpled sheet of paper was hidden in the darkness. He walked over and plucked it out of a small puddle, shook off the water, and straightened it. With his light flashing onto the surface a sense of encouragement filled him.

"I knew it!" he yelled.

"What?"

"It's Mick's handwriting." Tanner said, shoving the paper out for Andrew to inspect.

"What? No way. What makes you think it's hers?" He looked over the paper. "Half the girls in America have handwriting like that."

"Yeah . . ." Tanner replied shining his flashlight at the top of the paper, ". . .but half the girls in America didn't have world geography second period with Mr. Maughan.

"Let me see that." Andrew grabbed the paper away.

"There's your tangible proof, Mr. doubting Thomas," Tanner said with a big grin as he shoved Andrew in the chest. "Mick was here."

"I've got to give you credit T. I never would have believed it if I hadn't seen it myself. So why isn't she here now?"

"I don't know, but at least we know she was. Does the paper give any clues about where she might have gone?"

Andrew scanned the document. "Nope. It just talks about this cave. It's called the Mundus, and the stone that seals it shut is opened three times a year, allowing spirits from the underworld to escape into the city."

"That'd be *us*," Tanner said. "When is it opened?"

"According to this, it's opened August 24, so the seed-corn can safely be placed in here after the harvest, then on October 5 and November 8, when the seeds are retrieved for autumn sowing."

"What's today's date?" Tanner asked.

"I have no idea. It's whatever date the Time Room was set for I guess."

"Ah yeah, forgot about that little detail. Let's see if we can just open it ourselves."

The boys shined their flashlights around the space again. Sure enough there was a flat stone sealing what looked like an entrance above them.

Tanner quickly climbed until he was just below the stone and attempted to move it. It wouldn't budge. "Help me with this."

They had to do some maneuvering to get to where they both had enough leverage to push the stone.

"This was definitely not meant to be opened from this side," Andrew said with a strained voice.

The boys heaved as hard as they could several times. When they were about to give up, they finally heard a small creak. It was starting to move.

"One more time," Tanner said.

Another heave and the stone continued to slide until there was an opening large enough for them to fit through one at a time. Tanner had no idea what to expect as he slithered through the opening, but the one thing he didn't expect hit him like a ton of bricks.

"This place smells horrible," he warned Andrew.

Andrew pulled himself through the small opening.

"Gross." Andrew covered his nose and mouth. He looked around the small circular brick room they were in. "Why do you think this rotten food is all over the floor?"

"No idea, but if it didn't smell so bad, I'd be tempted to eat some," Tanner replied. "Don't you think it's odd that the door is so high above ground level?" Tanner pointed to the door ten feet in the air.

"I don't care, let's get out of here."

The boys sprinted for the ladder leading up to the door.

"Sure is a lot of noise out there," Andrew whispered.

"Wait," Tanner said. "Can you understand what they're saying?"

"Bits and pieces, why?"

"Well, if we're in Ancient Rome, then they should be speaking Latin, but I definitely understand what I'm hearing."

They both looked at each other with puzzled expressions.

"We're speaking Latin," Andrew said.

Tanner concurred. "I wonder how the Time Room did that."

"No idea, but it's pretty cool!"

"Yeah, I could have used something like that for Spanish class last year." Tanner climbed to the top of the ladder. "There's no way to open it from this side," he whispered as he climbed back down. "It looks like it's locked on the outside."

The sunlight that had been pouring into the space was gradually replaced with a flickering light, as if a flame were illuminating the wall.

"Shine your light up there and let's see if we can figure out how to get out of here."

"We can't," Andrew said. "It might tip someone off that we're in here. I think it's best if we get out on our own terms."

"Well, it's too dark without a light, so let's just call it a day. We'll get up early and try."

"Sounds good to me."

"We'll need to bring our A game tomorrow, so try to get some sleep."

The boys pushed the rotted food aside and lay down on the dirt floor. After about an hour, Tanner couldn't stand it anymore. "There's no way I can sleep with this smell. I'm climbing back down below."

"I'm right behind you."

❖ ❖ ❖

Andrew groaned as a small ray of light brightened the Mundus. "It can't be morning already. I don't think I slept at all."

"What a horrible night." Tanner stretched his arms in front of him, bending back and forth to work out the kinks in his muscles.

"I still don't understand why we didn't run into Mick," Andrew said. "We didn't touch the settings."

"Do you always think this deeply when you first get up?" Tanner asked.

"Or at least whoever used the machine last," Andrew replied, ignoring Tanner's comment. "I should have been more observant in the Time Room." He was clearly frustrated with himself. "This place definitely isn't designed for people coming from the direction we came. There's not even a handle to the door on this side." Andrew pointed to the door above.

"Well we will need to figure something out quick. That smell is never going to come out of these clothes as it is." Tanner took a sniff of his shirt and gagged.

It was a long morning. The pair tried everything they could think of to free themselves from what amounted to a prison cell. Before long they began to hear the commotion of the day outside.

"Well, we missed our opportunity to break out this morning," Andrew said. "Too much going on out there now."

"What else did Mick's paper say about this place?" Tanner asked.

"This is considered the center of the Roman Empire. Apparently, the founder of Rome, Romulus himself, had a pit dug here where fruit was sacrificed to the gods of the underworld."

"So that's why there's all this stale food."

"We're standing on centuries of sacrificed harvests," Andrew said. "No wonder it smells so putrid."

"We may have to eat some of this rotten stuff."

"I'm not *that* desperate . . .yet." Andrew looked a bit ill. "Hey. I think I know why Mick didn't arrive at the same time. I remember the settings on the time machine were moving. How long has it been since she went missing?"

"About five or six weeks."

"If the time machine was ticking in the same increments we have on the surface, that's probably how far behind her we are."

"Now that you mention it, I do remember some of the symbols were moving on that screen—like a counter." Tanner could see Andrew was crunching numbers in his head.

"So our only chance of survival is if Mick came through August 24." Andrew said.

"Why do you say that?"

"Come on Tanner, do the math. The Mundus is only opened three times a year. If *she* came on October 5, and we came five or six weeks later, then we're too late for the November 8 opening, and we'll be locked in here 'til next August. If she came November 8, we'll also have to wait 'til August. We've got a thirty-three percent chance of survival."

"Well, there's one way to find out."

Andrew looked at Tanner in shock. "How?"

"Check to see if there's any seed-corn down there."

"You know, sometimes you really surprise me."

The boys climbed back down into the cave and used their headlamps and scoured the place until Tanner spotted a small boulder that looked like it had recently been moved.

"Help me with this," he said.

The boys moved the boulder, and sure enough, they found a wooden crate full of seed-corn hidden safely behind it.

"We must have arrived between the August 24 opening and the October 5 opening," Tanner said. "So if Mick came on August 24, how long would it be until the Mundus is opened?" Tanner asked.

The boys went to work calculating dates.

"Tomorrow!" Andrew shouted.

Tanner quickly put his hand over Andrew's mouth.

"If she came in August, it's going to be opened tomorrow." He reiterated through Tanner's hands.

"We better get busy," Tanner said. "Anything else she wrote that might help?"

"Well, she said everything shuts down on those days because they're afraid the evil spirits that escape from the underworld will have a negative impact on business."

"You were in drama; how good of an actor are you?" Tanner asked.

"I don't know, why?"

"We just have to convince whoever opens that door that we're evil spirits, and we should be able to just walk right out of here," Tanner said. "If only I was as good as my dad was at making angry faces."

"We've got a little too much flesh and bone to fool anyone into thinking we're spirits. Besides, they are not going to just let evil spirits out if they can help it." Andrew started to go into his own brainstorming session and was talking to himself. "What do we have to work with? Hmm." He rummaged through his backpack. "That's it."

"*What's* it?" Tanner asked.

"We can get whoever opens the Mundus to drink some of the poisonous water from Acheron."

"We don't want to *kill* them," Tanner said alarmed.

"No. Remember, it's only supposed to fry your brain for a year or so."

"Okay, but there's no way they'll drink that disgusting stuff. Besides even if they did, how would we get past all the people that will be gathered outside? I'm sure a lot of people will want to make sacrifices to Demeter."

"Once their brains are fried we'll dress up in their clothes. We could just walk right past everyone."

"They're not going to drink it."

"We'll lure them with a note—as if from Demeter herself. It's not like they get the smartest people in town to crawl down into this rot fest. They'll be convinced it's from a god when they see how advanced the paper and pencil are. We'll say the drink is a magical elixir—which wouldn't even really be lying."

"I guess we can try it. Unless we come up with something better."

It was just before dawn when the boys poured some of the water into the lid and placed it with the note on the stone covering.

"They should be coming soon," Andrew said as they climbed down through the opening and carefully slid the stone back into position.

Minutes later, the boys heard the sound of someone fumbling with the lock above.

"This is it."

Their hearts pounded as they listened intently, knowing if this didn't work they might never be able to get out of the wretched place. The creaking sounds of the wooden ladder. Silence. Then the grinding noise of rock scraping against rock. "The Mundus is open," came a voice through the opening.

The boys listened carefully until it was completely silent in the chamber above them.

"Let's go see if it worked," Andrew said.

Slowly they climbed out of the Mundus and into the Umbilicus' chamber.

There was the cup. Tipped over on the floor.

"Do you think they drank it?" Tanner whispered.

"Doesn't matter. Even if they did, it didn't work fast enough. No one's lying on the floor in here. There's no way we can get out of here now."

"Sure we can. The door's open."

"We can't just stroll out in jeans and t-shirts. They'd lock us up or worse."

"Hmm. Good point."

The boys sat dejectedly on the floor.

"Ow. What was that?" Tanner asked.

Someone had thrown a handful of walnuts into the Umbilicus, and one had hit Tanner on the head.

"Must be throwing sacrifices to the gods," Andrew replied.

"Too bad they didn't throw down a nutcracker as well."

"Maybe we'll finally get some foods we *can* eat."

A handful of figs came flying down. Tanner fielded them like a true baseball player. Famished, he ripped one open and snarfed it down so fast he barely had time to taste it. Just as he made his last swallow the reflexes in his brain kicked in. "This is awful."

Seconds later he continued, "Oh no."

Tanner broke out in a cold sweat and began to throw up violently. With everything he had just eaten spewed across the floor, he looked over at Andrew with a drained expression and asked, "Aren't they supposed to sacrifice the best of their crops?"

"It probably was," Andrew laughed. "What you forgot is that eighty percent of taste is smell. Eating that fig in this reeking room made it taste horrible. Next time plug your nose."

Over the next few hours the boys enjoyed a shower of fruits, nuts, and grains, which they ate with their noses plugged. They continued to listen for a lull in the foot traffic outside, in hopes they could just climb up the ladder and walk out, but it never came. They discussed a variety of ideas for how to escape but never felt confident enough to actually try them.

"They're going to lock the door soon, and we're not going to have another shot at this," Andrew said.

"I think we're going to be okay." Tanner said pointing at the stone near his backpack. "Look at those handles. They've dissolved away where the river water spilled on them."

"Hey, you're right."

"We can just pour the water on the lock and sneak out of here. If we do it late enough, no one will see us."

"You surprise me sometimes, T."

The boys waited quietly for the Umbilicus to be locked up and all the noises outside to subside.

"I think we're good," Tanner said. "Give me the water."

"Don't get any on yourself."

Tanner climbed the ladder to the door. He reached up to the window with the cup.

Clank.

"It's too big to fit through the bars. What do we do now? I can't get the water to where the lock is. Have you got a smaller container?"

"Everything else I've got is plastic. It would just dissolve. What if we just dissolve the bars?"

"We don't have enough to dissolve the bars and the lock and we could never fit through that window," Tanner said.

"You're kidding, right? We're so close. And now, we're going to end up stuck here until November? There's got to be a way. "

"We should have just run out the door. Taken our chances," Tanner said in angst, realizing they had blown their chance. "There's no way we can survive in here for a month, and I don't have the energy to go back to the underworld.

"Wait. I've got it. Come down and give me that cup," Andrew said.

Tanner looked with a puzzled stare as Andrew climbed the ladder. "The hinges," he said turning around as he reached the top.

Sure enough, the hinges were on the inside.

"Apparently the Romans didn't want someone on the Surface to do what we're about to do, so they put the hinges on the inside. Grab your stuff. We're about to return to the surface."

Andrew poured the water on the hinges, and they immediately began to dissolve.

"Don't use it all," Tanner said. "That stuff may come in handy."

Andrew looked in the bottle. "There's still a little bit left."

"Help me pull this door open and let's get out of here," Andrew said.

CHAPTER 45

DECIMUS

(TANNER)

When Andrew and Tanner exited the Umbilicus Urbis, the imposing buildings of the Roman Forum seemed ominous in the darkness. Both boys had visited Rome a few years earlier and had been in awe of the scale of the ruins, but to see the structures completely intact and illuminated by nothing more than moonlight and some torches was intimidating.

"That must be the Temple of Concord." Andrew pointed to a massive temple directly in front of them.

"Looks a lot different than that pile of rubble we saw on vacation," Tanner said solemnly.

The temple was covered in the finest marble. On top was a golden statue of a winged goddess. Another statue was obscured in the darkness behind the pillars. To the right was a huge stairway. Behind the temple was a towering building built into the hillside.

"That's the Tabularium, where the official records of the empire are kept," Andrew said.

"How do you remember all this stuff?"

Andrew just shrugged.

They climbed the stairway and continued on until they reached the Tiber River.

"Maybe we should call it a night. I need some real sleep," Andrew said.

"Good thing it's summer. We should be able to just sleep under the stars."

They found a grassy spot near the river and lay down under an umbrella pine.

"Do you think we'll be safe here?" Andrew asked.

"Seems like we're far enough away from the city center that no one should bother us."

"I hope you're right. I don't want to be on the wrong end of a legionnaire's sword, that's for sure."

It didn't take long before both boys were sleeping soundly.

Andrew was startled awake by the sound of shuffling footsteps. He nudged Tanner. "Wake up. Did you hear that?"

"Wh-what?" Tanner mumbled.

"Look." He held his finger to his mouth signaling for Tanner to be quiet and pointed toward the bridge about twenty feet away.

In the darkness they saw the silhouette of two men.

"Where is everyone tonight?" a heavyset man angrily asked his companion.

"Kind of quiet," his companion replied.

"There's one." He pointed to a man walking on the bridge.

"Let's go."

The two men quickly made their way to where the man was.

The boys watched intently. The large man pulled a knife out from under his cloak and stabbed the man as his friend looked on.

The victim slumped to the ground.

"He just killed that guy." Andrew gasped.

"Shhh," Tanner said. He pulled Andrew down and covered his mouth. "If they figure out we saw it, we're next."

"Let's get back to the Mundus. I've seen all I want to see of Rome," Andrew nervously replied.

"Help me throw him in the river." The heavyset man said, looking at his companion as he stooped over and began to pick up his victim. The two of them threw the body off the bridge. Tanner and Andrew watched the body plummet thirty feet into the water below.

"We've got to see if he's still alive," Tanner whispered.

"No way. I'm out of here. I decided I don't like Rome."

"We can't split up. It's way too dangerous, and I'm not just going to let that man die."

Andrew reluctantly followed Tanner as he quietly raced down a staircase to the edge of the river.

"Do you see him?" Tanner whispered.

"Over there." Andrew pointed upstream. Tanner couldn't see the man clearly in the darkness but could tell he was struggling to keep his head above water.

"Are you coming or what?" Tanner said angrily as he jumped in.

Andrew followed and the two boys swam to where they had seen the man. When they arrived, he was no longer struggling and his body was limp as it floated down the river.

"What if the murderers see us?" Andrew asked.

"We've got to hope they don't. But we've got no choice. We've got to try to save him."

They dragged the man's body out of the water and onto the river's edge.

"Does he have a pulse?" Tanner asked as Andrew grabbed his wrist and put his ear to the man's chest.

"Yeah. Let's pull him over here where we won't be seen." Andrew motioned toward a tunnel that fed into the Tiber.

"What's that horrible smell?" Tanner asked.

"Smells like an acre of wet dogs to me."

"If that smell doesn't snap this guy into consciousness, I don't know what will."

"It must be the Cloaca Maxima," Andrew said.

"The what?"

"The Cloaca Maxima. Don't you remember when we were visiting Rome, how the tour guide told us about it? It's a sewer that runs underneath the city."

"Disgusting."

"Yeah, we might want to come up with a different hiding place."

The boys found another spot in the dark shadows where they were able to drag the man.

"Go get your first aid kit," Tanner said.

"I'm not going back up there alone."

"We've got to try to clean this wound and stop the bleeding. I'll go. You stay here and keep pressure on that wound."

"I'm not sure that makes me feel much better," Andrew replied.

"We've got to do *something*." Tanner cautiously sprinted for the stairs that led back up to street level, scanning in all directions as he went. He grabbed their backpacks and returned to the wounded man's side. Andrew began to clean and dress the wound.

"It's not helping. He's going to bleed to death," Andrew said.

"Hand me your water bottle." Tanner began to pull off the bandages Andrew had just put on the man.

"Your water bottle!" Tanner growled growing impatient. He grabbed Andrew's backpack and rifled through it until he had the water bottle.

"Tanner, that's water from Acheron," Andrew said nervously.

"Exactly."

"But it's poisonous."

"I know."

"Are you trying to kill the poor guy?"

"No. Don't you remember? The Acheron breaks off from the River Styx. Water from Styx is supposed to make you invincible. Remember how Achilles mother dipped him in the River?"

"Yeah, but what about the poisonous dissolving part?"

"We've got to take a chance. Otherwise he's going to bleed to death."

"There's only a little bit left," Andrew said. "Plus, do we really want to make him invincible?

"We're not dipping his entire body in the River. So what if he has an invincible stomach. We should be fine."

"But what if we aren't? We don't know anything about him. He could be a serial killer, and we're going to save his life and make him indestructible? This sounds like the kind of stuff that could blast a hole in the entire space-time continuum."

"He's going to die if we don't." Tanner poured the water on the wound.

"Noooooo." Andrew tried in vain to stop his friend. "I don't like this. This is not good."

The wound instantly began to heal and the water pushed back out of the hole where the new skin was forming. It began to spread across his entire body.

"I told you this wasn't good," Andrew said as they scrambled backward away from the man and watched helplessly.

A strange surface formed around the man's body and then disappeared.

Why was I so quick to use the water? Tanner thought.

"We've got to pour whatever's left on us," Tanner said. "We may need to be invincible ourselves if this guy turns out to be some kind of psychopath."

Andrew picked up the bottle and gave it a shake. Nothing. "It's gone." He tipped it upside down and a single drop fell to the ground. There was a sizzling noise, and a small hole quickly burned into the marble pavement.

"What were you thinking?" Tanner asked. "That drop could have been enough to make one of us invincible. We better hope this guy turns out to be good."

"No, *you* better hope this guy turns out to be good."

"We can't let him figure out he's invincible. If he doesn't know, all that power won't go to his head."

"I'm sure he'll figure it out eventually."

The man began to cough. Tanner and Andrew glanced around fearful that the two culprits might hear the noise.

"What happened?" he asked as he sat up.

"You were stabbed and thrown into the river," Andrew replied.

"I know that part, but how did I end up here?"

"We saw the whole thing happen and pulled you out," Tanner said.

"You saved my life."

"Who *were* those men?" Andrew asked.

"Nero and one of his henchmen."

"Nero? The emperor?"

"Yes."

"Why was he after *you*?" Tanner asked.

"I have no idea. I guess that proves the rumors are true."

"Rumors?"

"Well, people say he'll go out and randomly kill, as if for sport. He was wearing a wig for disguise."

"Then how can you be sure it was him?" Andrew asked.

"I'm sure he didn't think I would survive, so before he stabbed me he whispered something in my ear." The man coughed again.

"What?" both boys asked, leaning closer in great anticipation.

"He said, 'Consider yourself lucky. Tonight you're going to die at the hand of the god Nero.'"

"And it really was totally random?" Andrew asked fearfully. "You haven't done anything to provoke him?"

"Nothing. In fact, I've always spoken up for him and his policies."

Andrew and Tanner looked at each other, fearful of what they had gotten themselves into by going to Rome at a time when a crazy man ruled.

"It could just as easily have been us," Andrew whispered.

The man nodded in agreement. "What are the two of you doing out this late?" he asked. "It's not safe."

"Yeah, we can see that," Andrew said, glancing around nervously.

"How are you feeling?" Tanner asked. He wasn't asking just to be cordial. He wanted to know if the man could sense anything different about himself.

"I feel great! Never better. It's kind of strange, after what I've just been through." His hand went to his stomach as if feeling for the wound and he frowned curiously.

"Not the answer I was hoping for," Tanner whispered to Andrew.

"You're obviously not from here." He motioned at their clothes.

"Yes, we're visitors," Andrew said.

"From a faraway land," Tanner added, trying to be helpful.

The man eyed them curiously, looked down at his stomach once more, and then back at the boys. He began to nod his head as if he had come to some conclusion about the boys. Tanner braced himself, worrying that the man would call them out as sorcerers or worse. Instead he squinted at them one last time and then said, "You can't be seen in the city dressed like that. The emperor's men will lock you up on sight. Come with me. We'll get you some proper clothes and a good breakfast."

The boys looked at each other, unsure how to respond.

Possibly sensing their apprehension, he continued, "It's the least I could do after you saved my life. Name's Decimus."

The boys looked at each other again. Having an invincible man on their side might be exactly what they needed to survive. And they were hungry. They agreed to go with him.

"I'm Thaddeus," Tanner said, trying to quickly come up with something that sounded like an ancient name.

"And I'm . . . Julius," Andrew said.

Tanner glared at him with an "I can't believe you couldn't come up with anything more original than that" look.

"I live not far from here—over by the Vatican Hill. Follow me."

The boys followed as they crossed the bridge where Decimus had been stabbed and continued along the edge of the Tiber River. Each of them seemed to have his guard up, watching and waiting for someone to jump out and attack.

"What's that building?" Tanner asked as he saw another massive structure in front of them to the left.

"Nero's Circus. Lots of great chariot races held there."

"It's amazing."

The trio walked around the building on the north side.

"Just a bit farther."

Tanner's heart stood still as he looked up on a small hill next to the arena in the darkness. He could see the silhouette of six crosses, each with a man secured to it. Andrew nudged Tanner and pointed toward the crosses. Decimus turned around and saw the boys.

"Just some Christians," he said. "They deserve whatever they get."

Tanner was shocked at the callousness in his voice. He looked over at Andrew, who he could tell was in a panic.

"Don't believe in the divinity of the emperors, you know. They worship some other god."

Tanner wasn't sure if they should run for it or just lie low. It was obvious Decimus loathed Christians.

"Ah, here we are," Decimus said.

He opened the door and motioned for the boys to enter. He lit a small lamp and glanced down at the blood stain on his tunic. The boys watched as he lifted the garment up to look at the damage.

"Hey," he said. "Where's the wound? There's not even a trace. You're not Christians, are you?" he continued, the anger thick in his voice. "They're rumored to have strange magic. Some even say they have the power to heal."

"Uh . . ."

"Decimus! Is that you?" came a shout from another room.

Tanner looked over at Andrew, whose eyes were big as saucers.

"Yes, dear." Decimus said. By the look on his face, he was in trouble.

"Where have you been all night?"

"I was attacked in the city. Thrown into the Tiber. These two young men rescued me." The tone in his wife's voice changed instantly. "Are you all right? Let me see." She pulled Decimus closer to the light and looked at him questioningly when there was no wound.

"The knife must not have penetrated your skin," Tanner said quickly. "There was a noise, and they pushed you in the river." He looked at the woman.

"When we found him, there was a tear, but any blood must have washed away." Andrew said.

Tanner hoped she wouldn't ask why there was no scar or scab, but the woman's eyes lit up in gratitude. "Oh, thank you so much." She gave each of the boys a tight squeeze. The sun was just starting to come up, and the room began to lighten. "Please, please sit down, won't you? I'll get you something to eat."

"We really should go." Andrew said.

"I wouldn't hear of it," Decimus said. "After what you've done for me?"

"No, really we've got a lot to do today."

"You've got time for some breakfast. A person's got to eat."

"We need to get them some clothes as well," Decimus yelled to his wife as she scurried out of the room. "They'll never survive with those things they're wearing."

Tanner and Andrew tried to keep Decimus and his wife talking about themselves, fearful that Decimus would get back to his earlier question and discover they were indeed Christian. If he was as anti-Christian as he appeared, they had no chance if he turned on them.

CHAPTER 46

A New Ancient Friend

(Tanner)

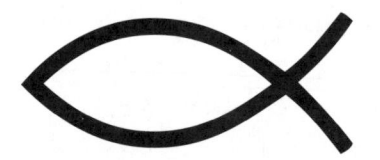

The boys changed into the clothes Decimus's wife found for them and, after a concerted effort, convinced their hosts they didn't want breakfast and needed to go.

"Thank you again," Decimus said. "You have no idea how much this means to me."

Unfortunately, I know exactly how much it means to you. That's the problem. Tanner thought.

"Maybe we'll see you again sometime," he added.

The boys walked out the front door.

"We never should have saved him," Andrew said.

"He was going to die."

"We're messing with time travel, T. He was supposed to die. We just altered history. If we get too involved here we're going to create an alternate future."

"Hadn't thought about that," Tanner replied. "But how different could it be? He's just one man."

"Don't underestimate the kind of difference one man can make. Think Steve Jobs."

"Decimus is no tech genius."

"Or Hitler," Andrew said.

"Come on, he's not going to become another Hitler."

"We don't know that. You saw how numb he was to those crucifixions. Once he realizes he's invincible, who knows what he'll do. Power goes to people's heads. Especially *that* kind of power."

"Maybe he'll never figure it out," Tanner said.

"He's going to figure it out. Didn't you see the armor in his house? He's in the military—a legionnaire. You know he's going to be in a position to die in that career field. When he magically doesn't, he's going to continue to rise in power until . . ."

"So what do we do?" Tanner asked. "You're not thinking we need to go back and kill him off, are you?"

"Even if I was, we can't do it," Andrew said. "He's invincible."

"Okay. Well we've got to keep an eye on him, then," Tanner said. "If things start to go awry, we may have to enlist some help from the underworld."

"Not sure I want to be the one to explain to the gods that we created an invincible mortal."

"If you've got a better solution, I'm all ears," Tanner said.

"Hopefully it won't come to that."

The boys were getting near the central plaza in Rome—the forum. Vendors wheeled their carts through the streets, ready to set up their wares for the day. There were wagons preparing to sell tunics, sandals, housewares, and lots of foods. Cheeses, breads, fruits, and nuts.

"What is everyone doing up so early?" Tanner asked.

"I know." Andrew yawned and stretched his arms over his head. "It would have been nice to get a little more sleep. Oh well, at least we got some clothes out of the deal."

"A pretty bad *deal*. Giving someone invincibility in exchange for a couple of lousy tunics and some old sandals? *Not* a good trade."

"So where should we go now?" Andrew asked.

"Well, we've run out of clues from Mick," Tanner said. "We've done everything she wrote about."

"I guess from here on, if we're going to find her, we're going to have to follow our guts."

"Speaking of following our guts, the effects of that sacrificed fruit have pretty much worn off," Tanner said. "How about if we look for something to eat?!"

"I agree! I'm famished."

"This looks like the biggest toga party ever," Tanner said as they entered the forum and began searching for breakfast.

"Hey, what's going on over there?"

There was a big commotion near the Basilica Julia. A crowd was quickly forming around the building.

"What's everyone looking at?" Andrew asked.

"That man's throwing money from the roof," Tanner said.

It was a heavyset man in an elegant purple toga. A man who, despite no longer having a disguise, looked somewhat familiar.

"Is that Nero?" Andrew asked.

"Yes, it's Nero," a stranger said in disgust. "He's trying to be like Caligula. *He* used to do this day after day to watch the commoners fight over the coins."

"This is our chance to solve our money problem," Tanner said, nudging Andrew with his elbow.

The pair quickly maneuvered into position where they would be able to gather some of the money. It was an all-out brawl. The look on Nero's face made it clear he enjoyed watching the fracas. By the time the melee was over, the boys had secured a fair amount of money and bruises for themselves.

"Let's get some food." Tanner rubbed at a particularly angry welt on his forearm. If he finally got to eat something substantial it would be worth it.

They crossed the forum to the Tabernae Novae, or new shops, and purchased some breads and cheeses, which they wolfed down in no time. As they finished, Andrew glanced to his right where a girl about his age was staring at the two of them. He wiped his mouth to make sure he didn't have any food on his face and then gave the girl an awkward smile before glancing away.

"Don't look now, but we have an admirer over there." He pointed toward the girl with his finger discreetly against his chest.

Tanner couldn't help himself and immediately turned to see the girl still staring their direction.

"You wish," Tanner said.

The girl approached. She directed her attention to the ground where she drew a small arc with the stick she was holding. Tanner was baffled, but Andrew enthusiastically grabbed the stick and drew an arc in the opposite direction. Tanner glanced at him, a look of confusion on his face. He stared down at the newly formed shape, which looked like the profile of a fish.

"What the?" Tanner said as Andrew and the girl exchanged a warm smile. The girl quickly brushed the sand with her foot, destroying the image, and Andrew gave Tanner an "I'll tell you later" look.

"Salve, my name is Marina," the girl said. "And you are?"

"I'm Julius," Andrew said.

Tanner rolled his eyes. "And I'm Thaddeus."

"You are strangers here, are you not?" Marina asked.

"Yes. How could you tell?" Andrew asked.

"The strange sacks you're carrying. I've never seen sacks like those." She pointed to Tanner and Andrew's backpacks, which they had forgotten they were carrying.

"Ah, where we come from everyone has sacks like these," Tanner replied.

"We're trying to find our friend," Andrew said. "She came here a few weeks ago. She's about our age, and has reddish-brown hair. We're afraid she's in danger."

"Follow me," Marina said. "My family is always happy to help fellow Christians."

Tanner gave Andrew a look of surprise. "How does she know we're Christian?" he whispered.

"I'll tell you later."

"We live not far from here, on the other side of the Circus Maximus."

"Okay," Andrew said. He appeared more than happy to follow Marina.

"Is this your first time in Rome?" she asked.

Tanner wasn't quite sure how to answer.

"Uh, yeah." Andrew finally said.

"Why did you hesitate?" Marina asked.

"Well, we've been lots of places, just trying to remember if we'd been here."

"I think you would remember if you'd been to Rome." Marina said laughing.

"Yeah, I'm sure I've never seen *these* buildings." Tanner winked at Andrew.

The three of them began to walk along the Via Sacra.

"Behind that temple is one of the most important buildings in the city," Marina said.

"That little thing?" Andrew replied.

It was the smallest, least important building they had seen.

"Centuries ago, a shield from the god Mars descended from heaven and a voice declared that as long as it was kept safe, Rome would be mistress of the world," she said. "The shield is stored in a special room, and eleven exact copies were made so if anyone wanted to steal the real one they would have to take all twelve."

"That's pretty cool," Andrew said.

"The Regia is also where the lances of Mars are stored."

"The what?" Andrew asked.

"The lances of Mars. The high priest shakes them and yells *'Mars Vigila'* to awaken the god and ask for his help whenever Rome goes to war. Supposedly it's a bad omen if they start to shake on their own."

"What do you mean?" Andrew asked.

"Well, they were shaking the night before Julius Caesar left the Regia and was assassinated."

Tanner whispered with a smile to Andrew. "Maybe if they start to shake again, something terrible will happen to you, my friend . . . Julius."

"You're never going to let me live that down, are you?" Andrew asked.

A covered two-wheeled carriage stopped in front of them, and a striking woman dressed all in white emerged.

"Whoa, who's that?" Tanner asked.

"It's a Vestal Virgin," Marina replied. "The Vestals are keepers of the sacred eternal flame, one of the three things that guarantee the continued rule of Rome."

"I had no idea the Romans were so superstitious," Andrew whispered to Tanner.

"What's that temple up there?" Andrew asked. "The one that rises above all the others."

"Oh, that's the Temple of Jupiter, the most important in Rome. There used to be shrines to other gods there, but the priests were able to get permission to remove them so that temple could be built."

"Permission? Who'd they have to get permission from?"

"The gods themselves. Terminus, the god of boundaries, was the only one who refused. So they built the temple around his altar and put a small hole in the ceiling to give it open exposure to the sky."

"Why did Terminus refuse to have his altar removed?"

"No one knows, but it has been interpreted to mean the borders of Rome will also refuse to move for any other civilization. It may be because of this that boundary stones, dividing one man's property from another, are believed to contain spirits."

"So do *you* believe these boundary stones contain spirits?" Tanner asked Marina.

"No, but a lot of Romans do. They make sacrifices to Terminus every year to assure the borders of their property are never violated." She stopped and looked at the boys as if assessing if they believed her or not then continued eastward. The boys stumbled along after her.

"My home is over there," Marina said as she pointed south, where Tanner saw the largest stadium he'd ever seen.

The boys stared in awe at the enormous building. They'd been to the site when they visited Rome, but it was nothing more than a big grass field and some rubble at the time. Mick had explained to them that the original structure sat nearly a quarter of a million people.

Tanner closed his eyes and tried to imagine what a chariot race in a stadium with that many people would look like. He knew their first order of business was to find Mick, but he knew he wouldn't be opposed to seeing some of the local culture. *I mean, when will we ever make it back to Ancient Rome?*

CHAPTER 47

MARCUS AND ANASTASIA

(TANNER)

A large marble slab with the name Anastasia inscribed on it was on the front of Marina's door. She opened the door and ushered the boys in.

"Hi, Cornelius," Marina said. "These are my new friends Julius and Thaddeus."

"Nice to meet you."

"Cornelius is a family friend."

Cornelius reached out and shook hands with the two boys. Tanner's knuckles popped under the man's firm grip. He had a square jaw and a muscular build, and even though his hair was graying and he looked a bit weathered, he still had a commanding presence.

"They're from a faraway land."

"Ah, what land?"

Tanner panicked as he tried to think how to answer. America wouldn't be discovered for over fourteen hundred years.

"Cornelius has travelled across many lands as a centurion," Marina explained.

Makes sense, Tanner thought. Cornelius had the look of a once powerful military leader.

"Can someone help me please?" a voice yelled from another room.

"Whew, that was close," Andrew whispered as they followed Cornelius and Marina into what must have been the kitchen.

Standing in the kitchen was a beautiful woman with straight jet-black hair, a dark complexion, and welcoming smile.

"This is my stepmother, Anastasia," Marina said.

"Welcome to our home," she said. "What brings you here?"

"We're searching for our friend. She indicated she was coming to Rome, but never came back. We're afraid she's in trouble," Tanner said.

"Well, it's definitely a dangerous time. Is she Christian?"

"Yes."

"Then you have good reason to be worried. We'll help however we can. Tell us about your friend."

Tanner was carrying a picture of her in his wallet, but was sure showing it would label him as a witch or sorcerer. Something like a simple photograph would certainly be viewed as strange magic.

"She's about the same height as Marina, with reddish-brown hair," he said. "She usually ties it back and is always smiling."

"What's her name?"

"Makayla, but her friends call her Mick."

"Interesting name," Anastasia said. "We'll spread the word and see if anyone has seen her."

"Where's Marcus?" Cornelius asked.

"He should be home soon."

"Who's Marcus?" Andrew whispered to Marina.

"My father. He's a merchant in town."

"Cornelius, Marina, can you help me set everything up for the meeting?" Anastasia asked.

"Meeting?" Andrew replied.

"Our home is a *domus ecclesia*," Marina replied.

"A what?" Tanner asked.

"A house church. As Christians we have to meet secretly in people's homes. My stepmother volunteered our house. Other Christians will be arriving throughout the afternoon. It's too dangerous for them to all come at the same time."

"Maybe one of them will have seen Mick," Tanner said hopefully.

"Why are Christians so hated?" Andrew asked Marina.

"The emperor has been declared a god, but we believe in a different god."

Tanner and Andrew sat through the meeting, which actually had the same feel as a Sunday service at home. Only at home, Mick would have been there with them. Not only was she not here, but none of the Christians in attendance had any information about her. They sat dejectedly wondering what they would do next when a young girl about five years old entered the atrium. She looked just like Anastasia with her straight black hair and a complexion that was slightly darker than Marina's.

"Hi, Livia," Marina said as she picked up the small girl. "What have you been doing?"

"Just playing."

"Everyone needs to change and come for dinner," Anastasia called from the other room. Andrew and Tanner looked at each other. The only Roman clothes they had were the tunics they were wearing. While Tanner would have loved to change back into the jeans in his backpack, he knew that probably wouldn't go over so well.

"I have some extra dining robes," Anastasia said as she walked past. "Let me get them for you."

She returned with some colorful lightweight robes she referred to as *cenatoria*. The boys were happy to change out of the tunics that had been a little too big for them.

Tanner knew Ancient Romans ate lying down, but it was strange to actually do it. The triclinium, or dining room, was named for the three beds that were placed on three sides of a small square table in the middle of the room. The fourth side was open for those who were serving. Along the edge of the beds closest to the table were long pillows used for resting their elbows as they ate. Because the Romans reclined perpendicular to the edges, there was room for nine diners—three on each bed. The boys watched closely to see how their hosts positioned themselves.

"Those are the seats of honor," Cornelius said pointing to the bed that allowed the diners to look out at the central garden. "Go ahead," he continued, motioning for the boys to lie down.

"Marcus, welcome," Anastasia said as her husband entered the room. "How was your day?"

"Extremely busy."

"This is Julius and Thaddeus. Friends of Marina."

"Actually, it's Tanner and Andrew," Tanner said.

"But you said—" Marina began.

"I know," Tanner said. "We weren't sure it was a good idea to use non-Roman names."

Cornelius nodded. "Probably not a bad idea to use Roman names when you're out and about."

"Well Marcus," Anastasia restarted her introductions, "this is Tanner and Andrew, and they've come from a faraway land in search of their missing friend. Tanner, can you tell my husband what she looks like? He has lots of contacts within the Christian community."

After Tanner described Mick, Marcus replied, "Yes, I actually met her at a youth gathering two or three weeks ago. She attended a few times, and then we never saw her again."

Tanner and Andrew could hardly contain themselves.

"Where is she now?" Tanner asked ready to jump out of his skin with excitement.

"Actually, she might have already returned home," Marcus said. "She said wanted to see how citizens make offerings to Demeter at the Umbilicus, and then she'd leave. The Umbilicus was opened yesterday."

Tanner and Andrew looked at each other.

"We may have just barely missed her," Tanner said his voice full of frustration.

"But we were in the Umbilicus the whole day," Andrew said.

Tanner gave Andrew a stern look.

"What?" Marcus asked.

"Nothing. Nothing," Andrew replied

"Will you help us look for her?" Tanner asked.

"Yes. We'll all help." Everyone in the room chimed in and committed to assist.

"Why don't you spend the night?" Anastasia asked. "We have an extra room. Tomorrow we can work out a plan to find your friend."

She appeared excited to have the boys stay in her home, as did Marcus and the two girls.

"Momma, I'm tired. May I go to bed?" Livia said.

"Yes, dear. It has been a long day," Anastasia said.

Tanner and Andrew saw this as their chance to leave the table as well. They hadn't wanted to be impolite, especially since they were given the seat, or bed, of honor at dinner. But having dined for several hours, they were stuffed and tired.

"I think we're going to call it a night as well," Tanner said.

"You do look exhausted," Anastasia said. "Livia let's show the boys their room."

"Yes, Momma," Livia said. "Do you think their friend is dead, Momma?"

Anastasia gasped. "No, of course not. God will help us to find her, Livia."

Tanner and Andrew looked at each other, worry covering both their faces. They knew this was a possibility; they'd always known. Even they had almost died more than once, but to have a five-year-old voice it so casually confirmed the fears they'd been trying to ignore. Livia sounded like she was going to add some more, but her mother shushed her.

The guest room was small. The paintings on the walls were of elegant landscapes with painted architectural elements like pillars and wainscoting that framed each scene. The feather-filled mattresses were relatively comfy, and Tanner was happy to be up off the ground. Their sleeping accommodations were far more primitive than their bedrooms in Brownsville, but better than anything they'd had since they left.

"Why do you think Mick stopped attending those meetings?" Tanner asked as they got ready for bed.

"I don't know," Andrew replied. "I worry about the whole Christian persecution thing, though, and the fact that we didn't run into her in the Umbilicus."

"Well, the good news is that we're the closest we've been to finding her yet. I don't think we've come this far in vain." Tanner tried to sound optimistic. "By the way, what was that whole fish in the sand thing?" he said, changing the subject.

"It's a way to show you're a Christian. A few months ago, my dad got a fish emblem for his car. When I asked him what it was, he explained that early Christians would draw a small arc in the sand when talking with a stranger. If the stranger drew an arc in the opposite direction to form the shape of a fish, they would know they had met another Christian—someone they could trust."

"You're kidding," Tanner said. "If your dad hadn't bought that, we never would have met Marina's family, and more importantly known about Marcus seeing Mick."

"Definitely a stroke of luck," Andrew said, nodding his head.

CHAPTER 48

ICHTHYS

(TANNER)

"Time to get up," Cornelius said.

Tanner mumbled an undistinguishable response.

"There's bread and oil in the triclinium. Come join us when you're ready."

The boys groggily made their way to the dining room. Tanner lay down on the couch bed and almost dozed back off again, but Andrew nudged him to keep him awake while they discussed their options in the hunt for Mick.

"Our best chance to find the girl is to talk with other Christians," Marcus said. "We have a good communication network. Once word starts to spread we should find her pretty quickly."

"We will need to split up to cover more ground," Cornelius added. "You will have to look for signs that identify Christian homes. For example, the sign of the fish."

Livia chimed in, "I don't like fish!"

"Me neither!" Tanner winked.

"Momma, that boy winked at me," Livia said, pulling on her mother's dress.

"Why *is* the fish used to identify other Christians?" Andrew asked.

"The phrase 'Jesus Christ, God's Son, Savior' is an acrostic."

"What's an acrostic?" Tanner interrupted.

"It's a phrase in which the initial letters of the words form a word of their own. In this case they spell the Greek word *ichthys*, or fish."

"Huh?" Tanner was confused.

"Well, the first letter of the Greek word for Jesus is *I*. *CH* are the first letters of the Greek word *Christ*. *TH* are the first letters of the Greek word for *God's*, *Y* is the first letter of the Greek word for *Son*, and *S* for the Greek word for *Savior*.

The symbol of a fish, or *ichthys*, is a way to tell someone you believe Jesus Christ is God's Son, the Savior of the world."

"That's pretty cool," Tanner said.

Cornelius gave him a strange look. "It has nothing to do with the temperature."

Marcus brought them back on task. "We need to start by searching areas with large Christian populations. Look for the *ichthys* on the front of the house. When you see it, you'll know it's a Christian home. Oh, and you may also see the sign of the wheel."

"What's that?" asked Andrew.

"Another symbol," Cornelius said. "We needed more than one. This sign looks like the wheel of a chariot."

"Have you seen my toy chariot?" Livia asked.

"Not now, honey." Marcus said, putting his arm around his little daughter.

"So what does the wheel symbolize?" Andrew asked.

"It's the Greek letters ΙΧΘΥΣ, which means *ichthys*. When they are superimposed, it makes the shape of an eight-spoked wheel. Watch for that or the fish. I put together a list of house churches I am aware of as well. Everyone will need to make a copy."

Cornelius left the room and returned with wax writing tablets and styluses. Andrew tried to draw a wagon wheel with his finger by superimposing the letters.

"Okay. Here's the list. Hopefully you can see it well enough to copy."

Tanner wanted to pull out his phone and take a picture, but knew he couldn't.

"Protect this list with your lives. In the wrong hands, it could lead to the destruction of the entire religion in Rome. Nero would light the streets with our burning bodies. So destroy the list if you find yourselves in danger. Good luck, and God be with you."

"Momma, can I go with the boys?" Livia asked.

"No, dear."

"Aw, please?"

"Hey, Livia, when we get back, we'll play with your toy chariot, okay?" Tanner said.

"Can we really?" Livia replied excitedly.

"For sure. When we come back, we'll play together."

"You swear?"

"I swear."

"Do we go together or split up?" Tanner asked Andrew. He was nervous. The thought of being in Rome alone with Nero on the loose was not pleasant.

After a brief pause, he answered his own question "We've GOT to split up. Mick's been alone in Rome for weeks now. We've got to find her as quickly as possible."

"We'll meet back here at dark," Andrew said. "Hopefully with good news."

❖ ❖ ❖

When evening came, everyone reassembled. Like the two boys, Anastasia and Marina hadn't found anyone who had seen or heard from Mick.

"One of the families I visited saw Mick ten days ago." Marcus told the group when he returned.

"Do they know where she is now?"

"No."

"Well, ten days isn't *that* long ago," Tanner said. "That's encouraging."

"True, but until we know exactly where she is, there's still the chance . . ." Cornelius didn't finish.

There wasn't much conversation at dinner. They had canvassed only a small number of *domus ecclesiae,* but there was a lot of communication among the Christians, so a single sighting didn't bode well.

Dinner hit the spot, not because the boys were big fans of Ostrich Ragoût, which was one of the six courses, but because they had put in a long day walking the streets and had worked up a huge appetite.

"Can we play now?" Livia asked.

"Sure," Tanner replied. He and Andrew followed Livia to the atrium where they began to play with some of her wooden toys. Tanner looked like a little kid himself.

"I'm going to bed." Andrew said as he turned toward the bedroom. Marina, who had just arrived at the atrium, stopped him.

"Tell me about the land you come from."

Andrew cautiously began to tell Marina about Kentucky. They walked over to a bench in the garden while Tanner and Livia continued to play in the atrium.

"Livia, time to go to bed," Anastasia called out.

"Aw, Momma. Do I have to?"

"Yes, dear. I'm sure Tanner will play again tomorrow."

"He's not Tanner, Momma" Livia said indignantly. "He's Musclosus, the great charioteer."

"Oh. I see. Well, say good night to Musclosus, then."

Anastasia pried Livia away and carried her off to bed.

Tanner sat thinking about his own little sister and the fun they had. His heart ached knowing he would never see her again in this life. He might not even see his mother again. As he walked toward the bedroom he saw Andrew and Marina still talking in the garden.

"Don't stay out too late," he said as he smiled and winked at Andrew.

Andrew shot him an evil glare and went back to talking with Marina.

It wasn't long before Tanner was sleeping soundly.

❖ ❖ ❖

Tanner and Andrew and their new friends continued to search for the next three weeks without anyone having seen Mick. The boys from Brownsville were tired, discouraged, and argued frequently about whether or not they should just give up and make their way home on November 8—the next opening of the Umbilicus.

"Get up sleepy heads!"

They dragged themselves out of bed and to the dining room, now a common routine. They helped themselves to hunks of salted bread they tore off from the flat round loaves that had been placed on the table. There was a small bowl of olive oil and another of honey for dipping. In addition, there was a selection of delicious cheeses.

"Today's the first day of the Ludi Romani," Cornelius said. "The streets will be packed."

"What's the Ludi Romani?" Andrew asked.

"One of our biggest annual festivals. The chariot races are this afternoon."

"Maybe we should check it out," Tanner said as they walked out the front door. "We might have as good a chance of finding Mick there as with what we've been doing."

"We need to stay the course," Cornelius replied. "We've almost visited all the house churches and homes of Christians."

Tanner opened the door and tripped over the threshold falling face first onto the street. "Watch that," he said pointing to the threshold as he dusted himself off.

"Okay. We'll see you tonight!" Andrew yelled, above the noises of the busy street, as they parted ways.

Tanner wound his way through the streets. The second family he visited had seen Mick less than a week earlier.

Encouraging.

As he continued to walk his route he spotted a house, that wasn't on Cornelius's list, with an *ichthys* wheel etched near the front door.

There must be more Christians than Cornelius thought. He was encouraged. *Maybe the small number of Mick sightings isn't as bad news as we were thinking.*

Excitedly Tanner knocked on the door. An extremely large, burly man answered.

"Good morning!" Tanner declared. "I noticed the mark on your door. I'm Christian too."

A look of consternation quickly turned into a look of anger.

"That's the mark of the true god Jupiter! Not your false Christian god!" the man shouted. He turned and yelled back into the house. "It's a Christian!"

The man lunged at Tanner but he dodged him and fled. A footrace ensued. The man and his friend were in hot pursuit.

I should be able to outrun these two, Tanner thought as his mind raced. *As long as I don't come across any dead ends.* His adrenaline was pumping as images of tortured Christians flashed through his mind. He darted in and out of the streets and around the vendors and wagons.

"Christian! Christian!" the men shouted.

"Grab him," someone else shouted as Tanner ran past.

More people joined the fray, hoping to become a hero for capturing a Christian. Tanner ran as if his life depending on it—because it did.

CHAPTER 49

BEGINNING OF THE END
(MICK)

"Where are you taking us?" Mick asked as a guard pulled her to her feet and led her out of the cell along with the other prisoners.

No reply.

"Probably to be crucified," one of her fellow prisoners whispered.

Follow my feelings you said? Mick began to converse again in her head with the gods. *I'm pretty sure you don't want me to do that, because right now, I feel like spewing forth a stream of obscenities that you wouldn't be very happy about.*

CHAPTER 50

THE ARENA

(TANNER)

I've got to get to Circus Maximus, Tanner thought. *With my complexion, I should be able to lose them in a crowd of 250,000.*

He made a couple of quick turns until he could see the arena ahead. A man grabbed at him as he darted past a vendor booth under one of the arched entrances. His tunic ripped as he spun free. Ahead he saw some stairs and quickly made his way up. He turned to continue his ascent in the other direction and then stopped. The men were about to the top of the first flight. Tanner leapt over the wall, putting himself behind his pursuers on the lower stairs. He scrambled down and pivoted into the main corridor. He tried to blend in with the thousands of fans walking toward their seats. He didn't dare look back, but listened intently for any indication that his pursuers had followed his trail. He couldn't hear anything out of the ordinary.

Did I actually get away?

In those few minutes of cat and mouse, the fragile nature of life became real. Tanner, for the most part, had always felt invincible, but running for his life with images of Christians being fed to the lions and used as human torches, changed all that.

What about Mick? No one's seen her for more than a week. Is she being tortured and beaten somewhere? Scourged? Has she been fed to the lions? He couldn't bear the thoughts that ran through his mind. His thoughts switched to Andrew.

I should have stayed with him. No one told us the ichthys *wheel symbol was also a symbol for Jupiter. What if Andrew makes the same mistake I did? He wouldn't have the speed and stamina to go through what I just did without being captured.*

Tanner followed the crowd down the corridor. He picked a set of stairs to climb and worked his way to a seat. As he contemplated his new reality, he was startled by the sound of trumpets. A hush fell over the crowd. Heads turned to the center of the north side of the arena, across from where Tanner was sitting. He looked just in time to see Nero emerge from his palace into the Imperial box. He had seen glimpses of the emperor already, but this was his first unobstructed view of the legendary figure. He had the prominent belly of a glutton. Nose in the air, he appeared callous and full of himself. Nero reveled in the pomp and circumstance surrounding the event and his role as emperor. The trumpets continued to blare and everyone stood to show their respect.

I can't stand, Tanner thought. *I can't show respect to this megalomaniac. He's a psychopath. He's crazy. He's . . . I have to stand. I can't afford to do anything that will make me stand out in the crowd. I can't give those men a chance to spot me.*

He sprang to his feet. The trumpeting stopped, and a hush fell over the crowd. Nero motioned, acknowledging the masses, and sat down. Energized by the prospects of the spectacle they were about to witness, the cheering crowd raised the decibel level.

Tanner had been to many sporting events and had seen raucous crowds of 23,500 at Rupp Arena gathered to watch the Kentucky Wildcats play basketball. But this crowd was more than ten times the size of that. A staggering quarter of a million people assembled to watch a few chariot races. As he tried to take it all in, he heard the sound of trumpets again and the crowd went silent. A group of young boys on horseback entered the arena from the left. They were dressed in regal attire. The crowd erupted. Following close behind were more boys dressed as legionnaires. They had red shields with yellow eagle wings painted on them and intricately designed helmets. Their silver breastplates gleamed in the sunlight.

Tanner's heart rate started to return to normal, and he marveled at the spectacle he was witnessing. The colors. The setting. The throngs of people. He had been so preoccupied with his pursuit of Mick over the past few weeks that he'd failed to take in the experience he was having.

Next in the procession came the charioteers. Tanner had seen *Ben Hur* and the famous chariot race, and he was about to see the real thing. There was a group of charioteers dressed in red, followed by one arrayed in white, a group in blue, and another in green. As the red charioteers passed directly in front of him, he heard the man next to him praying.

"Help me in the Circus today. Bind every limb, every sinew, the shoulders, the ankles, and the elbows of the charioteers of the red. Torment their minds, their intelligence, and their senses so that they may not know what they are doing, and knock out their eyes so that they may not see where they are going—neither they nor the horses they are going to drive."

Tanner looked over at the man in shock. Not quite the type of thing you were supposed to pray for. As each color passed in front of him, there was a wave of heckling, cheering, and booing. Men took amulets off their necks and threw them into the arena while chanting curses.

This is worse than a Yankees-Red Sox game.

Once the charioteers had all entered, a group of gladiators emerged. They were fully dressed in gladiatorial armor and lived up to what Tanner would have expected: a rugged group you wouldn't want to meet in a dark alley. The crowd began to chant in unison.

"Spiculus! Spiculus! Spiculus!" A particularly fierce gladiator acknowledged the crowd.

"Excuse me. Will the gladiators be fighting today?" Tanner asked the man next to him.

"No. They'll fight tomorrow."

"So how long does this festival last?" Tanner asked.

"A little over two weeks. The first five days are represented in the parade. For example, today are the chariot races, tomorrow are the gladiator battles, and so on. Each event's participants appear in the parade in order of their occurrence during the festival."

"Makes sense," Tanner replied.

He continued to watch the procession. Next were troops of dancers performing to musical accompaniment. They were wearing purple tunics and performing war dances using swords and spears. Following the dancers was a chorus dressed as satyrs. They had woolly tunics, hair standing out like horse ears on top of their heads, and long tails. The satyrs were in the attitude of mocking the dancers.

Day three must be a dance festival and day four, a play.

Following the satyrs was a group of men escorting chained lions, bears, boars, and dogs into the arena. The crowd erupted with their approval as these fierce beasts entered the Circus. Tanner was familiar with the fact that the Romans were known to have animal hunts in their arenas. Walking behind the animals was a group of humble looking people in chains. He knew right away they were Christians.

The Christians are going to be fed to the lions on day five.

As a Christian himself, Tanner envisioned himself in the shoes of those about to be ripped apart.

I can't believe Romans are that bloodthirsty.

He looked again at the lions as they roared and pictured their fangs sinking into his own flesh. Tanner shuttered.

He stared with sympathy on the . . .

A shiver of excitement ran through Tanner's entire body as he recognized a familiar face in the front row. Mick. She was alive.

And about to be fed to the lions.

His heart sank. He sprang to his feet, but quickly glanced around and sat back down. *I can't do anything about it. Not yet. Not alone. I've got to just sit right here and watch.*

Mick, look up here. Tanner knew it was a pipe dream. There was no way Mick was going to spot him in that crowd. *We'll rescue you. I don't know how, but we'll do it. Don't worry.*

Four days. That's all we've got. I've got to tell the others. We've got to start planning. Tanner started to stand up again. *No, I can't. I've got to blend in. Can't get myself captured.*

The stadium filled with boos and hisses as the Christians paraded in front of him. Tanner looked around in disbelief. As he listened to the continued roars of the beasts and jeering crowd, a terrible feeling of hopelessness entered every fiber of his being, and yet Mick was alive. He had seen her, so at the same time, it was the greatest feeling of hope he'd ever felt. The incredible procession continued but Tanner barely noticed. He couldn't keep his eyes off Mick.

She looks a bit roughed up, but she looks good.

The chariot racing that Tanner had been so excited to see dragged on and on. He was so anxious to go back to tell his new friends the good news and bad news and begin organizing a rescue. It felt like he'd been in the arena for days when the event finally ended and the spectators began to file out. There had been plenty of time for the exits to have been manned by anti-Christians who had teamed up with his pursuers, so Tanner was relieved when he was able to exit without incident.

He hustled to Anastasia's house. No one else was back. He paced anxiously back and forth.

What's taking so long? Where is everyone?

Finally, Andrew, Marina and Cornelius entered the house.

"I saw Mick!" Tanner exclaimed.

"Where? Is she okay? Why isn't she with you?" Andrew asked rapid-fire.

"She was in chains. She's going to be fed to the lions."

"What?" Andrew looked like he was going to be sick.

"How do you know?" Marina asked.

Tanner explained the events of the afternoon.

"What do we do?" Andrew asked.

"We've got to stay calm," Cornelius said. "Panicking isn't going to help."

"How can we stay calm?" Andrew asked. "Didn't you hear what Tanner just said? They are going to feed her to the lions!"

CHAPTER 51

FED TO THE LIONS

(MICK)

Fed to the lions? Fed to the lions? Mick asked the invisible gods as she was paraded into the Circus Maximus behind the ferocious beasts. *That's your definition of* success? *Or did I mess up? Was I supposed to go to the house church of Anastasia and not Priscilla? Maybe I would have been safer there.*

Mick wanted to believe that success meant she'd somehow escape, but looking at 250,000 angry faces jeering at her as she walked across the arena floor didn't make it very believable.

CHAPTER 52

THE RESCUE PLAN

(TANNER)

"Our best chance to free Mick would be to bribe the prison guards," Marcus said as they lay around the table after dinner.

"I agree," Cornelius said.

"I'm just not sure where we could come up with that kind of money."

"Perhaps we could break into the State Treasury."

"Really?" Marcus asked incredulously.

"We would be justified since it is the state that is unfairly sacrificing Christians," Cornelius said. "It is not heavily guarded. All we have to do is figure a way to lure the guards from their posts. If we can do that, I can round up some men to overpower them and secure the keys. Access to that kind of money would allow us to get Mick freed for sure."

"And you really think we could do it?"

"Absolutely. Don't forget, having been a centurion, I have enough inside information to pull it off; I've just never had the motive. But with Nero persecuting us the way he is, that has all changed. I would love nothing more than to rescue their friend *and* take down the emperor."

Everyone looked at one another in shock, but no one disagreed. Nero had to be stopped.

"If we can save the life of a Christian, that's good enough for me," Marcus said. "Tell us the rest of your plan."

"It would be difficult to get close to the treasury without being spotted, even in the middle of the night. However, there is a series of little known underground tunnels that were built during Caesar's time for use in the production of shows held in the forum." Cornelius began to sketch the layout of the forum.

"The passages form a grid. The longest corridor runs the length of the central plaza. There are smaller passages that connect to the main tunnel and run perpendicular to it. These shorter corridors are accessible through manhole covers on the surface. One of them opens right in front of the Rostra."

"Is that the raised platform next to the Umbilicus?" Tanner asked.

"Yes," Marcus replied. "And it's very close to the treasury."

Cornelius continued. "The Rostra is tall enough that after the boys climbed out of the tunnels they could hide along its front edge on the corner closest to the Treasury. Once there, they could lure the guards into an ambush, and you and I could dress in their clothes and take whatever money we need."

"Sounds good," Tanner said. "But how do we get into the tunnels without being seen?"

"I know a man who builds and repairs litters used to carry members of the imperial family, dignitaries, and members of the rich elite. Do you know what a litter is?"

"No." Tanner frowned. There was still a lot he didn't know.

"It's a portable seat in which the upper echelon is carried around the city."

"Oh, okay. I know what you're talking about."

"My friend could cut a trap door in the bottom of a litter. With the curtains closed we would carry the two of you to a spot above a manhole where, we would set the litter down, pretending to rest. One or both of you could slip through the trap door, remove the manhole cover, and climb into the tunnel. Then, in the middle of the night, you would emerge along the front edge of the Rostra."

"How would we distract the guards?" Tanner asked.

"We could use our laser pointers," Andrew chimed in.

"That would grab their attention," Tanner agreed, realizing they were beyond hiding their futuristic gadgets from these people who were willing to risk everything to help them save Mick.

"Laser? What's a laser?" Marcus and Cornelius said in unison.

"Oh, yeah. Sorry," Andrew pulled the laser out of his backpack and turned it on, flashing the light around the room.

"Wow, can I see that?" Cornelius said.

"Sure." Andrew handed the laser to Cornelius.

Marcus and Cornelius played with the laser for a while, looking entranced. "What is this used for in your country?" Marcus asked.

"Different things," Andrew said. "Sometimes as a level. Since the light runs perfectly straight, you can make sure your building materials are aligned."

"Pretty useful," Marcus said.

"I'm sure we could distract the guards with that," Cornelius said. "Once we have secured the money, my friend, Titus Octavius Verus, a member of the Praetorian Guard, would be glad to help us bribe the prison guards."

"Praetorian Guard?" Andrew asked.

"It's an elite group of soldiers that protect the emperor," Marcus said.

"And someone that closely associated with Nero will be willing to help us?" Tanner asked. "Why would you trust him?"

"About six months ago," Marcus said, "he began attending some of our meetings. Said he had been a Christian for quite some time, but he was afraid he might endanger the entire sect if he worshipped too frequently with us. He considered abandoning his duties, but felt being in the guard might prove beneficial to saving fellow Christians. Titus is just as anxious to stop the emperor as we are. Plus, he has access to the prison guards."

"And you're sure he won't double cross us?" Andrew asked.

"Absolutely. I would trust Titus with my life," Cornelius replied.

CHAPTER 53

TITUS OCTAVIUS VERUS
(TITUS)

"Get your hands off of her! NOW!" Titus said in a commanding voice. A much larger man cowered as he backed away. "And don't you *ever* threaten her again."

"What's going on?" a guard asked as he entered the room.

"Nothing," the culprit replied.

"Everything's fine," Titus added.

"Good. We can't have any trouble today. We received a dispatch from the emperor," the guard said. "He will be here soon. You will be required to be on your best behavior and will be rewarded if you provide him with a favorable report of our facility."

"Why would the emperor come here?" Titus asked.

"He did not state his motives."

There was a commotion near the doorway, and another guard came down. "Titus, the emperor has requested to speak with you alone." The guard opened the door wider, and Nero came down the stairs into the dome shaped cell.

"Titus," the emperor began. "I have spoken with the guards and have been informed that you have been a model prisoner."

"That's very kind of them," Titus said.

"Let me make one thing very clear to you. The empire means everything to me. I would do anything to see it preserved."

"Understood."

"There are those Titus, who feel very differently than I. Those whose personal interests and lust for glory, power, and honor would supersede their commitment to the general good. Is it true that you have, at the peril of your own life, protected the guards from other prisoners?"

"Yes."

"And the prisoners from themselves?"

"Yes."

"Then you understand the importance of order and loyalty and the destructive nature of chaos?"

"Yes." Titus stood still as the emperor walked slowly around him scanning him from head to toe.

"I've been informed that you execute orders with the utmost precision. You have no problem taking orders from a superior, is that correct?"

"That is correct."

"And do you have any political allegiances to the nobility of Rome?"

"No. I haven't been in Rome long enough to form any."

The emperor looked him in the eyes as if he were trying to read his very soul.

"Titus, can I trust you?"

"Yes, Your Majesty."

"Then I have come to ask for your help."

"What is it you need?" How could the most powerful man in Rome have need to seek help from a prisoner?

"I am concerned that my mother, Empress Agrippina, is no longer loyal to me and the empire. My informants say she has placed personal interests above the greater good. She would be willing to plunge Rome into chaos for her own gain. Everyone knows she poisoned her husband, Emperor Claudius."

"She couldn't have," Titus replied.

"She gave him a plate of mushrooms laced with poison. All so she could rule the empire with me, but I'm afraid she's going to murder me next. She's such a treacherous woman, Titus. She even had a woman executed because Claudius said the lady was beautiful."

"So how can I help?"

"I am searching for a man I can trust, a man worthy to be a member of the Praetorian Guard."

"Go on."

"To what lengths would you be willing to go in order to preserve stability?"

"What would it take?"

"Preserving the empire often pits family member against family member. The hunger for power can drive men mad. You must have only one loyalty—Rome."

"And why would you come to prison to seek out such a man?"

"The politics of Rome are complicated. Finding someone with no political allegiances or ambitions of their own is not easy. Your reputation for being a man of integrity without guile has reached royal ears. I can raise you from a dire situation into a life of luxury. But, by so doing, I would expect your undivided loyalty."

"What would you require of me?"

"I would need you to inform me of any signs of treason. Could I trust you not to be persuaded by those who would drag the empire into civil war?"

"If their cause is unjust, and they're willing to destroy the stability of Rome for their own aspirations, then I could not be persuaded by such individuals."

"I'm going to make you a member of the guard right now, then. If you're willing, I'm ready to make you a free man. I need you to be an extra set of eyes and ears to make sure the empress doesn't plot against me."

"I'll do it. But you must release the woman as well." Titus said pointing to a female prisoner. "She'll never survive this place without me here to protect her."

"Let's make it official." Nero said as they made their way out of the prison cell.

CHAPTER 54

PARANOIA

(TANNER)

Tanner woke up to the smell of freshly baked bread.

"Good morning," he said to Marina and her stepmother as he passed the kitchen. "I'm going to step outside for some fresh air." It had rained during the night and was still slightly overcast.

Ahh, just what I needed. The morning air helped him shake off the sluggishness he was feeling. The city was starting to come alive. Tanner could hear the sound of the merchants positioning their carts and preparing for the masses that would soon occupy the streets. A light drizzle began to fall.

He looked over at the main entrance of the Circus Maximus and thought about the events of the day before.

Glad we don't have to go roaming around this treacherous place looking for Mick today. That chase was a little too close.

He looked at one of the vendor booths and froze.

That's one of the guys who was chasing me.

The man disappeared behind the booth and into the shadows. Tanner's heart began to race.

Was it just my imagination? Am I becoming paranoid? No! I'm sure it was him. I have to alert the others. We're all in danger.

He quickly turned and entered the house. Everyone had gathered around the table and resumed their discussions from the previous night.

"Sorry to interrupt," Tanner said, breathing heavily, "but I just saw the guy who chased me yesterday. He was watching the house."

"Are you sure?" Cornelius asked.

"I can't be positive. But I got a quick glimpse of a man who looked like him staring my direction. He ducked behind a merchant's cart when I made eye contact."

"Maybe you were just imagining it? I mean, you had a pretty traumatic day yesterday," Cornelius asked.

"I'm pretty sure it was him."

"We're going to have to end our planning session," Marcus said. "We'll need to check the city and alert the other members of our congregation that we need to change the location of tomorrow's meeting. Too risky to meet here."

"Agreed," Cornelius said. "If Nero is behind this, and I suspect he is, he will stop at nothing to capture and have us all executed."

"Why do you say that?" Tanner asked.

"I'm sure you're familiar with how far he went to kill his own mother."

"No, I'm actually not."

"You never studied," Andrew said under his breath.

"On three occasions Nero attempted to poison Empress Agrippina. None of them was successful, so he had a collapsible ceiling designed for her bedroom."

"Is that how she ended up dying?" Tanner asked.

"No, one of the conspirators warned her."

"So how *did* she die?" Andrew asked.

"Nero invited her to a celebration. He had a boat built in such a way that the cabin would collapse and the boat capsize. When Agrippina arrived on her own ship, Nero's men 'accidentally' collided a boat with hers causing much damage. When she needed to leave, Nero offered her his rigged ship."

"Is that what killed her?" Tanner said.

"Not exactly. Agrippina's messenger brought Nero word that even though the ship collapsed and capsized, she was able to swim safely to shore."

"So how did she die?" Tanner asked getting agitated. They didn't have time for storytelling. They needed to know how psycho this guy was now and then figure out how to outsmart him and save Mick.

"I'm almost there. But hopefully you're getting the message that once Nero views someone as a hindrance to his schemes, he will not stop until they are exterminated."

"Don't worry, we get it!" Tanner replied.

"Nero claimed Agrippina sent the messenger to slay him. He immediately sent his men to kill her and then spread the story that when she learned her murderous plan had failed, she committed suicide."

"Wow. You're right. He *is* relentless," Andrew said.

Marcus jumped into the conversation. "He even killed his wife because she complained he came home later than he should have from the chariot races."

"Okay. We get the point," Tanner said. "We need to be extremely cautious."

"We best get moving," Cornelius said. "I'll swing by my friend's shop and ask him about building the trap door for the litter. Does everyone have the names of the families we'll be visiting today?"

The group nodded in unison.

"Make sure no one follows you, and don't talk to anyone who isn't on your list." Cornelius looked at Tanner. He squirmed, knowing his deviation from the previous day's list had almost cost him his life and had endangered them all. But at the same time, had he not had to run for his life, he may never have found Mick—at least not in time.

"In case we *are* being watched," Cornelius said, "we'll need to leave one at a time. We don't want to draw additional attention. Tanner, you leave first. If you see that man, drop this cloth at the front door and keep going as naturally as possible."

Cornelius handed Tanner a piece of white linen. "Whoever leaves next will wait a while, and if the cloth is there when he leaves, he'll pick it up and come back inside. Otherwise he'll proceed with his tasks as planned."

"Once you've confirmed that Tanner didn't see the man, some of you could go out the side door to be extra cautious." Anastasia added.

Cornelius grabbed Tanner by the arm. "If you see the man, wander around for a while after dropping the cloth and then return. If he is no longer there when you get back, pick the cloth up and leave. If he is still there, we will all wait and try again later. Any questions?"

Everyone shook their heads. They were all on the same page. The plan had to work for all of their sakes. For Mick's sake.

"Good luck, and God be with you."

A surge of emotion flooded through Tanner's body. He knew one or all of them might not return for their evening meal. His best friend was already in chains, and he had barely escaped in a harrowing chase only a day earlier.

"*In bocca al lupo!*" Tanner said. He had learned this Roman idiom meaning good luck on their trip two years earlier. He made eye contact with each member of the group, grateful that they were willing to take such risks for someone they barely knew.

"Are you leaving, Musclosus?" Livia said as she ran to the door and gave Tanner a big hug. It was apparent from her messy hair she had just climbed out of bed. Andrew gave Tanner a strange glance.

"Musclosus?" he asked raising an eyebrow.

"Well, isn't it obvious? Don't I look like Musclosus, the greatest charioteer ever?" Tanner puffed out his chest.

Andrew rolled his eyes.

"Musclosus has to go, but he'll return for more chariot racing later." Tanner told Livia as he walked out the front door. He scanned the faces of everyone he could see in every direction. No sign of the man. He breathed a sigh of relief.

Must have been my imagination. Paranoia.

He carefully began his journey to alert the families on his list, the white cloth firm in his hand.

CHAPTER 55

SUPERSTITIONS

(TANNER)

Everyone made it back safely by sundown. All were successful in warning their assigned families.

"There's a lot of fear out there," Marina said as she sat down near Andrew.

"But everyone seems determined to stand strong," Cornelius added.

"The crucifixions were weighing heavily on their minds, though," Marcus said.

"We should wear amulets to protect ourselves against evil spirits and provide us with good luck," Anastasia said, her hand at her neck as if stroking a charm that no longer was there.

"We don't believe in those things anymore. Don't you remember?" Marcus gently reprimanded her.

"Couldn't do any harm, could it?" she replied.

"Those are just silly superstitions. An amulet can't really protect you," Marcus said. "Only the superstitious wear them."

"Did you talk to your carpenter friend?" Tanner asked Cornelius.

"Yes, he said he should have the litter done sometime tomorrow."

"Perfect," Tanner said. They would finalize all their preparations tomorrow. *We're coming for you Mick. Hold on. Just one more day.*

❖ ❖ ❖

Tanner and Andrew stood anxiously by Cornelius's side as he knocked three times on the door of Lucius's carpentry shop near the Temple of Saturn. A short, balding man opened the door.

"*Salve*, Cornelius!"

"*Salve*, Lucius!" The men embraced as Cornelius entered the shop and made introductions.

"Thanks for helping us," Marcus said.

"About that. My son, who's been working with me for years, is making the changes."

"That's fine. As long as we can get it done today."

"No problem."

"I knew you'd take good care of us," Cornelius said.

"I'd do anything for you, Cornelius. You know that."

"I do." Cornelius clasped his hand around Lucius's forearm, and the friends nodded once in appreciation toward one another.

With litter preparations accounted for, they turned to go to their next stop. Tanner opened the door, and a black cat scurried across the threshold, running under a wooden table and crouching in a protective stance.

"Good thing my wife isn't here," Marcus said in a sarcastic tone. "You heard how she is about bad omens. She'd be doing something right now to reverse that one."

"So black cats are bad luck in Rome, too?" Andrew asked.

"Technically, it's considered a sign of impending disaster to have a cat enter a house," Marcus replied. "So since it was a shop and not a house, we should be fine."

"As long as the gods are technical, I guess." Tanner joked, but he wasn't thrilled that a black cat crossed their path. He was worried enough as it was. There was no need to add bad luck to the equation—real or not.

"Marina told me about some of the Roman superstitions, like the Flame of Vesta being extinguished and the lances of Mars shaking. What other things are Romans superstitious about?" Andrew asked.

"Lots of things. A snake falling from your roof or even just spilling wine, oil, or water," Marcus said. "Stumbling over the doorstep when leaving one's home is also considered a bad omen."

Tanner gave Andrew a concerned look. He clearly remembered how he tripped over the doorstep the day he was chased.

Is there really something to these superstitions? He wondered. *After all, Caesar was killed after the lances of Mars began shaking.*

Were the Romans so successful in war because they protected Mars's shield? Did Rome thrive for so long because they took these signs and omens seriously? They'd been to the underworld. Hades himself had chased them. The gods of mythology were not as mystical as he thought they had been during the school year. Perhaps there was more to superstitions than he'd ever imagined. *Was that black cat a sign that our rescue effort is destined to fail? Maybe I should ask Anastasia about an amulet when we get back.*

Marcus continued. "There are others too, like meeting a mule in the street that is carrying herbs to decorate a tomb. I could go on and on."

"No, no that's fine," Tanner said. He didn't want to find out any additional reasons why things weren't going to work out. His optimism was starting to waiver.

Cornelius was able to round up four pretty tough looking characters during the afternoon to help overpower the guards at the treasury.

"I think we may actually pull this off," Andrew said looking at the burly men.

Feeling good about their progress, they returned to Marcus's home. After dinner, Tanner and Andrew went to their room.

"Tomorrow's the big day," Andrew said. "I think things are coming along pretty well."

Tanner wasn't as confident, which was the reverse of their usual perspectives. "You didn't bring a rabbit's foot, did you?"

"Why in the world would you ask that?"

"Just wondering."

"You're not becoming superstitious on me, are you?"

"Just cautious."

"Now that I think about it, I guess you always have been superstitious."

"No, I haven't." Tanner scoffed.

"Then what do you call all those rituals you go through before your basketball games?"

"Habits."

"Yeah, right." Andrew rolled his eyes at him.

"It wouldn't hurt to take some precautions, you know. I mean, I tripped over the threshold the day I was chased. Then we had that black cat over at the carpenter's shop. Do you think those were coincidences?"

"Of course," Andrew said emphatically.

"With all those stories Cornelius was telling us about Nero, I think we need to do whatever we can to bring us some good luck."

CHAPTER 56

CORNELIUS

(TITUS)

"Quintus," Nero said in an authoritative voice. "Britannicus complains that his drink is too hot. Please pour him some of that water over there to cool it off."

The Praetorian Guard Titus Octavius Verus watched as the servant carried the pitcher of water to the table where Nero's rival stepbrother and other nobility of Rome were seated.

Odd that only Britannicus complained about the temperature, Titus thought as he surveyed everyone else drinking.

"Is that better?" Quintus asked after adding the cool water.

"Much," Britannicus uttered. He barely got the word out when his body violently convulsed, and he collapsed to the ground. Several attendees fled the room. Most stayed riveted to their seats, staring fearfully in Nero's direction.

"Happens all the time," Nero said flippantly. "Been having seizures since he was a baby. He'll snap out of it quickly enough."

A shudder ran down Titus's spine. The ice-cold heart of the emperor whose life he was protecting created a chill in an otherwise warm room.

"Titus!" Nero barked. "Come here."

Dragging his feet in his mind, Titus quickly made his way over to the emperor.

"Yes, Emperor."

"Divine Emperor." Nero corrected him.

Titus choked on the words as they came out. "Yes, Divine Emperor."

"You'll need to double your efforts. I didn't like the look Agrippina gave me when Britannicus had his little seizure. Looked like she thought I was responsible for his episode."

Titus—and everyone else in the room—was sure he *was* responsible.

"I wouldn't be surprised if she expands her efforts to overthrow or assassinate me. Enlist whoever you can. I need eyes and ears across the empire."

Titus wanted to rebel himself, but he was sure that, as paranoid as Nero had become, there were eyes and ears trained on him as well.

Sometime later, one of Titus's informants arrived at the camp of the Praetorian Guard.

"Cornelius, have you got something for me?" Titus asked.

"Nothing."

"You're not telling me the truth."

"Yes, I am. No information on conspiracies against the emperor."

"Then why are you here?"

Cornelius hesitated.

"Follow me," Titus said as he grabbed Cornelius's arm and walked with him away from the camp.

"Okay. What's going on?"

"Did you know Nero is plotting to kill his mother?" Cornelius asked.

"What? Why do you say that?"

"I overheard some men talking about building a collapsible boat meant for her."

"You're sure?"

"Positive," Cornelius said. "I need your help. They recognized me. I'm a dead man."

"Listen. There's a group of Christians who meet out on the Appian Way. They'll protect you."

"But I'm not Christian."

"They'll take you in."

"A centurion?"

"Sure. Just explain your plight. They know what it feels like to be hunted."

Titus explained how to find the meeting place, and Cornelius left.

CHAPTER 57

THE LYRE

(TANNER)

It was early in the afternoon—day four of the Ludi Romani, the day before Mick was scheduled to be fed to the lions.

"We need some food from the market," Anastasia said while Tanner was helping to clean up from a late breakfast.

"I'll get it," Tanner said.

"You sure?" Anastasia asked.

"I'll be fine." He was actually wishing he hadn't volunteered, but Anastasia had been so nice to let them stay in her home and had asked so little in return.

"Why don't you take Andrew?"

Tanner looked at his friend who was enjoying some time with Marina.

"No, I'm good." Tanner winked at Andrew and made his way out the side door, careful not to trip over the doorstep.

As he walked past the arena, images of the horrible scene that was set to play out the next day raced through his mind. He passed the Imperial Palace and could imagine Nero passed out in bed holding a drumstick in his hand and plate of exquisite foods, some wine, and bunches of grapes on the floor next to him.

He entered the forum from the east side. The city was teaming with people, but Tanner wasn't paying attention to the hustle and bustle. His eyes darted back and forth as he surveyed the planned route for later in the day. He walked under the triumphal Arch of Augustus and could see the Temple of Saturn, where, in a few hours, they would try to pull off the heist of the century.

He crossed the plaza, looking for the manhole where he and Andrew would disappear and spend the evening in the tunnels, waiting to emerge in the middle of the night.

There it is.

This is going to work.

He continued toward the new shops where he and Andrew bought food on their first day. While waiting in line, he looked to his left.

The Rostra.

It would be in front of this speaking platform that he and Andrew would position themselves to distract the guards.

Once we get that money, we'll be able to buy freedom for Mick—and possibly even others.

After buying the food, he walked across the plaza toward the Temple of Saturn, almost directly above the manhole they would emerge from later.

Exactly like Cornelius described. Should be easy enough to remove that from below, he thought. *Cornelius's guys should be able take them out.* Tanner slowed for a moment and carefully sized up the guards standing in front of the treasury door.

Feeling more and more confident, he passed the temple and walked along the base of a large cliff. A marble plaque attached to the rock read *Saxum Tarpeium*. It was the Tarpeian Rock. Tanner had learned all about the rock from a tour guide when he'd come to Rome in his own century. It was a site where the worst criminals and traitors to Rome were flung from the eighty-foot cliff to their deaths. It was considered a fate worse than death and reserved only for those who committed the most grievous crimes. Tanner could picture himself and his friends being cast off for their attempted heist.

There's no room for error. We're either going to save Mick or die trying.

As he approached Anastasia's house, he was still running through the plan in his mind. It took his brain a while to catch up with what his eyes were seeing. Tanner froze in silent devastation. His friends were being rapidly escorted out of their house in chains.

I've got to save them. He started to run toward the scene. Abruptly he stopped.

Too many soldiers.

One of the captors was the man who had chased him a few days earlier.

It wasn't my imagination.

He hid behind a merchant booth to better observe what was going on. He wanted to yell at Andrew to let him know he had seen what happened and would come to their rescue. But it was too dangerous. He had to remain silent.

Boom.

Tanner whipped his head around in the direction of the blast. The house that had become his home was engulfed in flames. He looked back toward where the guards escorted his friends. Had they all made it out? He tried to count, but there was too much commotion.

The fire spread rapidly. Fanned by the wind, the flames leapt over Tanner's head to some of the vendor booths near where he was standing. As he watched helplessly, the wooden seating of the Circus ignited along the southwest end and, before long, the entire arena was ablaze.

People ran around screaming, which gave Tanner the perfect cover to follow the guards that led his friends. He gave it his best effort to trail them at a safe distance, but menacing flames were springing from every angle. The heat itself was nearly unbearable. As he strained to spot Andrew, Tanner noticed another one of the men that had chased him earlier in the week.

"The Christians have done this," the man shouted, "to prevent the justice they were about to face in the arena."

What a lie! The fire didn't even start in the Circus. They've got to be connected to Nero.

His suspicions were confirmed a few minutes later when he watched the captors lead his friends to the Imperial Palace.

Within a few hours, a large section of the city was on fire. Looters ran rampant, and the narrow winding streets and irregular blocks encouraged the fire to jump from building to building, uninhibited. Tanner had no place to go. The house church had been torched. His friends were being held captive in the Imperial Palace. He was completely alone.

He wasn't only thousands of miles from home, he was thousands of years from home.

I have to figure out how to save everyone.

That weighed on Tanner far more than the isolation.

Mick and Andrew could be hours, even minutes from their deaths.

And his new friends, friends who had risked their very lives to help him, were about to pay for that friendship with those same lives. Tanner tried to assist shrieking men and woman and the helpless young and old, but it wasn't easy since everyone was cursing the Christians for destroying their city.

His mind was racing. He could hear his father's voice telling him to give up. That he wouldn't be able to save *anyone*. He tried to cast it aside.

This is all my fault. If I wouldn't have knocked on that stupid door, none of this would have happened.

It was about one o'clock in the morning when Tanner finally made his way, coughing and wheezing, back to the Aventine Hill area of the city that he had learned to call home for the past few weeks. He sat in isolation on the hill longing for Brownsville. Life had been so simple before Mick's disappearance. Why had all of this happened? He wanted his basketball. He wanted to go out in the yard and take out his anger, frustration, sorrow, fear—everything he was feeling—on the court like he had always done in the past. But he couldn't.

I can't fail. I have to save them.

He looked at his backpack. Luckily, he'd taken it with him when he'd gone shopping.

Andrew's backpack must be nothing but ashes. Tanner felt a pit in his stomach. Andrew was always better about packing things you would have never expected to need.

Mick's papers, he thought. *I hope there wasn't anything we need to get back home in there.*

Tanner took out his binoculars and scanned the smoke rising above the buildings. The fire continued to rage in scattered sections of the city. The normally dark Roman night sky was orange and black with the flames and smoke. He panned from right to left in disbelief. Straight across from where he sat was the pulvinar—the Imperial box where he'd seen Nero emerge to watch the chariot races. As Tanner looked at it through breaks in the flames, he saw the emperor walk up the corridor from the palace. He had a lyre in his hand. When he arrived at the imperial throne, he plopped himself lazily in the chair and threw his legs over the armrest. Nero gazed at the smoldering mess and began to play. Tanner had seen the callous look of the man at the chariot races, but this took evil to a whole new level.

Tanner's blood boiled. Somewhere in that same palace Andrew and his new friends were being held captive by one of the worst human beings in history. What could he do to save them? How long did he have? Mick facing the lions would surely be cancelled due to the destruction of the Circus Maximus, but did that give him more time, or would Nero want to make an example of the Christians at the crack of dawn?

I've got to come up with a new plan.

Ideas began to formulate in his head.

I'll need a snake and maybe a mule. The thoughts continued to enter rapid-fire into his head. *Some oil, herbs...where am I going to find this stuff? I'll need some help. But who can I get?*

Lucius. He's the only one I know that isn't in chains.

He fought his way to the carpentry shop through the chaos of gangs and fugitives fueling the fire with torches in order to plunder unhampered. Dawn was still several hours away when he arrived. Lucius was there.

"Lucius," Tanner said. "You're here." Relief spread through him. He wouldn't need to wait and waste precious time.

"Had to try to protect the place. Can you believe that fire?" Lucius asked. "Worst in history."

"I saw the whole thing start. Marcus's house just exploded, and it took off from there. Nero's men did it."

"But why'd Nero wanna burn down the city?"

"I don't know. Maybe it just got out of control. But one of his guys was running around blaming Christians"

"Where's Cornelius?" he asked, his brow furrowed in obvious worry.

"He's been captured, along with the others that were helping me. Last time I saw them they were entering the palace in chains."

"No." Lucius exclaimed sorrowfully. "The emperor never liked deserters, and that's what he'll consider a former centurion like Cornelius."

"I hope he's still alive," Tanner said. He hoped they were all still alive.

"You and me both. What about the robbery?"

"I'm still going to try to pull it off."

"Alone?"

"Unless you know of anyone else who'd be willing to help."

"Afraid it would be too much for an old man." He shook his head.

"I'll help," Lucius's son said from across the room. Tanner was shaken for a moment, realizing they hadn't been alone, but he was more than happy to accept the offer. It was all he had.

"I've got some ideas," Tanner said. "Would you be willing to round up the things on this list?"

Lucius's son reviewed the list. "I'll have them by midday."

"Thanks. Thanks so much."

Tanner made his way back to the Aventine Hill where he eventually fell asleep—a thousand questions running through his mind, a few ideas for a new plan, and less than restful dreams filling his subconscious.

CHAPTER 58

TWO PRISONERS

(MICK)

When Mick returned from the parade at Circus Maximus, there were two new prisoners.

"They plan to crucify us," one of them said when Mick asked why they were there.

"They're going to feed me to the lions." Mick shuddered. "Are they really that cruel? Will they really go through with it?"

"Of course," the man said. "They have no regard for human life." He extended his hand toward Mick. "I'm Paul."

"Mick."

"What's your story?" Paul asked.

Mick explained how she had come to Rome to prove both her father's and her ancestor's innocence. But she had failed. She would never escape the stigma of their possible wrongdoings now.

"You can't let your own or someone else's past determine who you are," Paul said. "There was a time when I was an accomplice to the stoning of a Christian. I was hated by them. But I put that behind me. There were those who didn't believe I could change and those who thought it wouldn't last. But I refused to let the past control my destiny. You have to decide for yourself who you want to be and then go do it."

"But you don't understand. For me it's the other way around. I come from a family with a stellar reputation, and it's going to come crashing down now that everyone knows who we are."

"But that's not who *you* are. You control your own future by the decisions you make today. Worrying too much about the past or the future takes away your ability to choose. The only time you can make choices is in the present."

"I guess you're right, but what about all the persecution?"

"Just let it go."

"Easy to say," Mick said with a dismissive grunt.

"It's easier if you know who you are. That's how I've been able to survive. Regardless of what happens, I know who I am. That's what you've got to do. No external circumstance will be able to change that."

"You sound so sure."

"I've lived it. You have to believe me. At least enough to try for yourself."

"I'll give it a try. I've run out of other ideas. Following Donald's journal definitely didn't work."

"Maybe it did. Maybe your entire experience was designed to help you find out who *you* are. Outside of your family tree or anything else."

"Hmm. I have learned a lot about myself that's for sure."

"Then hold on to that. Let *that* define you."

"But it doesn't matter now, does it? Sometime tomorrow who I'll be . . . is a dead girl."

"You never know," Paul replied. "Miracles do happen."

Mick lay in the cell thinking about what Paul had said for several hours before falling asleep. When morning came, she was surprised how peacefully she had slept. She hadn't slept like that since the night before she found the money.

"Hey, where's the older guy I was talking with," she asked another prisoner.

"They took him to be crucified."

Mick was devastated. She had heard about crucifixion, but obviously had never known anyone personally who had been crucified until now. And she knew it was less than twenty-four hours before she would be facing her own mortality. Visions of ferocious lions roared through her thoughts as she began to lecture herself about the lessons she'd learned.

CHAPTER 59

THE CAPTIVES
(ANDREW)

The group was sitting around the table discussing final preparations for the upcoming heist and rescue.

"I wonder what's taking Tanner so long," Andrew said.

"I would have thought he would be back by now, too," Anastasia replied. "He only went for some food. Hopefully nothing's wrong."

The front door crashed open and a handful of burly men dressed in military gear poured in. Cornelius grabbed his sketches, sprinted for the kitchen, and tossed them into the fire.

"No one move! You're coming with us," one of the Praetorians barked. "Nero wants to visit with you."

"What's the meaning of this?" Marcus asked as he entered the atrium.

"Your emperor, the divine Nero Claudius Caesar Augustus Germanicus is in need of some Christians to use as torches to light the city. The four of you will do just fine." The Praetorian pointed to Marcus, Andrew, Cornelius, and Marina. There was an audible gasp from everyone except Cornelius.

Anastasia and Livia were in the kitchen. Andrew tried to keep his eyes from shifting there, hoping they would remain hidden and not be subjected to whatever fate awaited the rest of them.

"Divine Nero?" Cornelius brazenly asked. "Did you *really* say 'divine Nero'? Well . . .I guess he *would* make a good partner for Invidia, the goddess of wrongdoing." Having been a centurion prior to his conversion to Christianity, Cornelius wasn't intimidated by the men.

"I don't know about that, but I do know that you'll be getting better acquainted with Vulcan—the god of fire," the Praetorian shot back. The others broke out laughing.

Cornelius responded in a majestic voice. "The emperor is the opposite of divine. He's controlled by the devil himself."

"Silence! This is treason," shouted one of the other men. "Nero is a god!"

"Show us your *libellus*!" yelled the leader, referring to a document that proved a person had performed a pagan sacrifice. Andrew knew it was a way to demonstrate loyalty to the authorities of the empire. "You know the punishment is death for anyone who cannot produce a *libellus*, and the emperor has chosen death by fire for you."

Cornelius shot back. "Nero is the anti-Christ!"

"Enough!" cried the oldest Praetorian. "Cornelius, if you had showed this same passion as a centurion, you would be a member of the Praetorian Guard yourself—like your friend Titus. What a waste. What happened to you? You had so much potential."

"Put them in chains!" the leader shouted. Within moments, the four of them were in shackles.

Once the small group was bound, the members of the guard pulled several large sacks into the home. They placed one in front of each of the doorways that opened into the atrium and central garden. Andrew wondered what they were until one of them tipped over and some straw fell out.

"Everyone out!" The leader barked. As they made their way out the front door, Andrew looked back just in time to see one of the Praetorians running from bag to bag and setting each on fire.

"Marcus!" He jabbed Marcus in an attempt to remind him that his wife and youngest daughter were still in there, without actually saying it.

"It's okay. They'll escape," he whispered. "Now us, I'm not so sure. You can't even imagine how painful Nero's going to make this."

Andrew had been so caught up in thinking about rescuing Mick he hadn't thought about the possibility of being captured and executed himself. It was at the front of his mind now. He was separated from his two best friends, at least one of whom was on the verge of being executed.

Tanner's probably been captured as well. I should have gone with him. What's going to happen? His thoughts drifted to his family. *I'll probably never see them again.*

The flames ascended behind the Circus. The small blaze had become a raging fire. The southeast end of the Circus was entirely engulfed in flames. The merchant carts and wooden seats of the arena were like kindling for the inferno.

"Go on, into the palace!" One of the guards pushed Andrew through the door of the imperial palace. To Andrew's surprise, the Praetorians had been telling the truth. They were about to have an audience with the emperor.

"The divine Nero has important business he is attending to at the moment," said a small wiry man tending the exquisite doors of the throne room. "He'll see you when he's finished."

The guards shoved the prisoners to the ground.

"Wait here."

The four of them sat nervously on the cool marble floor in the corridor. Eventually, the doors flung open, and the attendant yelled. "The emperor will now see you!"

This could be bad. If Cornelius spews forth the same anti-Christ, led by the devil tirade he unleashed a few hours ago, we'll be human torches before the sun sets.

As they entered the room, the emperor sat nonchalantly in front of them, his leg thrown over one arm of the throne, and a golden chalice of wine hanging from the hand that was dangling over the opposite arm. He was dressed in an exquisite purple robe with an elaborate multicolored trim, which Andrew was sure contained the most expensive fabrics available to man.

Images of the atrocities the man had committed flooded through Andrew's mind. How he had killed his mother and wife, how he crucified Christians, fed them to the lions, and used them as human torches.

"My dearest Christian friends," Nero said, his voice dripping with sweetness. "I brought you here to first thank you for what you have done. After expressing my gratitude, we'll find a nice way to dispose of you. You see," Nero motioned to the palace around him, "I am forced into living conditions that are below what a god like myself should have to endure."

Andrew looked incredulously around at the opulence that even by his own century's standards would be available only to the wealthiest.

"I am in need of a new palace. My architect has been busy drawing the plans, and, let me assure you, it's worthy of the god I have become. Some rooms will have perfumes sprayed from the ceiling, and in others, rose petals will flutter to the ground whenever I desire. It will contain the finest gold and jewels. There will be a spectacular lake along which exotic animals will roam for my viewing pleasure. It will be the greatest architectural feat the world has ever known. And why? Because it has the touch of one of the greatest artistic talents to ever grace the earth—the divine Nero."

Is this guy full of himself or what? I've seen some of Tanner's athlete friends that are pretty enamored with themselves, but they look like the humblest sinner repenting in sackcloth and ashes compared to this. He's a lunatic.

Nero continued. "My biggest dilemma you see, one that has been troubling me for some time now, was where to put this tremendous palace. Rome is sprawling with apartments and meager dwellings and has become so crowded. I could build a palace outside the city, but the people want me near them. They want to see the divine Nero and bask in the success of the empire."

Andrew had always hated people who referred to themselves in the third person. But none of those he had endured in the past referred to themselves as a god.

"And now, thanks to you, my dear Christian friends who have started this fire that will consume the entire southeast quadrant of Rome, I will have a place to build my palace and live as I should."

Andrew looked over at Cornelius, wondering when he was going to blow a gasket. Now that he thought about it, he was surprised it hadn't happened already. After the display at Marcus's home, he was shocked Cornelius had lasted more than a few seconds. But there he stood as calm and peaceful as could be.

How can he be so relaxed? He's got to be fuming under the surface.

"You see," Nero added, "my men have been busy wandering the streets blaming this fire on your cult. The Ludi Romani are the biggest games of the year, and everyone knows that tomorrow's event was the Christians versus the wild beasts. It will be so easy for the citizens of Rome to believe that you set this fire, trying to destroy the Circus Maximus, where the event was to be held. By morning the whole populace will want to crucify all Christians. And I will give them an offering. Watching you burn will help to appease them. Just think of yourselves as heroes. You may be saving thousands of your fellow Christians from mob violence by your willingness to be a 'light on a hill.'"

Andrew was about to snap. *How can this devil be citing a scripture as reference for our execution? Was it intentional or a complete coincidence?* Whatever it was, Andrew was on the verge of a meltdown.

"Off with them!" Nero commanded.

As they were being escorted out of the palace Nero continued in a sickeningly sweet voice, "And thank you again for your willingness to be my scapegoat. You have made my wildest dreams possible!"

Their captors led them out of the throne room on the opposite side from where they had entered. Andrew quietly was questioning Cornelius about how he kept his cool.

"Confronting Nero directly would only expedite our deaths. I have no intention of becoming a human torch, so picking a fight with him made no sense. Not at this point, anyway."

"But, back at the house . . ."

"Yeah, most of those men have known me for years. They really didn't want to be taking me away in the first place. They were more worried about what was going to become of me than what I was saying. They were only doing their duty out of fear of the emperor."

Again, the prisoners were forced to sit and wait on the floor of the corridor outside the throne room. Andrew was distraught. *Are we really only hours away from our deaths?* The sun had gone down, and it would soon be dark. *Will we be lighting the streets with our flaming bodies tonight?* Though he tried to block the thought, Andrew could vividly picture himself tied to a stake and set on fire. The thought flashed over and over in his mind.

After a couple of hours, the Praetorians returned, and the captives were led out of the palace into the burning city. Andrew panicked. He could see the Tarpeian Rock silhouetted against the flames rising above them to the left. He knew it was the place where traitors and criminals were flung to their deaths. It was a natural place for Nero to light the night with their burning bodies. Sometimes he wished he didn't think so much.

I wonder where Tanner is. Hiding in the tunnels, waiting to execute our plan by himself, or somewhere in chains or worse? Andrew knew one thing for sure—if Tanner was able, he would be doing everything in his power to rescue his friends. But would it be enough? And would it be in time? Andrew could see the Umbilicus Urbis, where this whole Roman drama had begun. *Why did Mick do this? And by herself. If we would have done this together, we probably wouldn't have found ourselves in this predicament. Why did I let Tanner talk me into coming along?*

Our poor parents. They'll never know what happened. I wish there was some way to get them a message.

The group was approaching the Scalae Gemoniae, the stairs that led up to the Tarpeian Rock. Andrew braced himself. His life flashed before his eyes.

Please, please, don't take us up the stairs!

Again images of himself and the others burning on stakes ignited on the stage of his mind. They were so real he could almost feel the scorching heat of the flames searing his body. They continued past the Umbilicus and the stairs. Andrew breathed a sigh of relief.

They must be taking us to the prison.

He had toured the place, near the Umbilicus Urbis, where the apostles Peter and Paul had been held, and now there it was in front of him, in much newer condition.

"They must not be burning us tonight" he whispered to Marina. "That gives us time to figure out an escape."

Andrew and his friends were led down the stairs of the prison to a pitch-black cell. It was more than just the lack of light that created a dark mood of despair. It was the ominous feeling of their impending executions. The guard shoved them roughly into the cell and slammed the door. It was too dark to assess his surroundings and look for assets he could use in an escape. He lay on the damp floor wondering how he could avoid certain death until he finally fell asleep.

CHAPTER 60

FRIEND OR FOE?

(TANNER)

The sun's rays, filtering through the fire and smoke-filled city, woke Tanner up. He put his elbow over his nose to try to filter his breathing.

Our seven to rescue one has turned into one to rescue seven, he thought, shaking his head in disbelief. *I'm the only chance everyone's got.*

He walked through the fiery ruins to Anastasia and Marcus's home.

Maybe I can salvage something from Andrew's backpack.

The house was still smoldering. It had been such a beautiful place. When Tanner and Andrew had been taken in by Anastasia and her family, they were tired, homesick, and discouraged. They had found comfort in having a place to call home, even though it was primitive according to the standards they were accustomed to. As Tanner walked through the torched rubble, he thought about his new friends.

What does Nero plan to do with them?

The more he thought, the more urgency he felt.

The heist has to be tonight.

As Tanner approached the kitchen, he was horrified at what he saw.

Anastasia! He cried out in agony.

She was lying dead against a cabinet. Anastasia had been like a second mother—and there she was burned to death, snuffed out by Nero's men.

Why didn't I notice she wasn't with the others?

His heart sank.

Could I have saved her?

He played the scene back in his mind.

Wait. Livia wasn't with them either!

"Livia! Livia!" He raced frantically through the charred remains knowing at any moment he might find her in the ashes as well. He scrambled from room to room calling for the little girl who had reminded him so much of his own sister. There was no response.

Please God, let me find her alive. Why didn't I realize Anastasia and Livia weren't there?

He remembered the explosion and how quickly the entire structure was engulfed in flames.

There's nothing I could have done. It all happened so fast.

He tried to convince himself, but there still was a terrible nagging feeling that he couldn't shake.

If Livia escaped, where is she? Tanner couldn't bear the thought that Livia might have died as well. She had brightened his day every time he entered the house. No one could ever replace his own little sister who had died so suddenly, but Livia had filled a small portion of the huge void Tanner had felt over the years.

He continued to walk through the ruins. Andrew's backpack was in the corner of their bedroom, but nothing was intact. Mick's papers were destroyed and anything else he'd brought had been burned beyond recognition.

Tanner fell to his knees and buried his hands in his face.

I can't do this. Where do I go? What do I do? Livia might be wandering the streets alone. She'll never survive. Do I go after her? Or are the adults in more danger? Nero is such a savage. I can't leave them in his hands for long or who knows what will happen. What do I do?

Come on. Think!

If I choose the adults, at least I have some idea what to do. We've been preparing for that. Once I rescue them, we could all go looking for Livia. Then he thought through the alternative. *But Livia is just a kid. She can't defend herself. She won't be resourceful enough to get food, water, or shelter. At least the others are adults. They could be working on an escape or have already escaped on their own. But then again, I have no idea where Livia even is. I don't have a clue where to start. She could be anywhere.*

This was the most horrible decision Tanner had ever faced.

Maybe I can do both.

There's no way I can rescue the adults alone, and I need help to find Livia too. If I can find some other Christians, I can do both. Marcus and Anastasia were so willing to help us. Surely there are other families that will be just as kind.

Most of the Christians Tanner had visited lived in the quadrant of the city that had been devastated by the fire. He began to walk the streets looking for help. Much to his disappointment, home after home was deserted.

I don't even know if these are the right houses. Most of them are burnt beyond recognition.

Time's running out, and I'm not any closer to saving anyone.

The catacombs! They're far enough away that the flames probably haven't reached there— plus I should be able to find Christians.

Tanner had enjoyed visiting the catacombs with Andrew's dad. He remembered they were somewhere on the Appian Way. He began to ask people how to get to the street and was happy to learn it wasn't far.

The Appian Way was like a long cemetery. Since burials were required to be done outside the city limits, this major road leading out of Rome was an ideal location for tombs.

I can't afford to wait until I get there to start asking for help.

Tanner awkwardly began to run up to anyone he saw and sketch the half fish.

After about an hour, a man sketched the other half. Tanner's pulse quickened.

"I'm Aquila. This is my wife Priscilla, my brother-in-law Erastus, and my sister Julia."

"Nice to meet you. I'm Tanner. I need your help!"

"Interesting name. Of what origin are you?" Erastus asked.

"I come from a faraway land I'm sure you're not familiar with," Tanner said trying to move the conversation along.

"Give me a try. I have met many foreigners and have become acquainted with many lands in the empire."

Tanner quickly responded so he could get on with it. "I'm from Brownsville. Brownsville, Kentucky."

"You're right I've never . . ."

"Sorry to interrupt, but my friends have been captured by the emperor. I desperately need your help."

Can I trust them? He wondered looking in their eyes. *I don't have another option. I have to.*

Tanner continued to explain his predicament.

"I'm sure they're all going to be executed soon, if they haven't been already. The Praetorians burned down the house I was living in. The mother was killed in the fire and her five-year-old daughter is missing. I need help finding her too."

"We understand," Priscilla said. "We had a guest in our home who was captured as well."

"It's a dangerous time," Aquila added.

Tanner wasn't sure he trusted the families enough to confide every detail, but shared as much as he felt he could.

"Can you at least help me get into the forum's underground tunnels?" Tanner asked. "I need four men to carry me in a litter above one of the entrances so I can slip through a trap door into the tunnels. Shouldn't be too risky."

Tanner knew storming and overpowering the treasury guards was far more dangerous, and he wasn't sure he could convince these new friends to risk that much. Besides, there was a chance the men Cornelius lined up still might show. He wasn't counting on it, but there was a chance.

"If you can just get me into the tunnels, I'll figure it out from there."

"We'll help," Aquila said. "And we'll bring a couple of friends as well."

"And *we'll* organize a search for the girl," Priscilla said motioning toward Julia. "What was her name again?"

"Livia."

Tanner gave Priscilla and Julia a detailed description of the little girl, and the women left.

"We've got to get moving," Tanner said. "We don't have much time."

The three men began to make their way toward the city center.

"I'm not sure you told us all the details of your plan," Erastus said.

"It's actually better that way," Tanner replied. "I don't want to endanger you any more than I have to. I'm already responsible for the situation my friends are in, and I don't think I could bear it if either of you were captured or implicated in my rescue. I've probably told you too much already."

Tanner was thrilled that his argument convinced Erastus to back away from asking for more details about his plan.

As they approached the center of town, Erastus asked Tanner, "Where did you say you came from?"

"Brownsville, Kentucky."

"I am surprised I have never heard of it," Erastus responded. "As chamberlain of Rome, I have contact with many lands both in and out of the empire. Anyone that has trade dealings of any kind with the city."

"What's a chamberlain?" Tanner asked.

"I'm responsible for the finances of the city.

Tanner froze.

"I work with Phaon, Nero's secretary of finance."

Oh no. Did I just tell the guy in charge of the treasury that I was going to break in and rob the place? He tried to re-create the conversation in his mind.

This whole thing is going up in smoke. Erastus is just going along long enough for me to get caught, and then I'm going to prison as well. I should have been more careful.

A million questions ran through Tanner's mind.

Do I scrap the whole thing? It was already shaky at best. No, I don't think I said anything, but even if I did, there's no time to come up with another idea.

As they approached Lucius's shop, Tanner thought through the plan.

My new friends will get me into the tunnels. Now, I just have to distract and overpower the guards, get the keys, load the money, wheel it away, and hide it—only a few minor details.

He laughed to himself, shaking his head.

How am going to pull this off? I have to. No choice. I've got to keep Erastus and Aquila away from Lucius. I don't want him implicated. Plus, he might say something about the treasury if I didn't already.

"Aquila, can you go get your friends and meet back here as soon as possible?" Tanner said before they reached the carpenter's shop.

"Of course," Aquila said. "We'll see you shortly."

"Thanks," Tanner said. "I don't know how I'll ever repay you."

After making sure the two men were gone, Tanner continued to Lucius's shop and knocked on the door.

"Welcome, Tanner," Lucius said, motioning for him to enter.

"Is the litter ready?" Tanner asked.

"Sure is. My son did a great job on it. Where will you store the money, now that Marcus's place burnt down?" Lucius asked.

"Still working that out."

"Store it here. Just be careful. Make sure no one sees you. I would prefer to not have my shop burned down too."

"I hear you. I'll be careful."

"Did you get some helpers?" Lucius asked.

"Yeah, but I may have ruined the whole thing. One of the guys is in charge of the city finances. I don't think I told him about breaking into the treasury, but I'm not sure. Lucius, please don't say anything. If he finds out, I'm dead."

"Don't worry. Secret's safe."

"Were you able to get everything on the list?" Tanner asked Lucius's son.

"It's all in that sack in the litter. Except the mule, of course," he chuckled. "That's tied up in back."

About forty-five minutes later, Aquila and Erastus returned. Tanner was relieved, but still uneasy about which side Erastus was on. The two men had only been able to locate one additional helper. Still, with the help of Lucius's son they would make it work.

Once everyone was clear on the route, Tanner climbed into the litter, and his friends positioned themselves on the four corners. Tanner slapped his hand a couple of times on one of the wooden sides, and said, "Let's roll!"

"There are no wheels," Aquila said, slightly confused.

"Sorry, just an expression where I come from," Tanner said. "It means let's get moving."

"Good luck!" Lucius said as Tanner closed the curtains. Lucius opened the door of the shop. Tanner could hear the noise and commotion of the city. His heart rate sped up. The rescue mission was underway.

Can I pull this off? Or am I going to end up in chains, too?

Tanner thought about how his baseball team had relied on him in their state tournament qualification game. *I failed them. It was because I believed him.* "You can't do this, You're not good enough." Tanner cringed as he thought about his father's voice and his own failure.

My friends' lives are at stake. I can't fail. His determined resolve gave him added strength.

The litter continued down the Vicus Jugarius street toward the Temple of Saturn. Tanner had two sacks with him—the one

Lucius's son had prepared and his backpack. He looked through his backpack one more time.

Smoke bombs, phone, external speakers, couple of laser pointers, lighter, knife, solar charger—that came in handy. Hatchet, mess kit...

Tanner felt the litter make a turn and go up the few steps of the plaza.

I should have tested that trap door.

Sometimes Tanner's lack of forethought came back to bite him.

That's one thing that was great about Mick. She always thought through the details, letting me ad lib and not pay for it.

He had gotten pretty good at improvising, though. He could usually turn a bad situation around in a hurry.

Tanner felt the men lower the litter.

We're here. You can do this.

He moved himself along the back of the litter and opened the trap door. He reached through the opening and slid the manhole cover carefully so that it would leave him room to jump into the tunnel but still be hidden by the litter. He knocked twice on the wooden frame of the litter as he jumped into the darkness. Tanner heard his friends slide the marble cover above his head and everything went pitch black. He flicked his lighter and nothing happened.

"Oh no." He groaned.

He flicked it again. A burst of flame, and then nothing. In the quick flash of light, he saw something scurrying around his feet. He shook the lighter and tried again and again. Still nothing.

Why don't these things ever work right?

He thought about using the flashlight on his phone, but couldn't afford to run down the battery.

He tried again. Finally the lighter worked. More scurrying. He was sure it was rats underfoot, but didn't want to look too closely. Making his way toward the central tunnel, he turned left. Part of the tunnel had collapsed, but he was able to squeeze through the small opening and continue to make his way to the far end. At the final intersection, he took another left, and after a short walk reached the end of the tunnel system—directly below the front of the Rostra.

CHAPTER 61

THE HEIST BEGINS

(TANNER)

Tanner pulled out his phone and began working on a recording while the plaza above was still noisy. After a few attempts, he felt he had a recording that, when played back with the volume cranked, would give the effect he hoped for.

Six hours. Maybe I can get some rest. It's going to be a busy night.

He set the timer on his phone, put on his headphones, and tried to get some sleep. As he lay in the darkness, he executed the plan over and over in his head. He focused on Mick and Andrew freed of their chains and the three of them returning to Brownsville and finally began to relax and fell asleep.

When the timer went off, it jolted Tanner awake. A few hours of sleep and a surge of adrenaline had him ready to go. As he slid the marble slab cover open, he remembered Erastus.

If I did tell him what I was doing, someone's going to be waiting to bust me when I climb out of here. He mentally kicked himself. *How would I have known Erastus was responsible for the city's finances?* He couldn't worry about that now.

Slowly he pulled himself out of the tunnel and peered into the dark plaza.

No one.

He sneaked behind the Rostra and climbed the stairs of the Temple of Saturn.

This has got to work. I hope the Romans are as superstitious as Marcus claims.

Tanner untied the sack Lucius's son had prepared. Inside was another sack, carefully secured at the top. In the darkness, he could barely see the outline of a snake.

Better be careful, in case this thing's poisonous.

Tanner had so much on his mind with all the events of the last few days that in his mad scramble to come up with a revised plan, he hadn't previously considered the snake might be poisonous. He had handled many milk snakes in the barn at Mick's house, but the thought of handling a poisonous snake terrified him. He knew what Mick was about to face was far worse, so he gathered up the courage to do it for her.

He opened the bag and strained to see its shape in the darkness.

Gotcha. He grabbed the serpent tightly, placing his thumb on the top of its head. *Now to scare some guards.*

A noise from behind startled Tanner and he whipped around to see if someone had followed him. Before he could realize what happened the snake had torqued its head free from his grip and sunk its fangs deep into his wrist. He bit his lip wanting to scream out in pain, but knowing he couldn't afford to make a sound.

Oh my gosh! Is this thing poisonous? Is that why snakes strike such fear into the Romans? Is that why Lucius's son secured the bag so tightly?

Tanner had originally considered it a silly superstition. He had chuckled about how they thought a snake falling from a roof was a bad omen.

When Lucius saw a snake on the list of things his son would be getting for me, I could see the fear in his eyes, but I thought it was just because it was a bad omen—not because snakes in Rome might be venomous. I might not even live as long as my friends.

"Just give up," he could picture his disgusted father telling him.

No. I'm not going to.

He threw the snake over the railing. His hand burned from the bite, but he had to focus on his plan. He shone the flashlight on the snake.

Perfect, Tanner thought as he heard the guards talking in panicked tones about the omen. *Even better than I hoped.*

His enthusiasm quickly faded as he thought more about the reaction. *Would those macho guards be that afraid of a harmless snake? Or did that just confirm the snake was poisonous?*

I've got to keep moving.

He quietly ran to the bottom of the stairs and temporarily forgot about his burning hand.

Off to get the mule.

Tanner paraded the mule in front of the guards.

"Excuse me," he said. "I'm taking these herbs to decorate a tomb. Could you please tell me how to get to the Appian Way?"

It was obvious by the expressions on the guards' faces they were well aware of the ominous nature of this omen as well. They babbled and had difficulty putting a complete sentence together.

Tanner was encouraged as he noticed one of the guards had two amulets around his neck.

"Thank you so much for your help," he said to the guards after they finally were able to give him directions. "Would you care for some water? You must be thirsty standing guard all night."

They agreed. They moved closer to Tanner. He could see the keys on the belt of the guard that wasn't wearing the amulets. He poured the water.

"Oops, so sorry!" he exclaimed as he spilled it on the guards.

They jumped back.

Obviously familiar with that omen as well. Tanner was pleased.

"I have another pitcher of water," he said. "Let me get you some."

He reached for the water. He had dissolved a few Nyquil capsules in this water and hoped after drinking it the guards would be sleeping like babies.

"No! No! We're fine." The guards responded with a frantic tone in their voice.

Tanner was devastated. He tried again to get them to take the water to no avail. His backup plan was destroyed. He was thrilled that the omens had been so successful, but his safety valve, making the guards sleepy enough that he could steal the keys, was out the window. He was kicking himself for not having them drink from the Nyquil pitcher before spilling the water.

"I told you you'd never succeed. You're too weak". Tanner fought the images in his mind. *Can't change the past. Got to keep going. Only one omen left. Got to stick the landing on this one.*

He scrambled around the temple and back up the stairs. He felt sick to his stomach, and his hand throbbed more than ever. He had learned in Boy Scouts that you were supposed to immediately stop and treat a snake bite, or the venom would work more rapidly through your bloodstream due to your activity.

Am I going to die myself, trying to save everyone?

Again, images of his father broke on to his mind's stage. *"You've got no common sense, boy. You might as well stop trying."*

He's not going to convince me this time! I've got to finish this thing off. I've got to succeed.

He hooked his phone up to his portable speakers and readied the audio recording. He had placed the stone that would become Terminus—the god of borders, on the stairs in preparation for this final omen. He hoisted it to the railing. Pain surged through his arm, causing it to weaken. He tossed the rock over the edge. It landed with a loud thud almost exactly where he had hoped. The guards jumped. He quickly lit the smoke bombs and tossed them over the railing as well. Smoke billowed all around the stone. He grabbed his laser pointers and focused them on the stone. He heard the most panicked conversation yet coming from below.

This might work. But am I going to survive long enough to finish it?

He pushed play on his phone. Even Tanner was impressed when he heard the booming, thunderous voice he'd created, now reverberating off the buildings in the vacant forum.

"I am the god Terminus. God of borders. You have witnessed the signs and omens this night. Your families are in danger. The borders of your homes have been violated by intruders. You must go save them. Leave the keys next to me, and I will protect the treasury. Now, go! Save your families before it's too late!"

Tanner was busy patting himself on the back for how impressive the whole act was, when he saw a commotion in his peripheral vision. One of the guards was fleeing his post.

Yes!

But what about the other? Why hadn't he fled?

Am I still going to have to overpower one of the guards?

"You wouldn't stand a chance. Are you kidding? Don't even try."

I will succeed. Tanner continued to fight through his memories. He waited. Nothing. *Should I go see what's going on?* Still nothing.

He heard a loud noise. It was the second guard. He was fleeing as well. Tanner's heart leapt for joy. His plan had worked. He scrambled down the stairs hardly able to contain his excitement.

I'm actually going to pull this off.

He ran to the pavement in front of where the guards had been stationed and looked. There weren't any keys.

CHAPTER 62

CORNELIUS'S PLAN

(ANDREW)

"Andrew! Andrew!"

Andrew was asleep on the floor of a prison in Ancient Rome, dreaming about the Angel's Landing hike in southern Utah. The last half mile was like a spine with massive drop-offs on each side. When he, Tanner, and Mick hiked the final leg, he had been ready to turn back and go to Scout Lookout, where the rest of their group was waiting below. In his dream, he found himself in the same situation. Mick was encouraging him to keep going. "Andrew! Andrew!" He began to walk toward her when the dream turned nightmare. He tripped and began to plummet the 1,500 feet toward his death. He could hear Mick screaming. Her voice was becoming more emphatic. The ground was rapidly approaching. Just as he was about to make impact, he heard a final call. "Andrew!" He woke in a cold sweat trying to get his bearings as he looked around the warm, damp prison cell.

When he began to clue in to his whereabouts and recognize his surroundings, much to his surprise, he heard the voice again.

"Andrew! Andrew!"

He rapidly scanned the room.

"Mick?" Then he saw her. "Mick!"

"Andrew! What are you doing here!"

"Rescuing you, of course!"

"It's so good to see you. I thought I'd never see you or anyone from home again. How did you get here? How did you know I was here? Wait. If you're *rescuing* me why are we both in prison?"

"Yeah, about that. The reason I'm in Ancient Rome is because I'm rescuing you. And now that we're both in this prison, I'm hoping Tanner will be rescuing both of us."

He squinted in the darkness to see his friend in the adjacent cell. It had been months and the sight of her face brought a smile to his face, even if she did look a little roughed up. She was alive. Mick was alive.

"Hold on. Are you telling me that Tanner is in Rome too? This is incredible. Where is he?"

"I don't know."

"What do you mean you don't know?"

"Well, we were staying with a family near the Circus Maximus. Tanner went to get some food, and before he came back, we were all captured. He had been gone quite a while himself, so we were all worried about him, but you know Tanner, he can usually get himself out of any bind."

"That's true. But this is different than anything we've ever been through."

"That's for sure."

"How did you get here?" Mick asked again. "How did you know where to find me?"

"One second. Let *me* ask *you* some questions. What were you thinking taking this on by yourself? We've always done everything together, and you make a discovery like this and don't even tell us?" Andrew was getting a bit worked up.

"Yeah, well what about you? Telling everyone I'm related to Donald Carlton. You promised you wouldn't say anything."

❖ 335 ❖

"I didn't. I swear it!"

"Then how did everyone find out?"

"I have no idea, but I promise it wasn't me. So why *did* you go this alone?"

"I wanted to prove that Donald was innocent."

"What does that have to do with Ancient Rome?"

"It's a long story."

"I'm not going anywhere," Andrew replied.

"I guess I didn't realize how hard it was going to be. I thought I would only be gone a couple of days at most. Unfortunately, I was unable to regain access to the Umbilicus Urbis. And now, here I sit about to be fed to the lions."

"You mean lit up like a torch?"

"No, *I'm* being fed to the lions. Today!"

Andrew explained about the great fire and how it had destroyed the Circus Maximus.

"Lucky for you, the Ludi Romani has been put on hold." Andrew shared the details of the meeting he and the other captives had with Nero and how the emperor was blaming the fire on the Christians.

"So I won't be eaten by wild beasts this afternoon, then?"

"No. I would guess that tonight or tomorrow night we'll both be lighting up the night sky."

"I think I might prefer the lions," Mick said.

"Really?" Andrew said a bit surprised

"You think being rammed on a pole and lit on fire would be better?" Mick replied.

Andrew cringed as he flipped back and forth in his mind between the two tortures.

"We've got to figure out a way to get out of here," he said with determination.

"Oh, I'm sorry," Andrew said, embarrassed by his lapse in proper etiquette. "These are my friends Marcus and Cornelius, and you may have already met Marina." He motioned to Marina, who was in the cell with Mick.

Marina gave Mick a "should I be jealous or not?" glance.

"They *were* helping Tanner and me try to find and rescue you."

"Thank you." Mick replied, making eye contact with each.

"We are still going to rescue her." Cornelius said with a steely resolve.

The group began to discuss possible options for escape. Andrew kept saying how he wished he had his backpack and how he would use this gadget or that gadget.

Cornelius interrupted. "We get it. You wish you had your sack, but you don't. I am not planning on becoming a torch, so let's stop talking about what we don't have and focus on what we do have."

"I have no idea how to get out of here," Andrew said.

"Come on Andrew," Mick said. "You could make a bomb from a piece of gum and a bobby pin."

"The problem is," he looked around at the dirty cell, "I don't have a piece of gum or a bobby pin."

He had nothing. This escape was going to have to be created from thin air because they had only the clothes on their backs and the chains that held them bound.

Cornelius was busy assessing everything in sight. The wheels were turning in his head full speed. Andrew could see it in his eyes.

"Our only chance is when they bring us our daily rations," Cornelius said. "The guard keeps the key with him. When he hands us the rations, we'll have to grab him and hope to be able to pull him hard enough that his head will snap into the bars and knock him out. Then, we can secure the key, free ourselves, and get out of this hole."

"I hope we live long enough to make it until our rations," Marcus said. "If they plan on burning us tonight, we may have already had our last meal."

"Nero's such a showman, though," Cornelius said. "Everything he does has to be theatrical. I'm sure he'll wait at least another day so he can spread the word and make a major event out of the whole thing."

"I hope you're right," Marcus responded.

Before long, the guard came down the stairs with their rations. Mick's cell got their rations first. Cornelius watched intently. The guard disappeared as he went to get the rations for Cornelius's cell.

"Do you think this is going to work?" Andrew whispered.

"It has to," Cornelius replied.

The guard reappeared with rations for the cell where Andrew, Cornelius, and Marcus were being held. Cornelius moved toward the bars.

"Here's your meal," the guard said in a rough voice. "Enjoy. This may be your last." He gave a sickening grin.

Quick as lightning Cornelius grabbed the man and pulled him to the bars. It was like a cat pouncing on a mouse. The other prisoners watched in awe as the guard slumped to the floor.

"It worked. We're out of here," Andrew whispered.

"Not yet," Cornelius said. "There's still plenty to do."

Cornelius grabbed the key. He opened the door and unlocked the adjacent cell. As he reached down and turned to unlock Marina and Mick from their shackles, the guards who were standing duty outside heard the commotion and ran down the stairs to the cells.

"What's going on in here?" They were all hampered by chains on their wrists and ankles, but began to fight. The guards were protecting the narrow entrance to the stairs that represented freedom to the prisoners. Andrew looked over at Mick and Marina and was awed to see them fighting like lions.

We're going to get out of here. Andrew's spirits lifted.

After all, it was five in chains against two who weren't. Unfortunately, the guard who had been knocked out, was at the end of his shift and, just as it looked certain they would overpower the remaining guards, his replacement walked in. Five in shackles against two without was a possibility, but three unfettered men against five who were restricted in such a fashion quickly became an unfair fight. The guards beat the prisoners severely. They were bruised and bloodied when they were corralled back into their cells.

"We were so close," Andrew said. He was beginning to come to the realization that they might not escape. The guards divided each of the prisoners into their own cell, making it impossible for them to coordinate another escape attempt.

The prison was hot and muggy. One of the guards smugly walked by and said, "You think you're hot now? Wait until tomorrow night." This was the confirmation they were wondering about. Apparently, the horrific massacre would be happening the next day. It was late when they finally fell asleep, hoping that their luck would somehow turn.

CHAPTER 63

THE PRAETORIAN GUARD

(TANNER)

Tanner looked frantically around, shining his flashlight in every direction. There was no sign of the keys. This most critical part of his plan. He couldn't get in the treasury without the keys. The whole brilliant scheme meant absolutely nothing if he couldn't get in.

"I knew you'd fail. You always choke." Tanner wondered if his father was right.

I haven't failed until I stop trying. Tanner thought. *But what do I do? Should I chase down the second guard? There's a 50–50 chance he was the one with the keys.*

Tanner began to run in the direction the guard went. Despondent at this latest setback, the pain from his throbbing hand was all he could think about. He felt sick, tired, and weak.

Is it because I've been running on adrenaline all week, or am I actually dying from this stupid snake bite? He panicked.

Gradually his run became a walk, and then he stopped altogether.

I'm never going to catch him.

Tanner was destroyed. He had come so close.

I failed again. When it mattered most. One little detail is going to ruin it all.

He kicked a small rock on the pavement as hard as he could to take out some of his frustration. Then he saw something shimmer on the ground near his foot. It was a gold coin. He saw another, and then another. He knew exactly what had happened.

The guard took some money for himself, he thought. He must have believed he would need it for a ransom to buy his family's freedom.

Tanner began to gather the coins even though he knew there weren't enough to buy his friends' freedom. They led all the way back to the door of the treasury. Then he saw it. The key. It was still in the door! Tanner's heart raced.

He had to move fast. The men would soon realize they'd been duped.

He loaded as many coins as he could into the wagon, made his way into Lucius's shop and pulled the door closed behind him.

Tanner had just pulled off the heist of the century or even the millennium.

I did it! I can rescue my friends! You were wrong, he said to an imagined image of his surprised father.

Excruciating pain surged from the snake bite up his arm. His head was reeling. The adrenaline that had sustained him, had given in to whatever was afflicting him; and Tanner slumped to the ground.

❖ ❖ ❖

"Did you hear?" someone asked Lucius on his way to work in the morning. "Nero plans to execute a group of Christians tonight on the Tarpeian Rock. Gonna burn 'em to death."

"Why?"

"For burning down the city, of course."

All of Rome was abuzz with the news. Nero and his men were busy telling the populace that the Christians started the fire to protect their own and that he was about to make an example of them. The carpenter had always been sympathetic to the Christian cause, although he had never converted himself. But he wasn't about to be an open sympathizer at this point. The whole city had turned on the Christians, and unless he wanted to be a light on the hill as well, he would have to keep his feelings to himself.

When Lucius opened the door to his shop, to his surprise, he saw gold coins spilling out of his wagon and Tanner sprawled across the floor in front of it. He quickly closed the door behind him, hoping no one on the busy street had seen what was stashed there. Fearing the worst, he put his ear near Tanner's mouth and grabbed his wrist hoping to feel a pulse. He closed his eyes as he tried to shut out the noise and confusion from outside and focus on Tanner.

"He's alive!" he said under his breath as he recognized a pulse. "Thank Jupiter!"

Lucius poured some water over Tanner's face, and he woke with a start.

"What's going on?" Tanner asked.

"Not sure. Just found you collapsed here with a cart full of gold. What happened?!"

Tanner reviewed every detail with Lucius.

"Wow! Incredible." Lucius said. "Oh, and don't worry. Snake wasn't poisonous. Just terrible omens, snakes are. Treat 'em with great fear in Rome, we do. Poisonous or not."

"Thank heavens!" Tanner replied.

Lucius told Tanner what he had heard on the streets.

"I've got to get moving!" Tanner said. "No time to lose!" And he was right. It was nearly noon. His friends would soon be escorted to the Tarpeian Rock.

"I've got to find the Praetorian Guard Titus."

The carpenter explained how to get to the camp of the Praetorian Guard on the outskirts of the city.

"You'll protect the money, right?" Tanner said. "I'm trusting you. The lives of my friends are at stake. If we pull this off, I'll make sure you're rewarded."

"I promise. They're my friends as well, you know."

"Wish me luck!" Tanner said as threw his backpack over his shoulder and opened the shop door.

"*In bocca al lupo*" Lucius replied.

Tanner sprinted for the camp. It was a race against time.

✧ ✧ ✧

"I need to speak with Titus" Tanner boldly stated as he arrived at the headquarters of the guard.

"And who may I ask is here to see him?" The reply came from a guard stationed in front of the camp.

"A friend of Cornelius. I have an important message."

Tanner knew mentioning Cornelius was risky. If Cornelius's conversion to Christianity was widely known, saying he was a friend was dangerous. But Tanner was willing to take that chance, because if the message got through, Titus would recognize the urgency and move quickly. Luckily, that's how it happened. Titus was almost instantly at Tanner's side.

"Walk with me," he said.

When they were about one hundred yards from the camp, Titus broke the silence.

"Who are you?" he asked.

"A friend of Cornelius. He told me to come to you for help. He was going to ask in person, but he's been captured."

"You're kidding!" Titus replied. "Where is he now?"

"I'm assuming in prison somewhere. I saw him being taken to the palace in chains, but I haven't seen or heard anything from him since."

"When was this?"

"The night of the fire."

"So Cornelius is one of those who will be burned to death tonight," Titus said. Tanner could see there were a million thoughts going through Titus's mind, and Tanner could understand why. As a member of the Praetorian Guard, Titus was one of the emperor's special forces, and here the emperor was about to burn one of his good friends. Tanner could see the conflict unfolding on Titus's face.

"How did this all come about?" Titus asked.

"Well, my good friend Mick was scheduled to be fed to the lions. Cornelius and his friend Marcus and Marcus's family agreed to help me rescue her. Some Praetorians found out we were Christian and began watching our every move. Everyone was captured but me. That is, except for Marcus's wife and youngest daughter."

"What happened to Marcus's wife?" came a rapid-fire response from Titus.

"She's dead." Tanner said, feeling pangs of guilt. "As I watched my new friends being led away in chains, there was an explosion, and Marcus and Anastasia's home was engulfed in flames. The Praetorians had set the fire. I'm sure of it. The next day I returned to find Anastasia dead in their home."

"No!" Titus cried out "Not Anastasia!"

Tanner could see the pain and anguish that filled Titus's eyes.

"What about little Livia?" he asked anxiously.

"I don't know where she is. I searched the rubble inside and out of their home. I couldn't find her anywhere."

"It's not possible!" Titus said. "I refuse to believe it. Anastasia dead, and Livia missing."

Titus grabbed Tanner by the neck. His backpack fell to the ground.

"You swear this is true?"

"Yes." Tanner replied.

Titus looked at Tanner. Then he looked at the ground and noticed Tanner's backpack. There was a long pause.

"What is that?" he asked.

"It's just my bag."

"It's a very strange looking bag."

"Yes, I got it in a faraway land."

"How far away?" Tanner began to wonder where the conversation was heading. Why was there such interest in the bag? Titus picked it up and studied every detail of the backpack.

"This is very strange workmanship. I have never seen anything quite like it. It is far more advanced than anything we have here in Rome."

Tanner was trying to figure out why the bag held such intrigue to Titus.

"Where is this far away land?"

Tanner gulped. What should he say? He hesitated.

"Answer me!"

Tanner tried to change the subject. "We have to save our friends. We don't have much time." Tanner was sure that would deflect the question. He was wrong.

"Answer the question!" Titus shouted. He was obviously irritated.

Tanner decided to let it go. He'd just blurt it out and be done with it. It had worked out fine when he had told Aquila and Erastus.

"I'm from a land called America. It's far away and very advanced. But don't worry, we're no threat to Rome."

Tanner was flabbergasted at the response. Titus gave Tanner a big bear hug and simply said. "Me too."

CHAPTER 64

TITUS IN ACTION

(TANNER)

"We've got to get to the prison," Titus said as he began to sprint toward the center of town.

Tanner's world had turned inside out.

"Just a minute!" He ran to catch up with Titus. "What do you mean, 'me too'?"

"I'm from America," Titus said continuing to run.

"Wait. What? You're going to tell me you're from America and then just keep running?"

"Okay. Okay. I'll tell you more, but time is wasting. I'll explain on our way."

Tanner couldn't believe what was happening. The man began to tell his story as they ran.

"My real name is Donald Carlton."

"What?" Tanner thought about the news article hanging in the police station. After he'd read it, he was convinced Donald Carlton had escaped Brownsville by using the portal as well, but he certainly hadn't expected to meet the man in Ancient Rome.

He was terrified. He'd never been face-to-face with a murderer. Let alone a four-time murder that was currently armed with sword and dagger—everything he needed to make Tanner victim number five. But he seemed so kind and was willing to risk his own life to help Tanner.

"I grew up in Brownsville, Kentucky," Donald said.

"I know. So did I."

"You can't be serious."

"I am. In fact, I read a newspaper article about your disappearance." Tanner winced inside after making the statement. *That was stupid. Now he knows I'm aware he's a murderer.*

To his surprise, Donald was completely unfazed.

Is he really that cold-blooded?

"You're really from Brownsville as well?" Donald asked. "It's impossible. How did you get here?"

"It's complicated," Tanner replied.

"Yes, my story is complicated as well."

Yeah, I know. Tanner decided to tell his story first. He started with Mick and her papers. "I'm sure there is a lot more we could talk about, but we really need to get working on this rescue," Donald said.

Tanner wondered if he just wanted to avoid talking about *his* complicated story. He wanted to run for it. Standing there talking with this man who acted so nonchalant, even after knowing that Tanner had read about his disappearance, was creepy. But at this point he wasn't sure he'd care if it was Hades himself he was talking to, as long as he could help Tanner rescue his friends. Instead of prying into Donald's story, Tanner told him what he'd done so far to rescue his friends.

"That's impressive, Tanner. Robbing the treasury single-handedly. Playing on superstitions. It was brilliant."

Yeah, you'd appreciate a good robbery, wouldn't you?

"Thanks," Tanner said, "but none of it really matters if we can't save my friends, does it?"

"Now that you have the money, I will be able to buy their freedom. The only issue we are going to have is timing," Donald said. "We have got to get to the guards before the legionnaires arrive. Once the legionnaires get there, too many people would be involved. I'm not sure we could buy the permanent silence of that many."

Realizing the urgency, they quickened their pace. "Where is this carpenter's shop?" Donald asked. "You said that's where the money is, correct?"

Tanner tried to read Donald's intent as he looked in his eyes. He tried to convince himself that he was interested in the money only as a means to help their friends.

"On the Vicus Jugarius street, near the Temple of Saturn."

"Great. That is near enough to the prison that we should be able to get back and forth without too many seeing what we are up to."

When they arrived at the carpentry shop, Lucius was there waiting.

"Lucius, this is Titus," Tanner said, careful not to reveal Donald's real name and all the questions that would come with it. "Cornelius's friend. He's agreed to bribe the prison guards."

"Pleasure," Lucius said.

"Likewise."

"Have you got anything we can put some of the money in?" Donald asked. "We can't take that much; a couple of small bags should be enough."

Lucius went to the back of the shop and returned with two small satchels. They quickly filled the bags. Donald hid his under his shield, and Tanner hid one under his tunic. It was mid-afternoon, and there would only be an hour or two until Nero would have the prisoners marched to their execution. They began to make their way to the prison. Across the plaza, Tanner could see a group of legionnaires.

"Surely they are the ones who will be escorting our friends," Donald said. "We have got to be quick."

"I'm Titus, a member of the Praetorian Guard," he said to the guards as he entered the prison "I'm here on official business."

"Yes, Titus, how can we help you?"

"In the name of Nero Claudius Caesar Augustus Germanicus, I come to ask for the release of certain prisoners. The emperor wishes to buy your silence on the matter." Tanner stopped himself as he began to shake his head in disbelief at how well Donald could lie. Donald opened his satchel and showed the gold coins. He looked over at Tanner signaling for him to do the same.

"Why has the emperor changed his mind?" the guard asked. "They were to be burned tonight."

Donald reacted quickly. "He wants it to look like an escape. He feels it will galvanize the anger of the populace against the Christians if the culprits not only burned down the city but escaped from prison as well."

Wow, Tanner thought. *He's good.* Tanner looked over at the guards who looked at each other skeptically.

"Do you really think we would have these funds if we weren't on Imperial business?" Donald continued. "I have sworn on my life to be loyal to the emperor. Now, accept the payment in exchange for your testimony against the Christians. And come with me."

The guards took the bribe. Donald was still in the doorway and leaned back looking out to the plaza. Tanner glanced in the same direction. The legionnaires had begun to make their way toward the prison.

"Only a few of the emperor's closest confidants know about his plan," Donald said. "He can't afford to have anyone expose it. We will have to let the prisoners run out as if they have truly escaped. I will inform the legionnaires about the escape. If we delay them long enough, they will not be able to capture the escapees and ruin Nero's scheme."

The guards were convinced. "Which prisoners do you want released?"

Donald named off the list that Tanner had given him.

"We'll get them." Two of the guards began the descent to the cells.

"You're *amazing*," Tanner whispered looking at Donald, who gave him a quick grin and then went back to his businesslike expression. At the same time, it was disconcerting to Tanner how easily he'd fabricated a story without flinching. Is that a skill you learned after you had brutally murdered people? As much as he needed Donald, he was also terrified.

"*You've* got to hide," Donald said urgently. "We can't afford to have your friends slow down when they see you."

As badly as he wanted to talk with Andrew and Mick, Tanner knew Donald was right. The legionnaires would be at the prison in a matter of minutes. His emotions felt like a shaken up can of soda. He would soon see Mick for the second time in Rome, and for the second time would be unable to speak to her, though he had a million things he wanted to talk about. He thought he was going to explode.

"Wait around the side of the building, over there." Donald pointed to the north side of the prison. "I will get you when it's safe to come out."

❖ ❖ ❖

"What's taking so long?" Donald mumbled as he walked over to the top of the stairs just as the guards were coming back up. Since he'd come to Ancient Rome he'd had to act many times, but this one felt like it had the most on the line. People from his own world needed him. He wasn't just Titus now. He was Titus and Donald. One man, two worlds. He straightened his shoulders and gave the guard a death stare.

"They refuse to leave."

"What?"

"They refuse to come out of their cells."

"Did they say why?" he asked.

"They demanded to know why we were releasing them, and when I told them about Nero's plan they said they weren't going to jeopardize the rest of the Christian community by playing into it."

"I told you not to talk about the plan with anyone," Donald said angrily. "You're going to endanger us all. Now, let me go talk with them," He scrambled down the stairs. "I've got to convince them to come, or we'll all be dead men."

"Titus! What are *you* doing here?" Cornelius whispered as he arrived at the cell.

"Freeing *you*. Now, get out of here. Quick."

"But Nero . . ."

"I made that whole thing up. But there's no time to explain. The legionnaires are on their way to escort you to your deaths."

"You don't need to tell me twice," Andrew said as he pushed Cornelius to the side and sprinted up the stairs.

"Take the stairs along the south side of the prison, just north of the Temple of Concord. Go straight to the *domus ecclesia* of Sebastian on the Appian Way," Donald told Cornelius. "I'll meet you there later."

❖ ❖ ❖

Once the prisoners left, Donald and the guards exited the building. Tanner joined them. "Follow my lead," Donald said.

Apparently, the legionnaires hadn't seen the former captives flee, since they were still crossing the plaza at a slow and steady pace.

Oh no. Tanner looked at the legionnaires. *It's Decimus!* With so much time and energy focused on saving Mick, he'd completely forgotten about the invincible man.

I can't believe this. I've got to get out of here. He'll make the connection for sure when he sees me and finds out a bunch of Christian prisoners have escaped. But, if I run for it that would just draw more attention to myself. I've got to stay. I'll just have to hide my face.

When the legionnaires arrived, Donald said with dramatic flair, "The prisoners have escaped!"

"What?" exclaimed one of the men.

"They overpowered the guards. The emperor will be furious." Donald stood before them with so much more confidence than Tanner felt.

"Furious isn't the word," replied a legionnaire. "He'll have us *all* killed."

"Do whatever you can to find them. They must be captured!"

"Any idea where they went?"

"The guards saw them head toward the Forum of Caesar," Donald said as he pointed in the direction opposite from where the escapees had actually gone. The guards nodded their heads in agreement.

"You must stop them. Now, go. Find them before Nero decides to burn all of *us* instead."

The legionnaires quickly made their way to the Forum of Caesar.

CHAPTER 65

A Defector

(Tanner)

An hour later, the legionnaires returned to the prison. Tanner stopped his pacing and tried to hide in Donald's shadow to keep from being recognized.

"Any luck?" Donald asked as the men approached.

"They're nowhere to be found."

"The emperor will be livid," Donald said.

The men nodded. "He'll probably execute whoever brings him news of the escape," one said. The other legionnaires concurred. They were all in fear of the emperor and what he might do to them. Tanner didn't blame them. He was afraid himself of what would become of these men. Yes, they worked for the bad guy, and yes, saving his friends was his top priority, but it was gut wrenching to know that if these legionnaires were executed, he would be an accomplice in sending someone to their death. He looked at Donald, who didn't fall out of his Titus character once. Tanner wondered if he didn't care if these men died, because he was so used to death.

"Someone has got to stop Nero from destroying the entire city," Donald said. Tanner looked up at him in surprise. What was he up to? But all the legionnaires seemed to agree with him.

"Since we are all connected with this escape, and because he considers it so important to publicly punish these Christians for the fire; he is going to light the city up with *us* instead."

Tanner could see from the dejected looks on their faces, they recognized that in his wrath, Nero was likely to turn on all of them.

"Aren't you overdoing it?" one of the guards whispered to Donald.

"Just stay with me," Donald whispered back.

"The timing is perfect for a revolt." He told the group. "A rebellion calling for Galba to replace the emperor is already underway. If we can build on that momentum, it may be our best chance to overthrow the emperor. Join with me. At this point, we're all going to be dead anyway if we don't unite against him."

Tanner scanned the legionnaires waiting for some loyal guard to object to the mutiny, but with determined expressions, they all agreed again.

"My friend owns a carpentry shop not far from here. We'll make that our headquarters. Follow me there."

The legionnaires followed. Tanner wasn't sure what to feel. What would Lucius say when they appeared on his doorstep. Donald continued as they approached Lucius's shop.

"We've secured some funds for an uprising. For the time being, I'll retain my role as a Praetorian so I can infiltrate Nero's inner circle."

Donald knocked on the door of the shop. "We need a place to headquarter a revolt," he said when Lucius answered.

Lucius appeared stunned to see such a large group standing at his door. "Be glad to help. I'm a dead man already for helping with the heist."

The men sat around a workbench and for several hours discussed plans for overthrowing the emperor. Tanner listened halfheartedly, spending most of his time looking at the door, wondering where his friends were and how they had managed after the escape. There was nothing he could do, though. He couldn't draw attention to the fact that he was worried about the escaped prisoners.

The sun began to set, and Lucius lit a few candles so they could continue their dialogue when one of the legionnaires stood up and shouted, "We have to warn our families. Once it has been discovered that we have deserted our posts, our homes will no longer be safe. Nero's men will come looking, and when they find our unsuspecting families, they'll be . . ." He couldn't continue. The thought of what Nero might do was overwhelming to everyone.

"I have friends hiding in the house church of Sebastian on the Appian Way," Donald told the men. "Take your families there. Once they are safely there, come back."

One by one, the legionnaires departed.

"I think I'll go out there myself," Donald told Tanner. "I need to make sure our friends are safe."

"I'm coming with you," Tanner replied.

"You need to stay here."

"Why?"

"The price on your head is too high. Plus if I'm seen too frequently with you, my cover will be blown."

"Price on *my* head?"

"Yes. Remember how you were chased, stalked, and then the home you were in was burned to the ground? Granted, it was part of Nero's master plan, but they also want *you* dead. You know too much. We have to minimize your exposure. Especially now that we freed the prisoners. Once word gets back to Nero, no one will be safe."

Tanner had no idea his situation was that precarious. He found a comfortable spot and lay down in Lucius's shop, trying to recover from the last twenty-four hours.

CHAPTER 66

Strange Magic

(Decimus)

I've got to stop them. Decimus reflected on what Titus and the others had been discussing. *Especially after what they did to my son. I'd be okay if they wanted only to overthrow the emperor, but I'm sure they plan to install Christianity as the state religion of Rome. We can't have that. But what can I do? I can't share their plot with Nero. He might recognize me from the night he stabbed and threw me into the Tiber and decide to finish the task. Especially if I tell him I was involved with the escaped prisoners. I'm going to have to take matters into my own hands.*

"Decimus? Is that you?" his wife asked as he moved toward the front door in the darkness.

"Yes."

"Where are you going this time of night?"

"I'm going to stop the spread of Christianity in Rome once and for all."

"What?"

"You heard me."

"How are you planning to do that by yourself?"

"You'll see."

Decimus really didn't have a plan yet. He was making it up as he went along, but he was determined to succeed.

"You know I support you. But be careful. Nero and his friends might be out on the streets again."

"I'll be careful. Remember, I'm doing this for us."

"And others like us." his wife replied.

Decimus opened the door and stepped out onto the dark street.

I've got to get my hands on their plans. If I can prove they intend to take over, I can get the backing I need to rid us of this plague. Decimus pictured the house church and tried to think where such plans might be held or who would have them.

The girl! Titus mentioned she was the whole reason for freeing the prisoners. If he was willing to risk his life to help some young girl . . . That's got to be it. There's something about her that everyone is rallying around. I have to kill the girl.

When he arrived at the house church, he carefully surveyed the site by moonlight to determine how to get in without being noticed. After an hour of scouting around, he found an upper story window he was able to enter through. He grabbed the handle of his sword and moved quietly through the house.

There she is!

He moved closer. Mick was asleep on the floor.

What's that? He looked at a backpack on the ground next to Mick. *That must be where she keeps the plans.*

Decimus saw someone stirring in the darkness. He waited until everything was still again.

Carefully he opened the bag and pulled out Mick's personal journal. He strained to look through its contents in the sliver of moonlight entering the room. *Strange magic,* he thought as he flipped through the pages and saw sketches of places Mick had been and things she had seen in the underworld.

Always heard the Christians had strange magic.

He placed the book back in the backpack.

This is exactly what I was looking for.

Decimus stood up from his crouched position.

Now to kill the girl and get out of here.

He pulled his sword from its sheath and raised it above his head.

Andrew leapt to his feet and charged Decimus, knocking him off his feet. His sword clanked on the ground.

Realizing he was greatly outnumbered, Decimus grabbed the backpack and fled up the stairs. "Stop that man!" Andrew shouted as the intruder jumped through an open window.

Decimus heard someone yell his name as he escaped down the Via Appia. He turned to see Titus pursuing him into the dark Roman night.

CHAPTER 67

WE CAN'T TELL MICK
(TANNER)

"Wake up," Lucius said shaking Tanner.

"Whoa, it's morning already?" Tanner asked rubbing his eyes. "Where's Don—I mean Titus?"

"I haven't seen him."

"He went to check on the others and never came back."

"Must be staying at the Praetorian Camp," Lucius said.

"I'm surprised he didn't at least stop by here last night. You think he's okay, don't you?" Tanner asked nervously. Why had he not come back? Was something wrong? Every time he felt like Donald was on his side, something like this happened, and Tanner remembered who Donald really was.

"Nobody'll mess with that man," Lucius said.

"I wouldn't want to be on his bad side, that's for sure," Tanner said. "Do you think I'd be safe going out to the house church of Sebastian on the Appian Way?"

"Sure."

"Titus didn't want me to go last night. He said there was a price on my head."

"Should be safe now. Rome's very different at night than during the day."

"Yeah, I've seen that," Tanner said, thinking back to the stabbing of Decimus.

"Just make sure no one's following you, and stay on busy streets."

Tanner got directions and carefully made the journey to the Appian Way. When he arrived at the house church and opened the door, his freed friends spotted him right away.

"Tanner!" Mick shouted as she sprinted to the door and nearly knocked him off his feet as she gave him a big hug. Andrew smiled at him from across the room. Tanner couldn't help but think it was a smug sort of smile, the type he himself gave Andrew whenever he was talking to Marina.

"Wow, have we got a lot to talk about," Mick said.

"No kidding!"

"Tidings can wait," Cornelius interrupted. "We've got to get moving. We have to relocate."

"In other words, we don't have time for your little hug fest." Andrew's grin grew more prominent.

Tanner gave him a look that made it clear he better zip it.

"Why do we need to relocate?" Tanner asked.

"One of the legionnaires defected," Cornelius replied. "He said he wanted to help, because of his hatred for Nero. But when he found out we were Christians, he claimed we needed to be punished for burning down the city."

Decimus.

"Did Titus come by here last night?" Tanner asked.

"No. Why?" Cornelius replied.

"He left Lucius's shortly before dark and said he was headed here."

"I hope he's not in some kind of trouble," Mick said.

I hope he hasn't double-crossed us. Rounded up everyone who is willing to conspire against the emperor, got us in one place so he could destroy us all. That was why the emperor made him a Praetorian in the first place.

"Titus can take care of himself. I'm sure he's fine," Cornelius added.

Unless it's an invincible legionnaire named Decimus.

"How do you know who to trust?" he asked, thinking about Titus, Decimus, and Erastus.

"It's not always easy Tanner," Cornelius replied. "But you can trust *me*."

I hope so, because my list of potential mortal enemies seems to be growing.

"We've got to go," Cornelius said. "The defector could be headed back here this very moment with a cohort. Nicomedis has a house church on the opposite side of town, not far from the Praetorian Camp. Marcus, you take Tanner, Andrew, Mick, and Marina. I'll take the legionnaires' wives using an alternate route."

With that, they left Via Appia.

Tanner was dreading it, but he knew he had to talk with Marcus. He gently approached his new friend. Tanner had never been in a position where he needed to break the news to someone that a loved one had died. He tried to remember how he felt when he got the word his sister had passed away and what might have helped him at that moment.

"Marcus, I don't know how to say this, but I found Anastasia in the rubble of your home. She's dead."

Tanner could see the devastation on Marcus's face. He threw his arms around his friend and gave him a hug. It would not be nearly enough comfort. Tanner was aware of that, but it was the only thing he had to offer.

"What about Livia?" Marcus asked, the pain obvious in his voice.

"I couldn't find her," Tanner said. "I scoured the house. In fact, I searched the whole block. When I realized I couldn't search for Livia *and* rescue everyone from prison, I found some women who agreed to organize a search party. They promised they wouldn't leave any stone unturned until they found her."

"How can I find these women?" Marcus asked.

"Their names are Priscilla and Julia, wives of Aquila and Erastus."

What ever became of Erastus? He has to know by now that I'm the one who robbed the treasury.

"Don't you have more to go on than that?"

"I'm sorry. I don't. I was in such a panic that—"

"Did you say Priscilla?" Mick interrupted.

"Yeah, why?"

"She's the one I stayed with while I was here in Rome."

"You're joking, right?"

Mick confirmed it was the same Priscilla and gave Marcus directions to her house.

"Why didn't I have Anastasia come with us when we were captured like you suggested? I really thought she had a better chance escaping the fire than we did of escaping Nero; and yet now we're free, and she's . . ."

He didn't continue.

"You can't beat yourself up for this," Andrew said. "You only did what you thought gave her the best chance for survival."

"I have to go search for Livia. You must understand."

Everyone nodded.

"I'm coming with you," Marina said.

"Good luck," Andrew said as he reached out toward Marina's hand. As she made contact he quickly pulled his hand back.

"Andrew, I've got something to tell you." Tanner said quietly as they cautiously walked the back streets of Rome. Mick was walking a few feet behind them, focused on the damage from the fire.

"What is it?"

"It's Titus. He's Donald Carlton."

"What?" Andrew sounded flabbergasted. "The Caveman? You're kidding me."

"Shhh."

"How do you know?"

"He told me."

"Wow. So he used the Time Room as well?"

"I guess so."

"Why would he tell you his name? Wouldn't a killer want to keep his identity a secret?"

"I know. That's what's got me. Either he's just so callous he doesn't care, or maybe he didn't do it."

"T, there's never been another suspect. Everything points to him."

"But he risked his life to rescue us. Maybe he's reformed."

"Come on. Four murders? People like that don't reform," Andrew said. "Who knows what his motives are. And where is he now?"

"He's such a good liar," Tanner said. "For all we know he and Decimus might have been working together leading us into a trap."

"But he *seemed* sincere," Tanner continued. "And Marcus and Cornelius believe in him. I just don't know. I don't know who we can trust."

"Me neither," Andrew replied.

"We've got to tell Mick about all this." Tanner turned around, but Andrew grabbed him by the arm, spinning him forward again. Tanner looked down at the grip Andrew had on him in shock.

"What are you doing?"

"We can't tell Mick," Andrew said.

"Why not?"

"Just trust me. We can't say anything until we know more about Donald. Mick will completely melt down. Don't you remember the school bus incident?"

"But we need to warn her about both of them."

"We'll just have to watch out for her. Believe me, we can't say anything unless . . . "

"Unless what?"

"Unless we can prove he didn't commit those murders. Just swear you won't tell her who he is. I don't think she could handle it."

Tanner had never seen Andrew this assertive. He nodded, knowing Andrew was probably right.

"You know the prison guards are gone now, too?" Andrew asked.

"What?"

"When they realized Titus—I mean Donald pulled a fast one on them they took off."

"Didn't anyone try to stop them?" Tanner asked.

"We tried, but they got away."

"That's not good. Do you think they'll turn us in?"

"Could," Andrew said, "but everyone's so terrified of the emperor at this point, I don't think anyone wants to even approach him."

"Are you sure we have to wait until the eighth to go back to Brownsville?"

Andrew nodded, a frown forming on his face.

CHAPTER 68

ONE LAST READ

(MICK)

Why would anyone break in and steal my backpack? Mick wondered as she settled in at Nicomedis's house church. She looked at the slightly burned secret journal of Donald Carlton in her hand. It was the only possession she had besides the clothes on her back. She had been flipping through its pages the night before and hadn't returned it to its designated pocket in her backpack before she fell asleep.

I've failed. Donald never even came through the Mundus, and all I've done was to make life worse for everyone. My two best friends nearly died trying to save me, I'm sure Mom and Dad are worried sick, Dad's probably in prison, and November 8 is only a couple of days away, and it's our last chance of the year to head home.

She began to read the journal again, looking for anything she might have missed.

August 3, 1810
A young Shawnee woman named Methoataske chased me down on her horse today. She had an incredible story to tell.
A few weeks earlier, her six-year-old brother dug up the skull of a giant. As word spread, the elders became concerned, since he had apparently violated a sacred burial site.

About a fortnight later, their fears were realized. A giant man appeared in the entrance of Methoataske's wigwam. He tied up the girl's mother and carried her away. Methoataske ran to get her father, who went in pursuit of the giant. When he returned, he explained that the giant stepped into an underground stream, and both he and their mother were eaten by the underwater man-eating serpent, Kinepikwa. For many years Methoataske had heard the legends of Kinepikwa.

The father ran to the river's edge to see if he could see any trace of them or the horned serpent, but there was nothing. Methoataske was not sure she believed the story and vowed to resolve her mother's disappearance.

The Shawnee had heard stories about my exploration of the cave so she came to find me. I knew her mother hadn't been eaten by Kinepikwa.

August 4, 1810
Last night I spent the evening torn about whether or not to tell the young Shawnee about the new land I had discovered. It has only been a few days since I even told Hannah. Now, I am compelled to tell a young woman I've only recently met.

I also have a new fear. Is there a race of giants that live in this new land? And if they were hostile enough to kidnap this girl's mother, what other hostilities might they be willing to commit?

August 7, 1810
Today Methoataske met me in the field, and we went to the cave. After making her take an oath of silence, I showed her how to pass into this new land. It gave her hope that her mother was still alive. I explained that when her father saw the giant and his wife slip through the portal, he must have assumed they had been eaten by Kinepikwa and that the legend must have grown from other Shawnee seeing the same kind of thing. It all made sense to her.

We began to search for her mother, and for the first time I brought a gun into the cave.

...

After having explored for some time, I told Methoataske that I needed to return home. She was desperate to find her mother and I resolved to help her in the coming days.

There's no way he could have killed the Shawnee girl, Mick thought. He was just trying to help her. But what about the other three murders?

August 9, 1810
...
As I was leaving the library, Methoataske was coming up the steps. We exchanged greetings, and I shared some of the things I had learned. I explained that I wouldn't be able to accompany her to the cave tonight.

August 17, 1810
I got up early and met Methoataske near the old dirt road that leads to the cave. We rode horses to the site.
...

Mick continued to thumb through the journal until she reached the final entry:

Methoataske and I were able to reach Mount Olympus. It was as beautiful as I expected. We described her mother to those we encountered and eventually found someone who had seen her. The man directed us toward a strange and beautiful building. It looked like a modern gothic cathedral with extensive blue stained glass. It had steeples on top and standing alone around the outside. It was round with six or eight entrances high above the ground. After explaining our cause, the bearded man kindly escorted us in and showed us where the giant and his captive had entered. He didn't say much about the building but treated it with great awe and respect. We carefully entered...

He then wrote a lengthy description of the interior including the Time Machine Room itself. Mick read the final line of the journal . . .

Methoataske and I plan to try this most unusual machine on our next trip into the cave.

No clues about where he might have gone. Nothing. Absolutely nothing. Mick thought. *What a waste. Why did you let me come this far if I wasn't going to find anything?* Mick asked the gods.

CHAPTER 69

STRANGER AT THE DOOR

(TANNER)

After spending the night at Nicomedis's house church, Mick, Tanner, and Andrew decided to go to headquarters to see if there were any updates.

"We've got to find Donald," Tanner said as they entered Lucius's' shop.

"Who?" Mick asked.

Andrew looked at Tanner angrily.

"No one." Tanner replied.

"Okay. Out with it," Mick said sternly. "What are you keeping from me?"

Knowing Mick wouldn't let up until he shared their secret, with hesitation Tanner replied, "It's Titus. He's actually Donald. Donald Carlton."

"What?" Mick looked completely stunned. "How long have you known that?" she asked.

"Ever since I first met him," Tanner replied.

"Why didn't you tell me?" Mick began shoving Tanner.

"It never came up. We were so busy with everything else that was going on."

"But you told Andrew?"

"Yeah."

"Then why not me?"

"He told me not to," Tanner said pointing at Andrew.

"But you knew," Mick said looking at Andrew.

"Knew what?" Tanner asked.

"Nothing." Mick replied.

Tanner looked over at Andrew.

"I saw what happened on the school bus," Andrew said, "and I ... I didn't want to say anything until we knew more about him. I was planning to tell you eventually. Really, I was."

"I actually met him. He was right here, but I didn't even know it, and now, I might never get to talk to him again, I might never get answers." Mick was talking out loud to herself as she paced in circles. "If he's dead, I've missed my chance. I can't believe this is happening."

"But you did talk to him," Tanner replied.

"Not as Donald Carlton."

"What's the difference? Have I ever told you sometimes you can be really strange?"

"The difference is Donald Carlton is the whole reason I came down here."

"Why?" Tanner asked.

"And how did you even know he was here?" Andrew added.

"It's a long story," Mick said.

"Well, we've got all the time in the world to hear it," Tanner said. "Literally."

Mick explained how learning she was a descendant of Donald had destroyed her sense of self-worth and how she became obsessed with clearing his name.

"Mick, your self-worth can't be tied to someone else," Tanner said.

"I realize that now. I've had a lot of time to think about how irresponsible I've been. I let my stupid pride nearly destroy my life and yours, too."

"But I still think we'll find him," Tanner said. "He's got to be around."

"Yeah, but will he be alive?" Andrew asked.

Tanner glared at him.

"What was he like, Tanner? You spent the most time with him."

"I think you can be proud of him," Tanner said with some hesitation, knowing that's what Mick would have wanted to hear.

"Did he actually commit the murders? Did he rob the bank?"

"I never dared ask. But based on what I saw, I'd be surprised. He didn't seem the type."

"I've got to hear it from his own mouth. He's got to be alive. He's just got to," Mick said. "I've got so much to ask him."

"So how *did* you know he was here?" Andrew asked.

Mick explained about the journals.

"I can't believe you did all of this on your own," Tanner said. "You were obsessed."

"I've definitely learned some major lessons, but I haven't gotten over my obsession with getting answers. That's why we've got to find him."

"Well, let's start looking."

The three of them spent the day cautiously sneaking around the streets of the charred city.

"It's getting too dark to keep going," Andrew said as the sun began to set. "The city's way too big. He could be anywhere."

"Let's head back to the shop. We'll keep searching tomorrow," Tanner said to soften the blow.

"We can't," Andrew said.

"Why not?" Mick asked.

"Tomorrow's the eighth. That's the last day the Umbilicus is open until August of next year."

"Well I'm not leaving," Mick said. "I've been risking my life for the last couple of months for this. I'm not going to give up now. Especially since I'm this close."

"But Mick, your family. They're so worried."

"Then you will have to tell them I'm okay, but I can't leave. I have to talk to Donald. Just trust me, it's important."

Tanner shook his head. "So we'll just go back and tell your parents you're in Ancient Rome? That'll go over real well."

"I'm sure you'll come up with something to tell them."

"Besides *we* can't go back without you," Tanner continued. "We broke into the police station and stole your papers so we could find you. If we go back without you we'll be doing time in juvie."

"Mick, you don't need to talk to Donald," Andrew said. "You've proven who *you* are. Before you found out you were a descendant of Donald, I can't think of anyone who was more in control of her own destiny than you. And look at what you've done *after* finding out. You discovered the Inner Earth. You found the lands of Greek mythology, and accessed the Cathedral of Time, which can take you wherever and whenever you want to go. You've become even more in control of your destiny than you were before you made your discovery.

"I can't do it. I can't just walk away." Tears welled up in her eyes. "I've got to know the truth about the murders. I've got to know what happened."

"I'm sure it's incredibly frustrating," Tanner said. Something was going on with Mick. This wasn't just frustration about an ancestor being a possible murderer. There was something she wasn't telling them, but by the look on her face, he knew this wasn't the time to push. He would just have to convince her somehow that staying was not an option. "For now, let's head back to Nicomedis's to get some sleep. We can continue our search in the morning."

"I think we should sleep at Lucius's," Andrew said. "It's closer to where you last saw Donald, and it's closer to the Umbilicus."

"Good idea."

Marcus, Marina, Cornelius, and Lucius were at the shop when Tanner, Andrew, and Mick arrived.

"Were you out looking for Titus?" Cornelius asked.

"Yeah," Mick replied.

"I'm guessing you didn't find him."

"Nope. Any idea where we should look?" Tanner asked.

"Not really," Cornelius replied.

Mick wandered to the corner of the shop and sat on the floor with her arms wrapped around her knees.

"I need some space," she said when Tanner tried to approach her.

"We'll organize a search party," Cornelius said. "With all this help, we're bound to find him."

"Trouble is, we really need to be going home tomorrow," Tanner replied.

"Surely you can stay a couple of more days, at least until we find him, can't you? Now, get some sleep. Tomorrow will be a busy day."

Tanner didn't sleep much. Most of the night he watched Mick who tossed and turned fitfully in her sleep. As dawn approached, the door burst open. Everyone sat upright, not knowing what to expect. Thoughts darted through Tanner's mind as he tried to clear his vision to better see the silhouetted figure standing in the doorway.

Erastus? Decimus? One of the Prison Guards?

The figure collapsed in the doorway. Everyone scrambled to see who it was.

"Titus!" Cornelius shouted as the others joined in.

He was bloody and bruised, with one eye swollen shut.

"Donald!" Mick said. "You're alive."

"Of course, I am." Donald replied weakly while giving Mick a strange look. "Oh, Tanner must have told you my real name."

"Yeah," Mick replied. "What happened?" she asked while assessing his wounds.

"I knew Decimus had defected. As I was on my way to Sebastian's, I spotted him fleeing the place with a sack similar to yours, Tanner. I went in pursuit, and he nearly killed me. Luckily, he thought he had, and he left."

"Let's get you comfortable," Lucius said. "Help me."

The men carefully moved Donald to a chair so he could sit up and wrapped him in some blankets. "I'm not sure if you've ever been formally introduced," Tanner said to him, "but this is your descendant, Makayla Brown. Makayla, Donald Carlton."

"I've got a million questions for you," Mick said excitedly.

"Wait," Donald said. "Did you say she's one of my descendants?"

"I am." Mick jumped in, a big grin breaking across her face. She gave him the type of hug you would expect from someone who had just found a long-lost relative.

Donald winced slightly. "I'm sorry," he apologized as he started to break down. "From which of my children are you a descendant?"

"From Bridget."

"Ah, my first child. Such a good girl. How I loved my little Bridget. Please continue, Mick." Donald Carlton was now talking to Mick with a certain reverence and enthusiasm that hadn't existed in his voice before.

Mick explained how learning he was her ancestor had devastated her at first, because of all the rumors that had gone around Brownsville, for so many years.

"Rumors? What rumors?" he asked.

"Well, there was a bank robbery the day you disappeared. Three bank employees were murdered. Since you went missing the same day, you were accused of the crimes. Many of the townspeople had seen you hanging around with a Shawnee girl before you disappeared. The whole town assumed you left your family and ran off with her for a life of crime. It was just a few years ago that her remains were found in Mammoth Cave. Everyone assumed you had murdered her as well."

"That's so far from the truth," Donald said as he began to explain the events of that fateful day.

CHAPTER 70

Confrontation in the Cave

(Donald Carlton)

"Don't move!"

Donald and Methoataske turned to see two men, sights trained on them with bags at their sides overflowing with cash.

"What do you want from us?" Donald asked.

"We want ya dead."

"What do you have against us?"

"Nuthin', just the fact ya know who robbed Brownsville Bank."

"I didn't even know it *had* been robbed," Donald said.

"Don't mess with us. Everyone knows."

The two men were using Mammoth Cave as a hideout. Donald began to work his way with Methoataske toward the portal entrance while he kept the thieves talking.

"Another step, and they'll be havin' a joint funeral down at the mortuary for you an' the employees down at the bank." The man cocked the gun and slowly moved it side to side from Methoataske to Donald and back. "Ya wouldn't want that now, would ya?"

"No sir," Donald replied. He tried to determine a strategy to distract the men long enough to grab Methoataske and jump through the portal.

"Do exactly what I do," Donald told Methoataske in a whisper.

"We'll let you take us captive, just don't shoot," he said as he raised his hands above his head. Methoataske looked at Donald in surprise but followed along. He began to walk toward the men. The portal was directly in front of them.

One more step, he thought. Donald and Methoataske stepped in the Styx, and they were gone.

Donald knew that if the men followed them, they would be disoriented when they first emerged into Inner Earth.

"We'll grab their bags and make a run for it," he told Methoataske.

"But the guns," she replied.

"Just trust me."

They waited impatiently, Donald wondering if perhaps their sudden disappearance had frightened the men out of the cave. Was it safe to go back? But then one by one the men appeared before them. Donald wrestled one of the bags away and fled with Methoataske right by his side.

Click.

The water in the gun prevented it from firing.

"After them."

Having been in the underworld a few times before, Donald and the fleet-footed Indian girl led the two men deeper and deeper into Inner Earth.

"We just have to lead them far enough in that they'll eat something," Donald said.

CHAPTER 71

PARTING FAVORS

(MICK)

"So you didn't kill the Shawnee girl either?" Tanner boldly asked.

"No," Donald replied, though he looked sad.

He continued his story and began to tell them about his arrival in Rome.

"When we first arrived, we changed our names to Titus and Anastasia and continued our search for her mother for the past ten years."

"Wait. Did you just say Anastasia?" Andrew asked. "Are you telling us that Marcus's wife was the Shawnee girl?"

"That's right."

"She never said anything," Tanner said.

"That was her way. Always very private."

"Then who is the Shawnee girl buried in Mammoth Cave?"

"I don't know. That burial site was there before I came to Rome."

Marina and Cornelius looked at each other with bewildered expressions.

"Do you have any idea what they're talking about?" Cornelius asked Marina.

"It sounds like my stepmother wasn't from here," Marina said angrily.

Donald looked over at Marina. "Marcus and your stepmother always planned on telling you once you got a little older."

"A little older? I'm fourteen years old! How long were they planning to wait?"

"I'm sure now that Anastasia's gone, your father will explain the whole thing to you."

"I sure hope so," Marina said. She angrily walked to a corner of the shop.

"Now it makes sense how crushed you were when you found out about her death." Tanner said to Donald.

"I *was* crushed. *You* know what it's like, the bond that develops when you are working together so closely on a rescue mission, risking life and limb, and trying to adapt to a culture so different from the one you're used to. Anastasia and I were lifelines for each other."

Going back to his story, Donald continued. "When Anastasia and I discovered the Cathedral of Time, I documented the time room settings. I wanted someone to be able to find me in case anything happened and we couldn't get back. We figured since we were only a short period of time behind the kidnapper, the settings for the room had probably not been altered, so we departed for Rome. After arriving, we were immediately taken prisoner."

"So Anastasia was the woman you were protecting in prison, and the one whose release you demanded from Nero when he made you a Praetorian." Tanner said.

"That's right."

"Wait," Mick interrupted. "When did you arrive in Rome?"

"AD 54."

"Did you ever find Anastasia's mother?" Tanner asked.

"No, we never did. She could have gone anywhere during those years."

Mick was busy checking the secret journal. She shook her head in disgust. The ink had been smudged on his drawing of the time room settings. She originally thought it read AD 64, but could see now that it really read AD 54.

That's why Demeter said no Surfacer had been through that portal in nearly a decade.

Donald looked at Mick curiously. "Is that my journal? How did you find that?"

"I wanted to prove you hadn't killed anyone or abandoned your family. I was sure there was more to the story. Eventually, I found a journal of yours. I read it over and over, looking for clues."

"And then you read the last paragraph." Donald said, nodding as if things now made sense.

"That's right."

"What was in the last paragraph?" Andrew asked.

"It was the clue that led me to this." Mick held the book up. "This is where I learned about Inner Earth."

"Where did you find that?"

"In Mammoth Cave."

"So why didn't you let us in on the secret?" Tanner asked.

Mick hesitated. "You saw what happened on the bus. The last thing I wanted was to say anything about the Caveman to anyone."

"I fully expected to see someone arrive in Rome at the same time we did," Donald said.

"Here's why I didn't," Mick said showing him the smudged ink.

"If only you would have come ten years earlier, we wouldn't be in this predicament," Donald said.

"Why didn't you ever go back to your family?" Andrew asked.

"After Anastasia and I gave up on finding her mother, we tried to go back, but every time we arrived back in Brownsville, it was much later than the year we left. I still can't figure out why."

"So all the sightings around Mammoth Cave over the years—they really were you," Mick said in amazement.

"But couldn't you have just set a new date on the time machine and returned to your time?" Andrew asked.

"We were never able to figure out a way to do that."

"Are you saying that *we* may never get back to our friends and families either?" Tanner asked. He looked at Mick, and she saw the same fear in his eyes as she felt.

"Not necessarily," Donald said, "but I *am* saying *we* were not able to."

"Well, that's just great!" Mick felt a surge of anger. Why hadn't the gods bothered to mention that?

Donald tried to reassure her. "I'm sure you can figure it out."

"What ever happened to the money from the bank robbery?" she asked. She'd come here with a mission, and if she was stuck here forever, she was going to at least get the answers she'd originally sought.

"I hid it near the River Styx. Not long ago I made another attempt to return to Brownsville. I took the bag with me, intending to return it to the bank. This time over 200 years had passed since I originally left Brownsville. Unable to find the bank, I hid the money the only place I could think of: my old barn—"

"In the hayloft!" Mick finished his sentence.

Tanner and Andrew looked at each other with puzzled expressions.

Dad didn't take the money. Mick was thrilled. She only wished she could go home and make things right with him.

Mick and the boys spent most of the day visiting with Donald and learning more about his life both in Brownsville and Rome. By late afternoon, they knew they had a tough decision to make. They had to at least try to get home, but the loss of vivacious little Livia still hung over the group like a dark cloud.

"What do we do about Livia?" Tanner asked. "We can't leave not knowing if she'll ever be found."

"But what about *our* families?" Andrew asked. "They're going through the same thing. None of them know where we are either. We can't continue to leave them in the dark."

"You're right," Mick said. "We need to at least try to get home." She turned to Donald. "Are you coming with us to Brownsville?"

"No. The life I had there has passed by."

"But you would have me and your other descendants."

"That's true, but it would be so difficult to not be able to reveal my true identity to my posterity. I think its best I stay here."

"We'll miss you," Tanner said. "Thanks for everything. Without your help, we never could have done this."

"I will miss all of you as well," Donald said. "These are memories I will never forget."

"Me neither," Mick replied. "Maybe we can come back and visit."

Tanner looked at Mick in shock. "I'm not doing this again," he whispered to Andrew.

Mick gave her sixth great-grandfather a hug. Tears streamed down his dirty, weathered cheeks as he wished her luck. Mick thought about how the whole adventure had begun. How she wanted to vindicate him, to restore his good name. And now, like Mrs. Barrett, she looked up to him and considered him a hero and knew Tanner and Andrew did as well. He was the type of person everyone said he was prior to the disappearance. Donald clasped arms with the boys one at a time and slapped them heartily on the back.

"Thanks for everything you taught me," Tanner said.

Mick wanted something more. She looked at Donald. "Do you think you could put some kind of document together that would in some discreet way, let everyone know that you didn't commit the murders or desert your family and would help them stop judging you so harshly?" *And your descendants.*

"Hmmm," he replied. "An interesting request. Let me see what I can do."

"Can I ask the three of *you* a favor?" Marcus inquired stumbling into the shop. "I'm sorry I didn't acknowledge that I knew where you had come from. Anastasia," he paused on her name, "made me promise to never tell anyone." He held out two linen bundles for them.

"What is it?" Mick asked, taking one while Tanner took the other.

"Anastasia always spoke passionately of the land of her fathers. She loved the world you come from. It would mean a lot to me if you would take her bones and bury her there. I've had them carefully prepared and wrapped nicely in linen."

"You know how important burials are to the Indians," Donald interjected. "See if you can find where her Shawnee village was."

"Sure thing," Mick said.

"It would be the least we could do," Tanner added. "Her hospitality made your house a home away from home for us."

"We've got to get going," Tanner said. "We haven't got all day."

"Actually we do," Mick whispered in reply. "The Umbilicus closes when the sun goes down."

Tanner rolled his eyes and smiled. "You're starting to sound like me."

"You'll have to be careful," Marcus said. "There are still a lot of threats in the city, and the three of you would make nice targets."

Marina began to cry. She ran to Andrew, gave him a kiss on the cheek, and then a big hug. Andrew's face turned bright red.

"Come with us," Andrew said, holding her hands in his. Mick and Tanner exchanged a surprised smile.

"I really can't, Andrew," she replied. "I need to stay and help with the search for Livia."

"I understand," Andrew said, clearly disappointed.

"But you'll come back, right?" Marina asked.

"We'll try," Andrew said. Tanner looked over at him like he was crazy.

It was late morning when the trio emerged from the shop.

"Sounds like a storm's rolling in," Andrew said as distant thunder rolled toward them.

They took a quick look around for any shady looking characters and made their way to the Umbilicus. On either side of the open door, was a guard, but they couldn't tell whether or not they were armed.

"We need a distraction," Mick said.

Andrew was already on it. "Tanner. Don't you remember when we first got here how Nero was throwing coins from the top of the Basilica Julia?"

"Yeah, why?"

"Don't you remember the havoc it created?"

"For sure," Tanner said. "I had bruises for weeks from the scramble."

"Let's go back to Lucius's shop and get some of the money from the heist. We'll approach the Umbilicus from the sides and throw coins directly in front of the monument. In the chaos that's created, we'll slip past the guards and be on our way."

"Great thinking," Tanner said.

They returned quickly to the shop and each got a couple of handfuls of coins they loaded into pouches. They deposited themselves on the back side of the Umbilicus and began tossing coins around the sides. In a flash, the crowd was scrambling for the money. The guards moved away from the entrance, and Tanner, Andrew, and Mick leapt into the Umbilicus Urbis. They moved the *lapis manalis* and climbed into the cave below.

"That was easy," Andrew said.

"Yeah, unlike about everything else we've done on this journey!" Tanner replied. "Darn. I never had a chance to thank Lucius's son for all his help with the heist. Without him, I never could have pulled it off. I never even knew his name."

"We can't go back now." Mick said.

"Hey, where's the door to the Cathedral of Time?" Andrew asked.

CHAPTER 72

MOVE THE LAPIS

(TANNER)

Tanner, Mick, and Andrew stood staring at nothing more than a rock wall.

"That's where it was isn't it?" Andrew asked.

"Yeah."

"Demeter? Demeter?" Mick called out.

"What are you doing?" Tanner asked.

"Calling for the goddess."

Tanner and Andrew looked at each other.

"I think she's lost it." Tanner whispered.

"Didn't you meet Demeter when you came through here?"

"Uh, no."

"Hmmm. She appeared when I was here. When I heard the *lapis manalis* begin to move, she appeared and caused a landslide to hide the door."

"Well, let's start digging, then," Tanner said. He didn't waste any time and walked over to the wall and began looking for rocks he could move. After failing to even budge the smallest rock, they sank to the ground dejectedly.

"The gods must not want us to leave," Mick said. "Welcome to our new home boys."

"I'm not buying it," Tanner replied. "I'm not going to let my destiny be determined by the whim of some goddess. I'm making my own way." He jumped up. "Get over here and help me and let's get these stones moved."

"Okay," Mick said with reluctance. "But trust me. If the gods don't want it, it's not happening."

"Wait." Andrew stood and paced around the cavern deep in thought. "Didn't you say Demeter hid the opening when the Mundus began to open? Maybe she only unveils the Cathedral entrance when the Mundus is closed."

"Did I ever tell you you're a genius Andrew?" Tanner asked.

"No."

"Well I'm not going to now either. That is the stupidest thing I've ever heard. Now, get over here and help move these rocks."

"Mick. Come help me move the lapis," Andrew said.

Tanner was stunned. He stood and watched as his two friends maneuvered to the opening and slid the stone, closing the Mundus.

"See. I told you it was stupid," he said when nothing happened. "Now come help me dig."

"We're never going to get those stones to move," Mick said. "We're either going to live out the rest of our lives in Rome, or we've got to figure out what the gods need us to do here so they'll open the entrance and let us go home."

Tanner wasn't listening. He continued to struggle in his attempt to move one of the rocks. Ever so slightly it moved. "Hey, it's working," he said.

The room quickly filled with light and Tanner fell backward onto the cave floor, as Demeter appeared. A few flicks with her wrists and the rocks moved out of the way revealing the door to the Cathedral of Time. As quickly as she appeared, she turned and left.

"Hey, wait! Is there a shortcut for getting home?" Mick yelled, but it was too late. The goddess was gone.

"Who are you calling stupid now?" Andrew said.

"Yeah, yeah." Tanner muttered.

"Do you think things will be different when we get back home?" Mick asked.

"What do you mean?" Tanner replied.

"Well, aren't you familiar with the butterfly effect?"

"No, what's that?" Tanner asked.

"It's the idea that small differences in what occurs at a certain point in time can cause wide swings in what happens in the future."

"I'm more worried about *if* we get home. I hope you have a plan Mick." Andrew gestured at Tanner. "Because brilliant over here didn't really think about the return trip before we set off."

"Tell me you've got that golden bough that guarantees we can get back out of here," Tanner said.

"No, I was just planning to go back the way I came."

"Pay up." Andrew held out his hand to Tanner. "And there's no way I'm going back down the Acheron, or climbing down the Cliffs of Erebus."

Mick looked confused for a moment. "Oh, that's right," she said. "You followed my papers. *I* just asked the High Priest of Delfi, and he provided me with transportation straight to Olympus."

"What?" Andrew asked.

"And then you snuck into the Cathedral of Time?" Tanner asked.

"No, I asked the gods, and they took me there."

"You've got to be kidding!" Andrew barked. "You mean we didn't have to go through all that stuff?"

"Well, asking the gods to get us back home is not really an option for *us*," Tanner said.

"Why not?" Mick asked.

"We basically broke into the Cathedral. I'm thinking the gods probably aren't very happy with us. And we can't go near the Kingdom of Hades. He was furious when he found out Persephone had granted us access to the Great Hall of Judgment when he wasn't there. We were lucky to get out of there alive."

"Plus, I don't want to leave my return trip to the discretion of the gods," Andrew added. "What if they don't *want* us to go back to Brownsville. What if they have some mission for us in the underworld or Rome or somewhere else?"

"Let them try to stop me," Tanner said just as an explosive clap of thunder from above shook the ground.

CHAPTER 73

THE RIVER LETHE

(TANNER)

"If we do make it back to Brownsville, do you think we'll get there in the same year we left?" Andrew asked as they opened the door and entered the Cathedral of Time.

"Of course, why wouldn't we?" Tanner asked.

"Weren't you listening to Mr. Carlton? He was never able to get back to his own time."

"Why do you think that was the case?" Mick said looking at Andrew.

"I'm not sure. It seems odd."

"We might never see our friends and family again," Mick said.

The three of them went quiet.

"We'll figure out a way." Tanner broke the silence. "We made it this far, didn't we? My mom always says, 'Where there's a will, there's a way.'"

They made their way to the command center and approached the glass panel that displayed destinations. Tanner held his finger to the arrow changing the destinations.

"Mt. Olympus. That's us," Andrew said excitedly.

"Okay. Here we go," Tanner said as he reached to press the green button that would send them to Olympus.

"Stop!" Andrew swiped away Tanner's arm from the panel. "We've got to check and see if there's anything that looks like a date on this thing."

The trio scanned the screen looking for anything that looked like a date. The symbols were all unfamiliar. If it weren't for the map, they wouldn't have even recognized Olympus.

"Right there." Andrew pointed to a group of symbols that were refreshing in one second increments. "Remember how we didn't arrive in Rome at the same time Mick did? It's because the Time Machine settings were continuing to tick forward from when the last person used the machine. Those symbols right there have to be the date. But I have no idea how to read them."

"Any ideas?" Tanner looked at Mick. "'Cause I've got nothing."

Mick was laser focused as she watched the symbols. "I think I've got it," she said as she leaned back away from the screen.

"What?"

"You know how the Arabic Numbers System we use is based on angles?"

"No," Tanner replied. Mick and Andrew smiled at each other.

"So the numbers are drawn the way they are because of the number of angles the symbol creates. The circle has no angles, so it's zero. One has a single angle, two has two angles, three has—"

"English please," Tanner said cutting her off.

"Okay." She rolled her eyes at him. "I've been watching the symbols increment, and each one has one more angle than the previous symbol, and their zero is the same as ours."

"Watch," she said.

A perfect circle flashed on the screen. "That's their zero." Then an upside down "V" displayed. "That's one—see, only one angle?"

"You're brilliant," Tanner said with a big grin as he shoved Mick's shoulder.

The three of them began to analyze the counter on the screen.

"It looks like we'll be returning toward the end of the summer the same year we left. It must be that no one has used the machine since us, because based on how long we've been gone, that's what date it would be back home," Andrew said.

"Then let's go!" Tanner pushed the green flashing button.

Arrows illuminated their path to the central platform and after a series of flashing lights, everything went dark. Flashing arrows again illuminated the floor, and the trio followed them to the corresponding exit.

"What do you think would happen if we opened one of the other doors?" Tanner asked gesturing around the cathedral.

"I don't know, but I'm not going to take a chance," Mick replied. "If we open the wrong one, we could find ourselves in the middle of the Trojan War or storming the Bastille."

"Kind of cool to think about, though, right?" Tanner responded.

"For sure, but right now, I just want my own bed," Andrew said.

"Amen, brother!"

"No place like home!" Mick added.

Tanner flung the door open and they exited out of the cathedral and onto Mount Olympus.

"We've got to find the golden orb and return to the underworld," Andrew said.

"Chances are we won't find it where we left it. If you remember, we kind of altered its normal course," Tanner replied.

"Why didn't you just land on the judgment platform and meet the twelve gods of Olympus?" Mick asked with a puzzled look on her face.

"No way," the two boys said vehemently.

"Why are you so scared of the gods?" Mick asked.

Tanner looked at Mick. "Come on Mick. Do you really think I would have ended up on Mount Olympus if I was being judged by the gods? More likely I would have been in Tartarus shoveling coal, weeping, wailing, and gnashing my teeth!"

They all laughed. Tanner knew he wasn't a bad kid, but he probably wasn't Olympus god material yet either.

"I bet the orb is parked on the Judgment Platform, right where it's supposed to be," Mick said.

"So wait. Are you telling us that you went through the judgment process and were considered goddess material?" Tanner asked Mick.

"Why would you seem so surprised Tanner?" Mick asked.

Tanner knew better than to answer that loaded question.

"Um, well, of course you're goddess material, but . . ."

"Nice recovery, T," Andrew said as he jabbed Tanner in the ribs with his elbow.

"But what?" Mick replied.

"Actually, there's no but," Tanner said. "I just wanted to hear about the whole judgment thing, that's all."

"Okay, but first let's go find the orb."

The circular pavilion where the gods sat in judgment was on the other side of an orchard, which provided cover as they tiptoed toward it.

"That's good news," Andrew said quietly as he pointed toward the orb in the center of the Platform. "Looks like most of the gods are there—probably not the best time to attempt a getaway."

"Once they've left, we'll be on our way," Tanner said. "I don't want to meet any of them face-to-face."

"All right," Mick said sounding put out, "but if you've got some repenting to do there's no time like the present to get it resolved." She gave Tanner a big smile.

The trio parked themselves under a tree and quietly discussed the adventure they had been through.

"Tanner! What are you doing?" Mick said as emphatically as you could without actually screaming. She slapped at his hand. Tanner had plucked a piece of fruit from the tree and had his mouth open with the fruit in it. He looked at Mick in question.

"What was that for?" he asked.

"Don't you know that if you eat food from the underworld you'll be forced to live here forever?"

"Ah, wow. I had forgotten. Good thing you're here Mick."

"Honestly, how did the two of you ever make it to Rome without me around?" Mick asked.

"I'm surprised myself," Tanner wisely replied. "I guess we were so bent on rescuing you that we were more focused than usual."

Andrew smiled and gave him a discrete thumbs-up. Tanner figured he had made up some of the points he lost with Mick about the whole goddess thing.

"Looks like we're going to get an unobstructed run at the orb," Tanner said as gods began to leave the pavilion. "Come on!" he said as he ran for the orb. Mick and Andrew followed quickly behind.

When they arrived, they remembered how small the interior was.

"This wasn't really built for three," Andrew said.

"Aw come on. It'll just be a little cozy," Tanner replied.

"Just make sure no one bumps the controls," Mick added.

"Let's take turns in the orb for our return flight to the underworld," Andrew suggested.

"Way too risky," Tanner said. "I'd prefer not to get separated again. Let's just make this work." He was thinking about how he had felt when both his friends were captives in Rome.

The three of them climbed in.

"Everybody in?" Mick asked.

"Looks like it," Andrew said.

"Go ahead and push that button, and let's be on our way!" Tanner directed Andrew.

In a flash, they were hurtling through space. They could see from the 3D displays that they were heading toward the Elysian Fields.

"We should be arriving shortly," Andrew said.

Moments later they touched down. When they exited the orb, they could see the Great Hall of Judgment in the distance.

A man approached dressed like a treasure hunter.

"Excuse me, name's Harvey Wilkins. Can you tell what building that is over there?"

Mick paused momentarily while her senses registered what the man said. Then, in an explosive moment, her heart leapt for joy and she flung herself into the man's arms giving him a massive bear hug.

"Harvey Wilkins! You're alive! So no one kidnapped *or* killed you?" She pulled away just enough that she could look him in the eyes.

"What?" Harvey exclaimed pushing Mick away.

"Nothing, nothing," she said. "Oh, and that's the Palace of Hades."

"Hey," he said looking like a light bulb had gone on in his head. "You're the girl I saw jump into the River Styx."

"Huh?"

"I saw you about to jump and yelled out just before you did."

"Ahh, okay. I thought . . . Never mind."

"What are you doing down here, anyway?" Andrew asked.

"Don't you wish you knew." Mr. Wilkins said.

Tanner looked questioningly at Mick and Andrew who just shrugged their shoulders and walked away.

"Running into Harvey Wilkins is good news Mick," Tanner said as they walked the opposite direction from the treasure hunter, "but I think you were a little over the top."

Mick rolled her eyes. "It just means that everything is going to be all right." She smiled. "There is more actually. Something I need to tell you."

Tanner looked at her expectantly.

"I saw your dad in Mammoth Cave."

"What?" Tanner replied, shocked.

"Shortly before I left, I saw him near Giant's Coffin."

"Why didn't you say anything?"

"Well, everyone was speculating about who killed or kidnapped Harvey Wilkins, and I thought you would be devastated if your father had only returned to Brownsville to kill the treasure hunter."

"So is that why you gave Harvey Wilkins such a big hug?"

"Only partly."

Mick explained the events that had led her to believe her father may have been the culprit.

"Makes sense now."

Mick couldn't wipe the smile off her face.

Dad's coming back. And he's about to find out I rescued Mick.

A big smile broke across Tanner's face as well.

"Oh, my gosh," she said and she turned and sprinted for Harvey. "Mr. Wilkins, mind if we take a picture?"

"No, I don't mind. You must be fans of the show."

"Uh, yeah," Mick replied, even though Tanner was certain she had never seen his show.

"Make sure there's nothing that gives away where we're at in the picture," Mick said as Tanner began to take pictures.

She took the phone back thumbing through the pictures as if to make sure Tanner had followed instructions. She nodded once and grinned at him. Tanner felt a surge of happiness that reminded him why he'd done everything he had to save his friend.

"Now to email this to mom," Mick said.

"You know we don't have service," Andrew said.

"Just thinking ahead. If we can at least get close enough to the surface that the email will go through, it may save my dad."

"You think of everything," Tanner said shaking his head.

The three of them thanked Mr. Wilkins and departed.

"Is that the Mnemosyne River?" Andrew asked.

"I think so," Tanner said.

They could see the river originated at the Great Hall. It was one of the two rivers that Persephone said they could drink from. There was a small boat anchored to the dock waiting.

"What? No ferryman for this boat? What a rip-off," Tanner said. "I'm going to complain to management!"

"I guess we'll have to navigate on our own." Andrew laughed.

Tanner was thrilled not to have to deal with Phlegyas, Charon, or someone similar. They hopped in and began to row down the river.

"I don't know if *you* drank the water from this river or not," Tanner said. "But, it was the best water I've ever tasted,"

"No, I never tasted it," Mick answered.

"It's amazing," Andrew said. "It cleared my head, and I felt so focused and sharp."

"There was something magical about it, that's for sure," Tanner said.

The three of them leaned over in the boat, cupped their hands, and shoveled the tasty water into their mouths. They couldn't get enough of it. Finally, when they had quenched their thirst, they leaned back in the boat, stretched their legs, and relaxed. Andrew pointed to a sign along the river's edge.

"Hey, that says we're on the Lethe."

"Wait!" Mick said, "I thought you said this was the Mnemosyne."

"I'm starting to feel groggy," Andrew added.

Ahead they saw a cave.

"I don't remember seeing *that* on the way in," Tanner said.

A small sign in front of the cave read Cave of Hypnos. No sooner had they read the sign than they felt the swiftness of the river increase significantly. They were in rapids and being pulled into the cave at high speed. They barely had enough time to process the significance of Cave of Hypnos when they found themselves entering its grasp.

"Hypnos is the god of sleep, and this is the river of forgetfulness," Mick said. "The myths say that those who sail down the Lethe forget their prior life before being reincarnated."

"So we're about to be reincarnated?" Tanner asked.

"I haven't seen one of the myths that wasn't true yet," Mick replied.

"Wait. What does forget their prior life mean?" Tanner asked in a panicked tone. "Does that mean we'll forget all about Brownsville? Or Inner Earth? Or both?"

Maybe Dad didn't really abandon us. Maybe he just found Inner Earth and sailed this same river and forgot about us.

"None of those sound like good options to me," Mick replied.

"Yeah, let's get out of here," Tanner replied.

He tried to move, but his body felt as though it was in a tremendous sleep that he couldn't pull out of.

"I can't move," he said.

"Me neither," Mick replied.

Andrew was fading so fast that the whole forget their prior life thing didn't even register. "When I'm reincarnated I want... to... come... back... as... a...", he said. That was as far as he got before he was out cold.

"Well, Andrew's gone, what have you got left?" Tanner asked Mick.

"Not much," she replied sleepily. "We've got to get out of here. I don't want to go back to earth as an animal!"

"And I don't want to forget my prior life!" Tanner added emphatically.

Tanner and Mick tried again to move, but neither could muster the energy.

The craft was headed for the dismal Stygian Marsh, which according to legend is the place where those from the underworld who enter its waters are reincarnated and returned to the surface.

"Thure's nooo waaay owwwt! I hooope I go back as a leop-uurrrrd!" Mick said.

"Yeah... a... leopard... would... be..." Tanner said.

Moments later all three were sound asleep and sprawled out in the boat.

CHAPTER 74

Return to the Surface

(Mick)

"Mom! Come quick!" Mick's younger brother said as he raced into the house.

"Today's the day!" he yelled. "Come and see."

Nathan, Addie, and Mrs. Brown ran to the barn. They all knew why Nathan was screaming. Three of the family cows were pregnant and one of them must have given birth.

"Which one is it?" Mick's mother said as they ran.

"You have to wait and see," Nathan replied.

"Aw, come on," Addie said as she trailed Nathan across the field. "Tell us which one it is."

"You have to see for yourselves," he replied.

When they arrived at the barn he flung the barn door open and to everyone's surprise except Nathan, all three cows had given birth.

"Can you believe it?" Nathan said. "Three new calves, all on the same day."

"Very unusual," Mick's mother replied. "Looks like we have two males and a female."

"Yep." Nathan said.

"This is definitely a big day at the Brown home," Mrs. Brown replied.

Little did they know just how big it really was...

The family remained in the barn admiring the newborns for a few hours. It was a miraculous thing to watch.

When Mick, Tanner, and Andrew came to, they found themselves lying in the underground stream Lethe in Mammoth Cave.

"Look at us," Mick glanced at their wet tunics and began to laugh. They looked like they had just come from a costume party. Their tunics dried quickly on the walk to their respective homes.

"Anybody home?" Mick called out as she flung open the front door. Since everyone was in the barn, there was no answer. She quickly checked the refrigerator and grabbed a couple of snacks before making her way up to her bedroom. She was exhausted.

I wonder where everyone is. Oh, well. I'm sure they'll be back soon enough. For now, I could use some sleep. She climbed in bed and was out in a matter of minutes.

CHAPTER 75

THE SUSPECT RETURNS

(TANNER)

"Tanner, Tanner. Wake up!" Tanner looked up to see his mother hovering over his bed. "You're okay." The relief was thick in Mrs. Hunter's voice.

"Yeah, I'm okay. What's going on?"

"Where do I start?" Mrs. Hunter replied.

"What are all the sirens?" Tanner asked.

"I had to do it Tanner. I didn't know what else to do."

"Do what?"

"I called 911. When I couldn't get you to wake up, I thought something was wrong. And since you've been gone for weeks, I couldn't take a chance. Tell me you're not responsible for Mick's disappearance. Tell me."

"What?" Tanner replied.

"Everyone suspects you and Andrew. After you stole those papers from the police station, fled, and then disappeared, the whole town turned on us. They're all convinced you and Andrew did something to Mick—especially her family. It's awful. Some people are even saying you're responsible for Harvey Wilkins's disappearance, and the strange sightings around the cave. Tell me it wasn't you Tanner. Please."

Tanner opened his mouth to reply.

"And now," Mrs. Hunter added, then paused as the sound of the sirens was growing ever louder, "you come back with this."

Mrs. Hunter unzipped Tanner's backpack revealing a linen cloth that she unwrapped to expose sections of a partially burned skeleton.

"It's not Mick's, is it?" she asked in a panic.

Ding dong

"That's the police. What do I do?" Mrs. Hunter moved toward the door, then back toward Tanner, then back toward the door again.

Tanner could hear her making her way down the stairs toward the front door.

He looked over at the TV his mother must have been watching during her bedside vigil. Her cooking show was interrupted with a special report.

"Brownsville police were violently confronted this afternoon by a man dressed in Roman military attire. Sheriff Gardiner indicated the man escaped into the woods on foot. Shots were fired unsuccessfully in an attempt to stop the stranger. If you have any information about the whereabouts of this man, please contact the Brownsville police department."

CHAPTER 76

THE WAX TABLET
(MICK)

Nearly three hours had passed from when Mick had climbed in bed. When she finally began to stir, she saw paramedics, her mom, and a police officer surrounding her bed. She was connected to an IV.

"What the heck is going on?" Mick asked.

"Are you all right?" a chorus of voices asked.

"Fine. I'm fine," Mick replied.

"Please. Give her some space," Mrs. Brown said as she tried to clear away the crowd in Mick's bedroom. "She's been through a lot. She's going to need some time."

Mick watched her mother herd the emergency personnel into the hallway. She could faintly hear the front door open and shouting coming from outside the house.

"Is she okay?"

"Did she say who kidnapped her?"

"Was it the Wheelwright and Hunter boys?"

Her mother closed the door and the noise subsided. She tried to sit up when she felt something uncomfortable underneath her. She moved out of the way to see what it was. Lying on her bed were a few gold Roman coins and a strange wooden object. It consisted of two small pieces of wood held together by leather straps like a book.

What's this? She thought as she opened the book. There was wax inlaid in each of the pieces. In the wax, she read:

I'm sure there are those who think I'm a murderer who abandoned his family, neither of which is true. In my attempt to find the kidnapped mother of a Shawnee girl, I was held at gunpoint by the actual bank robbers. We were able to escape by fleeing deep into the woods. A few days later, we were captured by a vicious people. To my horror, they killed the Shawnee. I am in the process of trying to overthrow their government and avenge the death of the girl and many other deaths and injustices. I miss my family, and think of them often. Though I've tried, I've been unable to get back home. If I continue to be unsuccessful in my attempts, hopefully someone will find this and determine the identity of the real murderers. I have and always will remain faithful to my family.

Mr. Donald Carlton/Titus

Mick leaned back in her bed and smiled. It might not be enough to prove his innocence to anyone else, but it was enough for her.

"But how did it get here?"

ABOUT THE AUTHOR

Stephen Thorpe, the son of a school teacher who made magic with her words by varying intonations and playing with pronunciation to add dramatic flare, grew up loving words.

But it wasn't until he sat down to document the flow of a video game he planned to create that he realized how much he loved to write. And so *Cathedral of Time*, the first in *The World of Agartha* series, was born. Stephen's love for Ancient Rome, and history in general, grew from his service as a 19-year old missionary in modern-day Rome. Stephen lives in Utah with his wife Maria and daughters Jenny and Mary.

THE ADVENTURE CONTINUES WITH BOOK TWO...

Toquchar's Prisoner

VISIT WWW.THEWORLDOFAGARTHA.COM

...AND THE UPCOMING VIDEO GAME...

REVENGE OF THE PRAETORIAN

VISIT WWW.REVENGEOFTHEPRAETORIAN.COM